THE YOU KNOW WHO GIRLS: FRESHMAN YEAR

Advance Praise for Annameekee Hesik

"*The You Know Who Girls* is a slam dunk of a novel. Open its pages and be whisked into a girl-on-girl world chock full of lovable characters and action-packed scenes that are both heartfelt and laugh-out-loud funny. The book is a winner!"—Alex Sanchez, author of *Rainbow Boys* and *Boyfriends with Girlfriends*

"I sure wish I had gone to high school with *The You Know Who Girls*! Annameekee Hesik has created smart, sassy, sweaty, sexy characters who tore down the basketball court and leaped into my heart. Readers of all ages will absolutely love this book."—Lesléa Newman, author of *The Reluctant Daughter* and *Heather Has Two Mommies*

"*The You Know Who Girls* is a delightful novel with a diverse cast of characters and a hilarious narrator that is impossible to resist. From the moment Abbey lays eyes on the irresistible Hot Dog on a Stick Chick to the very last page, Annameekee Hesik grips her readers' attention with her unique coming of age/coming out story that is heartfelt, funny, and a welcome addition to the positive images of LGBT youth. Thank goodness there's a sequel in the works!"—Ellen Bass, author of *Free Your Mind: The Book for Gay, Lesbian, and Bisexual Youth and Their Allies*

Visit us at www.boldstrokesbooks.com

THE YOU KNOW WHO GIRLS: FRESHMAN YEAR

by

Annameekee Hesik

2012

ISBN 10: 1-60282-754-0
ISBN 13: 978-1-60282-754-7

This Trade Paperback Original Is Published By
Bold Strokes Books, Inc.
P.O. Box 249
Valley Falls, NY 12185

First Edition: October 2012

CREDITS
Editor: Ruth Sternglantz
Production Design: Susan Ramundo
Cover Design By Sheri (graphicartist2020@hotmail.com)

Acknowledgments

The You Know Who Girls could never have made its way into the hands of readers without the help of many. First, a huge thank you to my family and friends for your constant cheerleading and encouragement. Thank you to Ellen Bass for your outstanding feedback and guidance and for introducing me to the incredible Lesléa Newman, who held my hand through the editing and publishing adventures. Thank you to Radclyffe and Ruth Sternglantz (Queen of Commas) at Bold Strokes Books and to all of the incredible folks at BSB who contributed to this finished product. Thank you to my webmaster and BFF, Casey Chafouleas, for being so attentive to my website whims and for making me laugh at things that aren't supposed to be funny. Thank you to the baristas across Santa Cruz County for blending my mocha shakes—sorry I sat at your tables long after I slurped down the last gulp. Thank you to my amazing students at NMCHS for being my biggest fans long before the book was published—you will always be my little chickadees. Finally, a special thank you to my wife, Mary, for everything you are, everything you do, and for being my one and only you-know-who girl.

Dedication

To all the you-know-who girls.

CHAPTER ONE

According to my best friend Kate, the purpose of our visit to the Tucson Mall today is to have my "never-been-kissed innocence get an ass kicking from my Beyoncé booty and Cameron Diaz legs." And this may be the closest Kate's come to paying me a compliment. I'm still not moving off this couch, though, because my plans for the day include rejecting all uncomfortable fashion trends and watching the twelve-hour *SpongeBob SquarePants* marathon. Yes, I know at fourteen-and-three-quarter years old I may be a little too old for cartoons, but I don't care. Kate will just have to torture me some other day. Besides, we've been friends since the day I threw up on her shoes in the third grade, earning me the nickname Abbey "Chunks" Brooks for the rest of my life. Kate got over the vomit incident, so I know she'll get over this, too.

I reach for the phone to tell Kate the bad news, and because I'm a giant dork who can't control her superlong appendages, I knock over my bowl of cereal and spill it all over the coffee table. I decide to mask the spill with my napkin, but then my mom walks in and says, "Abbey, I'm not really seeing this, right?" because she's the master at telling me what to do without actually telling me what to do.

"No, you're hallucinating again," I say and get up to grab a rag from the kitchen.

After she's satisfied with my cleanup on aisle three, my mom says, "Shouldn't you be getting ready to go? You don't want to miss the eleven-forty bus. Because you know, Abbey"—a sly smile appears on her face, and I know she's about to sing the public transit jingle, which is her not-so-subtle way of reminding me that a ride from her is out of the question—"Suntran…it's catching on!"

"Mom, that stopped being funny about a million years ago." I fall back onto the couch and watch SpongeBob prepare for a death-defying stunt on his bicycle. "Anyway, I'm not going. It's too hot to breathe, let alone walk around."

Then the phone rings.

"You weren't thinking of bailing on me, were you, Chunks?"

Damn Kate and her mind-reading skills. "No," I say and then let out a defeated sigh. "I'm getting ready," I lie and hang up, already sweaty from holding the phone to my ear.

We do have this thing called an air conditioner, but my mom refuses to employ its services. See, while the rest of Arizona's residents are chillaxing in their homes, we suffer like martyrs in hopes of ending global warming. In my opinion, Mom's using the earth's demise to her economic advantage, but I've noticed that everyone has stopped asking for my opinion on all topics of discussion.

But then again, since my dad died, Mom has been cheap about everything, even her creativity. She did get a huge amount of money from my dad's life insurance (she doesn't know I know this, but I saw the papers on her desk), but she's always worried about not having enough, and what-if-God-forbid-something-happened-to-her, which is why she's been working nonstop on this totally cheesy howling-coyote painting for commission (art inspired by cash). It's for Ventana Views, the new resort being constructed in the foothills of the Catalina Mountains. I consider pointing out that her art is going to be displayed in a 5,000-square-foot air-conditioned dining room built on land that once served as a habitat to javalinas and near-extinct bird species. But, then again, if she gets paid, maybe we can stop eating the always yellow and ever mysterious "casserole surprise" on Friday nights and start going out for pizza again. I have to play my cards carefully.

During a commercial break, I look over at her. It's the usual scene: Mom in her paint-splattered glasses, wearing overalls and a tank top with a cup of iced coffee on the table next to her. She carefully adds a gray line down the coyote's back, then rinses off her paintbrush in a jar of muddy brown water. I used to watch her so intently when I was a baby that Mom and Dad were convinced I'd become an amazing artist by the time I could babble *Picasso*. My artistic toddler efforts (like the one-eyed, armless "girl" with the purple Afro) still hanging around the house are proof, however, that I took after my dad: I'm book smart, scientific, and as linear as the crisscrossed grid of Tucson's city streets.

And according to my eighth-grade counselor, I'm also tenacious, so I give it one more try. "Whoa. Everything's getting blurry. Mom? Are you there? Where am I? Why is this giant frog staring at me? I can't feel my tongue. Is that normal?"

She laughs, but that's my only reward. "An Oscar-worthy performance, Abbey, but the air conditioner will remain off. It's not even ninety degrees outside," she says and dabs another empty spot on her canvas. I try to remember the last time she looked at me that closely, but can't. "Go take a cold shower and stop bugging me."

I almost say, "Dad would do it for me," but decide to save the dead-dad card for something more important. Instead, I collapse to the floor and belly crawl past her. "Water, water…please…just a drop…" And then feign death by dehydration at the bathroom door.

She finally looks up and smiles big enough to show off the new wrinkles reaching out from her lake-blue eyes. People say I look exactly like her. I used to think it was because of my blond hair and long legs, but now I see me in her eyes, and I'm glad to have inherited at least that part of her.

By the time I finish fake dying, showering, and getting dressed, I wind up missing the 11:40 bus. I don't even bother asking my mom for a ride but do ask for back-to-school-clothes money and then give her a kiss good-bye.

Thanks to my mom's recent yard sale shopping spree, it takes me a minute to free my dad's red bike from all the junk in the garage. I'm riding his now because long-tall Abbey here outgrew her bike last year. I tie a rag around the baked bike seat that has cracked open from too much sun exposure and strap on my helmet and backpack. As I coast down my driveway, I curse the infernal sun and Kate and low-rise pants, and start my forty-minute ride to the stupid Tucson Mall.

❖

Kate will be very disappointed if she finds me at the mall in a sweat-drenched shirt, so I clean up in the Macy's bathroom and change into a dry shirt I was smart enough to stuff in my backpack before leaving my house. I try to fix my helmet hair but give up and pull it back into a low ponytail. The lack of both effort and product I've put into my hair is going to bug her, but everything about me seems to irritate her these days, so it's not like I can win. Like the fact that I'm wearing my khaki shorts, plain white tee, and blue Converse shoes, which Kate says makes me look like a deckhand on a Carnival cruise ship. My choices in clothes and hairstyles didn't use to bother her, but ever since we became Future Freshmen, it seems like overnight she's become everything I'm not, and then some.

As I wait for Her Majesty, I work on my own list of important things to do before my first day of high school:

1. Rearrange glow-in-the-dark stars on my ceiling to reflect recent celestial changes.
2. Stop having nightmares about dead dad.
3. Develop addictions to all foods and drinks that stunt growth.

Then a shadow falls over me followed by a waft of some actress's new perfume and the smell of cucumber-melon lotion.

"You're such a freaking schoolgirl."

I look up and see my before-mentioned BFF with her brown hair cascading down her back, every curl in its place, the perfect shade of eye shadow to make her eyes pop, shimmery lip gloss, freshly painted fingernails, and coordinated clothes. None of which surprises me. What gets me is how much bustier she is than the last time I saw her. "Wow, have there been new developments in your life that you want to tell me about?"

"Jealous much? Pack up your little geek-party-for-one and let's go."

I put my notepad and pen away in my faded red backpack. "All right, let's get this over with."

She heads toward the wide open jaws of the nearest department store, and I dutifully follow.

We start at Kohl's, where I'm supposed to be looking for a "supertight shirt that matches my eyes and gives the illusion that I have boobs," but while Kate's distracted by the towers of jeans, I sneak out my notepad and work on my list:

4. Buy ultradry deodorant and new socks.
5. Make up a catchy cool saying.
6. Practice speaking Spanish.

I peek over a rack of shorts and see Kate scrutinizing a pair of jeans. They're pink corduroy, and the short zipper makes it easy for me to determine how much of my butt cheeks will be hanging out if I actually sit down while wearing them. I think we should all say no to crack, but the fashion gurus have a different idea. I send a telepathic message to Kate to put them down and walk away, but she adds them to the mound of clothes in her arms that I'm going to be forced to try on.

"It's time," she yells in my direction.

I have never met a fitting room I liked. First of all, fitting rooms are made for normal-sized people, not freakishly tall people like me. Because I'm five nine and a half, it feels like my nearly naked body is visible to everyone as they walk by. Plus, I always whack my funny bone on the stupid hooks protruding from the wall, which are placed at the most inconvenient level for Amazons like me. The worst part has to be the full-length mirror and bad lighting. I usually try not to look too closely, but today I glance over before slipping on one of the outfits Kate's picked out for me. I hate what I see: me standing there in my boring cotton undies and bra, with my bland face and scraggly long blond hair. The mirror seems to elongate my twiggy arms and legs more than ever, making me totally look like Elastigirl, minus the sexy thigh-high boots, secret identity, and boobs. I flash a fake smile at myself because my smile is the only thing I like. That and my inherited blue eyes, but neither are making me feel better at the moment.

"We don't have all day, Abbey," Kate says outside the door. "Come on. I promise I won't say anything mean."

"Yeah, right," I say and quickly put on the pink pants and the tight white shirt. I look slightly okay, but Kate will have the final word on that. I open the door and wait for the bullets to hit me.

"Oh my God, you look like a giant cricket. What's with your legs for days?"

This goes on for about fifteen more outfits, and then I change into the last one, open the fitting room door, hold out my arms, and do a slow 360 for Kate.

She looks up from texting and throws up her hands. "Why is it that we're the same damn size, and everything looks good on me, but you manage to look like a mutant?"

These comments used to bug me, but now I just shrug and let them go. "It is one of life's great mysteries, I guess. Can we go eat now?"

"God, you're such a freak, Abbey. We might as well just get a bedsheet and throw it over your head."

"I know, I know," I say, as I quickly strip and jump back into my comfy clothes. Before exiting, though, I add:

7. Buy new underwear and bras.

to my list. I don't dare tell Kate because she would have a heart attack from excitement and then drag me to Victoria's Secret for thongs and lacy push-ups. I'm only fourteen and I still like cartoons, so I'm not quite ready for sex-kitten status yet, but I may be ready for a bra with a little bow in a color other than nude.

As we slowly make our way to the food court, Kate alternates between texting Marisol and Sarah, gagging at how bad I look in the other outfits I try on along the way, drooling over the guys on the Abercrombie posters, and trying on every scented lotion at The Body Shop. Then she starts in on her "we are almost women, hear us meow" speech.

"I mean, Abbey, look at us."

I scan myself, then her, and see the obvious: Sure we're the same height and same pant and shoe size, but her long wavy brown hair and other parts of her do this supermodel sway when she walks. Her teeth and skin glow, just like the TV ads say they should. Plus, she knows how to apply makeup and waltz like a graceful dancer on her extra-long legs. My stride resembles Shaggy's from *Scooby-Doo*.

"We're practically women," she says and then glances over at me. "Well, at least, for the most part."

I cross my arms over my chest and remind myself that there's a lot more to her than finding the perfect pair of jeans and scamming on guys. She was there for me when I lost my dad. It was Kate who sat next to me at his funeral, and it's Kate who lets me talk about him whenever I need to. She's a good listener when it matters most.

But now I'm in a dressing room at Forever 21, and I hate her. The miniskirt she's making me try on makes me look like a sex worker who might be found strolling down Miracle Drive. I tear it off like it's contagious and come out dressed as myself. Before Kate has a chance to protest, I say, "No way. Not now. Not ever."

After two hours of dressing room torture, we finally arrive at the food court, and the first thing I notice isn't the group of guys Kate is trying to get me to see by stabbing her sharp elbow into my side. What I notice is we've missed a thunderstorm, and I'm bummed. See, in Tucson it can go from a hundred degrees to flash floods in a matter of minutes. The storms are so awesome and loud car alarms go off all over the neighborhood when the thunder rumbles. I love the power the monsoon storms pack.

Even though Kate and I are behind a wall of windows, I can smell the damp creosote bushes and clean asphalt. I close my eyes for a second, inhale, and think of the trips my dad and I took into the desert to record bird songs and collect rocks for the biology classes he taught at the University of Arizona.

Kate looks at her cell phone for the hundredth time today and then turns to me to deliver one last bit of advice. "Abbey, don't you think it's time you stop caring about the weather and start caring about something that really matters?"

I smile but keep quiet because there have been a lot of other things on my mind lately, things I think about way more than the weather. But they are things I can't ever tell Kate about, at least not yet. Sure, we've shared death, but I'm definitely not ready to tell her I enjoy the posters at Abercrombie as much as she does, but not because of the hot, barely clothed *guys*.

Kate gets a text from Jenn, her older sister and her ride home. "Well, hasta la pasta, girl," she says and gives me a quick hug. "I guess we'll have to hit the stores again tomorrow. Same time, same place?"

I look at my watch and don't respond, hoping that I can later say, "I never agreed to go to the mall with you," but Kate knows me too well and forcibly nods my head up and down with her hands.

"Great! See you tomorrow."

After Kate leaves, I look around and evaluate the food court lines. I nearly join the crowd in front of Eegee's, but the line at Hot Dog on a Stick is free and clear, so I beeline it over there instead.

I stand a little ways from the counter and gaze up at the menu to figure out what I want. Ordering french fries isn't normally a challenge for me, but I guess riding my bike fifteen miles in the hundred-degree heat and baking under the fluorescent lights in the fitting rooms like a Big Mac has sizzled my brain.

I have a bad habit of twirling my hair when I'm thinking, so that's what I do, as I stand there, spacing out at the menu like a moron.

Then a straw wrapper sails through the air and hits my gaping mouth.

And standing behind the counter, twirling a clean straw between her fingers, is a girl in her red, yellow, blue, and white striped polyester tank top with a whole lot of black hair stuffed under her matching striped paper hat. I have always loved those outfits, especially recently. I used to think it was because I associated the outfits with food, but now I'm definitely beginning to wonder if it isn't something much more involved than that.

"Is the menu too complicated for you?" she asks. She's smiling, and her teeth are bright against her cocoa-brown face. It's a smile I feel like I've seen before.

I feel my face turn red like an instant sunburn, but then I do something I've never before done to a girl like her: I smile back. Then I stammer, "Uh, sorry. I'll have a regular fry and a small lemonade, please."

I watch her peck my order into the register and see that her fingertips on her left hand are rough with calluses. My dad's fingers looked like that because he played guitar all the time. He was really good. Mostly he played the Beatles, which is why he wanted to name me "Abbey Road" Brooks, after one of their later albums. My mom said no way, of course, because she's a total bore. So, instead, they named me plain Abbey Brooks. But now that Dad's dead, Mom calls me Abbey Road. I'll never get her.

Now I'm wondering how long the girl with the nice smile has been playing guitar and where the heck I know her from. I try to look at her name tag, but it's hiding in a fold of her uniform and I'm afraid if I look there for too long it'll look like I'm checking out her boobs, which I'm currently not doing. I mean, not really.

"That'll be six dollars and twenty-five cents," she says.

Where could I have met someone cool like her? It's not like I go to concerts or coffee shops or wherever cool people hang out. Then I notice she's reaching for another straw and I snap out of it. At that exact same moment, her name tag is finally revealed, but it's plastered with stickers from Chiquita bananas.

As I reach into my backpack for my wallet, I can't hold back a goofy smile. See, my dad used to put Chiquita stickers on my nose every time we shared a banana, and I've spent the last five years sticking Chiquita stickers all over my wallet to keep that memory close.

The girl, I'll call her the Hot Dog on a Stick Chick, notices our shared affinity for bananas. "Nice wallet."

"Thanks." I smile bigger, if that's even possible. "Nice name tag."

I've only been around her for about two minutes, but I think…no, I *know*, I want to be like her and near her. She seems so confident, like she knows what she wants out of life and how she's going to get it. I wonder how people get that way.

She repeats my order to the guy working the fryer and then says in a voice that's cooler than the frigid mall air conditioning, *"Y, apúrale, gringo. Tenemos una morra bien loca que tiene mucha hambre."*

With my junior high Spanish skills, I know she's just said I'm crazy and really hungry, which is pretty much true. I smile again and then sneak a peek at her eyes while she gets my change. They're brown with tiny flecks of gold sprinkled in like glitter.

She asks for my name and I panic before I realize that it isn't for any special reason; it's so she can call me up for my order. *"Tu nombre…?"* she asks again and poises her finger over the register keys.

I open my mouth with every intention of telling her my name, but all I can think of to say is Chunks. "Um-uh," I say to try to buy time, but she's already typing something on the keypad.

The name *Amara* illuminates on the screen.

"Okay, Amara, I'll call you in a sec." Then she turns away to get my drink and…*did she just wink at me? Whoa, this is definitely a first*, but then I get a reality check and convince myself that she just got some lemon pulp in her eye.

I sit down at a nearby table because, for some reason, my knees are shaking and I feel like I might collapse. I want to look at her a little longer, but instead of staring at her like a hungry puppy, I count the Nikes walking by. A minute later the Hot Dog on a Stick Chick calls *Amara* on her loudspeaker, but I don't make the connection because I'm too busy trying to count the Nikes walking by and trying not to obsess over how she is making me feel. Then she says it again, follows it with a laugh, and I finally realize she's calling me.

I bolt up to the counter, but then slow down so I won't look too desperate for the french fries or to talk to her again.

She slides the tray to me and flashes her stunning smile again. "Here you go, Amara. Enjoy."

I look down at my tray because she makes me feel so shy. Then because I'm a professional idiot I say, "Oh, uh, I paid for a small lemonade, not a large. I mean, I don't want you to get in trouble," and pick up the drink to hand it to her.

She takes it, but puts it back onto my tray. "Sure, Amara, the lemonade police are going to bust through the door to take me away for giving you a bigger size." Then she laughs and winks again, and this time I'm almost sure she winks on purpose.

I laugh, too, because I don't know what to say or do with myself. I'm on uncharted ground, so I stand there, hold tight to the tray, and wait for my brain to send the message to my feet that it's time to go.

Just as I'm about to finally make my escape, she puts her hands on my tray, her right index finger nearly touching my left pinky. "Hey, Amara," she says easily, as if this new name is the one my parents had finally decided on.

I don't dare move an inch. I'm sure if our fingertips touch I'll implode.

She leans across the glossy red counter. "Come here. I've got some advice for you."

I move in a little closer, but I can't speak or even blink. I reach for my ponytail to twirl but force my hand down and wait for her next words.

"Amara, the next time you are given more than you expect, just say thank you and walk away." Her voice is heavy and sweet now, like cold maple syrup.

Then the Hot Dog on a Stick Chick just looks at me, and something about the way she does this activates a memory I didn't even know I had. She's *that* girl from elementary school. I still can't remember her name, but I know she's at least three grades ahead of me. She was the one who beat every boy at tetherball, and she never wore socks or hair bands that matched her outfits. And then I remember how she ate her string cheese very carefully, tearing each strip with the precision of a surgeon, unlike me who would just bite into it like the ogre that I am.

The memory feels like a jolt of something unfamiliar in my body, and all I want to do is get out of there. "Okay, thanks," I say way too loudly and yank my tray toward me. The giant lemonade teeters but doesn't spill.

"Wait a minute, Amara."

I freeze again. *Oh my God, she can tell.* What she can tell I'm not so sure of, but maybe she knows me better than I know myself, which seems very possible.

"Do you go to Gila High?" She leans on her elbow and squints at me. "You look really familiar."

I mumble something about being a freshman.

"Oh, then you went to McCormick Elementary, right?"

I nod and wonder why no one else in the whole entire mall wants a corn dog or fresh-squeezed lemonade. It's like we're suddenly alone. Very, very alone.

"Yeah, I remember you now. What was that crazy Halloween costume you wore one year?" She taps the counter with her hard fingertips.

I beg the greater beings of our universe to help her forget, but I know from experience that the universe works in magical and sometimes hateful ways.

"Oh yeah, you were a guitar-playing rock." Then she laughs at me for the third time. I like her laugh, though, even if it's at my expense. "Very creative."

I could save the entire moment by simply saying, "Thank you," but instead I say, "Well, I was actually a piece of metamorphic rock. Gneiss, to be exact, which is formed by the intense heat and pressure surrounding it. It was supposed to symbolize the pressure rock stars are under, kind of. Um, I mean, well, it was my dad's idea. I wanted to be a unicorn." My dad would have been so pleased that I remembered the rock facts, but I totally regret the words as they leave my mouth.

"Good to know, Amara." Then the Hot Dog on a Stick Chick nods at the woman who has apparently been standing behind me, waiting for her turn to order. "I guess I'll see you at Gila next week."

"Yeah, I'll probably be there. I mean, of course I will. I have to go to school. It is the law. Besides, where else would I go?" Oh, how I wish I could go back to being a smiling, but voiceless, idiot. "So, see you soon. Or whenever," I say, then grab my tray and hurry away like an Olympic speed walker.

And this is how my crush on the Hot Dog on a Stick Chick begins.

CHAPTER TWO

A nd don't cheat, Abbey," Kate says, as she washes down a spoonful of raw brownie batter with a gulp of Mountain Dew. "I'm not, so shut up already." I lean in closer to the screen to read the next question.

It's around two in the morning and it's our last sleepover at my house before our big first day of high school. My mom said good night four hours ago, making us swear we wouldn't stay up past midnight. We did promise to go to bed, but after my mom takes her prescribed sleeping pills she's pretty much in a coma. I guess I'm not the only one who still has dead-dad-caused sleep issues.

So here we are, strung out on brownie batter and Mountain Dew, enjoying our last night together before high school. Sarah and Marisol are sharing the earphones of Sarah's iPod while simultaneously beautifying themselves, and Kate's forcing me to take a stupid online personality quiz titled "Which Condiment Are You?" I'll admit I'm thinking about lying on some answers, but I don't because I know they will double check them. Being the founding sisters of the Doolen Junior High Geek Pack, we take tests very seriously.

"What does any of this have to do with my personality?" I ask after answering a question about how long I leave conditioner in my hair before rinsing.

"Just freaking do it," Kate says, throwing my U of A Wildcats pillow at my head.

Cherry or Vanilla Coke? I hate both but pick Cherry because it seems to have a sexual connotation, which I hope will increase my score. Gap, Wrangler, Levi's, or Lucky jeans? I pick Lucky for the same reason as above.

Marisol leans over my shoulder, smacks her gum in my ear, and reads the next question out loud. "'Who would you most enjoy grinding on the dance floor with? Katy Perry, Madonna, Miley Cyrus, or Lady Gaga?' Yeah, that was a tough one."

That's when I close my laptop and push myself away from my desk. I make pretty good distance in my wheeled chair on the wood floor. "Hey, I know. Let's do something else. Who wants to torture me with makeup?"

"Nice try, Abbey." Kate kicks my chair, and I'm back where I started. "Open up your flipping computer and answer it."

"Yeah, who's it gonna be?" Sarah says, blowing some loose strands of blond hair out of her face. She's hunched over, painting her toenails, her turquoise thong peeking out of the back of her yoga pants. No one says anything, so I guess that's the style. Then Sarah says, "I picked Madonna because I don't really like dancing and she'd probably get tired faster being that she's a hundred years old." She finishes her toenails and moves on to do her fingernails. She changes the color of her nails so much I am convinced she's lost some brain cells from the toxic polishes and remover. In fact, she nearly got kicked out of the Geek Pack when she got a B in Science, but Kate let her stay because Sarah has a giant trampoline at her house and a sister who works at Old Navy who gives Sarah and all her friends the employee discount.

"I don't know why they all have to be *gringas*." Marisol usually complains in Spanglish, which Kate hates because she can only half understand her.

Sarah and I get it, though, because we took Advanced Spanish in junior high seeing as we live in Arizona and all. Kate, on the other hand, took German because she wanted to be different. Sometimes, on very rare and beautiful occasions, Marisol uses her wonderful native language to tell Kate off. I enjoy those moments.

"Besides, brown girls are where it's at," Marisol says, as she straightens another lock of her thick black hair. *"Prefiero bailar con Shakira que con alguna de esas vacas."*

"What the hell are you saying, Mari? Are you talking about me?" Kate asks then smacks me again. "Just pick one, Abbey."

"Yeah, Marisol, Shakira is a good dancer, but I guess I'll pick Lady Gaga." I click on her name. "There. I'm done."

"That was my second choice," Sarah says. "She's got a nice ass."

But Kate gags and says, "Nah. She's too freaky. She'd probably try to make out on the dance floor."

I remind myself this is straight-girl talk; my friends are so very, very not gay and that's why they can talk like this. But for me, the one who is crushing hard on the Hot Dog on a Stick Chick, this is a tricky situation.

The website slowly contemplates my condiment.

"Read it to us," Kate demands.

"I will. Hold on. There's nothing to read yet." Then a giant pickle appears on the screen, which I'm predicting is not a good sign.

"Well?" Marisol and Sarah say in unison.

"Okay, it says, 'Congrats! You are relish: though you are rarely wanted, you are good to have in the back of the fridge and sometimes you can be sweet.'"

They all bust up laughing.

In between gasps, Kate manages to say, "Abbey's smothered all over wieners!" and they all cackle again.

I stare at the screen in disbelief. Relish? Why not salsa like Kate—fresh and spicy, and good with every meal? Or at least mustard like Sarah—packs a punch and offers many flavors to please everyone. But, no. I get stupid pickled relish. I spin a lock of hair between my fingers for comfort while my friends laugh at me. Unlike the Hot Dog on a Stick Chick's laughter, theirs makes me feel like crap.

"Hey, Weiner Sauce, take notes," Kate says after finally catching her breath. "It's time to make our new list of rules for high school."

Glad to change the subject, I pull a piece of paper from my printer tray and take on my duties as the official Geek Pack secretary.

The Geek Pack is our not-so-secret club. It was founded in seventh grade, which was precisely when we discovered that if the four of us stuck together, we could continue to earn the highest grades in class while helping each other fend off cheaters and other classmates who found our genius irritating. In junior high, we displayed our A+ grades proudly on our bedroom walls and celebrated every honor roll and student-of-the-month certificate. In fact, mine are still taped to my closet doors around the edges of my Beatles posters.

"First of all," Kate says, pointing her brownie spoon at each of us, "from this point forward, the Geek Pack is null and void."

Sarah stops blowing on her nails and nods her head in agreement because that's what she always does. Kate could say, "From this point forward, Sarah will cluck whenever we eat pizza," and every time we sat down for a slice at Mama's Pizza, Sarah would start clucking away. Marisol hesitates, runs the straightener down her hair to think on it, and then agrees that it's time to end our little haven of intellectual security. I'm usually the most argumentative one, but I feel too tired and shocked, so I write, *Rule #1: The Geek Pack is dead.* And just like that, when I feel like I'll need it most, it's gone.

"Rule number two," Kate says, as she eats another spoonful of batter, "we can enroll in honors classes, but we should *not* sit in the front row or raise our hands to answer questions."

"Why not?" Sarah asks.

Kate glares at Sarah with great exasperation. "Because hand raising is for dorks."

Marisol looks pensive and finally says, "What if we have to go to *el baño*?"

Kate looks at me.

"The bathroom," I translate.

"Obviously, you can raise your hand for that, Mari."

Then Sarah asks, "What if the teacher is asking something like, 'Who wants to get out of class early?'"

"Next rule," Kate continues. "Rule number three—no dating loser freshmen boys. No exceptions. Rule number four—no asking about extra credit assignments. Rule number five—no helping teachers grade papers. Rule number six—absolutely no displaying of report cards." After this one she looks over at me and then looks at my closet door.

"Whatever. I'll take them down tomorrow." I wonder if I'm the only one who already misses the old us.

When Kate finishes her rules, my whole page is full. Most of them are as stupid as Rule #14, which states that pink shall only be worn on Tuesdays. The only one I do like is Rule #20: We will eat lunch together every day. This makes the loss of Geek Pack feel a little less tragic. Like there might still be a chance for a reunion tour senior year.

By around three o'clock, the brownie batter has settled uncomfortably in our stomachs, the Mountain Dew wears off, and we decide we're all too sick and tired to stay up any longer. We pinky-swear in the new rules with our never-to-be-used-again song: "We link our pinks and swear to keep this promise 'til we sink."

While Marisol and Sarah, still connected by Sarah's earphones, sleep on an air mattress on the floor, I lie next to Kate in my bed, holding tight to the edge of consciousness and to the side of my mattress. I have to stay awake because if I let myself fall asleep, I might slowly slip into the middle and our bodies might touch. I don't think of Kate in *that* way and never have, but if I accidentally snuggle up to her in my sleep and she finds out about my crush on the Hot Dog on a Stick Chick and she freaks out and we are never friends again... well, I'm pretty sure I'll die.

So I'm awake, watching the minutes tick by on my bedside Beatles clock that sings "Here Comes the Sun" when the alarm goes off. I want to pass my time thinking about the person I haven't once stopped thinking about since I saw her in the mall, but considering my current sleeping situation, that's not such a good idea. Instead, I think about the person I usually think about before I fall asleep: my dad.

I think about how I'd do anything to have him back, especially now that I'm starting high school. He used to tell me stories about how much fun he'd had at Gila High and how I was going to love it, too. I was even going to join the club he started way back in the day: Future Scientists of America Club. I try to stop myself, but now I'm remembering the accident and the way his car looked like a crushed Coke can, then the funeral, then coming home and knowing he'd never be here again. I wish I could remember him without remembering any of that.

I need to focus on something else, so I start thinking about how the official start of high school is just forty-five hours away and that I have a lot of work to do. Since my encounter with the Hot Dog on a Stick Chick, I know it's going to take a lot more than new clothes and makeup to leave my nerdy self behind. I quietly take out my notepad and, by the light of the glowing faces of Paul, John, Ringo, and George, I make some changes to my to-do list. I cross out *Change glow-in-the-dark stars*, add *Buy scented lotion*, and draw a heavy, urgent circle around *Practice Spanish daily*.

❖

I make it through the night on two hours of restless sleep, and in the morning, after Marisol and Sarah are gone, Kate and I have some breakfast while we wait for her sister Jenn to pick her up.

In between bites, Kate lectures me on the expected behavior of high school girls. "I mean, Abbey, boys aren't going to like you if you don't like yourself. You have to, you know, put some effort into how you look, or you're going to end up going to your first formal with a group of other lame-ass girls who couldn't get dates, or worse, you won't get to go at all."

I try to act interested, but I'm not convinced she can know so much about a place she has never been. Jenn, on the other hand, is a much more reliable source. That's why when she talks, we all listen.

Jenn's going to be a senior at Gila High, and even though she usually ignores us or calls us names like the Freak Pack and Dorks R Us, she sometimes tosses out little morsels of highly desirable high school info. Naturally, I keep a list of these secrets in my notebook. They're mostly about which teachers to avoid (Schwartz and Ponsi), how to sneak off campus (like I would ever do that), and how the fastest snack-bar line is always run by the oldest lunch lady, but I'll take whatever I can get.

Jenn arrives and waits for Kate to polish off her cereal.

I get up for more cereal and can feel Jenn's eyes follow me as I cross the kitchen. I sit down again, fold my long legs in my chair like a contortionist because it's how I'm most comfortable, chew my Cheerios, and wait for Jenn's always-uplifting commentary on my body, as if I need more reasons to feel self-conscious.

"Damn, girl," she says, "I'm pretty sure your mom had an affair with Big Bird about fifteen years ago. Have you asked her about that yet? Seriously. Legs for days? More like legs for months."

I just roll my eyes and take another bite of cereal.

"Speaking of which, you guys are going to try out for basketball, right?" Jenn says, as she grabs another handful of Os from the box. "I mean, you kind of have to. Between the two of you, the janitors won't need a ladder to get the spiderwebs out of the rafters."

Kate and I have never discussed trying out for any sports, so I don't really acknowledge Jenn's suggestion/put down.

But then Kate shrugs and says, "We're going to wait and see."

"Uh, yeah. We're not sure," I say, playing along and successfully hiding my heart attack.

"Come on," Jenn says, "are you kidding me? You two are, like, bred for hoops." Then she asks, "Dude, you're not going to bail on tryouts just because of all the lezzies on the team, are you?"

This time Kate has nothing to say, and therefore, neither do I. Though, now I'm feeling something I haven't yet felt when the topic of going to high school has come up: I'm a little excited. But Jenn saying "lezzies" in my kitchen also makes my left eyelid start to twitch. I grab a lock of hair to twirl and look down the hall to make sure my mom is still in the bathroom. This is not a conversation I want her to walk in on.

"I mean, you guys have heard about them, right?" Jenn asks, looking right at *me*.

Kate glances over at me, too, and raises her eyebrows. I'm glad to see she's equally shocked. "Of course we knew," she says, "and by the way, that is so gross. But we're just not sure if we want to try out. So lay off."

"Yeah. We're just not sure if we want to try out," I say like a parrot, but in my head all I can think is that maybe I'm not going to be the only girl at Gila who, maybe, likes girls.

❖

Later on that night, to honor our last moments of summer break, Kate and I go to the movies. We choose a comedy instead of our usual slasher films because I think we're both feeling anxious enough. And even though Jack Black's performance makes us laugh, we're both pretty quiet, as we sit on the warm cement wall in front of Desert Cinemas waiting for my mom to pick us up. I don't know what's on Kate's mind, but there's only one thing on mine.

Then Kate turns to me with an ugly look on her face (like someone has just totally ripped a fart, which I haven't) and says, "Abbey, can you believe that stuff Jenn told us about the girls' basketball team? I mean, do you think it's true?"

My hands start to sweat and my voice seems a million miles away. "I don't know. Why?"

"Well, they better stay the hell away from us. That's just sick and wrong."

"Yeah," I say quietly but can't help but wonder what makes Kate so sure those girls would like her. I mean, yes, she's really pretty, but is she the kind of pretty that they'll like? Am I the kind of pretty that they'll like?

After that, we don't say anything for a few minutes. I listen to the crickets, and I think about what it would be like to see the Hot Dog on a Stick Chick in the hall at Gila. Will she remember me? Will she say hi? Or will she just walk by, laughing with her friends, and be untouchable like the goddess she is? Then I almost laugh, because in my little fantasy, she is wearing her cute uniform, which I know is ridiculous, but it's all I have.

"Earth to Abbey." Kate's voice slaps me back to the wall in front of the theater and out of the crowded hallway where my chance meeting with the Chick was about to take place.

"What?" I snap, and her eyes kind of bug out at me in shock, so I quickly take it back. "Sorry, I'm just tired. What's up?"

"I have another rule for our list."

"Okay." I take out my handy-dandy notepad and pen.

"Rule number twenty-two? Twenty-three?"

"Twenty-four."

"Right, twenty-four. Are you writing this down?"

"No, I'm just holding this pen in my hand for fun."

"Okay, rule number twenty-four—no matter how much taller we grow, we will never try out for basketball or be friends with those you-know-who girls."

My hand wants to refuse to write it down, but she's watching me, so I force the letters onto the page.

When I'm finished, she sticks her pinky out. "This will absolutely be our last pinky swear."

At this exact moment, even though it has always been as strong as the cement wall we are sitting on, I feel our friendship crack down the middle. I don't know if it can ever be fixed, but I do know I have been right not to tell her about the feelings I have for the Hot Dog on a Stick Chick. And I know that the one friend I thought could help me through whatever this is, might be the last person I should ever tell.

CHAPTER THREE

S hut up, Abbey. The weather report is on."
I haven't actually spoken since Kate told me to shut up ten minutes ago when her favorite song came on the radio, so I continue to stay silent even though I feel like screaming at her for making me arrive at her house an extra hour early. But she doesn't care that I had to get up at 5:00 in the morning to get here by 6:30 so we can start walking to Gila by 7:00 because school starts at 7:45.

Now it's 7:05 and she's still doing her hair. We could very possibly be late for our first day at Gila. It's times like this that I wish I had puked on someone else in the third grade.

"Oh my God, Abbey, look at the humidity level. Damn monsoons," Kate says, as she throws down her straightener. "Do you know what this means?"

All I know is we're going to be late if she doesn't get a move on.

"Now I have to rewash my hair and wear it curly because there's no way it's going to stay straight in this stupid weather." She storms off and slams the bathroom door.

"What's up her butt?" Jenn asks, as she gathers her bag and car keys.

"Humidity," I say and look at my watch again.

"Good luck with that, Crappy Brooks. See you at school."

❖

Thanks to her mom giving us a ride, Kate and I cross through the gate of Gila's barbed-wire fence at exactly 7:30, leaving us only fifteen minutes before the first bell. When I played this first-day-of-school scenario in my mind last night before I fell asleep, I had plenty of leftover time to find all of my classes, locate my locker, practice spinning in its combination, and go pee before first period (Jenn advised us to avoid using the restrooms after break, when they usually get the most use). Now I'll be lucky to get to first period before the tardy bell.

Sarah and Marisol are loyally waiting for us on the front steps, inseparably bound with the headphones from the iPod. When we all meet up, we laugh hysterically for no reason like we just drank iced double-shot lattes for breakfast. Marisol, Sarah, and Kate look like an ad for a new high school sitcom. Kate made me wear khaki capris instead of shorts, and a white button-down short-sleeve shirt instead of a T-shirt, but I finally see how I kind of look like I should be on the deck of a boat. "Ahoy, mates!" I say as a joke, but no one notices.

"*Ay Dios*, do you see all the sexy boys?" Marisol whispers. *"Voy a hacer pipí."*

"Stop it, Mari." Sarah bites her hand and squeals. "You're making me have to *pipí*, too."

Kate looks around and seems to be in a mixed state of euphoria and anticipation. It's like she's an elite athlete and this is the Olympics. I can tell she fully expects to win gold.

Meanwhile, I'm secretly scanning the crowds for the Hot Dog on a Stick Chick or any of the you-know-who girls, but I can't find her and don't know what the heck the others look like. I mean, how do you tell? Do they wear a certain color like the gang members? Is there a secret handshake? I see the Populars, Goths, Punks, Stoners, Pseudohippies, Hicks, Drama Geeks, Band Freaks, Emos, Scene Kids, Jocks, Homies, Preps, Preppy Punks, Gleeks, Wannabies, Realbies, Hacky Sackers, and every other group Jenn has told us about, but not one of these cliques appear to be the one I'd like to see myself being a part of.

We join a long line and quickly find ourselves flanked by upperclassmen dressed in pajama bottoms, flip flops, and T-shirts with not-so-subtle allusions to sex and drugs that the teachers probably won't get. It seems, by the expressions on their faces, this older crowd finds everything irritating and boring, not exciting like us. So, to fit in, we stop squealing and shuffle grimly along like orange-jumpered, shackled prisoners.

At 7:43 I finally reach the front of the line to receive my locker assignment and my first-semester schedule. But instead of listing a class in my Period One slot, it says *See Counselor*. I show Kate, who already has her schedule and is comparing it with Marisol's and Sarah's, but she just shrugs like it's no biggie.

"God, Abbey, you're already in trouble?" Sarah teases. "Nice."

"Show me," Marisol says and grabs my schedule. "*Chingale!* Sucks to be you."

"But I'm supposed to have Algebra 2." I grab my schedule from Marisol and flip it over. "Where is my Algebra 2?"

"At least we all have PE together," Sarah says.

Then the bell rings and my friends disappear down the hall like we're playing hide-and-go-seek and I'm it. Now I'm alone.

Someone with a kind heart has posted directional signs all over the walls to help the new kids like me, but then some jerk turned all the arrows down and wrote *Go to hell, Freshmen* on them. This explains how I nearly walk into the boys' bathroom, running into Jake Simpson with my giant size-ten feet. Jake Simpson, Mr. "I'm So Cool I Go to Concerts on School Nights," is a year older than me, which is why we have never spoken before now.

I cover my face quickly and back up into the hall, as soon as I realize where I am. "Oh my God," I say too loudly. "I'm so sorry."

"It's all good. I'm decent." Then he laughs, but not at me, which is nice of him. "Where are you trying to go? I mean, I'm guessing you didn't mean to walk in here. It's Abbey, right?"

"Yeah, I'm Abbey Brooks." I show him my schedule like a lost tourist. "I'm supposed to go to the counselor's office," I say then look over my shoulder, hoping for some reason that Kate might walk by and see me talking to him.

He pushes a lock of his curly black hair behind his ear. "Cool, I'm going there, too. Come on. I'll take you on your first official high school field trip."

The hallway is clear and we walk side by side without having to avoid all the short people in our way. And when I talk to him, it's at eye level. This is new for me, since the eye level of most boys in eighth grade was right at my barely there breasts.

We arrive at the office and he opens the door for me. And for the first time ever, I feel kind of girlie. I decide high school boys might be slightly more evolved, not like the middle school boys who used to follow me around making Chewbacca sounds.

Other students are already in line for the counselors and are nonchalantly leaning against the wall like they're waiting for a bus, so I join them, trying to look just as cool and aloof. Then I turn to say, "Sure is crowded in here," or something equally dumb, but Jake is already talking to some friends in the front of the line. I pick at my cuticles instead.

Thirty minutes into first period and the line outside the counselor's office is ten students longer and we haven't moved an inch. I've already memorized the inspirational poster (Teamwork Gets the Job Done), the suicide hotline number (800-WE-SAVE-U), and counted the pieces of gum stuck to the bottom of the principal's bulletin board (three pink, five yellow, ten white, fifteen gray). To make matters worse, I still have to pee. The smart thing to do would be to keep my mouth shut, but instead I turn to Jake, who is now standing next to me, and say, "Cool shoes."

What follows is a brief conversation about his flame-covered Converse. And when that topic runs its course, I ask, "So, are we, like, going to get a first period at all?" I know I sound very geeky, but I have to know.

He laughs in a nice way again. "No worries, Abbey. Ms. Morvay's hella nice. She'll hook you up with whatever class you need." The line starts to move finally and we scoot along the wall together. He makes me think it wouldn't be so bad to have an older brother, and I find his tallness reassuring and comforting.

Then my name is called.

"See you around, Abbey," he says, as I walk toward the open door of the counselor's office.

"Okay, later," I say and wave good-bye with stupid enthusiasm because talking to him made me nervous, which doesn't really make sense considering my current crush situation on the Hot Dog on a Stick Chick. Do I think it would be cool to have a brother, or do I like the idea of having a boyfriend? God, what's wrong with me?

I sit down opposite Ms. Morvay, grab a lock of my hair, and begin to twirl because now I am totally experiencing inner turmoil and could not care less about Algebra 2.

"So"—she leans back in her black leather office chair and takes a long drink of her coffee—"I suppose you would like something to do during first period besides smoke cigarettes in the girls' bathroom."

"Yes, please," I say. Her humor is nice, but I still twirl and shake my leg like a spastic junky. I must look like a freak, but she's probably used to freaks, being the counselor and all. "Seriously, though, am I going to have a first period? I was kind of hoping for early graduation."

She types something into her computer and then looks at me again. "Didn't you just get here?"

"Yes." I don't see her point.

She adjusts her black-rimmed glasses. "And you're already hoping to leave early?"

"That's the plan," I say with confidence.

"Well, I bet that I'm not the first to say that you are very ambitious."

I shrug. I haven't actually told anyone about this plan and I am getting the feeling she thinks it's a bad idea.

"Well, don't worry. We'll get you out of here as fast as we can."

I watch her as she types and notice she's prettier than I thought she would be. Her brown hair is cut short but styled in a fashionable, non-old-lady way, and her blue silk shirt and black suit jacket make her look professional, like how I imagine looking someday when I get a real job.

As she scrolls through what I guess is my official district file, she notes my impressive academic record. "No 'Unsatisfactory' behavior marks and perfect attendance every year"—then she pauses—"except second grade." Then she scrolls a little farther and must see a note explaining my sudden absences and weekly therapy sessions. "Hmm..." is all she says. "So, Abbey, you'll have to wait to take Algebra 2 until next semester because all of our algebra classes are full. But I can sign you up for an elective since you aren't taking one. Which elective sounds fun to you?"

I stop twirling my hair and stare at her in confusion. It hadn't really occurred to me that I could take a class for the fun of it.

Glancing through a packet of papers on her desk, Ms. Morvay asks, "How about woodshop?"

"Not really my thing," I say and have a flashback to when my dad helped me make my mom a new end table to put her coffee on while she painted. It was so crooked, when you stood it on its legs, it swayed like a drunk giraffe. Instead, we turned it upside-down and used it as a log holder next to the fireplace.

"Mechanics?" Ms. Morvay asks.

I make a face. "I can't even drive yet."

"Sign Language?"

I shake my head no.

"Keyboarding."

"I already type sixty words per minute."

"Home Ec?"

I sigh. "You might as well call the fire department right now."

Ms. Morvay turns to the last page of the electives packet. "How about Beginning Guitar? The class is small and I know the teacher is excellent. What do you say?"

I say nothing at first, but I like the idea of being able to play the songs my dad used to play for me.

She leans back again and drinks more coffee. "It's either that or burned casseroles."

"Okay, I'll take Guitar."

"Great." Ms. Morvay types some changes into the computer. "Okay, Abbey, here's your new schedule and your pass to PE. Anything else I can help you with?"

I easily come up with a long list in my head, but say, "No, thanks." I don't know her well enough to trust her with what I really need help with.

❖

Five minutes later I find myself face to face with Mrs. Schwartz, my PE teacher. According to Jenn, she's the second toughest teacher at Gila, the first being Mr. Ponsi, the mechanics teacher and weekend Harley rider who has reportedly failed kids for accidentally dropping a tool.

Mrs. Schwartz trusts no one. "Ms. Morvay?" she questions, as she inspects my pass carefully.

"Yes," I stammer. "They ran out of room in Algebra 2, I guess."

"I don't need your life story," she says and looks at me through sharp gray eyes that I am pretty sure have seen things that would make my dead-dad dreams seem almost pleasant. "Regardless of your excused tardiness," she says, tearing up my pass then tossing it in the garbage, "you are currently failing PE."

I nearly barf. "Failing? But I..."

"No excuses"—she looks down at her roster—"Abbey Brooks is it?"

"But I was at…"

"The only *butt* of yours I want around here will be at the track at lunch to make up the mile you already missed. Got it?"

"Yes, Mrs. Schwartz."

After my encounter with Sweat Suit Satan, I'm finally able to rush over to Kate and tell her what happened to me this morning. As we walk into the locker room, Marisol and Sarah join us. I know they'll be impressed that Jake knew my name, which seems like a stupid reason to be excited, but whatever.

❖

Spanish 2 is next. It's normally a sophomore class, but I tested into it this summer thanks to my Advanced Spanish teacher in eighth grade. Anyway, I have exactly seven minutes to make it over to the Foreign Languages wing from the gym. Remembering a bit of advice from Jenn, I take a shortcut down the first floor corridor before heading upstairs. Walking the halls, I discover, is just like riding my bike through town: you just have to know the right routes and be familiar with all the possible obstacles that can get in your way.

As I bolt up the second-floor ramp, I accidentally hit the arm of a football player with my backpack, which could be just as dangerous as the time I accidentally rode into the side of a Suntran bus on Grant Road.

"Watch it, freshmeat!" Number Twelve yells.

I keep walking and try to ignore him because it's my only defense, and my dad always told me, "Never engage with the enraged." Dad was talking about wild animals, but I think the Gila High football player qualifies.

"You hear me, freshmeat? Are you a retard or something?" he yells, which causes his teammates to laugh and a few other students to stop and stare.

Apparently my tactics aren't working out, so after I reach the top of the ramp (distance for safety), I turn around. "Sorry," I stammer and hope I will live to eat brownie batter one more time.

"Yeah, you are," he retorts and slaps Number Thirty-four's hand.

I'm sure my face is bright red and I want to disappear, still I can't help but wonder why the stupidest people in the world always seem to have the most power. Seriously, how does this happen?

Suddenly I hear a girl's strong voice yell, "Get a life, losers!"

Then another girl shouts from behind me, "Yeah, pick on someone from your own species. Morons!"

I nearly lose my breakfast for the second time today. I am sure we're all going to be put into garbage cans or given swirlies in dirty toilets, but the guys just flip us off and walk away.

"Don't let them get to you," says a green-eyed girl who is now standing beside me. The tight Wonder Woman shirt she's wearing shows off her curves, but I quickly divert my eyes to the other girl.

"Yeah, they're just jealous that you hang out with rad girls like us," says the shorter one with supercurly blond hair. She's wearing a T-shirt that has a picture of a gila monster dribbling a basketball, with the words "Gila Hoops Rocks!" underneath it.

I can't even believe they said that stuff to the jerks, but I'm even more shocked that I might have found *them*: the infamous Gila High girls' basketball players. But I don't act too excited. That would be weird. I just stick out my hand and introduce myself as casually as possible. "I'm Abbey."

"Garrett," says the Wonder Woman girl while shaking my hand. Her brown hair is back in a ponytail and she's got on a tiny bit of eye makeup, but she isn't all plastic and horrible like Kate insisted everyone at high school would be.

Neither of them are what I expected, actually. They both have on shorts, T-shirts, and worn-in Nikes, but they don't look like slobs. They just look comfortable and cute. And even though they don't look like her at all, the way they act reminds me of the Hot Dog on a Stick Chick: cool, calm, and collected.

"This is Stef," Garrett says.

"Hey," Stef says and gives me a quick wave.

"Thanks for saving me," I say, but instead of responding right away, they just stand there smiling at me, sizing me up like they're trying to figure out if I can fit in a pair of jeans Garrett has in her backpack or something. Then they look at each other and nod.

"No sweat, Abbey. See you around," Garrett says and they turn and walk away, talking too low for me to hear what they're saying.

I look up and down the hall and panic because it's nearly empty. Then the late bell rings above my head, motivating me to sprint to 204 before the campus supervisors write me up for being tardy because there's no way I can fail a class and get detention on the first day of school.

Lucky for me, there is still a seat in the row closest to the door (Jenn's advice: sit close to the door to avoid bad smells in the corners of the classrooms). It doesn't take a mastermind to figure out we're supposed to be copying down whatever *Señora* Cabrera is writing on the board, so I unzip my backpack, take out my binder, and get busy.

When the note drops onto my desk ten minutes later, I begin to pass it forward to the girl in front of me. Being a founding member of the Geek Pack, I have never been one to receive notes in class unless someone's asking me for the answers on a test. I lean forward to pass it, but someone from behind me kicks my chair. I turn in my seat and there's Garrett. Sitting across from her is Stef.

Garrett finally manages to stop laughing long enough to whisper, "It's for you, Genius."

I'm reaching my saturation point of people laughing at me, but I whisper, "I knew that," and glance around to locate *la profesora*. She's writing stuff on the board again, so I put the note in my lap, like I've seen other girls do, and quietly open it.

Hey Abbey,
Do you play b-ball? If not, you should totally try out anyway. You're supertall and we need you. We're both sophs on the JV team. Tryouts are coming up. I better see you there. ☺
Write back! Garrett

Not only do I start to freak out because I actually got a note sent to me that didn't include the words, "What's the answer to number..." but I'm also flipping out because *they* want me. Sure, I'm not positive she's one of *them*, but knowing my bad luck (or is this good luck?) Garrett is. Then I think, or maybe hope, this is some sort of incognito way of asking me out, which of course causes my pits and hands to sweat profusely.

I'm way too paranoid about passing notes to respond, so I slip the note into my back pocket and pretend to follow along with *la profesora's* lesson on greetings. But in between the *holas, igualmentes,* and *mucho gustos,* all I'm thinking about is my pinky promise with Kate: no basketball and absolutely no lezzies. Suddenly that promise is being challenged by two strangers that I actually think I want to get to know better.

When the next note plops onto my desk, my stomach dives down to visit my knees and I can feel my heart trying to pound its way out of my chest.

Hey Abbey,

It's a simple question. Are you trying out for b-ball? The freshman coach is intense. She'll teach you everything. September 15th, 4:00 in the main gym. That's a Monday—don't forget. Actually, Stef and I will remind you tomorrow, and the next day, and the next day. Hey, you owe us. We did, after all, save your freshie ass.

Hearts, Garrett

P.S. I'll see you at tryouts.

P.P.S. If you're thinking this is me hitting on you...chill out, you're not my type. I like my girls like I like my ice cream: chocolatey!

After reading those last lines of her note I know two things for sure:

1. My new ultra-strength deodorant is failing miserably.
2. I definitely am not the only girl at Gila High who maybe likes girls.

CHAPTER FOUR

After dropping my backpack on the couch, I head to the backyard for the annual Abbey's First Day of School ritual. Okay, ritual makes it sound a little too tribal; I guess I'll call it what it is—a tea party in which my mom drills me about my day and then gives me a celebratory, yet academic, present.

"There she is," my mom says, as she gets up from her chair and hugs me hard. "My little Abbey Road is home from her first day of high school."

"Can't...breathe...Mom."

"Okay, okay." She releases her death grip and we sit down at the patio table under the paloverde my mom, dad, and I planted on my fifth birthday. I guess when we planted it in the ground way back then, the tiny tree resembled what its name means in Spanish: a green stick. But now its branches shade most of the yard and half the pool like a giant umbrella, which makes sitting back here nearly tolerable. "So, how was it? Tell me everything." She pours me a glass of lemonade and puts a homemade chocolate chip cookie on my plate.

"Well, let's see," I say, then gulp down the entire contents of my glass to buy some time. The day was certainly eventful, but for the first time since kindergarten, I don't really want to tell her everything. "I'm not taking Algebra 2 like I thought."

"Oh, yeah?" She pours me more lemonade. "What happened?"

"I guess all the algebra classes were filled up."

"So now what?"

"That's the cool part. I signed up for Beginning Guitar instead. It was that or Home Ec and you know how dangerous that would be for the school," I say and laugh. I'm trying my best to be funny because I can already see tears in my mom's eyes.

"Guitar?" she asks, and it's hard to tell if she's sad, proud, or just reminiscent.

"Yeah. Is that okay?"

She forces a smile on her face. "Oh my gosh, yes, Abbey. It's great. It'll be…" She looks away from me to gather herself. "It'll be great to hear music in the house again."

I poke at the cookie on my plate. Grabbing a clump of hair with my other hand, I paint my cheek with its tip and feel bad for making her miss him and wonder if talking about him will ever get easier.

"So," my mom finally says, "did you meet any new and interesting people?"

In my head I think, *Boy, did I ever*, but say, "Yeah, there are a couple of cool sophomore girls in my Spanish 2 class."

"Terrific. What about Kate? Did she have a good day?"

The only thing I know about Kate's day is that she had Chemistry with some idiot jock named Daniel or Darren or Dumbass, or something with a D, and she's now apparently in love with him, which is all I heard about at lunch after I ran the mile I missed in PE. "Yeah, I guess she did," I say.

"What else? Come on, spill it! You used to talk forever without breathing after your first day."

You mean you want to hear about how Jake Simpson knew my name, or how I nearly got an F in PE, or how I passed notes in Spanish with a genuine lesbian, or how I told that lesbian a whopper of a lie about why I can't try out for basketball? Sorry, Mom. Instead, I say, "Nothing else to say, I guess. It was just an ordinary day of school."

"Hmm. Okay," she says. "Well, I do have something for you, but now I think I'll hold off giving it to you until your birthday."

"What! But that's not until November."

"Don't worry, sweetie. I've got something even better for you. Come on." She takes my hand and leads me to the garage.

She starts handing me random items from a pile in the corner, and since I don't know what to do with them, I make another pile behind me.

She holds up my rusty red tricycle. "I can't believe you used to be this tiny."

I take it from her and chuck it on the other pile. The hellish temperature of the garage is slowly suffocating me and I've already worked up a sweat. "How much longer?"

"Hang on. I'm almost there," she says, as she moves aside some Christmas decoration boxes to make a path to the shelves that hold our more valuable possessions.

My first-day-of-school present hasn't ever come from a box in the garage, so I'm kind of disappointed. Plus, I thought for sure she'd bought me a cell phone, since I've been begging for one all summer. But she's old, old school. We just barely got cable and voice mail.

"Seriously Mom, I'm about to pass out."

"Got it," she says and emerges from behind a tower of boxes, bikes, and wrapped up paintings. She's got a guitar case in her hands. "This is the one."

Back inside we sit down on the couch. My mom puts the closed guitar case on the coffee table in front of us. Before opening it, she says, "I gave this to your dad on our third wedding anniversary, when I was pregnant with you. We didn't have a dime to our name with me sitting at home about to burst and your dad finishing up graduate school, but I wanted to get him something special. He'd been talking about this guitar for months, so I marched down to the store, and you know what I did?"

"No, I don't, but I hope I wasn't a prenatal accomplice to armed robbery."

I make her laugh, which is always my goal when I'm around her. "Better. I told the owner of the shop that his small store was hard to see from the road. He agreed but said he couldn't afford to do much about it. So that's when I offered my services. I told him I'd paint a bright, eye-catching mural on his storefront for trade. For this guitar," she says and points to the guitar case in front of us.

I had no idea that my mom was such a wheeler and dealer. "And he gave you the guitar?"

"Well, not exactly. He thought my artwork was worth even more than this guitar, so he threw in the case, a bunch of spare strings, and a hundred dollars. The store and my mural are gone now, but your dad used to love to drive friends by my mural and say, 'Now that's a masterpiece.'" Then she finally opens the case.

We both silently stare at it nestled in the red velvet and remember the music Dad used to make. He was such a serious science guy most of the time, but when it came to playing his guitar, he'd let it all out. Maybe playing guitar will have the same effect on me, too.

❖

Neither my mom nor I know anything about tuning or restringing or caring for a guitar, so we decide to take it to a music shop to have someone look at it. Since the store is near our favorite pizza joint, I suggest to my mom that we drop it off and eat some pizza while we wait. Much to my amazement, she agrees.

I'd been to All Strings Attached a few times with my dad, so when I walk through the doors I have another one of my missing-dad moments. The noise level doesn't really match my mood, though. It sounds like there are five horrible rock concerts going on at once. My mom and I weave through the tight pathways between the instruments and other customers and wait for help at the register.

"I'll be right with you," a girl shouts, as she walks behind the counter. She's hidden behind a tall stack of folded T-shirts balanced in her arms. She carefully places the stack on another counter, and suddenly all my favorite parts of the Hot Dog on a Stick Chick are revealed: her smile, her eyes, her...other parts. Seeing her makes me gasp, which causes my mom to look over at me, which causes me to scowl back at her hoping to confuse her. I pray it works.

The Hot Dog on a Stick Chick tosses her heavy black braid over her shoulder and dusts off her hands to indicate she's done with that task. "*Hola*, how can I help you?"

I'm thinking, *Oh, Hot Dog on a Stick Chick, you had me at 'Hola,'* so thank God my mom's there to intervene.

Mom puts the case on the counter and opens it up. "We don't know exactly what it needs."

The Hot Dog on a Stick Chick raises her eyebrows like she's shocked. It must be because the guitar is so old or dirty or cheap or needs lots of work. After all, it has been hiding in the overheated garage for a long time.

"Is it still playable?" my mom shouts over the banging of drums and screeching of electric guitars. "Can you fix it tonight?"

The Hot Dog on a Stick Chick glances over at me, and I give a little wave to her then roll my eyes to convey that I don't normally do geeky things like go to music shops with my mom. I also congratulate myself for knowing her fingertip calluses are from playing guitar. Then I wonder how she manages to work two jobs and go to school.

"Well, it usually can't be done that quickly, but I'll give you the Gila High special and get her cleaned up for you tonight," she says to me then closes the case and gently leans it against the wall behind the counter like she knows how much the guitar means to us. "I'll have her ready for you by nine o'clock. That cool?"

She's talking to me again, but I've stopped breathing, so I nod my head instead of speaking.

My mom is satisfied with the transaction and is already halfway to the door. I'm about to follow her, but then the Hot Dog on a Stick Chick says, "*Adiós, Amara*," and winks at me...again. And because there aren't any lemons around, I am thoroughly convinced that this time she did it on purpose.

Dinner with my mom is a blur. I think there are black olives and mushrooms on the pizza, but it might as well be anchovies and onions because I am way too distracted to notice. I manage to appear like I'm listening to my mom's stories about her high school days, way back when Madonna was much closer to being like a virgin than now, but the only reason I know when to nod and laugh is because I've heard them all a million times before.

After dinner I tell my mom to go to the car, and I'll just run in to get the guitar. She gives me a wad of cash and I bolt across the street while she climbs in our junky blue Volvo station wagon.

The store is much quieter and looks bigger without all the customers crowded in trying out the goods. I arrive at the counter, but no one's around, not even the Hot Dog on a Stick Chick. I wait patiently and try to appear cool by tapping my fingers to the music playing in the background. It's a guitar instrumental of "Something" by the Beatles, which is the song my mom always asked my dad to play. Then a woman's voice starts singing along, and that's when I realize the guitar isn't coming from the speakers mounted around the store, and neither is the voice.

The live music is coming from behind a wall of Jimi Hendrix posters, so I peek around the corner and can't believe what I see: the

Hot Dog on a Stick Chick playing my dad's guitar. Her eyes are closed, and as she releases the sweet lyrics they feel like soft whispers floating by my ear, sending goose bumps down my arms.

Realizing that she might think I'm weird for spying on her, I turn around quietly to pretend I was never there. She must have sensed me watching her because she opens her eyes and stops singing, but keeps on playing my guitar.

"Do you always go around sneaking up on people, Amara?" she asks with a huge smile on her face, which tells me that she must not think I'm too weird.

I cross my arms over my chest, smile back, and then shrug because, once again, I can't breathe or speak. It's the way she says *Amara*, like she knows how it makes me feel. I had decided during dinner that I would go ahead and tell her my real name, but after hearing my pretend name again, I change my mind. Amara is close enough.

"I hope you don't mind. I was just trying her out," she says. "Man, she's a beauty. It's a Martin D-35, right?"

I have no idea who Martin is or what she's talking about, so I shrug and smile again.

She picks up on my confusion and tries to help me. "What I mean is, it's a really, really rare guitar. Where'd you guys get it?"

"Some guitar shop guy gave it to my mom in exchange for painting his wall," I say, and now the Hot Dog on a Stick Chick is confused.

Thankfully, she changes the topic to something we can both understand. "So did you enjoy the free concert, you little spy?"

"Oh. Yeah, it was…" I struggle to find the perfect adjective to describe the music she made but only come up with "nice." Then I watch her wind up some cords. She has nice tennis-player arms; they are strong, but not too muscular. Then out of nowhere, I say, "How do you do that?"

"Wind up cords?" she asks and laughs in her smooth sort of way.

What I am thinking is, *How do you make the music float across the room and land in my ear like a kiss?* But what I say is, "No, how do you move your fingers that quickly when you play? I'm never going to be able to do that."

"Just takes a little practice," she says, looking too closely at me, like Garrett and Stef did in the hall at Gila. "You don't play, huh?"

That was a question and I know I need to say something, but all I can think about is the dream I had about her last night. She was behind the counter at Hot Dog and was teasing me with a french fry, pulling it away from my mouth when it was so close I could feel the steam warm my lips. "It's not mine. It's my dad's," I finally say.

She snaps the case shut. "He must really love her. She's in great shape."

"It is? He's dead," I say without meaning to.

"Oh, I'm sorry." Then she changes the subject. "So, what are you two going to do with her? You know she deserves better than the highest bidder on eBay, right?"

"Actually, I'm taking a guitar class at Gila. It's for beginners." I grab a lock of hair to twirl but force myself to let it go.

"Really," she says, as if she's doubtful for some reason, so I explain.

"Yeah, I don't know why I chose guitar. I mean, I'll probably suck at it. I'll never be as good as you. It was a stupid choice. I should have taken typing or something." I pinch my freckled arm with one hand and begin to twirl my hair with the other.

She smiles and walks to the front of the store with my guitar. I follow her.

"Actually," she says, "Mr. Chase is a pretty good teacher, Amara. You'll be fine. Besides, you can do anything you put your mind to." She opens the front door for me. "It just takes a little time. Everything will fall into place when it needs to. Trust me."

I do. I trust her completely.

As she hands me the guitar, our hands touch. I feel my body flush and my head spin but still manage to remember I haven't paid her. "Wait, how much do I owe you?"

"It's on the house. Besides, I should be paying you for letting me hold something that rare in my arms." She embraces me in her gaze.

I respond with my cheesiest smile and wish I could stay in the store forever, but with my mom waiting across the street, maybe even watching us, I have to stay focused. I start to get the cash from my back pocket, but she grabs my hand to stop me. I try not to faint from the serious lack of oxygen to my brain.

"Keep your money, Amara. Don't you remember what I told you last time?"

I haven't forgotten any part of our previous meeting but want her to say it again.

"When someone gives you more than you expect, just say thank you and walk away." Then she puts the pick she's been using in my palm. It's warm from being in her pocket. "You'll need this for class tomorrow," she whispers.

I swallow loudly and whisper back, "Thanks." I don't know why we're whispering, but it feels like the right thing to do.

"Now you're learning," she says and looks into me again. I wonder what she sees that's worth looking at. *"Buenas noches, Amara."*

"Okay, yeah. I mean, you, too. And thanks." I turn to leave the store, forcing myself to keep walking across the street instead of turning around to look at her. Though I'm pretty sure I look totally drunk as I cross the road, I manage to make it to our car on my wobbly legs. I get in, shut the door, and buckle my seat belt.

"Any change?" Mom asks and slowly accelerates down the street.

"Nope," I say, "no change."

CHAPTER FIVE

W hat's with that thing?" Kate asks, as she sprays another layer of perfume across her pushed-up boobs.

I'm on her basement couch waiting (again) for her to finish getting ready for school. "It's called a guitar."

"Are you trying to become a band geek or something?"

"They don't play acoustic guitar in band. Duh."

She laughs. "Okay, well, you're an even bigger geek for knowing that."

"Are you ready yet?"

"Just one more," Kate says and showers her hair with another dose of hairspray. "Okay. Now we can go."

Our walk to school begins, and as we trudge down her street and then cut through the grocery store parking lot, Kate starts her morning rant. "I can't believe my mom shrunk my favorite pair of jeans and Jenn better replace my eye shadow because if she doesn't…"

And that's about when I tune out and instead think my own, nonshareable thoughts. I have the Hot Dog on a Stick Chick's pick in my pocket, and each time I reach in and touch it, I replay how she opened my palm and placed it gently in my hand. And how sexy she looked when she played my dad's guitar and how after I got home last night I actually hugged my guitar in hopes that her talent or perhaps her fresh, just-out-of-the-shower scent might rub off on me.

"And you know what else?" Kate asks.

I can tell from her intonation that I need to participate in the conversation again. "No. What?"

"I was talking to Jenn last night, this was before the eye-shadow incident, and you know how she's on the girls' varsity basketball team at Gila?"

I switch my guitar to the other shoulder and grimace at the sweat mark the strap has left on my shirt. "Yeah. What about it?" I say, wondering if I sound too defensive or guilty. I have successfully avoided telling Kate about how Garrett and Stef had bugged me about trying out, so I can't believe she's bringing up the subject at all. Then I wonder if Kate's doing her BFF mind reading thing. Maybe she already knows everything.

"Well, Jenn started in on me again about trying out for the team."

"Really?" I use the corner of my shirt sleeve to wipe the sweat dripping down my temple. It must be about ninety-five degrees and our conversation isn't helping me stay cool. "What did you say?"

"I told her no way in hell, of course, but Jenn was pretty insistent we do it. And she said there aren't really that many of the"—Kate lowers her voice—"lesbians on the team. I think she said there are only two main couples and maybe one other." We enter the noisy hallway of Gila, but the cool air doesn't help my sweaty condition. "And, I don't know. Jenn made it sound like it could be sort of fun."

"Fun? Humph," I grunt. But what I'm actually thinking is that Kate's attempting to trick me into confessing I've been thinking about trying out, too. "What about our promise? What about not knowing at all how to play?"

"Well," she says, as we approach our lockers, "I made a list of pros and it's pretty long."

"Ah, the pro-con list lives on. And I thought I was the only geek left."

"Whatever. Just listen to me and be serious for once."

I've never been more serious about any conversation we've had, but she can't know that.

"First of all, we get to go on road trips and get out of school early sometimes."

"I guess that wouldn't suck," I say.

Our lockers are side by side, thanks to some tactical moves given to us from our insider Jenn, and we spin in our combinations.

"Plus," she says, "we'd get to be on a team that didn't require polyester blazers and electing officers."

"Well, that would address rule number twelve, avoiding groups that have a high geek and polyester ratio."

"Exactly." Then she looks down at her shoes. "And there's one more thing."

"We'd get in shape?" I say, as I struggle with opening my locker.

"Actually, it's better than that."

I've seen this look in her eyes before and know what she'll say next is related to a guy.

"I found out that Derrick plays basketball, too, so I'm thinking if he sees me as more than just a genius in chemistry class then maybe..."

"At last. The truth." My locker finally opens, and I hang my backpack on the hook because I don't think I'll need it for guitar class, and I have enough to carry. "How do you know he's even into you, anyway?"

"Oh my God, did I not tell you how I totally caught him looking at my boobs? That's a good sign, right?"

"Why don't you just join the cheerleading squad? Then you can flash him your underwear without appearing to be a slut."

"Not funny," she says, as she looks in her mirror to fix her hair. "Besides, if I do it, you're doing it, so get over it."

I slam my locker shut. "No way, and you can't make me."

"Yes way, and I will make you. I always do."

She has a good point.

"Besides, what are you so afraid of anyway, Abbey? It's not like you're one of them, so who cares. Right?"

And I have nothing to say to that.

Room P3 is in the deepest depths of the performance hall, and apparently, I'm really early for guitar class because, as I walk in, the room echoes with silence. Even though this isn't an honors class, I follow Rule #2 and sit in the seat farthest away from the front. With nothing better to do, I take out my guitar and strum the only note I can remember from my dad's lessons—D, D, D, D, D—which doesn't make for a pretty song. I try to remember the other notes my dad taught me but can't, which really bums me out.

Five minutes later, the final bell rings and I find myself surrounded by grungy boys with long hair, wearing black T-shirts printed with the names of bands I've never heard of: Keat's Kills, Los Payasos de Mars, and The Spazmodic Fire Monkeys. I wait for a girl to walk through the doors to latch on to for solidarity and security, but it's just one boy after another. Eventually I stop watching the door, look down at my Converse, and pout. Stupid guitar class. I should have taken Home Ec.

Mr. Chase makes his entrance from behind the blue velvet curtain and rolls out a portable chalkboard. It's filled with notes entitled "History of the Guitar."

"I see some of you are ready to get started on actually playing the guitar." He looks over at me and smiles. I hadn't yet noticed, but I'm the only one with a guitar out. All the boys laugh, and I slowly die in my chair. "But, before we get to that, just like I promised, we have to fulfill some requirements from The Man."

The class groans, and I panic. Everyone else has their binders and backpacks, but mine are in my locker. As much as I hate doing it, I have to ask someone if I can borrow some supplies.

I scan the circle of slimy boys. I skip all the ones with multiple face piercings because they weird me out. That leaves five guys to choose from. One is wearing a wifebeater and has really hairy armpits. I fear his odor. The next three won't make eye contact with me. Then my eyes fall upon an oasis in my Sahara Desert of grossness: Jake Simpson. I don't know how I missed him coming in, but I am totally relieved to see his tall self.

Jake sees me, too, holds up a notebook and a pen, and raises his eyebrows. I nod my head, put my hands together to thank him, and he passes them around the circle to me.

Mr. Chase is all the way down to the third bullet on his list, so I start frantically taking notes as soon as the supplies arrive. I'm so completely engrossed in my note taking that I almost don't register that someone else has entered the classroom.

"*Buenos días, Señor* Chase," I hear. "Sorry I'm late."

I stop writing, look up, and nearly upchuck my Cheerios.

The Hot Dog on a Stick/Guitar Chick hands one of the coffees she's carrying to Mr. Chase and sits down on the stage. And me? Now my mouth is a mailbox left open, agape and empty of expression. She looks my way, nods her head toward my guitar, and smiles. In return, I give her a poorly performed closed-mouth grin. My mom says it's cute when I smile like that, which means I must look totally stupid.

"Lady and gentlemen that are new to class, this is my student aide, Ms. Reyna Moreno."

"But you can call me Keeta," she says to me, and to the rest of the class, I guess.

I repeat both her names in my head over and over again. I don't want to ever forget them, as if that's possible.

❖

Taking guitar is the best thing I've ever done, is what I'm thinking on Monday morning, as I walk to Spanish 2. Yes, after five days of being in the same room with Keeta, I'm in high school heaven. I wasn't even fazed when I got another lunch detention from Mrs. Schwartz for supposedly talking during her badminton presentation. In fact, I'm as happy as can be when I sit down in my usual seat in Spanish, take out my book and binder, and wait for Stef and Garrett to arrive.

Stef's backpack lands in her seat with a loud thud and I'm jolted out of my Keeta daydream. "Well, if it isn't Ms. Lying Her Ass Off," Stef says. "Look at her, Garrett. What a *mentirosa*."

Garrett leans over my shoulder and slams my book shut. "Yeah, what a liar. You know, Abbey, you really had us fooled."

If this was junior high, I would have quickly called out for the teacher to intervene. But I'm a big high school freshman now and they both have slight smiles on their faces. I decide to wait before calling for backup. "What's up, guys?"

"Well, we had a little chat with one of the varsity players," Garrett says, "one by the name of Jenn Townsend."

My stomach does a triple backflip and sticks the landing. Perfect ten.

"And your name came up somehow."

"Yeah?" I say quietly.

"You'll never believe what she said when we told her about a really tall girl named Abbey in our Spanish class who said her mommy wouldn't let her play basketball because of all her bad grades last year."

Even though Jenn is the reason I'm in this jam, I refer to her advice on what to do when you're caught in a big lie: I'm going to keep my damn mouth shut. There are only two more minutes until class starts. I can totally make it.

Stef chimes in again. "Turns out you're best friends with her little sister, Kate."

My mind races, as I try to come up with a new lie to cover the first one, but it's becoming clear that lying isn't really working out for me.

The tag team continues. "Yeah, once Jenn recovered from laughing, she told us that you and her little sis have made honor roll since the day you were born." Then Garrett shakes her head and tsks like my grandma does when I beat her at a game of cribbage. "I feel so betrayed."

"So, Abbey," Stef pats me on the back, "I guess we'll see you at tryouts. I can't wait. Oh, and by the way, you're a crappy liar."

The bell finally rings and *Señora* Cabrera bursts into the class dressed in an oversized skirt and matching blouse. *"Hoy aprenderemos el vocabulario para las fiestas Mexicanas. Viva!"* she shouts.

"Viva!" the class shouts back, but I'm freaking out and can't function. Not only have I just been caught in my first high school lie, but it appears I'm going to be trying out for the Gila High girls' basketball team.

CHAPTER SIX

After school on tryout day, Kate and I meet up in the locker room to get ready to humiliate ourselves on the basketball court. As I review chapter 10 of *Basketball for Dummies*, she gives me the play-by-play of today's chemistry class and her nonexistent relationship with her pretend boyfriend, Derrick.

"Anyway, after I told him I was trying out today, he totally told me to call him afterward to tell him if I made it. He said if I did make it, I could help him with his chem homework and he could show me some moves on the court. And then, oh my God, so I was all, 'How about you call me,' and then I grabbed his cell out of his pocket to add myself to his contacts and he was all, 'Damn girl, be careful what you're reaching for in there.' Isn't he so funny?"

"Gag," I say and turn the page. "Wasn't he just shoving his tongue down some girl's throat at lunch?"

"That skanky slut Roxy?"

"Right."

Kate walks over to the mirror to fix her hair for the tenth time in the past five minutes.

"Abbey, don't you see she's totally insignificant?"

I reread the page on layups, which is a shot I've been really focusing on since I've heard it mentioned often by Jenn while describing some of the "awesome" games she's had. "Well, if you ask me…" I say absentmindedly to Kate.

"Abbey, please," she says, interrupting me midsentence like I knew she would because she never does ask me. "It's obvious he doesn't really like her because if he was really into her, he would be hanging out with her and the rest of his friends at lunch at the jock table, not making out against the gym because she's a skank. And, by the way, I can't believe you are reading that book in public. Your continuous geekdom is a huge disappointment to me."

I nod because I know she's right. I am a complete geek for checking this book out from the library and reading the whole thing over the past week. I even practiced the foot- and hand-work for defense, jump shots, and layups in my backyard—all without a basketball. My mom thought I was choreographing a modern dance routine for PE, and I didn't bother correcting her because I didn't feel like explaining what I was really doing until I absolutely had to. Like this morning when I shoved the permission form in front of her while she mixed paints at her easel.

"Anyway, he is so totally mine," Kate says triumphantly, doubly pleased because her ponytail is centered on the back of her head and the curls are going the right direction. "And he's so yummy. Have you seen his muscles, and his smile, and his tattoo? And have you seen his"—she looks behind her to make sure no else is around—"have you seen his ass?" she whispers. "Double yum."

"Double gross," is all I have to say about that, and we head out to the gym to what could potentially be the most regretful day of my high school experience.

Kate and I stop at the sideline of the court, as if it's the edge of an ominous body of water. Like if we step out on it, something slimy and scary will grab hold of us and pull us under. We aren't the only ones who seem afraid, either. No one else has dared to step on the glossy court.

I can tell Kate is making spot judgments of the misfit pack of girls who are waiting for tryouts to start, so I check them out, too. A few girls have painted nails and makeup on like Kate, and others seem like your run-of-the-mill athletic types, but a couple others stand out to me. They have on superbaggy shorts, real basketball shoes, and low ponytails, not the high-on-the-head ponytails like Kate wears. After assessing the crowd, I conclude that I look more like those low-ponytail girls than anyone else. My ponytail is set sort of in between high and low, but I'm wearing baggy shorts and a T-shirt. Though my shoes are just my old cross-trainer Nikes.

Kate looks over at me, and I hope she doesn't notice me staring at the girls who I have decided to call "possible friends of Stef and Garrett."

But she doesn't seem to care where I'm looking. "We own these tryouts, Abbey."

"Okay, sure."

"We do. Come on, say it. We own this."

"No."

"Say it, or I will tell everyone here you have a crush on Jake Simpson and you want to jump his bones."

"We own these tryouts," I say meekly, but I am pretty sure I'm not going to own anything after tryouts, except maybe more time alone in my room.

Coach Kimball enters the gym, or I should say *glides* because I've never seen anyone that tall look so graceful, and I'm happy to see it's possible. She's wearing a white polo shirt with a little green gila monster embroidered on the chest and perfectly fitted navy shorts. Like me, she's got legs as tall as a saguaro cactus, and I feel like we have an immediate bond. But that feeling fades because a little ways behind Coach, pushing a rack of basketballs and dressed in the same outfit Coach has on, are two people I'm slightly sick to my stomach about seeing: Stef and Garrett.

Coach Kimball blows her whistle, and we all forget our fear of the court and run over like trained dogs. Stef and Garrett stand beside her and are introduced as sophomores on the Junior Varsity team who are there to help her pick the freshman team. They look official with their clipboards and whistles, but all I can think about are the two of them hovering over me in Spanish, catching me in that stupid lie.

Coach Kimball prompts Stef with a nonchalant nod and Stef blows her whistle signaling that she's in charge now. "Let's go. Lines of five, everyone," Stef says with authority, and all us freshmen know just what to do because this is how Mrs. Schwartz leads us in stretches for PE.

Kate and I hide in the back row like usual because our long legs make our shorts too short, thus revealing a little more leg and butt than we'd like. Bonus for today? It's a good place to hide from Stef and Garrett.

"Okay. Sit it, spread 'em, and touch 'em," Stef yells. We don't know what she means because that was something Mrs. Schwartz has never said, so we have to wait to follow Stef's lead. She sits on the court, spreads her legs, and then stretches out to touch her toes. We all do the same.

A girl passes a clipboard to me, but it takes me a second too long to notice, which gets Kate all irritated. "You better pay attention, Abbey," she whispers to me, as she adds both our names to the list. "We're making this team together. Got it? Who owns this?"

I roll my eyes, but she looks a bit psychotic, so I give in. "Okay. God, we do," I say, and this time I mean it. After all, I'm here. I might as well do my best and try to get Garrett and Stef to forgive me.

After we stretch, Coach Kimball blows her whistle. "Let's start with ten warm-up laps, girls. And let's see some hustle, okay?" The fact that she's asking instead of demanding with threats like Mrs. Schwartz makes me want to do anything for Coach K, so I run laps like never before.

On my seventh lap around the gym, I make sure Kate isn't looking and then wave hi to Stef and Garrett, as I pass them. Garrett waves back and Stef grants me a smile, so I run even faster on the remaining three laps.

Next are defensive slides. Garrett shows us how they're done. I notice then that her long brown hair is pulled back in a ponytail that is a bit on the low side. "Start here on the sideline," Garrett explains. "Bend your knees and get low. If you stay too high, you'll lose the girl you're guarding. Then point the lead foot in the direction you want to go. And never cross one foot over the other." She shows us a couple of times and my confidence soars. It's exactly how I've been practicing. "Okay, your turn," she says, and we line up.

Even though she told them not to cross one foot over the other, a few girls do and end up tripping and falling, but I stay low and shuffle with ease. Kate stumbles once but doesn't fall.

The last drill of the day promises to be my most challenging. Sure, I practiced the footwork for layups, but I don't have a basketball hoop at my house, or a basketball for that matter, so I'm not really sure if I can dribble, run, and shoot at the same time.

"Crap, I can't do these," Kate says after running to the back of the line with me.

I've already tried and missed three times. "I know. I suck, too." But no one has made any shots, which makes me feel a tiny bit better.

"How are you supposed to do all that and get the ball in the basket?" Kate asks and wipes her face off with her sleeve. I'm surprised she isn't complaining about how sweaty she is or how her makeup is running. She almost seems to be having as much fun as I am. Maybe basketball could be the one thing we could actually enjoy doing together.

We scoot up in line, and I'm about to go again when Kate says, "According to Jenn, it's all about finding a rhythm, but I can't find a rhythm to save my ass."

"Rhythm?" I have about as much rhythm as I did when I was three years old, banging pots on the kitchen floor with wooden spoons, but I try to stay positive.

I catch the bounce pass from Coach Kimball who says, "You can do it, Abbey," and I begin my long dribble down the court. It's my last shot of the day, my last chance to show them that I am worthy of wearing blue and white on the court. I start my fancy footwork and then, just as I am about to go up for the shot, the ball slips from my hand. I try to grab it but end up kicking it into Stef who is standing behind the basket to rebound.

"Nice try, Abbey," she says. I think she's being sincere, but I'm way too embarrassed to even look at her, so I just run to the back of the line and try to accept that I probably didn't make the team.

Coach Kimball blows her whistle and calls us over to the bleachers. "All right ladies. Good effort. Get some water. We'll be back in five with our decisions."

We all fall onto the wooden bleachers and gasp like fish out of water from our two-hour workout.

"God, I blew it. I should have practiced more at home," Kate says after cooling down. "You were pretty good, though. I guess that stupid book paid off."

I shrug and say, "I guess," but the idea that I might be better than Kate at something makes me warm and fuzzy inside.

Then some girls enter the gym with a bag of basketballs. They wave to Stef and Garrett, who are on the other side of the gym with Coach K, so I figure they're on the JV team. They all look really tough and mature and have arm muscles, real basketball shoes, and seemingly confident attitudes. After they pass by us, I look down at my skinny twig arms and legs. And, because I suffer from white-girl syndrome, my skin is bright red and blotchy. That's when I decide I can't go through with joining the team. Even if I do make it, I'll politely decline to save myself from being killed.

"Gross, I'm all freaking sweaty," Kate says, reverting back to her pretty-girl persona. "And I need some water in a bad way." She gets up and walks over to the fountain.

I'm dripping with sweat, too, so I peel my sweaty ponytail off my neck, put it up in a haphazard bun, and lift up the bottom of my shirt to wipe my face and neck. Of course, that's right when Keeta walks in.

I immediately throw down my shirt and try to look less nasty. Luckily she doesn't notice me, but I watch each step Keeta takes as she heads to the girls' locker room. I wonder what she's doing in the gym but figure she just came to use the bathroom since, according to Jenn, they are the cleanest ones at Gila.

Keeta stops at the water fountain, but Kate's leaning over in front of her, gulping down the city's entire water supply. As she waits, I take mental photos of Keeta in her baggy jean shorts, bright orange shirt, and long black hair gathered in a loose ponytail, which is sitting very low on her head. Kate told me once that no one can pull off orange, but Kate's obviously never seen Keeta in orange.

Finally, Kate wipes her face and makes her way back to me. I've just become aware of my gaping mouth, so I close it and throw in an eye roll for no reason.

"What's wrong with you?" Kate asks, as she sits down next to me.

Keeta is bent over sipping water now. I try to look away from her, but I'm transfixed. "I'm fine. Why?"

"Why'd you roll your eyes?" Kate asks and looks in the direction of the drinking fountain. "You know her or something?"

Keeta slips into the locker room and I wait for the door to fully close before answering Kate. "Her?" I untie and then retie my shoelace and think of a safe answer. "Yeah, she's the teacher's aide in guitar." And then add, "She's weird," even though it's a lie.

"Really? She looks cool."

"Yeah, I guess," I agree, and smile slightly.

"What's so weird about her?"

How she makes me want to leap into her arms like a ballerina is what I'm thinking, but instead I say, "It's nothing, I guess. She's just…"

"Oh, here comes Coach K."

"Oh good," I say with secretly relieved enthusiasm.

Coach calls us over and then waits for everyone to settle down and get quiet. "Okay, the following girls are Gila High's new girls' freshman basketball team." She looks down at her clipboard and begins to read the names. "Courtney Marzan—"

Courtney covers her face with her hands and squeals while Coach waits patiently for her to compose herself before moving on.

"Ashley Reyes, Emily Barrett, Casey Pierce, Raquel Goodlander, Kate Townsend…"

Kate gasps and grabs my arm. As we listen to the rest of the names, her grip gets tighter and tighter, making my arm tingly and numb like those blood pressure cuffs we used to play with at the drug store.

When Coach K finishes reading her list and congratulates the girls on making the team, Kate releases my arm and looks at me. Out of the corner of my eye, I see Stef and Garrett glance at me then smile at each other, like they're especially pleased I didn't make the team. Man, they sure can hold a grudge.

I shrug, trying not to act too bummed out. "It's okay," I say to Kate who still can't believe it. "At least you made it."

But then Coach K continues. "Now, I know the rest of you may be disappointed, but here's some good news. We had a lower turnout for the JV tryouts, so we need to fill two spots on the JV team. I agreed to let Coach Riley have the top two girls who tried out today to fill those spots."

"No way," Kate and I say in unison.

"So, I won't torture you any longer. The two freshmen we would like to join the JV team are Tori Galvan and Abbey Brooks. Congratulations, girls."

Kate looks over at me again, but now she has what appears to be a little jealousy added to her look of shock.

I shrug again, but this time I'm smiling. I guess Stef and Garrett have forgiven me after all.

CHAPTER SEVEN

Today I'm riding my bike with great speed and excitement to the Tucson Mall because I finally get to shop for something I actually want: basketball shoes. Even my mom, who seemed to doubt I would even make the team, thought my Nikes were too old, and forked over some cash for shoes, workout shorts, and sports bras.

Since Kate's positive that I am incapable of finding anything at the mall on my own, she insisted on meeting me there. Then Marisol said she needed to come, and we didn't want Sarah to feel left out so she's tagging along, too.

After I arrive at the mall, I lock up my bike, take the Macy's escalator upstairs to the bathroom, and try to make myself look presentable. Part of this effort is for my friends, who think the mall is as sacred as church and you should always look your best. But I'm mostly doing it for one special person who may or may not be working at the Hot Dog on a Stick stand today.

I brush and braid my hair to hide the sweat, apply my new tangerine-flavored Chapstick, and make my way over to our meeting spot. I join Marisol and Sarah who are already waiting on the purple couch in the center of the mall and wait for Kate.

"Congrats on making the team," Marisol says.

"Yeah," Sarah adds. "Snaps for even trying out, especially considering the situation with some of the girls."

I'm mad that Kate blabbed to them about that, but I hide any emotion and say, "Whatever. It's not really that big of a deal, you guys."

"Well, sure, for them," Marisol agrees, "but what about you, Abbey? I mean, it sucks for you." And then she adds, "I'm just saying. You should be careful."

"It's not like they're going to..." I start to say, but then we see Kate descending the escalator, and I gladly drop the subject.

She has her back to us and is laughing at something Dorkass Derrick said. He's standing two steps above her, and I can tell he's spending most of his time looking down her shirt from his convenient position. When they reach the bottom, she fakes a little stumble as the steps disappear, and he reaches out on cue to catch her before she falls. I have to fight the urge to regurgitate my granola bar. Maybe it's because I'm jealous of what they have, but I think it's mostly because I can tell he's a sleaze. Kate throws her head back and laughs again. Her perfect brown hair cascades down her back, just like I am sure she had practiced in front of the mirror all summer. She hugs him good-bye, then slowly makes her way over to us.

"Oh my God," Marisol says, and I know what she's talking about. "She is so wearing a Miracle Bra."

Sarah covers her mouth to hide her laughter.

"Ladies," Kate says, "always remember to leave them wanting more." She turns and smiles at Derrick, while also somehow making her new cleavage pop.

"It's hard to believe she's the same girl who cries every time we watch Nemo get fish-napped," I say to Mari and Sarah.

"Haha," Kate says, "let's go."

We hit Lady Foot Locker, Finish Line, and Journeys, but they're a bust because they don't have any women's basketball shoes that I like in size ten, and I refuse to wear men's shoes like the salespeople always suggest I do. Finally, we try Champs.

"How about these?" Sarah holds up a pair of bright red Converse that is on display. A sign above it says, *You know what they say about guys with big feet*..."These are a men's seventeen. Is that big enough for you, Abbey?" she says and laughs.

"Good one, Sarah," Marisol says giving Sarah a high five.

I flip them both off and continue searching for the perfect shoes. And when I say perfect, I mean like the ones Garrett and Stef have. "Hey, these are the ones," I say and hold up a pair of blue-and-white low-tops. "Do you have these in a size ten?" I ask the Champs employee who seems more interested in helping Kate work the treadmill. He looks doubtful but goes in the back to check.

When he emerges with a box in his hand, Kate says, "I guess miracles do happen."

I slide my foot in, lace them up, and jump around a little to make sure they're not too small. "They fit!" I say and then get butterflies in my stomach. Even after just four days of practice, I feel like I belong on the team. "I'll take them."

❖

We all go our separate ways after arriving at the food court. Kate, Sarah, and Marisol stand in line for burgers, and even though Keeta's not standing behind the counter looking irresistible in her colorful polyester uniform and cap, I opt for a corn dog, french fries, and lemonade. We meet up again with our trays, and I suggest a table near Hot Dog on a Stick in case Keeta's just on a break or she comes in for the second shift. Kate decides it has enough guy-viewing potential, so we sit down.

While I innocently munch on my fries, my friends discuss the "screwability" of the boys who pass by.

"Ooh, in line at Eegee's, the guy in the black shirt," Marisol whispers.

"No way," Kate says. "Check out the one in line at Chick-fil-A. Now that's what I'm talking about. His legs are almost as muscular as Derrick's."

As they continue their lusting, I use the opportunity to review my basketball gear list. Basketball shoes? Check. Now all I need are sports bras, more socks, and maybe some new shorts. Blue shorts like Garrett and Stef wear.

"Girl, are you listening to a thing we are saying?" Marisol asks and pulls on my ear like I'm five.

I continue to contemplate my list but say, "Yeah. I am." Because I'm a good multitasker, I know they've moved on to talking about the dance, some Back to School Fling, or whatever. "And no. I'm not going."

"Abbey, are you kidding? Jake and you should totally go," Kate says and starts to bounce in her seat with excitement.

Marisol joins in. "*Dios mío*, you have to ask him."

"Um, no. I actually don't have to ask him."

"But you guys are so perfect for each other," Sarah says with a dreamy smile on her face.

"You're both so tall."

"Yeah, I can totally see it now," Kate says. "You guys would be like two friendly giants, strolling through the hall, ducking through doorways."

Marisol nearly shoots Dr Pepper out her nose. "Totally," she says after recovering.

"Shut up, you guys. It's not like that with him. I mean, he's cool, but…" I pick at the gum stuck under the table, then get totally grossed out when I realize what I'm doing. "Ew. I need to wash my hands. I'll be right back."

"You can run, but you can't hide," Kate yells over her shoulder, as I walk to the bathroom.

I wash my hands and then stick them under the air blower. I rub my hands together vigorously as instructed, and think more about Jake. He is cute, I guess, in a dude kind of way, and part of me really wishes I liked him like Kate likes Derrick. It would make everything so much easier. But no. No, the person I really like has to be the one person I probably can't ever have. She's a senior, for crying out loud. Um, and a girl, for crying out loud. Yep, she's just a dream that will never come true, and I feel so stupid for letting myself think Keeta sees me as anything more than a girl who likes french fries and can't play guitar.

I give up on the dryer and wipe my damp hands on my shorts. On my way back to our table, I glance over at Hot Dog on a Stick. That's when my whole world sparkles again because there's my dream girl working at the register. As I pass by, she looks up, sees me, and sends a stunning smile my way. I smile back, download the image of her flawless face into my brain, and force myself to walk back to the nearby table of torture and ignore my sudden urge for more french fries.

While my friends continue to stare at boys, I have the tip of my braid between my fingers and am painting my face and staring over at Keeta, who's slowly moving back and forth over the counter, as she wipes it down. In my mind I'm replaying the last time we looked at each other over the counter's shiny surface. As she cleans, I notice how defined the muscles in her arms are and figure it must be from playing the guitar or maybe from making so much lemonade. I sigh and wonder how someone can be so perfect.

"You want another corn dog or something?" Kate asks.

I usually notice when they stop talking, but this time I guess I was too distracted. I can feel them all staring at me, so I slowly adjust my gaze. "No. I'm not hungry. Why?"

"Well, you're looking over at the hot dog stand like some sort of psycho." Then Kate spots Keeta. "Hey, isn't that the guitar class helper chick?"

Marisol and Sarah crane their necks like giraffes to look over at Keeta, who is now pounding lemons with the lemonade-making contraption.

"Shouldn't we get going?" I pick up my backpack and stand up. "Those thongs aren't going to buy themselves, ladies."

But Kate grabs my backpack and yanks me back down. "I'm not done eating yet. Park it, sister."

"Oh yeah, I've seen her around Gila," Sarah says.

"Your point?" I know I sound defensive, but I don't like that they're looking at my secret crush. They have this way of ruining things for me and I don't want them to ruin this.

"What's her name?" Marisol asks.

"Keeta," Kate says, like she and Keeta are longtime friends or something.

I stay quiet and fidget with my backpack straps. I need to think of a way to get them to quietly exit the food court.

"Omigod." Sarah squints at Keeta to get a better look because she's supposed to wear glasses or contacts but can't remember to wear either. "She's one of those dykes on the basketball team," she says way too loudly.

I slap Sarah's arm. "God, you don't have to scream it." I quickly glance over at Keeta again.

She's taking an order from a mom with a bunch of kids and I pray she can't hear us. I regret choosing a table so close to her.

"And she doesn't play basketball," I say, ignoring the other part of Sarah's comment because it's too much for me to handle. "She plays guitar."

"Well, I don't know what rock you've been living under," Sarah says, "but she definitely plays basketball. She's on the varsity team.

She practices when my brother practices. He told me about her and the others. Wait, she's in your guitar class?"

"Yeah, so?" I look over at Keeta again and she looks right back at me. No smile this time.

Then Sarah remembers more details about Keeta. "I think she's with that one girl with the blond 'fro."

"Isn't that the girl you have Spanish with, Abbey?" Then Kate turns to The All Knowing Sarah, "Her name's Stef, right?"

"That's the one," Sarah says then whispers something to Marisol and they both laugh.

"What's your point?" I yell, suddenly feeling sick to my stomach. Keeta and Stef? That can't be right.

"Damn, Abbey. You're like a lezzie magnet!" Marisol says, and they all bust up laughing. "And you're going to play basketball with them? Ha. Before you know it, you'll be hanging on the arm of some girl at prom." Marisol bumps knuckles with Sarah, and they crack up some more about my future lesbian life. Even Kate's laughing.

I don't know how this happened, but I know I have to stop it. If I overreact, though, they might get suspicious. So I do what I do best when I'm around my friends: follow their lead.

"Oh my God, Mari, you're right." I force myself to laugh really loud. "They are totally after me. I should get some Extra Strength Gayoff. Does Walgreens carry that?"

It works. They laugh even harder and fall in each other's laps.

"Maybe I can buy it in bulk at Costco."

"Stop!" Kate gasps "I'm going to pee my pants!"

With the fake smile still on my face, I accidentally look over at Keeta one more time. The screaming kids are long gone, and she's just standing there, looking hard over at our table. Then she shakes her head and turns away. She must have heard everything. My fake smile melts faster than a snow cone in July.

I panic inside, but what can I do? If I go over to Keeta, my friends will know something weird is going on. Plus, I've just gotten them off my back about the whole lesbian thing. So I do the worst thing I've done since I lied to Stef and Garrett: I sit here and do nothing.

My friends finally recover from their laugh attack and we leave to finish our shopping duties. Using all the telepathic power I have, I try to get Keeta to look at me so I can apologize with my eyes, but she pretends to be engrossed in dipping hot dogs in the batter and doesn't look up as we pass.

We go to Macy's and I grab the first sports bras and socks I see. "Um, I'm going to buy these and then I gotta go, you guys. My mom wants me to clean the house today, or else."

They look up from the three-tier tower of thong underwear. "Yeah, sure. See ya, Abbey," Kate says.

"Cool," Sarah says.

And Marisol adds, "*Adiós, chica.*"

My departure from the group seems too easy, so I get all paranoid that they know more than I want them to, but I have to brush that aside. I've got bigger worries.

The number one worry I have at the moment is that Keeta heard what I said to my homophobic friends and has already decided never to talk to me again. So now I'm rushing through the mall to get back to the Hot Dog on a Stick stand to undo some of my stupidity from earlier. I don't know exactly what I'm going to say, but it's going to be the truth...for once. Not the whole truth, of course. Like, not the part where I think about her every waking moment of the day. I'm sincerely sorry, but I'm not crazy.

I maneuver around the crowds and lines as fast as I can, but when I arrive at Hot Dog, Keeta's not at the register.

"Hey," I say to the girl behind the counter. I recognize her from Gila High. "Is Keeta still working?"

She shrugs then yells at the other worker in the back, "Hey, D! Is Keeta still here? Some chick wants to talk to her."

"Nah. She took off ten minutes ago."

The girl behind the counter figures I've gotten my answer and helps the next customer.

❖

I hate myself, and I hate my so-called friends, and I hate not knowing what Keeta thinks of me. I usually don't mind the death-defying rides down Grant Street, but today I want to be alone, so I take a sharp left onto Catalina Avenue and pedal down the wide residential street until I'm zooming down it in a blur of rage. A minute later, I feel the wind pick up and a few tumbleweeds roll across the road. The wind tries to slow me down, but my anger continues to fuel my ride.

Besides feeling mad at myself about what I did back at the mall, part of me is actually mad at Keeta for not telling me that she's gay. But what do I expect her to do? Say something like, "Hey, I'm Keeta. Oh, and you should know, I'm a lesbian." People just don't do that. And after the way me and my dumb-ass friends acted, I can see why. And how was I supposed to know she played basketball? I thought she was at the gym to use the clean bathroom.

And I'm mad at Stef for not telling me Keeta is her girlfriend. But I guess that's my fault, too. I mean, I've never actually told Stef and Garrett that I'm taking guitar because I don't want them to think I'm a dork (more than they already do). Anyway, how would Stef ever have had the chance to tell me who she was dating? It's not like I ask about their girlfriends. No wonder Stef knows so much Spanish without ever doing her homework.

After thinking about all that, I try to not think about what's really on my mind: the angry look in Keeta's beautiful eyes, the way her black braid rests against her back when she's bent over helping someone in guitar class, the sweaty-palmed reaction I have whenever I see her, the flamed guitar pick I hold between my fingers every time I strum my guitar, which makes me think of her.

And, of course, there's a part of me that's thrilled. Keeta is a real lesbian! Maybe she really was winking at me at Hot Dog and All Strings Attached; maybe I'm not imagining it after all. Then I give myself a reality check. Stef's dating Keeta, which means Keeta's taken and there's nothing I can do about it.

There's a distant rumble of thunder, then a giant raindrop hits my face, then another, which makes me pedal even harder because I'm not in the mood to be drenched by the monsoon. In fact, I want to scream like I used to when I was little. I want to cause a great big scene until everyone gives me what I want. But I don't because I'm almost fifteen and that would be pretty much the most uncool thing for me to do in public. What I do instead is scrunch my eyes shut and beg the universe to help me stop thinking about Keeta from this point forward.

I only close my eyes for a second or two, but within that short blip of time, the wind pushes me off course. And just as I open my eyes, I see that I'm about to catch my handlebars on the driver's side mirror of a broken down car. Like usual, I overreact to the situation, turn the handlebars too far, and down I go.

When I land on the asphalt, the reality of pain consumes my mind, leaving very little room for Keeta-fantasizing or any other confusing thoughts. I look up at the darkening clouds, which, combined with the metallic smell in the air, tell me the monsoon is about to unleash completely upon me. Within seconds, I'll be soaked.

I try to scream for help, but now sobs are spewing out of me too quickly and preventing speech. I'm on my side and my legs are intertwined with my bike's frame. I look down at my knee; it's hamburger meat. Then there's my ankle. It's throbbing from being tangled in the chain and frame and is twisted at an unnatural angle. My backpack, which has already been rescued twice from the giveaway pile, didn't do much better than me, and the stuff it once held is spewed out on the road like backpack barf. And here comes the rain.

By the time I can push my bike off me and attempt to sit up, I am drenched from head to toe. One of my soggy socks is full of blood and my ankle resembles a watercolor painting of a sunset. Red, blue, and purple are all blending together.

Sitting in the middle of the sleepy, abandoned street, I curse my mom for being too cheap and weird to buy me a cell phone, and I cry a little more. Then, after shoving my new clothes and shoes in my pathetic excuse for a backpack, I use my bike as a walker and hobble to the gas station down the street.

I call my mom collect because I lost all the change that was in my bag.

"Abbey, what's wrong? Who's hurt? Are you okay?"

I thought I could calmly tell her that I need her to pick me up, but when I hear her voice I start to cry again. "Mommy," I sputter into the phone.

"Oh my God, Abbey. Where are you?"

"I fell off my bike. I'm at the Exxon on Campbell and Grant."

"I'll be right there, honey. Five minutes."

When she arrives, she totally freaks out. This is obvious because she keeps on repeating, "You're okay. You're okay. You're okay," as she drives me to the urgent care at St. Joseph's Hospital. After we check in and I get put into an exam room, she finally calms down a bit.

"We're going to get you all fixed up, my Abbeyroo. Mommy's here, okay?"

It feels kind of nice to be her little Abbeyroo again, so I don't laugh when she says it. Instead I say, "Okay, Mom. Thanks," because it's good to know I'm loved by at least one person in this messed-up world.

CHAPTER EIGHT

"Why don't you rest one more day?" Mom asks, as she helps me pull up my shorts while I lean on her for support. "Missing one day of school won't kill you, Abbey Road."

"I'm fine, Mom," I say between clenched teeth, trying to hold back a scream because she accidentally bumped her arm against my annihilated knee. I am still pretty banged up on the outside, and I rested all weekend with my ankle elevated, but my guilt never let up. All I could think about was Keeta and the moronic way I acted in the mall. I've memorized my apology and written it down for reference. Now I need to face Keeta and get it over with.

Mom drives me to school, and we pick Kate up on the way. I can't maneuver my crutches and carry my guitar, backpack, and foot pillow, so Kate, very unwillingly, carries my guitar over to the performance hall for me. She's about to dump it on me outside of the building, but it's obvious I'm not going to get far if she doesn't at least open the door.

"Geez, Abbey." She rolls her eyes and swings open the door. "Here you go, gimpy."

"Thanks," I say and stick my tongue out at her.

"I suppose you want that door opened, too?" She points at the double doors down the hall, that lead into the music room.

"Yes, please."

"I swear. You really need to get better soon. This is going to get so old."

Once we enter the empty room, she pushes me down in my chair and tosses the guitar on my lap, barely avoiding my oozing knee wound, drags another chair over, yanks the pillow out of my hands, lifts my foot, sets it on its comfy resting spot, and leaves in her usual loving manner. "Later, klutz."

There are still ten minutes before the first bell, and I'm bored and lonely. I unzip my case and pull out my guitar to practice the new song we're learning. It's called "Moon Shadow" and it's a total hippie song, one I think my dad would have loved, but it's easy to play. Before my accident, I had it down, but now trying to go between D and G in a smooth way is a little tricky due to the bandage on my left hand. Plus, my fingertips haven't developed any tough calluses, so they're still sore from the metal strings. I almost get through it twice without messing up, but then I hear a noise behind the curtain.

"Hello?" I say, but no one answers. "Hello?" Nothing again.

Then, thanks to the horror-movie marathons Kate and I have every summer, I imagine a masked killer leaping out from behind the curtain and strangling me with a guitar string or bludgeoning me with a trumpet. "Tell me who you are, or else…" I yell.

"It's just me," Keeta says finally.

"Oh." I run my fingers through my hair and grab a clump to twirl. Here's my chance to apologize, but my mind has turned into a bowl of soggy corn flakes and all I can say is, "Hey."

"Keep on practicing," she says from behind the curtain. "Sounds like you need it."

I know I deserve her burn, but it still hurts. Then I take a deep breath and say more than one syllable this time. "Keeta?"

But she's gone back to ignoring me.

"Keeta, come on. Please," I beg.

"Yeah, what?"

"I need to…could you come here for a sec? It's so *Wizard of Oz* talking to you behind the curtain like this."

She parts the curtain and walks through. Her face is stone hard as she approaches, but when she looks up and sees my bandages, it softens. *"Ay, Dios mío,"* she says and steps off the stage.

"Yeah," I say, trying to sound extra injured so she'll feel obligated to be nice to me.

She stands over me with her hands on her hips like a superheroine and asks, "Are you okay?"

Whenever people ask me if I'm okay when I'm not, I always start to cry. I guess today the tears help me because instead of being angry at me, Keeta sits down beside me, moves my crutches to the side, and puts both of her hands gently on my ankle. "Amara, what happened?" she asks. Though she knows my real name by now, I am glad she still calls me Amara, even if I'm not sure why she calls me this and I wonder what it means.

I sniff back the waterworks and look at her. Hearing my special name again is all I need to know that whenever I actually get around to apologizing, she will forgive me. "Oh, you should see the other girl."

"*Estás loca*. Look at your knee…and your hand." She takes the guitar off my lap and places it in its case. I feel naked without it. "I guess you're not playing basketball anytime soon."

I wonder how she knows about my being on the team, but then realize Stef probably told her. I bet they tell each other everything, like about the moronic way I acted this weekend. I have to stop avoiding it. "Keeta?"

"*Sí, Amara.*"

I melt again.

"What's on your mind?" she asks.

"Why do you call me that?" I ask, deciding the apology can wait.

"Why do I call you what?" she says, pretending to look confused.

"Come on. You know."

"Well, what do you think it means?"

"Monkey face? Clumsy girl? Goddess of dorks?"

She laughs, and I love that I can make her laugh. "No, try again."

"*Ándale dime,*" I say and playfully shove her shoulder. "Come on, tell me." That's when I realize flirting comes a lot more naturally when you actually like the person you're flirting with.

"Hmm…" She gathers her hair and tosses it on her back, exposing her neck. I notice a cute freckle by her ear. Is it weird that I want to kiss it? "I'll tell you under one condition."

I try to stay focused. "Okay. What?"

"You tell me why you're always so nervous to be around me."

"What? Now you're the crazy one," I say and pull at the strings of my hoodie until I nearly choke myself.

She laughs again. "Oh, I'm the crazy one now?" she says and then looks down at my foot.

"Yep, that's what I said." My big toe is sticking out of the ACE bandage, and because I feel self-conscious of its nakedness, I wiggle it and then wince. This makes her even more concerned than before.

"You know what I think?" Keeta says with a smile on her lips.

At this point I would give up brownie batter and *SpongeBob* for the rest of my life if I could just know what she was thinking.

"I don't think you're like the rest of your friends. Are you, Amara?"

Here's your chance. Don't screw it up! "No. I swear I'm not. I'm so sorry about how we, how I, acted. They were being so stupid and I didn't know what to do. I'm sorry."

Then she looks up at me for what seems like a million minutes. The walls disappear and I'm so far away I don't even notice when the classroom door opens.

"Boys have the worst timing," Keeta says under her breath. Then she gets up, dusts off her pants, and hops up on the stage again.

I don't think I ever felt so unhappy to see someone, but I smile politely as Jake walks toward me.

"Oh man. What happened, Abbey? Are you okay?"

Weird thing is that when *he* asks it, I don't cry. "Yeah, I'm fine."

Jake spends the rest of class asking if I need anything, and I spend the rest of class watching Keeta walk around the room, helping the guys with their finger placements, wishing it was my hand she was touching instead of theirs.

❖

I hobble late into Spanish, and Garrett yells, "What the hell happened to you, Abbey?"

Then *Señora* Cabrera tells Garrett, *"Cuide su lenguaje, por favor."* And now everyone is staring at us.

I sit down and carefully prop my leg up on Stef's empty chair. After sitting in guitar and then all during PE to file emergency contact cards for Mrs. Schwartz, I'm developing a sore butt to match my sore crutch-bruised armpits. This whole situation blows.

Garrett leans forward to question me more, but *Señora* Cabrera clears her throat and gives Garrett the scary teacher stare, so Garrett writes me a note instead: *OK, how long 'til it heals? Just give it to me straight. You know I don't usually prefer things straight, but this time I'll make an exception.* ☺

I turn the paper over and write: *Ha, ha. The doctor said it wasn't too bad a sprain, so like two/three weeks. Then, take it easy and see how it goes. Don't freak out, I'll be better in no time.*

Then Garrett adds to another blank spot on the paper: *You'll pay for this. But since we're friends, I'll try to forgive you. FYI, you're a damn klutz.*

Señora looks our way and scowls a little, but I don't really care. I've already missed whatever it is she's teaching. Besides, Garrett just called me her friend, so our note passing has just become way more important than learning the names of Things in the Market.

I write back: *It's not like I meant to use the road as a slip and slide.* Then remembering my teammate duty, I ask about Stef: *Hey, where's your sidekick? Sick? Hungover? Maternity leave? By the way,* tú eres una chica extraña.

Hey, I know I'm a crazy girl. It's what all the ladies love about me. Anyway, Stef and her g.f. are fighting in the locker room. She'll probably be MIA for the rest of class.

This is the first time we've ever talked about girlfriends or anything closely related, and it feels good that she trusts me, so I make sure she knows I'm cool with it and reply: *That sucks. I hope she's okay.* Then I can't help but ask a slightly selfish question, revoking any kindness or coolness I just displayed: *They fight a lot?*

Garrett's reply comes back on a new sheet, which is a good sign; she wants to keep writing to me. I must have passed the cool-with-the-lesbianism test. *Kinda. I mean, you've met Keeta. FYI, she told us you're in her guitar class. Nice try keeping that a secret, you freakin' geek. Anyway, Keeta* es una coqueta. *Like, she'll flirt with any girl. And she's a* mentirosa. *I mean, like a big-time liar. They should break up already, but whatev.* Wáchale. *I think Mrs. C is on to us.*

❖

After the longest sixth period ever, I slowly make my way to my locker and drop off my Spanish and social studies books. Then, as I slam my locker shut, someone's clammy hands cover my eyes.

I lean on one crutch and feel the hands. They are big, rough, and not girly. "Jake?"

"How did you guess so quickly?"

"It's a gift," I say, not admitting he's the only boy I know, therefore making him the only possibility.

He has my guitar in one hand and a soft drink in the other.

I'm sort of, I don't know, angry that he took my dad's guitar from the safety of the instrument closet, but I let it go. "Wow," I say in the most enthusiastic girlie voice I have. "That's so cool of you. I was just imagining the pain I would have to suffer to go and get it." Should I hug him or punch his shoulder or something? I mean, I sure as hell am not going to kiss him. I opt for the half-hug-slug-nudge. "Thanks."

"No problem." He takes my backpack off my shoulder and puts it on over his own. He looks like a double-humped dork. I kind of like that someone is willing to look like a dork for me. I doubt Keeta ever looks dorky for anyone.

"Thanks," I say and smile sincerely. And it's right about then I realize I seem to be into any kind of positive attention, girl or boy. When have I become such a player?

"Oh, this is for you, too." He hands me the sweating soda.

I slurp down a big gulp to show my appreciation and my eyes water from the fizziness. "Thanks," I say, trying to hold back a burp.

He takes the drink from me so I can walk with my crutches, and as we stroll he asks me more questions than I thought teenage boys were capable of asking. He starts with the simple ones: "How's your ankle?" And eventually goes into more personal ones: "Do you have a big family? What does your mom do? Have you seen Fearful Gnats in concert?"

When I tell him about my family, I say, "It's just me and my mom."

"Oh, yeah. Sorry," he says, I guess remembering what happened to my dad. "So, who's your favorite teacher?" he asks, trying to recover.

"Oh, Mrs. Schwartz. Hands down."

"Yeah, she's pretty stellar," he says, and I like that he can keep up with my sarcasm. "So, you ever hiked up Sabino Canyon at night?"

I wonder if this is his way of suggesting we do so, but I'm not ready for that, so I say in a parental tone, "You should know better than to hike at night. Haven't you ever heard of mountain lions, rattlesnakes, and scorpions?"

He laughs. "But that's what makes it exciting." Then he asks, "So, how do you like Gila so far?"

I don't feel like I can answer this question without sounding schizophrenic, so I just say, "It's cool. How about you?"

"At first I thought it was sort of lame. I mean, the same people hanging out with the same people. But, you know, it's not like that all over. Like, I was really surprised to see you in guitar."

"Yeah?" I feel that flirty urge inside me again, so I go with it. "Why's that? Girls shouldn't learn how to jam?"

He laughs again and I'm pleased with myself. "No, I mean… you're just…I mean, when you were at Doolen, you just mostly seemed interested in making the rest of us feel stupid. And I mean that in a nice way."

For the first time ever, I'm glad to shed my nerdy persona. "Yeah, well, people change, I guess."

By the time we reach the double doors of the gym, I've told him a thousand times more about my life in our ten minute stroll than I've ever told Keeta and decide that he's actually a pretty cool guy, as far as guys go.

"Well, here you are," he says.

"Yep," I say. I look inside the gym and see Kate with the rest of the freshman team warming up. "So, thanks again for getting my stuff. And the soda." I motion toward the drink in his hands.

"Sure."

"So," I say, not knowing how to end it.

"Um, Abbey?"

Okay, he's either going to tell me that I suck at guitar and should quit while I'm ahead or he's going to ask me out. Either way, I'm breaking out into a sweat.

He clears his throat. "Uh, you don't seem the school-dance type."

"I'll take that as a compliment."

"It is. And, well, I don't really do dances either. So I'm not going to ask you to the Spring Fling."

I laugh because this is nothing like I've seen on TV. "Well, thanks for the heads up on that."

"But do you want to go to a concert with me?" His smile is frozen on his face, as he waits for my reply.

"Uhhh," is all I can say. "I, uh…"

"There's this band. Death Becomes Her. And there's this chick in the band. She plays guitar. You remind me of her."

"Really? Wow, um…well, I…"

His smile slowly thaws.

God, just say something, Abbey! "It's just that, I…"

"Hey, it's cool. You're not into it. That's okay," he says and opens the gym door for me. We walk in and he puts my stuff down against the wall.

Then I have an epiphany right there in the gym. I realize no boy has ever asked me to do anything and this might not ever happen again. Ever! "Wait, Jake." I grab his hand, and I think we're both momentarily shocked into stupidness from the unexpected contact of our flesh. Then I say, "That sounds cool."

"Nice," he says and gently kicks his foot against my good foot. "Our Cons look sort of good together."

"Yeah," I say.

"See you tomorrow in class then." He turns and leaves the gym and that is that.

I, Abbey "Chunks" Brooks, have a date with a boy.

CHAPTER NINE

After Jake leaves me standing there in the gym, Kate runs over. "Oh my God, you and Jake Simpson?" She grabs my crutches and nearly knocks me over. "I knew it, you little liar."

In my mind I'm already trying to come up with a way of getting out of this date with Jake, but at the same time, I'm enjoying Kate's attention. "We're just going to a concert."

"Well, whatever it is, I'm insanely jealous, but not really. Wait until you hear what happened in chem today."

I hobble over to the bleachers and she carries my stuff.

"So, okay, Derrick, yummy, finally broke up with that skanky slut during lunch, right?"

"Okay, sure."

"And then in chem, when we were in the middle of our lab, he leaned over and whispered in my ear that he, and I quote, 'really likes me' and he knows that I like him. And so then, I was, like, trying to play hard to get. So I was all, 'What makes you so sure I like you?' And he was all, 'I've been watching you watch me since the first day of school.' And I was all…"

Her story is making me cringe, like when I watch my mom scrape dry paint from underneath her fingernails. But then Coach Kimball unknowingly saves me with a blow of her whistle.

"I'll tell you the rest later, 'kay?" Kate shouts as she runs to the baseline, as if I'm on the edge of my seat.

"Can't wait," I yell back at her.

I have an hour until JV practice starts, so I prop my ugly foot and my pathetic self on the bleachers and take out my bio book. I intend to do homework, but what I busy my brain with isn't bio or even the thing that just happened with Jake.

"Don't strain yourself too much, Abbey," Garrett says and throws down her stuff, which includes her green messenger bag with an upside down rainbow triangle patch and a button that reads, *I'm not gay, but my girlfriend is.* Geez, even her backpack is cool.

Garrett sits down next to me and points to my closed book and blank binder paper. "Got something on your mind?"

With Kate so distracted with her Yummy Dummy Derrick, I've felt like I don't really have anyone to talk to, and I think maybe Garrett might be a good second choice. "Yeah, I guess."

Garrett waits to hear all about it, but it's harder than I thought it would be to say it. "Well I was wondering…how do you…you know… um, how do you…"

"Knot a cherry stem with your tongue?"

I roll my eyes. "No."

"Change your tampon while you're driving?"

"Gross. No." *Just say it,* I yell in my head. "Okay, so how do you know for sure if you like someone or if they like you?"

"Oh, love advice is my favorite. Though the cherry-stem thing may apply here because having that skill tends to turn people on," she says and moves in a little closer. "So, what are we talking about here? Boy or girl?"

I can't believe she's just asked me that, so I just stare at her with my eyes popping out of my head.

"Hey, anything goes, Dear Abbey. I'm just being open, but I take it by the look on your face you're talking about boy stuff. No problem. I've dated boys before."

"Really?" She seems so into girls, at least she seems pretty into the supergorgeous, tall black girl she's dating. I can't picture her liking a guy. "Why'd you stop?"

She pops a piece of gum in her mouth and shrugs. "You know, it just happens. There I was, liking boys, and then bam! I fell for a girl. It's not that uncommon. I mean, you've heard of being bi, right?"

I roll my eyes again and try to act casual. "Yeah. Duh." I want to ask more about that, but then I worry she'll think I'm too curious.

"Anyway, so how does it feel when you like someone? You know, a boy. Like, how do you know it's more than just a friendly thing?"

"Oh my God, Abbey, you're so..."

"Stupid?"

"I was going to say cute." Then she leans back on her elbows to get comfortable. I try not to glance at her cleavage, but she's made it impossible with the shirt she has on. No wonder she has a girlfriend. Who wouldn't want her? "Okay. Let's see...first of all," she says, after gathering her thoughts on the matter, "when you're around someone, I mean a boy"—she looks at me and winks—"that you really like, you spend most of your time trying to think of something clever to say, but instead you say things that make absolutely no sense."

This sounds familiar to me.

"And when you're around him, it's, like, not enough. It's like, you want him even closer and you sit around conjuring up ways that might make him touch you. I used to steal my girlfriend Tai's shoes and force her to chase me around the locker room and tackle me for them. You can borrow that one. It works like a charm."

"Okay. Thanks," I say, thinking of Keeta chasing me down the rows of lockers. It does sound like fun.

Garrett continues, "But if you really, really like someone, you— Hey, there's Stef." Garrett calls and waves Stef over to sit with us. "Abbey needs love advice," Garrett says over the bouncing basketballs, but the entire freshman team still looks over and stares at me.

"Thanks for that, G."

She pats my leg and laughs. "You're welcome."

I smile as Stef approaches and we exchange *holas*.

"Love advice? Jesus, you need to fix me first," Stef says, as she sits down next to Garrett and sighs.

"What happened?" Garrett asks. "Are you guys cool?"

I don't know if Stef wants me to be involved in the conversation, so I pretend to read my bio book.

"I dunno, G. Half the time I feel paranoid that she's cheating on me, and the other half of the time she *is* cheating on me. She's so messed up."

"Did you find out who that girl was?" Garrett asks.

"No, Nikki just said that some chick came by Hot Dog on Saturday, asked if Keeta was there, but didn't leave her name or anything. Keeta said she has no idea who it was and I'm crazy."

I look up after I hear that last part, and for some horrible reason, Garrett glances over at me and our eyes meet. My face burns with shame and I bury my head in my bio book again.

"Sounds like a supersized serving of lies, girl," Garrett says to Stef.

"I know, but it's not just that, G. It's everything. My mom is threatening to kick me out again and Keeta's not allowed over. I have to sneak out to see her. *Chale, odio esto.*"

"*Qué gacho*, Stef," Garrett says.

"Yeah, it sucks big time. Why does everything have to be so hard with her?"

"Well, do you love her?"

Stef pulls at her shoelaces and I hold my breath. "I guess I do, but I just don't know if she is worth all this crap I'm going through."

"That's something I guess you'll have to figure out."

Garrett is good at love advice. But I have a feeling she's good at everything.

"I doubt she even cares about me anymore, let alone loves me."

"I don't know. I think she does, Stef. At least when she's with you she cares. That's how Keeta is. You know she's just as desperate for love as the rest of us. Except maybe she's so afraid of not having it, she gathers it from lots of places so she'll never run out."

Stef laughs. "Yeah. When she's with me it's fine, but what about all the other hours of the day?"

"That is a lot of leftover hours, girl."

Stef nods, leans toward me, and says, "You can stop pretending you're not listening, Abbey. It's cool."

I come out from behind my book. "Sorry."

"No worries. How's your foot?" She takes a closer look and makes a sad face. "Keeta told me it was pretty bad. She wasn't kidding."

"Yeah. I mean, no she wasn't, I guess."

Then Stef elbows Garrett. "Hey, did you know our little newbie here has an upcoming date?"

"Oh my God. How did you find out?" I whisper, feeling embarrassed for some reason.

"What?" Garrett yells and slaps my good arm.

"You mean you haven't heard?" Stef says. "Well, let me tell you—"

"Seriously, who told you?" I interrupt.

"Doesn't matter. What matters," she says to Garrett, "is Little Miss Freshmeat is going to the Death Becomes Her concert at Club Congress with Jake Simpson."

"Ah ha," Garrett says. "So that's what all the questions were about? You have a little crushy-poo on Jakey-poo? God, what a relief. I thought for a second there you were going to declare your love for me."

"Dude, Abbey does not swing that way," Stef says. "I mean look at her."

Garrett smiles and shrugs. "You would know, I guess. Though I do have a way of making the ladies beg for my love."

I look at myself and wonder how Stef can be so sure about me.

"Don't be offended, Abbey. All I mean it's clear you like boys. You're going out with Jake, right?" Stef says. "I think it's great. At least he doesn't seem like the kind of guy who will cheat on you like some people we know. Which reminds me—are there any other girls in your little guitar class?"

"No," I say truthfully, "it's just me and a bunch of lame-ass boys and, uh, Jake. Why?"

"I'm just trying to figure out who that girl was that stopped by Keeta's work this weekend."

I swallow loudly. "Well, we don't talk a lot in class so I don't know anything." Sure, we stare a lot, but not many words had been exchanged until this morning.

"No," Stef says, "she wouldn't bother talking to you. She apparently only talks to girls she can get into bed."

I'm too shocked to respond.

"Oh, come on," Garrett says and slaps the back of Stef's head. "She's not that bad."

"I call it like I see it, G."

They're making me crazy with all their lesbian sex talk, and I'm feeling so confused about what's going on in my screwed-up head. I guess that's why I get defensive. "Well, it's like I said, we hardly ever talk."

"Thanks anyway," Stef says. "No worries, 'kay?"

While Garrett and Stef laugh at the freshmen shooting layups, I do the opposite of what Stef tells me to do. I worry.

I worry that Stef will find out it was me that went to go see Keeta. I worry that Garrett knows, just by looking in my eyes for that split second, that I have something to hide. And I worry that Stef and the whole entire school might see what I hope to keep secret forever: I can't keep my mind off Keeta. I know I'm headed for trouble, and the worst part of all is that all the worrying in the world isn't going to help me.

CHAPTER TEN

"Again!" Coach Riley screams at Garrett, who is our team's point guard. "I've got no plans tonight, ladies, so we'll be here until we get it right," he says, as Garrett slaps the ball to send the play in motion, as if we ever suspected he had a life beyond the walls of this gym.

Today Coach Riley is teaching us a new offense he calls Desert Storm, which involves a lot of screening, running the baseline, and fake outs. It's completely confusing to my teammates on the court, but I have a bird's eye view in the bleachers, as I sit on my butt taking notes because of my sprained ankle, so it seems easy enough to me.

"No!" Coach screams when Tori goes the wrong way again. "Baseline!"

While they run suicide lines, I doodle in my notebook and think about my day. In guitar class I did my best to avoid eye contact with Keeta because I'm trying not to be a whore who flirts with her friend's girlfriend. Jake helped distract me by singing his new lyrics to "Let It Be," which went something like, "When I find myself coming out of the bathroom, Abbey Brooks walks right into me. Seeking some direction, after I pee." And then he played "Mary Had a Little Lamb," but changed the words to, "Abbey had a little booboo, her knee was as gross as road kill." He's pretty funny, I guess.

Then we finalized our plans for Friday. "So, my bro is driving because I can't drive yet," Jake said toward the end of class. "But he's cool. Can we pick you up at six? That way we can get some grub before the show." Keeta walked by as Jake was laying out the night's plans, and I got weirdly quiet, which then made Jake say, "I mean, if you're still into going."

"Oh yeah, for sure," I said to reassure him, though I haven't even asked my mom if I can go. I'm hoping, like the playing basketball thing, I can just dump the idea on her as I race out the door Friday morning.

After guitar, I took the painful journey to PE on my crutches of doom and sat in Mrs. Schwartz's office filing emergency contact cards. I was just about to consider suicide by paper cut, but then I noticed the name on the card in front of me: Moreno, Reyna (Keeta). I considered stealing the card but then realized that could result in Keeta's death if they didn't know she was allergic to penicillin. So instead, I got all *Mission Impossible* and stealthily rolled my wheeled office chair to the copier and made a duplicate of Keeta's card. Now I know everything! (Insert evil laugh.) Including her address, her phone number, that she lives with her grandma (no parents listed), and that her birthday is on August 13, making her seventeen, not eighteen like I previously thought. That means we're only three years apart, two really, once I turn fifteen in November.

"Brooks!" Coach Riley yells, bringing me back to the present.

I jump in my seat and slam my notebook shut. God help me if anyone ever saw that I had written "Abbey Moreno" in the margins. "Yes, Coach?"

"Can you tell Ms. Woodside where she is supposed to go after the ball gets passed to Ms. Church?" The scary vein in his neck is pulsating.

"Uh," I stammer and search through my notebook.

Meanwhile, Ms. Woodside (aka Stef), is standing at the top of the three-point line with her hands on her hips. "I know where to go, Coach. You don't have to ask Abbey. She's not even playing."

Uh oh. Coach's face turns insta-purple, as he marches over to Stef. Then he swings his finger in her face like a tiny baseball bat. "Are you talking back to me, Woodside?" he screams down at her, showering the top of her head with spit.

Stef doesn't even flinch. "Just stating the facts, sir."

My mouth is not the only one that's dropped open, and I know my teammates are thinking the same thing I'm thinking: she's insane.

"On the bench, Woodside! Giuriato, you're in."

Eva runs onto the court and Stef marches off. She passes the bench and heads toward the locker room.

Like the rest of us, Riley can't believe it. "Woodside, what do you think you're doing?"

Stef stops but keeps her back to him and the rest of the team.

"If you walk out of this gym, don't expect to be welcomed back in."

Without hesitating, Stef strips off the blue mesh practice jersey, tosses it on the floor, and leaves the gym.

"Lines!" Coach yells at the rest of the girls.

The team obeys, but I can tell by the way Garrett looks over at me that she wants me to do something. This isn't the first time Coach Riley has kicked someone off the team during one of his practices, but he always lets them back after they apologize. Since Stef is our best outside shooter, I'm sure she'll be back tomorrow, but it's not like her to act like this. I guess that's why Garrett wants me to see if Stef is okay.

I quickly get my stuff together and carefully approach Coach on my crutches. "Um, Coach Riley, I need to call my mom to make sure she's still able to pick me up."

He waves me off and I go in search of Stef. After I enter the main locker room, I hear loud voices echoing through the empty rows. I hobble toward them but then stop and lean up against the wall outside the exclusive varsity locker room when I realize who it is. I know I shouldn't listen, but I want so badly to know more about what it's like to be them.

"I don't give a crap about Riley, Keeta," Stef shouts. "Don't you get it? My mom's going to make me leave my own house."

"Stef, she's not going to kick you out," Keeta says, remaining calm. "She's your mom. She'll get over it."

"You don't know that, Keeta. You don't know what I have to put up with. Just because your grandma couldn't care less about where you go and who you're with, doesn't mean it's like that for the rest of us."

"What the hell, Stef." Keeta gets irritated, but then quickly changes her tone again. "Look, I told you already. Move in with me."

Stef slams her locker shut. The wall I'm leaning against vibrates in my chest. "Why the hell would I do that? You're nothing but a *mentirosa*, Keeta."

"That's bs, Stef. You don't even know what you're talking about."

"Oh really? Then who stopped by to see you at work the other day?"

"I told you already. I don't know."

"Whatever."

It's quiet for a second, then Keeta says, "You're the only one I want, Stef. Come on, you know it's true."

My guilt quickly turns to jealousy, and I tell myself for the hundredth time this week that I'm an idiot for liking Keeta.

Instead of falling into Keeta's arms like I would, Stef laughs. "Keeta, don't embarrass yourself. I read the letter you wrote her." Then I hear the rustle of Stef getting into her backpack. "Here, you should have it back. It's so damn beautifully written. Actually, better yet"—Stef rips it into what I assume are very small pieces—"she should never see it. I wouldn't want anyone else to have to put up with you and your lies."

"Why are you going through my stuff?"

"Isn't it obvious, Keeta?" Stef yells.

"Stef, *hazme caso*—" Keeta starts, but I don't think Stef wants to listen to anything Keeta has to say anymore.

"Keeta, just leave me alone."

"Stef, come on. *Calmada*," Keeta tries again. "If you would just calm down and listen to me I can—"

"*Púdrete*, Keeta! I mean it." Then Stef starts to cry. "Go to hell."

"Dammit, Stef!" Hearing Keeta's voice turn sharp and mean makes me want to run out to the gym. But with all my injuries, I'm incapable of moving faster than a wobbly-legged toddler. "God, you know what, Stef? *Como quieras*. Have it your way. I'm done with your drama," Keeta yells, then swings open the door of the varsity locker room and leaves Stef with these final words: "I don't need this crap, and I don't need you."

I wish I had run earlier because now my only option is to hop over to a dark row of lockers and hope Keeta won't notice me hunched in the corner, trying to will myself invisible.

I almost look up when I hear an unlucky locker get punched, but I keep my head down until I'm sure Keeta is out of there.

Without the two of them screaming at each other, the air is quiet and cool again like after a monsoon storm. But the silence is soon replaced with the sounds of Stef crying. I think about sneaking out, but I can't just let her sit in there alone. She needs a friend, and even though I'm pretty sure I'm currently her worst option, the least I can do is try to help her.

I push the door open and see Stef sitting on the long wooden bench, gripping the edge so hard her knuckles are white. Her tears have decorated the cement floor below her with tiny wet polka dots.

I whisper her name.

"Go away, Abbey. I don't want to talk."

"Okay," I say and try to back out of the room on my crutches.

"I just feel so stupid, you know? God, everyone warned me about her. They told me she was like this, but I just wouldn't listen."

I take it she does want to talk, so I sit down on the bench next to her and lean my crutches against the wall.

"You probably think I'm crazy."

"No, I don't. I swear," I say.

"The thing is, Abbey, she always hurts me, but I can't seem to get it through my thick skull." She takes off her sweaty T-shirt, screams into it, and then throws it against the lockers. It lands in a damp heap on the floor. "I hate her and I love her and I can't stand it."

"I'm sorry," I whisper and wish I could say something more useful, but I'm a little distracted by the fact that she's now sitting here in her semi-see-through white sports bra. Her pale skin is bright red and blotchy like mine gets after working out.

"God, Abbey, she doesn't even know the half of it. My mom is making me go to therapy. She thinks I have mental problems because I like girls. She said if I don't stop seeing Keeta, she's sending me off to a boot camp in California for, like, delinquent kids. Can you believe that?"

"No," I say honestly and wonder what I'm getting myself into. It's not that my mom is a gay basher or anything, but maybe she'll feel differently when she finds out her only kid is gay or bi or whatever the heck I am.

"What kills me is that letter. She compared some girl's eyes to, and I quote, 'two deep pools of blue sky, sprinkled with stars that sparkle even in the daylight.' God, she's never written me anything like that."

The floor is littered with torn-up binder paper, and I try to read more of the words on the scraps that lie at my feet. "Who was it to?" I say, totally not meaning to speak those words out loud.

"Oh, Keeta's an expert at lies and deception. She never puts real names on that stuff. It was probably for some bitch at Sabino High. She's always had it for this blond slut on their team."

I feel foolish that for a second I thought the letter could have been written to me.

"It just hurts, Abbey," Stef says, as another round of tears begins to fall. Then she collapses in a heap on the bench and, somehow, ends up resting her head on my lap.

My body instantly tenses up every muscle because now there's a half-naked lesbian resting her head in my lap. What if someone sees us like this? I mean, I know Stef doesn't like me like that and I haven't ever thought of her like that, but still.

"I hope I never see her again," Stef cries.

I consider shoving her off me, but then I remind myself that this is obviously just a friend thing. If it were Kate, I would console her if her heart had just been broken, even if she was in a sports bra. It shouldn't be any different now.

I look down at Stef and push back a lock of her curly blond hair that is stuck to her wet cheek. Then I say the only thing I can think of to say. "I'm so sorry, Stef." And I really am. I'm sorry for everything.

❖

Thursday after practice, I find myself standing in front of my mom's easel with the intention of telling her about my date with Jake. The last minute approach I had planned was questioned by Kate and Garrett, so I decide to be more mature and give my mom at least twenty-four hours' notice.

"Are you just admiring my work or is there something you need to say?" my mom asks after five minutes pass and all I've managed to do is help the paint dry with my heavy breathing. She looks up at me over the rim of her glasses and can instantly tell I'm on the verge of confession. "Okay, spill it, Abbey Road. What did you do?"

"God, Mom. Nothing."

"Well, then, what is it?"

"I just was wondering, uh, what you're doing tomorrow night."

She drops her brush in a glass of cloudy water and picks up her coffee. "Tomorrow night? You know, the usual one-woman Scrabble tournament. Why? What do you think you're doing?"

"Uh…" Is it this hard for the ordinary teenage girl to tell her mom she's got a date with a boy? I don't know, but I have a feeling this conversation is a lot easier for other girls and probably involves a shared squeal and a special mom-daughter shopping excursion afterward.

"Can we speed this up a little, Abbey? I need to start dinner soon."

I grab a lock of hair and remember Garrett's suggested tactic: don't ask for permission, just nonchalantly inform her of your plans. "Well, there's this guy in guitar who wants to take me to an all-ages concert at Club Congress and I was thinking I'd like to go. No biggie."

"I see. And does this guy have a name and an age?"

"Jake. He's sixteen?" I say like a question because I can't tell how this is going.

"And who else is going to the concert?"

"Just me and him, and the other hundred people who show up," I say before realizing that it was the totally wrong thing to say.

Now my mom looks only slightly less freaked out than me. "So this is a date?"

"Well, I guess if you need to label it you could call it a date."

Mom nods her head slowly, like she's having a side conversation with an invisible person. "Right," she says, getting her cool back.

"As in 'all right'?" I ask. Is she saying yes? In my head, I hadn't quite imagined that I'd actually go through with this date with Jake. Surely, like everything else in my life, something would go wrong. "I can go?"

"Not quite, honey. I guess I should have told you this sooner, but Dad and I discussed this a long time ago and we decided no dating for you until sophomore year. Sorry."

"But, Mom, that's not fair. He already bought the tickets," I say in a whiny, spoiled-brat way because it's one thing to not want to go, but it's entirely different to be told you *can't* go.

"He'll just have to sell them or take someone else because you're not going. End of discussion." She gets up and walks into the kitchen to start cooking, making her decision more final.

I follow in hot pursuit. "But, Mom, I'm almost fifteen. You can change the rules. Dad's not even here. How would he know?" Even as I say the words, I know I just pushed the worst button on the keyboard that runs my mom's emotions.

She pops up from behind the fridge door with a combined look of anger, shock, and disappointment. "Abbey Road, how dare you say that? Your father will always be here."

She's right, but because I'm mad I don't tell her so. Instead I yell, "Whatever, Mom," and storm to my room, in a slow, clumsy sprained-ankle sort of way.

❖

Later that night, I end up over at Kate's house because that's where I always go after my mom and I fight. Because I'm still hurt, though, I have to ask my mom for a ride, which takes the powerful punch out of my planned silent treatment. But my mom wants me out of the house, anyway, so everyone wins.

"You must be totally bummed," Kate says, as she grabs another handful of Spicy Nacho Doritos. "And I can't believe you said that stuff about your dad."

"I know. It just came out." I adjust the pillow under my foot and scratch around my healing knee scab. "Anyway, now I have to tell Jake. This sucks," I say, hoping to convince Kate that my canceled date is tearing me up inside, when really I feel relaxed for the first time since he asked me out.

"Well, anyway, Derrick is so wonderful." Leave it Kate to change the topic to Derrick without any logical lead-in.

"Wow, a new record. Five minutes without talking about him," I say and flip through the muted channels on the TV.

"Did I tell you I moved into his locker?"

"Yes, only about ten thousand times."

Then we hear what sounds like a bowling ball slowly *thunk-thunk-thunk*ing down the basement stairs. We both look over to see Jenn, the Queen of Mean, but we return to our conversation before she has a chance to call us names.

"Yeah, my chem book and his chem book sit side by side, like they're kissing all day long."

"Oh God," I groan.

"I know. It's disgusting, huh?" Jenn says. Normally, this is when she would ask/demand for us to leave, with threats, so she can have the basement all to herself, but instead she tosses my crutches aside, plops on the couch next to me, and sighs heavily. Her behavior is definitely odd, but I figure it has something to do with her recent breakup.

Jenn lets out another long sigh then says, "Boys suck rat diarrhea through straws."

"I agree," I say, like I'm an authority on the topic.

"Not all boys suck," Kate chimes in.

Jenn and I give Kate a synchronized eye roll. "Just because you think you're in love doesn't give you the right to stick up for them," Jenn says. "And, FYI, I'll seriously beat the crap out of you if I hear any talk of you losing your goddamn virginity to this idiot. I'm serious, Kate. I'll kick your ass back to last week and kick his to next year."

Kate's mouth opens, and closes, then opens again. It's a remarkable thing when she's speechless. I don't blame Kate for not talking back, though. Jenn's scarier than ever these days. Even so, I wish I could have a sister like Jenn who could kick someone's ass for me.

"Anyway," Jenn says casually, like she hadn't just threatened Kate's life, "I was wondering if you guys wanted a ride to school tomorrow. Since I don't have to pick up that loser anymore, I have more time to pick you up, Abbey." Jenn pats me on the knee. She's never actually touched me before, so I jump a little and look over at Kate. *What the hell?* I say with my eyes.

"Sound good?' Jenn smiles at me.

We really can't tell if she's for real, so neither of us says a word.

"Okay, fine." She gets up to leave. "Your loss. I was just trying to be nice," she says, as she starts walking up the stairs.

"Why?" Kate dares to ask.

Jenn stops and turns around. "Do you guys think I'm some sort of bitch or something?"

Kate plays with the pile of chips in her hand, and I pull at my blond arm hair while simultaneously twirling a lock of hair with my other hand.

"Okay, so maybe I have been a bitch," she says, then pauses for a second. "Well, get over it. I'll see you tomorrow, Abbey, at seven sharp. Don't make us wait."

I'm now convinced love can totally mess you up. On one hand, Jenn's being nice, which is very out of character. And on the other, Kate isn't doing an ounce of homework, which is beyond unnatural, even for the new Ultracool Kate. I just don't get how she can let her life fall apart for some dumb boy. I mean, I like Keeta, but I'm not going to let my wishful thoughts of her distract me from everything else in my life.

CHAPTER ELEVEN

This morning, Jake walks into guitar smiling and whistling. He even leans down and gives me a hug, our first ever, then sits down next to me. "This concert's gonna blow your mind, Abbey. Wait 'til you see Perla Paul jam. You won't be able to take your eyes off her."

Keeta is within listening distance, writing notes on the chalkboard, and I swear I hear her laugh and say, "I bet she won't."

I tug at the bottom of my T-shirt. "Yeah, about tonight..." I know I have to break the news to him, but he's so happy. I didn't think this was going to be this hard. "I bet she's awesome, but I won't be able to see her."

"Are you serious? Why not?"

"Well, it's my mom..."

"Yeah?" he says, leaning forward and pushing his curly hair behind his ears. "She okay?"

I consider telling a lie because the truth just seems so humiliating, but I kind of want out of this dating-Jake thing for good. And there's only one way to do that: tell the truth. "Yeah, she's okay, I mean, besides having a brain disorder and thinking we live in the freaking fifties or something."

Jake's not catching on, but why would he? It's not like I'm making any sense.

"Bottom line is I can't go to the concert with you tonight because my mom just decided to inform me last night I can't date until I'm a sophomore."

I hear Keeta laugh again, and this time I am sure it's at my expense.

"Dude"—Jake sits back in his folding chair—"that blows."

"I told her you probably already bought the tickets, but she was all bitchy and was like, 'I don't care!' and then got all crazy and grounded me." Slight exaggeration, but he doesn't need to know that.

"Well." He looks over at me and smiles. Is it weird that I like the way he looks at me, even if I don't feel much in return? "I would be lying if I said I wasn't disappointed, but mom's rules always trump, huh? It's cool, though. I'll go with my bro. He'll be stoked to get out of the house."

"All right. Sorry, again." Then I don't know what to say or do next. I mean, it's not like I hate him. "But, hey. I'll Google Perla Paul tonight and check her out."

"Cool," he says and nods.

"Cool," I say back. And that's the end of that.

At lunch, Sarah, Isabella (Sarah's unexpected new iPod earphone friend from English), and I are spread out on the grass in the quad. After dumping Jake in guitar, my mood has steadily been getting better and I'm enjoying the less intense October sun on my face, as we eat lunch. Then a skinny shadow falls over us. It's Kate, and remarkably, her face is detached from Derrick's. Actually, it's the first time she's associated with us at lunch since she started dating him. So much for Rule #20.

"Stranger danger," I say, as Kate sits down.

Kate ignores my remark, slips on her new Gucci sunglasses (a gift from her barf-bag boyfriend), and asks, "Got room for one more, ladies?"

"I don't know," Sarah says. "This is sort of an exclusive group. There's a secret handshake, dues, etcetera."

I hide my laugh in my hand. Sarah's funniest when she's making fun of people who aren't me.

"Ha, ha," Kate says then slaps Sarah's arm and sips on a soda like nothing has changed and she's still in charge. "So, what's new?"

Sarah and I shrug our shoulders.

"Nothing. This is Isabella," Sarah finally says and points to the new girl connected to her by a white cord. She already seems a little frightened of Kate.

I get as quiet as a bug and make a little pile of yellow grass on my empty nacho tray.

"Where's Mari?" Kate asks.

"I don't know. Off making out with a guy, I guess. You know how people can be...*totally self-absorbed, and stuff.*"

"Very subtle, Sarah," Kate says then slaps my knee. "How come you didn't tell me Mari has a boyfriend?"

I don't feel like looking at her so I speak to the grass. "Sarah's delusional. Mari joined some debate club that meets at lunch or something, but she didn't want to tell you due to the high polyester count in the jackets. Besides, I hardly ever see you anyway. When exactly would I have told you? It's not like you call me anymore." I want to say some other stuff that's been on my mind, like, how since she started dating Derrick she's dropped us like we're a handful of peeing gerbils. But I don't.

"Geez, Abbey. I've been busy." Then she laughs at me, like my feelings are a huge joke, and adds, "God, you sound like a jealous girlfriend or something," which really pisses me off.

I say, "Whatever," and try to hide how I feel smaller than the little black ant making its way to a giant glob of nacho cheese sauce on my tray.

But Sarah and the new girl laugh because Kate is back so they fall right in line and take her lead.

"Come on, Abbey," Kate continues, "don't tell me all the rumors are true. Are those lezzies finally making their moves on you? I knew it!" And then she laughs some more.

Sarah laughs harder, too, which makes it seem like it's not the first time she's heard this rumor.

But it's definitely news to me. I had no idea people were talking about me because I've never been anything worth talking about. I want to run, but I know my only option is to stay and deny everything. "What the hell are you talking about, Kate?"

"I mean, it kind of makes sense," Kate says. "You have always been obsessed with Marilyn Monroe and continue to be resistant to makeup and skirts."

Then Sarah, who is finding this way too funny for no reason, keels over and grabs her stomach. "It's true," she sputters. "And the only boys you have up in your room are the Beatles."

It isn't in my nature to yell, but they've gone too far. "Shut up, you guys!"

Other students are staring at us now, and the new Kate doesn't like that at all. Her smile finally fades. "Abbey, forget it. I was just kidding. I mean, they are saying stuff, but it's just the usual stuff, you know."

"No, I don't know."

"Oh my God, chillax," Kate says, using my word. "And don't act all shocked. I mean, you're friends with Stef and Garrett, and this is high school, people say stuff. But it's stupid. Don't sweat it."

"We told you there'd be trouble if you played with them," Sarah says and throws up her hands.

"What *stuff*, Kate?" I demand.

"What does it matter? It's not true, so who cares? Right?"

I glare at her then try to console myself. *They're just stupid rumors. Nobody knows anything.*

"I mean"—she looks at me with the same disgusted look she had when she made me swear we would never join the team—"unless it *is* true."

Now I regret my choice to stay.

"Well, Abbey?" Kate says, flipping her long hair off her shoulder then smiling, but I can tell it's kind of fake. "You can tell us the truth. We're your friends."

I look down at the pile of grass I've made on my tray and at the ant that has changed its course for the tenth time. My dad once told me that to an ant, a tall blade of grass can seem like Mount Everest.

Kate, Sarah, and Isabella are waiting for an answer, but I don't even have an answer for myself, let alone for them. I'm so angry that they believe any of it, though. I've played along with all their straight games all these years, so there should be no doubt in their minds that I'm just like them. None. All I have to do is deny it, laugh and say how dumb people are. But my friends have let me down, and I'm getting tired of their laughter at my expense. So instead of playing along as usual, I say, "You guys suck." And as I struggle to push myself up and limp away from my *friends*, I finally get what my dad was trying to teach me about the ant and the grass.

I end up in the locker room in the familiar dark row where the lights don't work. The bell rings for fifth period, but I stay. It rings for sixth period, and then the final bell of the day rings, but I stay. I can't face the hallway. I can't stand the thought of seeing Kate. So I lie there wondering how my friends could believe those rumors; then I have my second epiphany of the day and understand why Stef and Garrett are so tough: they have to be. They're guarded because they can't really trust anyone. They trust me, though, and that just makes me feel worse.

So here I am, swimming in the middle of my ocean of sorrow, slowly sinking into the dark, icy core, when a voice calls me back to the surface. *"Estás bien, Amara?"*

I sit up quickly. How did she know I'd be here? I pretend that I'm brushing my hair out of my face, not wiping tears away. I feel too embarrassed to look at Keeta, so I stare at the ground. "I'm fine," I say quietly and think, *Now that you're here.*

"Okay, if you say so. Well, I brought you your guitar. It was getting late and I know you wouldn't want anything to happen to it. Anyway, here." She places the guitar carefully against the wall. Then she stands there beside me like she's waiting for something. "You sure you're okay?"

"Yeah, thanks." My voice cracks. Why does she have to be so nice to me? "I'll see you later," I manage to say, as tears roll down my face again.

"Amara, Amara, Amara." She whispers and gently takes my chin in her hand, moving my head up so I can see her when she speaks. "It's just gossip. *Chismes.* That's all. It'll blow over. Next week they'll be tearing up someone else. That's how it works around here."

Even though her soft vanilla-lotion-scented touch is making me feel so much better, I lean back against the metal lockers when I remember why I can't let myself do whatever it is we are doing.

"Entiendes, Amara?" Keeta says softly.

"Yeah, I understand, but you don't get it. Even my friends believe it." I hate myself for letting her see me like this. I always look hideous and puffy after crying, so I'm glad it's dark.

She kneels in front of me. *"No te preocupes, Amara.* Really, don't worry. It will get better, and hey, I do understand. Believe me." Her hair falls forward and slides across my knee. It feels cool and soft like silk against my skin. And it's just like Garrett described to me that day in the gym. All I want is Keeta's touch, all her attention on me.

But I can't have it. I promised I'd be loyal to Stef. I know firsthand now what it feels like to have crappy friends. Plus, I don't want them to be right. I just need to ignore these feelings, and then (eventually?) they'll go away.

I brush her hair off my leg. "Keeta, what are you doing here? I mean, you can't do this. I'm Stef's friend. We can't act like this. You're just…"

"Just what, Amara?"

Just making me feel like I'm special and beautiful and happy. "You're just confusing me." I look back at the wall. "Please, just leave me alone."

"How am I confusing you?" Her breath grazes my neck and sends a shiver down my back. "*Dime*. Come on. Tell me, Amara."

What am I supposed to say? I mean, she obviously likes or, I should say, *loves* Stef, since they are back together again. And even so, there was that love letter Keeta wrote to someone who wasn't Stef and I'm 99.9 percent sure it wasn't to me.

"Nothing," I say. "It's just that I don't know what to say to you. I'm really…I don't know. Besides, I'm not like you, Keeta." I don't know what I mean by that. Nothing's making sense. "Just leave, okay?"

She ignores my request, leans forward on her knees, and looks down at my ankle, which is now aching with pain. And then, as if she can read my mind, she picks up my foot and puts it in her lap. My lip starts to quiver again. All those nights I've wished for her warm touch, and here she finally is. And here I am, crying and being a total bitch.

"Eternally beautiful," she says, looking down at my swollen foot.

I swallow down another round of tears. "You think my foot is beautiful?"

She laughs and looks up at me. Even in the dim lighting, I can see a thousand pieces of gold scattered in Keeta's eyes, like a treasure chest spilled open. And, just like always, the rest of the world disappears. No more padlock jamming in my back, no more throbbing in my foot, and no more confusion. "Amara. The *apodo* I chose for you that day at the mall. It's Greek and it means eternally beautiful—like I'm sure you will be." Then she takes my hand in hers, turns it over, and kisses my palm.

The instant her lips touch my skin, electricity shoots through me, and the queasy feelings I've been having all year explode into something that no words in any thesaurus could describe. I'm being lifted away, far from Gila High, far from the smelly hallways, the mean cafeteria ladies, and the scary truths. I let myself briefly melt into this moment. This must be how floating on a cloud feels.

Then there are footsteps and voices. I jump out of my dreamy state and open my eyes, which I don't even remember closing.

Keeta carefully puts my foot back on the ground, stands up, and looks over her shoulder to judge their distance. Then, still holding my hand, Keeta whispers the five words I secretly dreamed that I might hear: "That letter was for you."

CHAPTER TWELVE

Yesterday my doctor *finally* cleared me for basketball practice. Now I'm in the mood to celebrate all sorts of things, so this morning I abandon my boring khaki shorts and hooded sweatshirt to put on black capris and a tight blue boob-shirt Kate made me buy on one of our summer trips to the Tucson Mall. And for that extra special touch? I wear my hair down instead of in a ponytail and spread some sparkly lip gloss on my lips.

"Morning, Mom," I say with more cheer than she's heard in weeks.

"Well, good morning," she says, looking up from the paper and raising her eyebrows. I think she notices the new look but stops herself from making a big deal about it, which I appreciate.

I kiss her good-bye and walk out to Jenn's car before her second honk.

"Wow, you actually look halfway decent. Way to go, Chunks," Jenn says to me after I get settled in the passenger's seat. Kate stopped riding with us the day after Derrick got his new Mustang, so it's just me and Jenn from now until whenever. And because of Kate's absence, Jenn and I have actually been becoming friends. Her almost-compliment is my proof.

"Ahh, shucks," I say. "I'm pretty sure that's the nicest thing you've ever said to me."

"Well, don't get used to it or anything, okay dumbass?"

"Okay, but the Eggies are on me today."

"Right on," Jenn says and heads over to Rickey D's.

As we sit idling in line at the drive-through, Jenn lowers the volume on the radio, turns her body my way, and then looks—very serious-sister-like—at me.

I look back at her, very scared and skittish-like. "What, Freak?"

"Nothing." She pulls up a little closer to the ordering screen.

"Okay, whatever." I'm used to her oddness by now, so I go back to pretending to read the billboards, though I'm actually wondering if Keeta will notice the smell of my fruity-scented lips or my new hairdo.

"You know, Abbey," Jenn finally says, "I've been playing basketball at Gila for four long years."

Information I do in fact already know. "Uh huh," I say.

"I'm just letting you know because..." She releases the brake to let her car coast up in line, but instead it dies. She uses her favorite swear words to command it back to life. On her third turn of the key, it finally obeys. "After all those years, you start to get a sense of people."

You know those instincts everyone is born with? Like running away when danger is near? Well, at this point I know I should flee like a gazelle galloping across an African prairie escaping the jaws of a hungry lioness, but I'm a moron lacking all natural instincts. "Yeah?" I say in my usual stupid way.

"I'm just saying, Abbey, I know a lot of the girls on the team." It's finally our turn to order, so she shouts our usual into the speaker then slowly coasts forward. "I know a lot about what they've gone through, things they've experienced. It wasn't always this easy to be yourself at Gila High. We've had to fight a lot of battles and we stick together. You know what I mean?"

"I guess," I say, trying hard to sound confused, but I know just what she means and who she means it about. And I know I'm lucky that I don't go to school in some scary conservative hick town.

"I'm telling you this because I want you to know if you need to talk, I'm here for you." She smiles sweetly and pats my knee for the second time in her life. I wonder briefly if she smoked out in the basement before picking me up. "I mean, if you need someone, okay? I know it must be hard going through life without a fabulous older sister like me."

I check her pupils while she stares at me; they appear normal and she seems like she actually means it, so I let down my guard. "Does Kate know?"

She pays with my money and hands me my Eggy breakfast sandwich. "Well, she suspects, but she's convinced that there's no way you would keep something this huge from her."

I have to force myself to swallow my first bite.

"I mean, that's what you told her when you guys made up from that weird lunch thing, that it wasn't true. So what's there to know, right?"

I grip the door as if what I'm going to say next might cause Jenn to veer off the road and kill us both. "Well, maybe there is something to know. But what I don't get is how everyone else can seem to know when I'm not even sure myself. I've never even..." I look out the window, embarrassed because I've said way too much. "I mean, I don't know what I am, so why is it anyone else's business and why is everyone talking about me?"

She pulls onto Dodge Road, cutting off a carload of Gila High students who honk and flip us off. "Well, you're always hanging out with Stef and Garrett, who are, like, the lesbian poster children of Gila. And some chick in my physics class said she saw you getting close with Stef in the varsity locker room, and that's how that one got started. Dude, you might want to chill with the cuddling in the locker room if you don't want people to talk."

"I was just consoling her," I shoot back and throw my Eggy back in the bag. "That's so stupid. I don't think of Stef like that."

"I know, okay. I get it all the time. I never thought I'd have to prove my straightness as much as I do."

"But she's just my friend. Can't I just be friends with someone?"

Jenn pulls into a spot in the back of the parking lot, and her car dies before she has a chance to turn it off. "Nice timing," she says to it then turns to me. "Abbey, I don't know why this stuff never gets old, but it doesn't. You just have to decide what matters more to you. Do you care what everyone else thinks? If so, then quit the team and stop talking to Stef and Garrett. And if you don't want things to get worse, stop crushing on Keeta. It's that simple."

"Who says I like Keeta?" I can feel my face turning as red as ketchup.

"That's my point, kiddo. Whether it's true or not, you have to decide if it matters because they'll eventually find out or they'll make it up. Just make sure you don't let the people who care about you the most find out in the hall before you tell them yourself. That's the kind of thing that can ruin a friendship."

I know she's right. I have to face some truths. But I hope I have time to figure out exactly what they are before everyone else does.

There's a sudden increase of activity on campus, which means the bell's rung and we have to wrap up our mini-therapy session. Jenn grabs her backpack and slams her door. "Laters, Abbey. And try to stay out of trouble."

"Yeah, I know. I'll try."

❖

Garrett and Stef both called me last night, so they knew that I'd be able to practice today. That's why, when I get to Spanish, there's a cupcake on my desk decorated with little candy basketballs. I bite into it right away and thank Garrett. Stef's not in class, again.

"Hey, G," I say in between bites, "we really need to get our act together in this class. I haven't done any homework in, like, a week or two…okay, three."

She points at my new outfit and nods. "First of all, I like what you've got going on here." Then to respond to my previous comment, Garrett makes a frowny face. "Yeah, I'm so behind."

"We're screwed," I say, then ask, "So, where's your BFF?"

"Hey, I have a plan to get us out of grade trouble in *Español.*"

"I'm listening," I say, aware she's avoiding my question. "What's your plan?"

"It will unfortunately rely on you developing skills as a liar. So I'm feeling less than confident, but I think maybe you've changed. You up for it?"

Finally, a chance to move up a rank or two in coolness levels. "Yep, I'm in." I don't ask about Stef again. Besides it's obvious she's with Keeta somewhere since Keeta never came to guitar class this morning. What a waste of my special outfit and flavored lips. "So, what do I have to do?"

Garrett doesn't get a chance to answer because *Señora* Cabrera starts class, already glaring in our direction. Twenty minutes pass, and I figure Garrett's forgotten about the plan, but then a note gets dumped on my desk like a giant piece of doggie doo. The delivery is so obvious to everyone, especially *Señora* Cabrera, who scoops it up before I have a chance to react.

"Well, well, well." *Señora* Cabrera unfolds the note. "Let's just see what you two have to say that is so important."

"No, *Señora* Cabrera! *Por favor, no lo lea.* We promise never to pass notes again," Garrett begs, in an obviously overdramatic way, but *Señora* Cabrera doesn't catch on.

I sink as low as I can in my seat. What if the note says something about Keeta? If it does, I will drop out of school and become a cave dweller.

I peek up at *Señora* Cabrera and it appears that the look of irritation has left her face now that she's halfway through reading the letter to herself. She looks down at me, then at Garrett, and smiles slightly. "I'll see you two after class," *Señora* Cabrera says and actually gives the note back to me. And that's when I know I've been right all along about Garrett. She *is* good at everything.

After class, *Señora* Cabrera explains that she also lost her dad at a young age, and she totally understands why I'm so sad around the anniversary of my dad's passing (which is not anywhere near today), and I'm lucky to have such a good friend who would give up so much of her time to help me through this "dark period." Then she gives us both an extension on our late homework. She even says she'll talk to Mr. Hughes, my social studies teacher, about the overdue project I've only halfway finished.

I wait until we're all the way down the hall before slapping Garrett's arm. "Oh my God, G, where do you come up with this stuff? You're freakin' crazy."

"What can I say? My mom taught me well," she brags. "Plus, my girl Tai listens in on every conversation she can while doing her duty as a student aide in the office. She could be CIA by the time she graduates, I swear. She's the one who gave me the scoop on *Señora* Cabrera and the scoop on you."

"Wow, you two are a good team in a scary sort of way. I guess I better watch my back around you and Tai, huh?"

"Yes, it's true. My power knows no bounds!" Then she throws her head back and laughs insanely, "Muahahahaha!"

Her laugh makes me laugh, too, which helps me get rid of the guilt growing in my gut. This is the first time I've ever used (or let someone else use) my dad's accident to get away with something, but what Garrett said in that letter worked. Now, all we have to do is make up our homework and we're golden again. It was definitely worth it because now, instead of worry, I feel something unfamiliar: happiness.

And it's all because of Garrett. She makes me feel like, I don't know, like a regular teenager, not an unsure freshman or someone who has something to hide.

But as soon as we see Stef leaning against my locker, her eyes bloodshot from crying, all fun comes to an abrupt stop.

"Dude," Garrett says and links Stef's arm in hers, "it looks like we need an emergency girl-talk session in the bathroom."

After finally getting a sufficient amount of toilet paper from the one-square-at-a-time dispensers, Stef blows her nose and tells us what's wrong. "I'm moving," she says and then starts to cry again.

Good thing Garrett is there to be concerned and upset because I'm too busy choking on a bit of relief and earning points in the Crappiest Friend of the Year contest that I am apparently participating in.

"My stupid mom accepted a job transfer and we're moving to Phoenix. She said it wasn't because of anything related to me being, whatever, in love with a freaking girl, but come on. We all know what a bunch of bull that is."

"Damn," Garrett says. "Well, at least it's only like an hour and a half away."

"Then, of course, we had a big stupid fight last night, so I snuck out to Keeta's and my mom came over there at like two in the morning to get me, and Keeta was so ticked off she started yelling at my mom. I thought she was going to punch a hole in the wall, but then Keeta's grandma came out and calmed everyone down. I was so embarrassed. I hate my mom so much." At this point, Stef kicks the metal trash can, which slides across the dirty linoleum and slams into the wall. "I'm so pissed! This whole thing is stupid!"

"Hell yeah, it is," Garrett says.

Then it's quiet and I know it's my turn to say something, anything, so I say, "I can't believe your mom would do that."

Garrett glances over at me, and I sense she's using her powers to see through my friendly façade. Then the bell rings and saves my pathetic self. "Shoot, I have to go you guys. I can't be late again." I pick up my bag and move toward the door.

"Dude, Abs, where's the fire?" Garrett asks coolly.

"You guys might not care about getting detention, but my mom will totally..." Then I realize I don't know what she'll do. I haven't actually ever really gotten in trouble at school before. "Anyway, she'll lose her mind."

"What class do you have next?" Garrett asks.

"English with Mr. Davison," I say quickly and peek out the bathroom door. The halls are clear, and in a matter of seconds, the supervisors are going to be sucking up meandering slackers like a Hoover vacuum and writing them up.

"Relax, Abbey," Garrett says. Then she takes a small pad of paper out of her backpack and starts to fill in the blanks.

I lean in for a closer look and see it's an official school hall pass. "How did you get ahold of those?" I'm definitely in awe and, if I had room in my manic head for it, I swear I could start to crush on her, too.

"Oh, I've got my connections."

Stef laughs. "Yeah, like she's sleeping with the fifth-period office aide."

"Man, you are so lucky," I say and make a mental note to look into becoming an office aide next year.

Garrett smirks and signs the pass. "I know you're both jealous, but she's mine."

"See, Abbey? Being a dyke has its advantages," Stef says while putting on makeup to try to disguise her tear-streaked face. "Too bad you'll never know the joys of dating girls. Just think, you could be me right now."

The thought has crossed my mind. What if I told my mom I was gay, or whatever…that I thought I liked a girl? Would she kick me out? Would she send me off to get electroshock therapy? The worst thing she could do to me, though, is be disappointed. The worst thing she could say would be, "I'm glad your father isn't here to see this." I'd rather be put out on the street than hear that from her.

Garrett tears off the pass and hands it to me. The signature is totally unrecognizable but looks very grown up. "Thanks, G. See you guys at practice."

❖

Since we have a game on Friday, we'll be spending the next four days running our plays. And since I'm no longer injured, I finally get to be part of the team again.

"Hey, Crutch, welcome back to the court," Garrett says and the other girls laugh.

Eva high-fives Garrett and says, "Excellent. From this point forward, Abbey will be known as Crutch." Eva laughs and slaps my butt, which I am still not really used to, but I roll with it.

"Okay, I guess I deserve that one," I say to her, like I'm bugged by it, but inside I'm actually ecstatic. The only other team nickname I've had was Amelia Earhart, which I got from the Doolen mathlete advisor because my mom and I got lost on my way to the middle school mathlete finals in Scottsdale and missed the whole thing. Now I'm not only Amara, but I'm also Crutch. And I like being these people so much more than just plain Abbey.

Later at practice, after a painfully boring hour of watching my teammates run plays, Coach finally says, "Brooks, you're in for Galvan."

"Yes, Coach." I quickly stretch my quads and take my position on the glossy painted floor. We run through the play and, as my virgin sneakers squeak on the court, I imagine the stands full of cheering fans screaming my new name: *Crutch, Crutch, Crutch.* I'd get a behind-the-back pass from Garrett and go in for a layup but then slam dunk it instead, shocking the crowd. There would be postgame interviews in the locker room with Channel 4 and replays of my sweet moves on the ten o'clock news. And of course I'd give my adoring fans waiting outside all the autographs they want.

Back in the real world, though, I end up on the wrong side of the key, which causes me to ram right into Garrett as she's running by trying to set a screen for Stef. Garrett lands hard on her butt and, instead of cheers, all I hear is my pathetic voice apologizing profusely, as I help her up. "I'm so sorry, G."

She laughs and pats my head. "It's cool, Crutch."

"Brooks! What the hell are you doing?" Apparently, Coach doesn't think it's at all cool. "Where are you supposed to be right now? Can you at least tell me that?"

I start to speak and point, but before I can make a sound, he blows his whistle. We all head toward the baseline to get ready for another set of suicides, which is a fitting description for the endless running on the court from end line to end line that we're about to do.

I only run half the lines at half pace due to my healing ankle, but we run for so long I'm convinced I'll need new shoes before the end of the day. However cruel and unusual Coach's punishments are, they definitely work because I don't mess up again.

At the end of practice I get another chance to redeem myself when Coach puts me back in during a rundown of our full-court press play. I took meticulous notes on this play and can do it with my eyes closed.

Tori slaps the ball to signal the play, so I set the screen for Eva, fake out Natalie, break through the press, catch the long pass from Tori, and make the layup at the other end. My teammates give me high fives and Coach nods in approval. It feels so amazing, and I can't hide my smile as we set up to run it again.

Then I see Kate standing in the locker room doorway. She's grinning and clapping quietly like a golf fan. I know she's teasing me, so I curtsy and blow a kiss in her direction, which is a little risky considering the latest rumors, but I'm too happy to worry. She's my best friend again, and I know I have to make sure I tell her the truth. Or at least make sure she never finds it out from anyone else.

❖

"Listen up people," Mr. Zamora says at the start of bio. "So far, only three of you have turned in your project. Now, I don't know what you're doing with yourselves after school, but you might want to consider…"

And that's right about where I lose interest. I used to be one of the students who did the homework, but now I'm the one ignoring the lecture that's supposed to inspire me or scare me into doing my work. I should probably feel like a loser, or at least a little ashamed, but I'm feeling…I don't know, okay about my life. Like, it's finally on the right track. I love being a part of the basketball team, Kate and I are friends, I'm successfully avoiding serious contact with Keeta, and my mom is too busy finishing a painting for an art show to notice I'm not spending much time on homework.

Then, just as Mr. Zamora concludes his rant and tells us to read silently as a punishment, in walks Tai. Of course, Tai and Keeta are, like, best friends. And I've seen her with Garrett in the hallway but have been too shy to approach them when they're together, so I always avoid them, which seems stupid now that I think about it. Tai's as tall as me, maybe even taller. And, to quote Garrett, Tai's skin is "the color of dark chocolate." What I notice most about her is the way she walks into a room; like Keeta, Garrett, and Stef, she's got so much confidence.

Tai hands Mr. Zamora the note and I glance down at my book so it won't look like I'm staring, but when I look up again, she's the one staring at me. I hold my breath until she leaves the room, and then I sort of freak out because the last thing I need is for a rumor to go around that I'm after Garrett's girlfriend.

"Abbey, you're needed in the office. Finish your chapter, then come and get your pass."

"Okay, Mr. Z," I say.

I shade my eyes with my hand and to try to focus on the small textbook print, but now I'm too nervous to concentrate. Since the day of my dad's accident, being called out of class has made me feel sick with anxiety. So instead of reading, I twirl a clump of hair and move my eyes over the words to fake it because it's all stuff my dad taught me before he died. He used to buy old high school science books from the Salvation Army thrift store, and for fun, we'd read through them and then he'd quiz me at dinner. My mom entered us into the father-daughter Jeopardy tournament, but we weren't selected because I was too young. I bet we could have wiped out the competition and taken home thousands.

When I think an appropriate amount of time has passed, I pack up and get my pass from Mr. Zamora. It says to report to Ms. Morvay's office "at the teacher's convenience," which makes me feel a little relieved.

This time there's no line, so I walk right up to Ms. Morvay's door and knock.

"Come on in, Abbey," she says.

I enter and close the door behind me. "Hey," I say and do my usual hair-twirling, spastic-leg-shaking thing right after I take the seat in front of her desk. "What's up?"

She does her leaning-back-in-her-black-leather-chair-while-drinking-coffee-and-looking-at-me-thoughtfully thing then says, "Well, I'd like to talk to you about something."

I feel a little more comfortable with her this time, so I get us right to the point. "Is this about my grades?

"Yes, that's part of it," she says.

"Okay, I'm totally going to fix everything. In fact, I've already talked to *Señora* Cabrera and Mr. Hughes and they gave me due-date extensions on my late work."

"Yes, Mrs. Cabrera told me you've been very distraught about your dad and that it has been causing you to get behind in class." Then she gives me a look that says something like *and we both know what a bunch of bs that is.*

So my lying either has to continue, or I can try telling Ms. Morvay the truth…the whole truth instead of the little bits I tell everyone else. I take a few breaths to summon my courage and say, "Um, do you have, like, a patient-doctor confidentiality rule or something?"

"Well, kind of, but you're not my patient and I'm not a doctor. I am required by law to report if a student tells me they have been physically or sexually assaulted by someone or if they plan to hurt themselves or others. But"—she glances at the door to be sure it's closed—"if you just want to talk about what's on your mind, I can listen and maybe even help."

I decide I can trust her. "My dad didn't die in November," I confess.

She smiles and nods like she's proud of me for telling the truth.

But I don't feel at all proud. All I feel is my stomach knotting up. "You probably think I'm pretty pathetic."

"Well, I suspect you have a good reason for lying."

I shrug my shoulders. "No, actually, I don't."

"Really? Because I think I know what it is." Ms. Morvay leans forward in her chair. "Let me give it a shot."

"Okay…" I say, baffled at how the entire world seems to know what's going on with me, except me.

"Everyone takes time to adjust to high school, Abbey. Everything's confusing and you're trying to figure out your place in the world." Ms. Morvay puts down her mug. "What you're going through is completely normal. I see it all the time with my freshmen."

The old *adjustment to fill-in-the-blank* theory? I'm disappointed but say, "You're right. It is a lot to get used to, I guess. And it was hard at first, but things are getting better."

She nods slowly but doesn't respond.

I pick up my stuff to try to make a quick getaway and mutter, "Well, thanks for checking up on me, but I'm okay."

"Are you sure things are getting better, Abbey?" Unlike most of the adults in my life, it appears she's not buying it. Then she asks, "Are you really doing okay?"

That's when my stupid bottom lip begins to quiver. I bite it hard to try and hide it but can't.

"Abbey," she says softly, coaxing me in with her voice like I'm a lost puppy. "My office is a good place for crying. I own stock in Kleenex."

My eyes are welled up with hot tears, so I give in and sit down again. I don't know where to start, so I just sit there looking at my hands, and we both listen to nothing for what seems like forever.

Finally, Ms. Morvay hands me a tissue and ends the silence. "Why don't you just tell me how you're feeling at this very second?"

I blow my nose and find my voice. "I don't know. It's like…like I'm trying to figure out who I am, but I don't really know how to do it. I've become this giant liar and all I can do is keep on saying, *I'm not like this, this isn't me*, but it must be me, because I keep on doing it." I wipe more tears off my face.

"What else, Abbey?" She asks like she can read the tear gauge on my face and knows I'm not even close to empty.

I let out a gasping sob. "I mean, I think I like…this"—I can't say it—"this person, but what if I'm just being influenced by, um, this person, I mean…her, and the other girls on the team? I just don't know for sure if I'm that way. Okay, maybe I am, but what if I'm not? How can I risk everything for nothing? What if I'm totally crazy and imagining it all? What if it's just a game they play with all the new girls on the team?" I look up at her. "But what if I'm gay?"

I can't believe I'm saying any of this out loud and I can't believe Ms. Morvay is still looking like she cares. Or maybe she's looking contemplative because she's thinking up a list of insane asylums to tell my mother about.

"I know you're scared, Abbey," she says, "but what you're feeling is okay. You're young and you're figuring out who you are. It's totally normal."

Normal? How can all this madness in my head be normal?

Then I start to cry again and more truths make their way to the surface. "But I don't want to be like them. I don't want to be stared at. I don't want to be laughed at. And I could never tell my mom."

Ms. Morvay frowns sympathetically and says, "Let's take one thing at a time here. First, try not to judge yourself. Just go with what feels right. I bet if you just listen to your heart, you'll know all you need to know. But, at the same time, don't be afraid to change your mind. You're allowed to do that."

Her advice is kind of confusing, but once I figure out what she's saying, I realize she's right. I know the answer. I know who I am. I just can't figure out how to be brave enough to accept it.

"And," she adds, "your mother doesn't need to know everything that's going on in your mind. But what makes you so sure that she won't love you for who you are?"

I finally look up at her. "I don't know. I'm just scared."

The corners of Ms. Morvay's mouth turn up in a slight smile, but not in a mean way. It's like she really gets it. "Abbey, you have to believe me when I say it will be okay. Trust yourself and be true to who you are. You'll see."

I take a deep breath. "Yeah, okay."

"And my door is always open, so come see me if you need to," she says, as if she can tell I'm done crying for now, which I am.

"Thanks, Ms. Morvay." School is almost over, and I know I don't want to have that emotional-basket-case look as I walk through the halls, so I change the subject and ask about my algebra class and if I'm going to be able to take it next semester.

"Yes, we have a section of Accelerated Algebra and a new teacher already lined up." Then she laughs and says, "Still hoping to graduate early?"

I shrug and a tiny smile gets out. "No, I guess it's not that bad here." Finally, I'm not lying. I mean, minus all the things that are making me cry, I'm sort of enjoying high school.

After my eyes clear up and my face feels less red, I leave her office with very clear sinuses and less worry. Talking to Ms. Morvay made me feel a million times better, so maybe it's time I talk to Kate, too.

CHAPTER THIRTEEN

I'm in the locker room changing for basketball practice when Garrett turns down my row and surprises me. I instinctively cover my chest with my shirt even though I'm wearing a sports bra.

"Girl, how many times do I have to tell you?" Garrett says and sits down to tie her shoes.

"Oh right"—I play along—"you're taken. Oh cruel, cruel world."

"Yeah, someday you'll get over me, Abbey. In the meantime, what did Ms. M want with you yesterday?"

"Oh, nothing. Just checking in," I say. It feels like more than a day ago that I talked to Ms. Morvay, and I thought telling her the truth might have a more permanent effect on me, but my lies continued as soon as I got home. I wonder if my mom even believes me when I do it. Like when she asked me last night if I did my homework, and I told her I finished it before practice. Did she believe me? Or when she came into my room before going to bed and asked if I was okay, and I said I was fine. Did she buy that or has she figured me out, too? Sometimes I feel like I've told so many lies that if each one were a snowflake I could cover Gila's football field with a six-inch layer of powdery white…lies.

"Come on, Abbey. Ms. Morvay doesn't pull kids out of biology just to check in and say hi."

It bugs me that, thanks to Tai, Garrett knows my every move, but I play it cool. "So, Tai tells you everything, huh?"

"Yep. Everything. Speaking of my g.f., I've never asked you what you think of her. Pretty hot, huh?"

I wager the risks of telling the truth and decide Garrett will probably like to hear it. "Yeah, she's a total hottie," I bravely say. "How long have you guys been together?"

"It'll be ten months next week."

"Wow." I want so badly to know how it all happened. Like, who asked who out? And how did Garrett know Tai liked girls, too?

"Go ahead. Ask me."

"Ask you what?" I say as I brush my hair, wondering how all my friends can read my mind so easily.

"Whatever it is you're trying not to."

I'm scared to ask the questions, but here's my chance. "Okay." I put down my brush, lean back against the lockers, swallow loudly. "Did you think she was, you know, cute when you first met her? I mean, did you *like her*, like her, right away?" With that simple question, I feel like I've just given Garrett the final confirmation she needs that I'm a you-know-who girl, too.

"Yeah, I guess I did like her, but for a long time I just thought it was because she was so cool and she was paying attention to me. It's nice to be the object of someone's attention, you know?"

"Yeah," I say, way too dreamily.

"I bet you do," she says, then continues with her answer. "Anyway, it all started on this road trip to Douglas last year. I was a freshman and Tai was a sophomore. So, Stef and I were sitting together, and then Tai and Keeta sat in the seat behind us and talked to us the whole ride there. Mostly, though, Tai talked to me, and Keeta talked to Stef. But it wasn't just talking going on. Tai did stuff like try to braid my hair, feed me Doritos, and make me laugh every time I drank my Gatorade. By the end of the trip, I realized Tai was doing more than being nice. Of course, Stef helped me see the light because that same night Stef confessed to me that Stef and Keeta had messed around a few times already."

As Garrett tells her story, I am right there with her on that bus. But instead of seeing Garrett and Tai talking and flirting, I see Keeta and me talking and flirting. Everyone else on the bus becomes fuzzy and soft around the edges and everything sharp and mean about them disappears.

I must look as far away as I feel because Garrett clears her throat loudly and slaps my forehead.

"What?" I say, jumping back into reality.

"Girl, you've got it bad."

I bend forward to look for something in my bag so she can't see me as I add another white lie to my snowstorm. "Whatever, G, I don't have anything."

She pulls me up by my arm to force me to look at her. "Come on, Abbey. I know you like her. I'm not surprised. I mean, why wouldn't you? Those amazing brown eyes, that long black hair, that sexy muscular body. Admit it, something about Keeta's got a hold on you."

"I don't know what you're talking about."

Garrett rolls her eyes and lets go of my arm. "You're such a bad liar," she says but then leaves me alone. "Anyway, after that trip to Douglas, I felt like everyone could tell I liked Tai. Like I was walking through the halls holding a big sign over my head that said *Garrett Church likes girls!* You know what I mean?"

I know exactly what she means. Every time someone ends a conversation when I walk into a classroom or laughs as I pass by in the hall, I'm convinced they're talking about me, seeing through my heart like a window. And inside, there's Keeta, kneeling like Princess Charming and kissing the palm of my hand.

"You know what, though?" Garrett says thoughtfully. "No one really noticed."

"But it seems like everyone knows about you now. Doesn't that scare you?"

"Abbey, there are people in my life that I care about, whose opinions actually matter. Then, there are the other thousand or so morons at this school. I had to stop worrying about what they think. I could have hidden forever, but I couldn't think of enough reasons why I should."

I feel like I've had the opposite problem: too many reasons why I *should* hide. But playing a really long game of hide-and-seek can get tiring. You know, like one of those games where your hiding spot is so good eventually you have to jump out and say, "Here I am!"

❖

"Gatorade and water?" Kate reads from the list we made up last night on the phone.

I look in the giant duffel bag I've packed for our first long-distance away game. "Check. My mom even froze two for us so they'd be cold after the game."

"Travel games and deck of cards?"

"Check."

"Assorted flavors of M&M's?" she continues.

"Peanut, mint, and dark chocolate. I couldn't find the peanut butter ones, so I got some Reese's instead."

"Two major dorks?" Jenn says from the bench she's sprawled on, as we wait for the bus in front of Gila. "Check."

She, Stef, and Garrett are laughing at us now, but at least Kate and I won't be crying for water on the way home.

A decrepit yellow school bus pulls into the parking lot and parks in front of us. The toxic exhaust gets us all moving very quickly to get on, but keeping with tradition, the varsity team boards first. I wait outside and watch as Keeta and Tai walk the length of the bus to claim the long seat in the back. JV goes next. Naturally, Stef and Garrett join their girlfriends, and if it weren't for the fact that I'm pretty much in love with Stef's girl, I would have loved to sit back there, too. I actually feel like being as far away from them as possible so I won't have to witness their lovefest, but I've been told the front seats are for shy loser freshmen and coaches. So I end up picking a seat in the middle, but a little toward the front.

Once my JV teammates and I are settled, the freshmen climb aboard. Kate approves of my seat choice but then says, "Move it, loser. I get the window."

"Bossy much?" I complain but move to the hotter aisle seat.

Even though no one is listening, the bus driver gives her obligatory speech about emergency exits and procedures. Then the front door closes and the bus jerks forward, beginning our journey.

As soon as the bus pulls away from the front steps of Gila, one of the varsity girls suddenly shouts, "Stop the bus! I forgot my shoes!"

The bus driver hits the brake, the cards Kate's been dealing out for a game of Speed slide off the seat, and all the varsity girls laugh hysterically. Coach Stahl, the varsity coach, apparently forgot to warn the new driver of this obnoxious tradition. "Ignore them," he says to the bus driver, and we're on our way, again.

While Kate recounts the cards, I remember my fantasy about Keeta talking to me and flirting with me, as we ramble through the never-ending desert in our yellow vessel of love. For a second, I hold out a secret hope that it might come true but then remind myself that Stef is on this bus to Nogales, too, so I quickly get over it.

Twenty minutes into the trip, Kate's beaten me twice at Speed, which is very rare, but I'm distracted because I have to pee and because I can't stand the thought of Stef and Keeta cuddling in the back. Then, a wad of paper hits my shoulder as I'm shuffling the cards.

"Hey," I say then pick the note up off the floor and look toward the back of the bus.

Garrett blows me a kiss and laughs. "Read it," she yells.

As usual, I do as I'm told.

The writing is nearly illegible, but as far as I can tell it says, *Abs, we want you*—then it skips a few lines, as if that's the whole note—*to give us some food. Bring us your stash or risk being pantsed during the game. We are not kidding, either. G and S.*

Kate wants to read the note and I let her, but I don't like the way my two worlds are colliding. I barely won Kate back, with my lies, and I can't stand to lose her again.

"They can threaten me all they want, but they aren't laying their grubby hands on my loot," I say and shuffle my cards around in my hand. "Moochers."

Kate doesn't say anything and I feel the tension creep up between us again.

"Too bad for them," I say but look at Kate for a subtle sign of permission to go back there. It might kill me a little inside, but I like that they want what I have, even if it's just my junk food.

Stef calls my name and yells, "Hey, Abbey. Hope you wore your good *chones* today."

"Oh my God," I say. "Do you think they'll actually do it?"

Kate hands me the bag. "It's cool. You should give them some."

I act nonchalant and shrug like I wasn't waiting for her approval. "Yeah, I guess I should."

To avoid the embarrassing "Get in your seat!" announcement from our driver, I crawl to the back of the bus on my hands and knees with my bag in my teeth. "Hi, losers," is all I can think of to say when I arrive.

"Yeah, Abbey!" Garrett cheers and grabs my bag. "Oh, Tai, this is Abbey."

"Hi," I say.

"Man, I've heard *all* about you. Nice to meet ya officially." Then Tai smiles a little too big at me, and I can only imagine what Garrett has told her.

While Stef and Garrett pilfer the food, I try to keep my gaze down because it's weird to see them all sitting so close on that long bench seat, and it's especially painful to see Stef sitting between Keeta's legs, holding her hand. Keeta doesn't say anything to me or even look my way. She just stares blankly out at the desert on the other side of the dirty window.

I shouldn't be surprised, though. I've done such an amazing job avoiding Keeta in guitar. Besides, that whole locker room hand-kissing thing was probably just a moment of temporary insanity on Keeta's part, and maybe that "letter was for you" bit was just a lie. I mean, if I'm lying twenty-four-seven, why should I think everyone else is telling the truth?

After Garrett and Stef clean out all the good stuff, I go back to Kate with a near-empty bag and more questions about Keeta than ever before. But I shove them down and pretend that everything's okay. I have to act normal for Kate. I feel like I owe it to her.

❖

I don't dress out for the game because Coach isn't convinced I'm healed enough. Maybe that's why our team kicks some serious Nogales butt. In fact, all three of our teams win, and like they promised, the coaches let us celebrate at the nearby Pizza Hut. We eat, drink large amounts of soda, and are merry. Then we all have to pee.

There's only one girls' toilet in the whole restaurant, and it seems as if all three rosters of players are lined up against the wall in the dark, cramped hallway with our legs crossed. Natalie's banging on the door demanding that Jenn hurry up. When Jenn finally opens the bathroom door, we all cheer, and Nat races in, barely shutting the door before her pants are down.

Since I'm caught up in the fun and trying not to pee my pants, I forget to avert my eyes when Keeta exits the bathroom a few minutes later and makes her way down the narrow hallway to go back to the dining room. There's only one naked lightbulb illuminating us, but I can still clearly see the glow of Keeta's entrancing brown eyes when she looks into mine. Then, just as she's squeezing by me, she slyly reaches out and runs her fingertips across my stomach. *"Perdóname, Amara,"* she whispers.

Her touch and smile make me feel like someone's pushed the pause button on the world and we're just silently floating in space, waiting to be put into play again.

I don't speak to her, but maybe I don't need to. It seems like she knows everything I want to say. Her hand lingers on my stomach for one second more, and then she's gone.

When I recover, I look at Kate to see if she noticed our clandestine exchange, but she's laughing with the other girls who are cheering and scooting along the wall. Maybe time *had* stopped.

On the ride home, I'm unable and unwilling to stop thinking about Keeta. Under the shelter of my sweatshirt, I press my hand onto my stomach like Keeta did an hour earlier, and a million butterflies take flight inside me. I want to jump into the aisle and scream, "Here I am! Big Gay Abbey Brooks! And I am falling for Keeta Moreno! And guess what! I think she might be falling for me, too!"

But, instead, I snuggle my face into the hood of my sweatshirt and smile the entire ride home. Ms. Morvay was right. My heart knows exactly who I am.

CHAPTER FOURTEEN

A bbey, we need to talk."

Nothing good has ever followed those words. When I was five, it was about Santa Claus and the Tooth Fairy. Then, at seven, it was time for me to start sleeping with the light off. At nine, it was the worst.

"Abbey, we need to talk. Your daddy was in a car accident."

Now it's six thirty on Saturday night and I'm about to embark upon another pathetic night of attempting to play sappy love songs on my guitar, that I dream of someday playing outside Keeta's bedroom window.

But then, my mom says these five feared words to me, as I try to slip past her in the hallway on my way to my bedroom: "Abbey, we need to talk."

"Is it the dishes? I'll do them later, I swear." Another lie.

"As a matter of fact"—she puts her hands on either side of the wall—"it's about the dishes, and the laundry, and your homework."

"Mom—" I try interrupting, but she's on a roll.

"And it's about me, and Kate, and your grades, and basketball."

This last part makes my heart do a freefall to my feet. What does she know about me and basketball? Is she going to make me quit? I've finally found a team I can be proud of being a part of, and I think I'm getting pretty good at it. I can't lose basketball. Especially not until I know for sure about Keeta and me.

Then she takes my face in her hands, which is also always a bad sign. It's her I'm-serious-Abbey thing that she does. "I'm worried about you. It seems like all you do these days is hang out in your room. You don't even talk to me anymore. Why are you avoiding me, Abbey Road?"

She's right. I've been doing everything I can to avoid her, but I'm not the only one avoiding people. Kate has been doing an impressive job of avoiding me, which kind of makes sense since the latest rumor at school is that she and I hooked up in Nogales and are now dating.

After a long moment, my mom finally lets go of my face. "Abbey, I'm going to ask you something, and I just want you to tell me the truth."

I break eye contact with her and look down at the carpet, a sure sign of a liar. "Okay."

"Are you doing drugs?"

I laugh. "Drugs? Mom, are you serious?"

"Do I look like I'm kidding?"

No, she doesn't.

Then she says, "You've been distant, tired, cranky, and lazy in your schoolwork. What else should I think? You're not yourself, Abbey. There has to be something going on."

Now I'm presented with an interesting conundrum. If I claim to be addicted to drugs, my odd behavior will be explained, the questions dropped, and I can go on with my life, overdosing on Keeta fantasies every night. The downside is the NA meetings and a possible visit to a drug rehab facility.

So I come clean, sort of. "Mom, I swear I am not doing drugs."

She looks at me carefully. "Okay, I believe you." But there's something different in her eyes. The thing I am seeing more and more when she looks at me: doubt.

"Don't you believe me, Mom?"

"Abbey, I do believe you. I just wish you could trust me. If you're not doing drugs, then what's wrong with you?"

There's no way I'm going to tell her I'm falling in love with the Hot Dog on a Stick Chick, but what I do tell her has to be something believable. Then, thanks to Ms. Morvay, I come up with a good one. "I guess I'm just adjusting to high school. You know, friends, classes, basketball, and"—I look down again, as I say the last item on my list—"you know, boys. It's just hard to figure it all out sometimes."

Success. My mom kisses my forehead and says, "So this is about Jake? I'm sorry about the house rule. Maybe we can work something out. After all, you are going to be fifteen in a week. I had my first date when I was fifteen."

Man, I didn't see this coming at all. "Um, okay."

"It's not good to keep everything all bottled up, Abbey Road. You know you can talk to me about anything. Especially about boy stuff. I dated boys in high school, so I know all about it," she says, like she's relieved, or maybe that's just my warped interpretation.

"Thanks, Mom. From now on, I promise to be less emotionally constipated," I say because I have been waiting for a chance to try out that expression since I heard Garrett yell it at Tai when they were fighting in the locker room about something stupid last week.

"Emotionally constipated?" my mom repeats, which makes her laugh. This is not my intention, but I'm glad she's smiling. "Honey, I'd settle for a 'Hi, Mom' or 'Love you, Mom' once in a while. And maybe when you're sad, you can talk to me and let me tell you everything's going to be okay. Do we have a deal?"

"Deal," I say.

Then she hugs me close to her like I'm about to leave for summer camp or something.

After she finally releases me, she kisses my forehead again. "I love you."

"Love you, too, Mom," I say, and then I'm finally allowed to complete my hallway journey. I shut my bedroom door behind me and hope my fake truths will get her off my back for a while.

As I strum some notes to a Cranberries song I've been trying to learn, I think about the real truths I can't tell my mom. Like how I can't get through my forty-five minute guitar class without dreaming of kissing Keeta. And how I go to Spanish and Stef's all nice to me and I feel like the worst friend ever. When did I become a backstabber? The whole thing is wrong on so many levels and I know it. That's when I vow to stop drooling over Keeta, at least until Stef moves to Phoenix and things are settled between them.

I fall asleep with new confidence and determination.

❖

Monday morning I feel Keeta's arm link around mine as I'm walking to guitar class, and she easily ushers me off to the side of the performance hall where no one can see us.

"Sorry I had to do this to you," she says with a cute but mischievous smile on her face. "But you've been making it hard to talk before class, or after class, or before practice, or after practice." She pushes me gently against the brick wall. "If I didn't know any better, Amara, I'd say you were avoiding me."

"That's crazy," I say, looking down into her eyes, trying to hide my satisfaction that she's noticed.

"Is it crazy?" She leans on the wall beside me. "Look, I know you're probably really freaking out right now, but you don't have to."

I almost say she's crazy again, but I don't want to tell such a big lie, so instead I shrug and look down at our shoes; my purple Converse and Keeta's Nikes look better together than mine and Jake's.

She turns toward me, reaches for my hand, and holds it sweetly in hers; any coolness I have in me melts like gummy bears left in a hot car.

"The truth is, Amara, I can't stop thinking about you and I can't keep my eyes off you. *Dios mío*, all I want to do is kiss you."

Kiss me? *She* wants to kiss *me*. I look away because if she doesn't kiss me I think I might cry. *Please, please, please kiss me, Keeta.*

Now Keeta's standing so close I can feel her breath on my cheek.

"I've never felt this way about anyone before," she says and runs the fingers of her free hand through her hair. "Damn, girl, you've got a hold on me. I can't explain it, but I also can't stand being ignored by you when I know you feel the same way."

It's like I dreamed it would be. She likes me, too, and she's saying all the right things, but it's happening too early, before Stef has left. I should run, but I'm so tired of fighting it.

I take her other hand in mine and look into her eyes instead of at her shoes or the oleander bushes we're hiding behind. "I do. I mean, I like you, too," I whisper.

"You do?" she asks, like she thought I might actually turn her down.

"Keeta, I can't stop thinking about you either and I *am* freaking out, but I don't care anymore because..." I bite my lip.

"Because what, Amara?"

For a second, I think about Stef and I know I'm a bad, bad, bad friend, but that part I keep to myself. "I want to kiss you, too."

"Really?" Keeta whispers and then leans in even closer so our lips are only millimeters apart.

I don't reply. Instead, I close my eyes and wait for her lips to touch mine. When they do, I finally understand how time and space can bend and sway like a tree on a windy day. And I finally understand what it means to be in love.

Ding, ding, ding goes the bell over our heads. We both jump and stop kissing, and I develop a hate for that bell that is stronger than my hate for dressing rooms and low-rise pants combined.

After we look at each other and smile, Keeta kisses me once more and I'm 100 percent sure I can spend the rest of my life kissing Keeta behind these shrubs.

"I'm glad we had a chance to talk," she says then gives me one of those hypnotizing looks, slips out from behind our secret spot, and walks into the performance hall.

And me? I lean against the brick wall for support until I can be sure I can stand on my own. I can't believe I've just been kissed by Keeta, and I can't believe I didn't screw it up.

I somehow get through guitar without imploding, but I'm not sure how much longer I can keep it in. I want to scream it into the office PA system during homeroom or hire a plane to fly over the school at lunch with a sign trailing behind that reads: *Keeta and Abbey kissed!* But I know better; this is a secret that must never be found out by anyone.

I change for PE, and keeping to my usual routine, I wait for Kate, who has taken to changing in the bathroom instead of next to her locker in order to avoid changing next to me. I guess I understand why she does it with all the gossip going around. But, even if I do like girls (okay, okay, I do like girls), it doesn't mean I'm going to start hitting on Kate. She's my best friend, nothing more, and I wish everyone could see the difference.

I spot her shoes in the third stall and bang on the flimsy door. "Hurry up, Kate! We're going to be late."

"Whatever, go away."

At first I think she's joking, but then Kate pushes open the door and nearly knocks me over as she rushes by.

"Whoa, qué te pasa? Estás bien?"

"I don't know what you're saying," Kate says, as she stands in front of the mirror to put her hair up in a messy ponytail. "You must have me confused with your *other* friends."

"What's going on, Kate?" I can't believe how mean she's being. She turns from the mirror to look at me. "You tell me, Abbey."

"What? Why are you so mad at me?" I don't know what she knows, but she definitely knows something and it's not something good.

I can tell she wants to scream at me, but she won't because she doesn't want to draw any attention to us. Instead, she glares at me as she says, "I don't even care that much, you know? But you seem to have no problem lying to me, and that's what really pisses me off. It's like everything we've been through is a joke."

"Kate, wait," I start, but there isn't a ladder big enough to get myself out of the hole I'm in.

"Save it, Abbey. I'm sick of your lies."

She storms out of the locker room leaving me alone with my guilt and a dozen classmates thinking that the rumors about me and Kate are true. In less time than I spent kissing Keeta, the best day of my life quickly turns into one of the worst. I could blame it on someone else, but I know it's my fault. I got caught. My lies have to end, or my friendship with Kate has to end. The problem is I want it all: Keeta's kisses and Kate's friendship.

Kate ignores me all during PE, which means Mari and Sarah ignore me, too. Things would be a little bit better if I at least had third period to look forward to, but I dread seeing Stef and Garrett. I'm sure they have built-in radar that can detect lesbian love.

"Hey, Abbey!" Stef's enthusiastic greeting is like a knife in my gut. Garrett doesn't say anything and waves because she's busy copying Stef's homework before the bell rings.

I fake a smile—"Hey, guys"—and throw my stuff down on the floor, trying not to look as guilty and crapilicious as I feel. "What's up?"

"Don't you think you should tell us?" Stef asks.

I almost go into cardiac arrest, but she's smiling, so I figure I'm still okay. "Tell you what?"

Señora Cabrera starts class, so, like always, we have to resort to our sneakier form of communication. I must say, I'm really getting a knack for passing notes while still being able to appear like I'm paying attention in class. I guess it's like playing basketball or guitar or, in my case, lying. It just takes a little practice to get good at it.

Stef slyly drops a note onto the floor and covers it with her foot. When I see an opportunity, I drop my pen, get the note, and open it in my lap:

So Crutch,

U thought u could keep it a secret? Haven't you learned by now that nothing gets by us? You're dealing with the freakin Lesbian Mafia, dude.

I look up to check in with *Señora* Cabrera. She has her back to the class as she scribbles some vocabulary on the board.

Back to Stef's note:

Yeah, we found u out, Girl. Time to swim with the fishes.

My great day that quickly went worse is now seemingly done for. I start to sweat profusely and read on:

But we talked it over, and you're forgiven. So, this Saturday, we're taking you out for a night you won't forget. It's BYOBB—bring your own barf bag. Ask no questions.

Stefarino Soprano

I turn in my seat and roll my eyes at Garrett and Stef then fold up the note and breathe a giant sigh of relief. My special secret is still safe for now, I think.

At least they want to take me out on Saturday, instead of my actual birthday on Friday. I guess they figure my mom would want to do mushy mom-daughter stuff, which is the case. I play along for my mom, but I'm usually glad when it's over. Sure, my birthday used to be my favorite holiday, but after my dad's accident, it became another reminder that he's not here anymore. And there's something kind of lame about waking up to find only one other person in the house who is happy you were born. I guess it could be worse. At least I don't have to wake up in a house where someone actually wishes I had never been born at all. Maybe that's how Stef feels with her mom. Great, now my guilt has multiplied and I can't breathe again.

After Spanish, my day continues on its sucky downward spiral toward hell. Stef's niceness makes me feel incredibly guilty, and my best friend ignores me when I see her in the burrito line at lunch and before her practice in the gym. And because I mess up twice during our inbound play, Coach makes me run four extra sets of lines after practice.

While on my first set, the girls' varsity team starts coming in from the other gym. I see Jenn and Tai and nod my head to say hi. Then in walks Keeta. The second I see her, I'm reminded of why today is still the best day of my life.

As I run, I replay our morning kiss in my mind and I wonder if she's thought about it all day, too.

After I'm done running, I gather my stuff and head toward the locker room. I try not to, but I can't stop myself from looking over my shoulder. I guess I want to see if what happened before school today was real and if it meant anything to her.

The wink she sneaks to me tells me everything I need to know.

CHAPTER FIFTEEN

The next morning when Jenn picks me up for school, she hardly waits for me to get in before she throws the car into drive, causing my head to slam against the headrest. "I warned you, Abbey," she growls.

She doesn't have to explain what she means. She did warn me, and I should have listened. But it's taking me a long time to figure out that everyone's getting slammed by my lies. My mom, Kate, even Jenn, and soon enough, I figure Stef is going to feel it, too. "I'm sorry, Jenn. I know I should've told Kate. I was just too afraid."

Jenn stops hard at a yellow light and looks over at me. "So you flat-out lied to her?"

"I know."

"I told you to tell her before it was too late."

A telephone pole stabbed with a million rusty staples stands on the corner. I wish I could trade places with it. "I know," I say again.

"That's all you're going to say? You know?"

"No. I mean, how did she find out?"

"I told you she would, Abbey. I just can't believe it was with Keeta. I hope you plan on telling Stef yourself."

"I will." I want to cry because I feel like scum. No, I'm worse than scum. I'm what scum eats for breakfast.

Jenn blasts her horn at the car in front of us for not turning when they had the chance.

I'm scared for my life and hope we get to Gila in one piece.

"It was Jake," she says as we turn left onto Speedway.

"What? How? Why? When?"

"Calm down and listen. Kate went looking for you yesterday before school started. She didn't see you in the music room, so she asked Jake where you were. He told her he saw you and Keeta walking toward the side of the building."

"Why was she looking for me?"

Jenn changes lanes, cutting off an old lady in a giant Cadillac. "I don't know. You'll have to ask her. Anyway, she said she saw you two holding hands."

"Is that all she saw?" My first-kiss memory is now tarnished by the image of Kate glaring at me with disgust from behind her Gucci sunglasses.

"God, Abbey, you're walking a thin line," Jenn says and turns up the stereo, so we ride in an earsplitting silence the rest of the way to Gila.

❖

When I enter the music room, I don't see Keeta, so I sneak behind the curtain to see if she's there. I find her prepping the chalkboard for the day's lesson.

She turns toward me as soon as I appear and wipes her chalked hands on a rag. *"Buenos días, Amara."*

"Hi." It feels so good to be near her again. Maybe my mom is right. I am addicted to a drug, and her name is Keeta.

"Dichosos los ojos que te están viendo." She reaches out and pushes some stray strands of my hair behind my ear.

"Thanks." Even though she just told me it's good to see me, I still feel miserable.

"Hey, what's wrong?"

"It's my best friend," I say. "She saw us, um, yesterday."

"Chale," Keeta says then turns back to finish writing the notes on the chalkboard. "What did she say?"

"Nothing, really." I don't want to tell Keeta that Kate confirmed what a liar I am. That doesn't seem like a good way to begin our relationship. "But now she knows about me, about us, or whatever. I don't know. Everything's messed up. And then there's Stef. What if she finds out? I'll feel even worse, and I'm pretty sure she's going to kick my ass."

"You didn't seem to feel too terrible yesterday," Keeta says with a tone that slithers out of her mouth like a snake.

"I know, but now…" I reach out to touch her shoulder.

But she shrugs off my hand. "Abbey, I get it. You can't be with me. People will find out and talk. You were just confused before and now you see that it was all a phase. I'm fine with it. Really."

"What?" I massage my forehead. "I was just going to tell you that I have to try and figure out how to fix things with Kate, that's all."

She keeps her back to me and says nothing.

"Come on, Keeta. I've been crushing on you since that day you blew a straw wrapper at me," I say, telling more truth than I've told anyone in a long time.

She finally turns to face me again. "*No manches*. Really?"

"Actually, I have pretty much been crushing on you since second grade, and I'm not about to give you up already."

"Since second grade? That's so cute." She takes my hand, pulls me over to her, and lays a long kiss on my lonely lips.

I'm in that faraway galaxy again, floating away with her in my arms. I even forget about Kate and Stef for a moment.

Then she pulls away. "You do what you need to do. But, Amara, it'll all work out," Keeta says, sensing my worry. "You'll see. You worry too much about everything, *chula*."

Keeta calling me cute makes me feel a little better. "Yeah, I know." She gives me another kiss, which makes me feel all the way better. Then I slip through the curtains to take my seat before the boys arrive.

But today, instead of spending my time in class messing up on purpose so Keeta can have an excuse to lean over me and breathe on my neck, I spend my time thinking about what I'm going to say to Kate.

❖

After guitar, I race over to the PE locker room to make sure Kate isn't already changing in one of the bathroom stalls. They're clear, so I wait by her locker so I don't miss her.

A minute later, she turns down the row, sees me, and scrunches up her face in an ugly way. "What do you want?" she asks, spinning in her combination.

"Kate, please hear me out. I know you saw me and…" I can't say Keeta's name. "Anyway, let me explain why I didn't tell you before. Please."

"Whatever."

I don't know if that's a yes or no, so I start my practiced apology, "Okay, so, umm, here's the thing—"

"Why should I believe anything you say?"

She has a good point, so I tell her so. "Kate, you're totally right and I am so, so, so, so sorry."

Other girls start to arrive in the locker room and begin to stare and whisper about us. At least, that's how it feels to me and Kate.

"Can we talk later?" Kate says, glancing over at Diana and Monica, two girls we have always hated, who are obviously trying to listen in.

"Meet me on the track so we can run the mile together?" I plead.

She agrees.

❖

I'm stretching next to the bleachers when Kate walks up. "Let's go," she says and takes off in front of me.

To ensure privacy on the track, Kate sets a ridiculously fast pace. I'm gasping for air after about fifty yards and am pretty sure I might collapse, but I have to tell her my side of the story so I delay passing out. "Look, I know I lied to you," I say and wipe away the sweat that is already rolling down my face. "I felt horrible as soon as I did it. I never thought it was okay. It was just—" I stop talking to sort out my thoughts and catch my breath. "It's just that...I don't know." But I do know. I know I was scared I would lose Kate if she found out. "I thought you would be grossed out and hate me. I kept on thinking about the way we freaked when we heard about the girls on the team and about the pinky swear we made."

After I say that, Kate rolls her eyes and runs faster on our second lap. "Abbey, I'm not just some bitch in the hall."

I steady my breath and tell her the rest of it. "I know. It's just I couldn't stand to lose you because, well, because I love you."

Kate slows down to a fast walk to let a bunch of girls run by. She waits for them to pass before saying, "Abbey, what are you saying? I'm not like them, or you."

I have no idea what she's talking about, but then I get it and I nearly laugh. "Oh my God, Kate. I don't mean like *that*. You have Derrick and that's cool, I just mean I love you as my best friend. And I just couldn't stand the thought of you hating me for being like, well, you know...like that. I guess I'd rather have you hate me for lying. Then at least I would know it was because of something I did, not because of who I am. Or who I think I am." I really can't tell anymore if I'm making any sense. "You know what I mean?"

Kate looks at me very seriously and I try not to look away. But then Mrs. Schwartz blows her whistle at us. "You two better kick up some dirt or there will be two detentions waiting for you at the end of class!"

We start running again, which means I have only one more lap left to win back my best friend.

"Abbey, it just sucks that I'm the last one to find out. I thought you trusted me."

"But I do and you aren't. I didn't actually tell Jenn—she just figured it out, I guess. Actually, I haven't told anyone anything, not even Garrett. I swear, Kate. I'm telling you the whole truth." I don't think Ms. Morvay counts, so I still think it's the truth.

She's breathing hard, but her face seems to soften.

Then I say, "I'm sorry I lied."

Kate turns around and runs backward in front of me. "Okay, I'll forgive you if you promise me one thing."

What if she asks me to stop seeing Keeta? Could I go back to lying that quickly? "Okay. What?"

"I don't want you to lie to me ever again. I don't care what it is, just tell me the truth."

A huge smile spreads across my face. "Okay," I pant, "I promise."

Then she sticks out her hand. "Pinkies?"

"I thought we were done with those."

"One more, for old time's sake."

I reach out and grab her hand and try to link my pinky with hers, but my gigantic foot steps on one of her giant feet. She stumbles, pulls me forward, and down we go like...well, like a couple of idiots trying to pinky swear while running. She lands on her butt, then pulls off a backward somersault, and somehow ends up on her feet again. I fall next to her, but with a much less glamorous performance. My ankle survives without injury, but I fall hard on my nearly healed knee.

Even though I'm in excruciating pain, I'm so happy we're friends again that I start to laugh. When Kate tries to help me up, she doubles over, too.

Mrs. Schwartz, however, is not feeling the love. She blows her whistle again and promises the detentions as soon as we finally make it across the finish line. We both explode again and roll around in the dirt like we're back in third grade, like we don't care what anyone else in the world thinks. And it feels like the coolest thing ever.

❖

My knee requires some cleaning before I go to Spanish, so we sign our detentions, change out of our PE clothes (Kate still changes in the bathroom stall), and head over to the nurse's office as friends again.

We walk in silence at first, but then Kate asks, "So, are you guys, like, girlfriends?"

The idea that I might have a *girlfriend* makes me freak out inside. Plus, I don't actually know if I have a girlfriend and that seems stupid, so I stall. "Uh, why do you ask?"

"Abbey, no more secrets remember?"

"I know, I know," I say and have no choice but to tell her the truth. "See, the thing is, I don't know if we're dating, or girlfriends, or what you would call us."

"Really?"

"Yeah. And you want the whole truth?"

She gives me a look of exasperation, so I take that as a yes.

"Um"—I can't look at her when I say it—"she's still sort of dating Stef, I think."

"Well, when is Keeta planning on breaking it off with Stef?"

"I don't really know."

"Don't you think you should find out?"

She makes it sound so easy. "I tried this morning. Kind of."

"So, how long have you and Keeta been, you know, more than friends?"

"We just kissed for the first time yesterday. So, like, not long." It's so weird talking to Kate about my private kiss with Keeta, and I wonder whether honesty really is the best policy.

Then, just outside the nurse's door, Kate asks me one more question. "Do you even know anything about her?"

It's a simple question. Easily answered with a yes or a no or with details about what I know about Reyna Moreno, who goes by Keeta for some reason. When she asks it, though, I feel a rush of fear shoot through my middle. I know pretty much nothing about Keeta except for her first and last name, that she plays basketball and guitar, and that she's perfectly willing to cheat on her girlfriend with a dork of a freshman like me. That isn't much to go on, so I shrug my shoulders. "No. Not really."

Kate rolls her eyes and says, "Well, I have to go. See you later," and leaves me standing here feeling like I have a giant L on my forehead—L for loser, not for lesbian.

❖

After Spanish class, Stef, Garrett, and I walk over to my locker to make plans for my Saturday Night Birthday Extravaganza.

"Hey, I know, let's go bowling," Stef says. "They have those cool lights where everything glows, and I think it costs like three dollars per bowler or something."

My guilt about what I did to Stef is seriously killing me on the inside, but I hide it by saying, "Yeah, that sounds superfun!"

Garrett scrunches up her nose. "Nah, it has to be special. Something mature. Our little baby is growing up."

"Oh please," I say, "spare me. I've already got my mom in tears every time she looks at me. It's not like I'm dying. I'm just turning fifteen."

After my third attempt, I get my locker open, and as I search for my social studies book, a note falls out of my locker, landing face up onto the gritty linoleum floor. Written across the front in beautiful lettering is my secret name: Amara.

I see it. And Garrett sees it. But Stef, who is yelling down the hall at one of our teammates, doesn't see it. My muscles go into atrophy and I'm unable to do anything to save myself.

Thankfully, Garrett was born with the common sense I lack and she quickly covers up the note with her foot. I know Stef told her about the letter she found in Keeta's bag, so even if Garrett doesn't know about my special name, Garrett probably recognized Keeta's handwriting and is smart enough to put it all together. We both glance quickly at Stef, who is now digging in her backpack for something.

Garrett takes hold of Stef's arm. "Well, we will figure out the appropriate affair for the Duchess's celebration," Garrett says in a perfect British accent. "In the meantime, we will see you after school at practice. Come along, Ms. Woodside. We must be off." She turns on her foot but doesn't lift it.

"Ta ta, Abbey darling," Stef says over her shoulder.

As they walk away, Garrett kicks my letter behind her, looks over her shoulder, and smiles coolly at me.

I think I manage to smile back, but inside I'm totally confused. She has covered for me without giving it a second thought, keeping my secret closer than I did. What kind of friend is she to Stef anyway?

As soon as the coast is clear, I pick up the letter and dust off Garrett's shoeprint. I wait ten more seconds to be sure they're out of range then unfold it in my locker and read Keeta's words:

Amara,

Hey girl, why'd you leave guitar so quickly? I wanted a kiss good-bye! Anyway, I hope you feel our kisses as deeply as I do. You know, at first I was freaked out about how I felt for you because you're like soooo much younger than me. I mean, a senior with a freshman? But I think you're more mature than most girls I know. I just hope I don't make you too nervous. Maybe I'm not your first, but if I am, we can take things slow, okay? You just let me know what you need. No te quiero apresurar. *Though I did like your kisses this morning, so I wouldn't mind getting more of those really soon.*

I'm smiling right now just thinking about you. When I close my eyes, I picture your lips, your fiendishly flirtatious sparkling blue eyes, and your long, silky blond hair. Not to mention your legs. Chale, *I've never felt so short in my life, but I'll get over it. Haha.*

So, this might sound really weird, but when I'm with you, the whole world seems to disappear, Amara. It's like tú eres mi mundo. *I even had a dream about you last night. I am not going to give you all the details because it's way too embarrassing, but you were there and I was there and the moon was very full.* Órale, *it was an interesting one. Hmm, if you come to guitar class early again tomorrow, maybe I'll tell you about it. Geez, maybe I'll have a new dream to talk about.* Quién sabe. *All I know is you're different, Abbey...in all the good ways.*

Okay, I've said way too much already. Ya me voy a historia. *I can't wait to see you tomorrow in guitar. Which reminds me, you better stop practicing so much or I won't have a reason to stop by and "help" you. (wink, wink)*

Te estaré mirando,
Keeta

CHAPTER SIXTEEN

Come on, Abbey. It's time to get up," my mom says, standing over my bed.

My "Here Comes the Sun" alarm is also going off and the combo attack of the two of them is driving me crazy. "I'm up!" I shout but roll over and cover my head with my pillow.

"I'll make you some good-luck pancakes, but only if you get up right now."

"Mom, please just let me sleep." I'm groggy and cranky because last night I tossed and turned like a sock dancing in the dryer while worrying about today's game against Saguaro High. Though my ankle is better, Coach didn't let me play in or even dress out for our first game. Then yesterday at practice he told me I'd be starting as center today. About 1.4 percent of me was excited when I heard that bit of news, but the other 98.6 percent wanted to run away and hide in the caves.

And my mom is only making things worse. When she's nice to me like this, I feel like a rotten daughter. Like, it's just another reminder that I can never break it to her that her only child is falling in love with a girl at school. This fear is totally unrelated to the real issue at hand, that I'm too nervous to play in the game, but every worry is torturing me this morning.

"You don't want to miss your chance to show off your hard work, honey," she yells from the kitchen. "And, just so you know, I'm not falling for your usual sore-throat act."

I whine, but know she's right. What's the point of practicing if I hide in my room whenever we have a game? "Okay, okay. Start the dang pancakes."

❖

After a well-balanced meal and a hug from my mom, I leave the house feeling somewhat confident. Maybe it's the push-up bra I borrowed from Kate, maybe it's the eyeliner and mascara, but when I walk into guitar and Keeta notices my new mature look, I feel even better. Keeta's kisses in first period definitely sweeten my day, too. But by fifth period, I'm back to feeling nauseated and am starting to regret the extra jalapenos I piled on top of my nachos at lunch. I'm just about to ask Mr. Zamora if I can be excused, when Tai waltzes through the door exuding her usual generous amount of coolness.

After she hands Mr. Zamora the pass, she looks right at me, smiles big, and then leaves, shaking her head like she knows something I've done and should be ashamed of doing.

Mr. Zamora holds up the square of paper but continues writing on the overhead. "You'll need to take your things, Abbey. Class is nearly over."

I don't look at the pass until I step outside the room. It's addressed to Mr. Zamora from Mrs. Guzman, the librarian. I haven't checked out any books, so I'm a little confused about why the librarian wants to see me.

"Don't worry," Tai says, leaning against the wall, out of view of Mr. Zamora's classroom. "You're not in trouble. She just *had* to see you."

"The librarian?" I ask.

My innocent question makes Tai laugh. "Garrett says you're a pretty smart girl, but I'm beginning to wonder."

I stare blankly at her.

"Girl, it's K. She's in the library waiting for you."

I try, but I can't hold back my smile. Then my stomach sinks again. Tai *does* know something I should be ashamed of. I wonder if it was Garrett or Keeta who told her. More importantly, I wonder how much longer I have before someone spills it to Stef.

"I gotta tell you, Abbey, K's my best friend, but you should be careful. She's the kind of girl who always gets what she wants."

At first I'm embarrassed by Tai's warning, but then I say, "Is it really so bad to always get what you want?" and I think I shock us both with that.

"Well, damn, I guess not." She hands me a new pass. "Give this one to Mrs. Guzman. Oh, and Keeta's waiting for you in the poetry section."

"Poetry?" I smile wider. "Thanks, Tai."

"Sure. And, hey…"

"Yeah?"

"Try to stay out of trouble, freshie." She pulls another pass out of her pocket. "Speaking of trouble, time to get my girl out of chemistry. She really shouldn't be around combustibles. *Basta*."

❖

Just like I was told to do, I give Mrs. Guzman my new pass which is addressed to her from Mr. Zamora. I wonder how Tai memorized all their signatures but then realize that maybe teachers don't really pay as much attention to these things as we all think.

I have no idea where the poetry section is, but I don't dare ask and risk blowing our cover. So I just wander around looking very intent and focused. Finally, Keeta grabs my arm and pulls me behind a tall shelf of books.

"I can't believe you, Keeta. We could get so busted," I whisper and look over my shoulder.

"Shh…we won't get caught. Mrs. G never leaves her station. I promise we're safe."

"Why here? Why not the locker room or instrument closet? I mean, I'm so happy to see you, but it's not very private." I want to kiss her so badly.

"I know," she whispers, "but I wanted you to see my favorite hangout." She takes a book off the shelf and sits down.

She pats the carpet and I sit on the floor next to her. At least the poetry section is sort of secluded from the rest of the library.

"Now close your eyes and listen."

I do as I'm told and she reads a poem to me.

There's a word for what you've done to me; the only one that says
*   it all.*
This word captures the surprise in my eyes when I first saw you.
It tells the story of my heart and what it wants to do.

It explains why I dream of you day and night.
It describes how your smile lights up my life.
Yes, there is a word for what you've done to me; the only one that
says it all.

When she finishes reading, I don't know what to say. The only poems anyone has ever read to me were by Shel Silverstein, and those are the opposite of romantic.

"That poem kind of says how I feel about you, Amara."

I look at her and lose myself in her eyes. "Yeah?"

Her smile reassures me.

"Who wrote it?" I ask when I finally recover.

"Well, did you like it?" she takes a piece of paper from the book and hands it to me. For a moment, she looks sort of shy, which is definitely the first time I've ever seen her look anything but certain.

"I liked it very much. It was sweet," I say then unfold the paper. "What's this?"

Her confidence returns. "It's the poem. I wrote it…" She hesitates. "For you." And then she kisses my cheek.

I can recognize her handwriting and see her name on the bottom but ask, "*You* wrote this?" I guess my astonishment isn't exactly a compliment.

"Yeah, Amara, I write poetry. There's a lot more to me than basketball and my nice ass."

The mention of her butt makes me blush, but I change the subject back to a more serious topic. "That's just it, Keeta. I feel like I don't know anything about you. The only thing I know for sure is I want to be around you every waking minute of the day." Maybe I shouldn't have said that, but it's how I feel and I'm just trying to be honest for once.

She slides her hand into mine. "Yeah. Okay. I get you."

"I mean, I feel so…I mean, I don't even know where your locker is or what you have third period." I don't use this opportunity to mention that I do know where she lives, her blood type, and her home phone number.

"Well, I suppose I should at least give you my digits and my locker location since I now have yours, thanks to Garrett and Tai."

Hearing their names makes my hands sweat. "Do they know?" I whisper.

"I also found out some other interesting things about you," she says instead of answering my question.

I know I'm being ignored, but Keeta must have a good reason, so I let it go. "Great, what else did those losers tell you?"

"Well, loads of stuff. But most importantly, it's your birthday tomorrow."

"Yep, it is." I hadn't thought about how having a sort-of girlfriend might improve my birthday spirit. I mean, it could be fun to celebrate with Keeta, instead of with my mom, Kate, and a couple of other friends like usual.

"So can I take you out Saturday night?"

I feel like screaming, *Yes, yes, a thousand times yes,* which is an entirely different reaction than I had with Jake, but then I remember my weekend plans. "*Chale.* I can't. Garrett and…well, we're already going out that night."

She nods her head but doesn't say anything for a second, so I see another chance to get something off my chest. "Hey, Keeta?" I ask, this time louder. "What about Stef? I mean, she's my friend. This is not something I'd normally do to a friend."

"I can tell," Keeta says and pats my leg.

"It's just that, when are you going to break up with her? What if she finds out about us? I mean, I don't know if you've noticed, but it seems virtually impossible to keep secrets around here." I swallow loudly and continue. "I just don't know if I can do this."

She pushes my hair behind my ear and runs her fingers through it, which is totally unfair because now I can't concentrate. "Amara, I will take care of it. I promise. *No te preocupes.*"

"But won't G and Tai tell Stef?"

Another soft kiss lands on my cheek. "How about Sunday morning? I can make you breakfast at my house."

I'm incapacitated by her kiss, so I look at her and nod. No one else seems to think what we are doing is a big deal, so maybe it's time I stop caring, too.

"Good, because I make a mean omelet. And, Amara?"

I blink twice.

"I promise that by the end of our time together on Sunday, you will know all you want to know about me. *No guardaré ningún secreto.* No secrets."

"Okay." I still have a ton of ugly worries sprouting in my head like annoying weeds, but right then I just want to hear her read more poetry to me. It's by far the most romantic thing that has ever happened to me in a library, or anywhere else for that matter.

I rest my head on her shoulder. *"Léeme más poesía, por favor."*

"Whatever you want, my Amara."

She flips through the book she had taken off the shelf earlier. It's called *Contemporary Poetry for Lovers*. I'm surprised the book is in Gila's library, but maybe Mrs. Guzman is a hopeless romantic just like the rest of us.

CHAPTER SEVENTEEN

Oh my God. This is a disaster." I'm standing in front of the varsity locker room mirror, seeing myself in my uniform for the first time. "Why do these shorts have to be so short? And why do they have to ride up between my cheeks like butt floss?" It's an hour before my first basketball game. I'm about to puke from nervousness and my uniform isn't helping matters at all. "I look so bad."

"You'll get used to it," Garrett says, trying to reassure me.

Stef shoves her clothes in her locker. "Yeah, after a while, you might even start to enjoy it," she says and laughs.

"Gross," Garrett says.

"I don't see how that's possible." I pull at my shorts again and then try to stretch out the tight polyester tank that's smooshing down any bit of boobage I have. Garrett and Stef don't look at all hideous in their uniforms, but they have much nicer bodies, with curves in all the right places. I just look like a skinny boy in mine.

Stef gathers her curly blond hair in two small ponytails on either side of her head. Now she looks like a sixteen year old toddler, but that's still a better look than what I'm rocking. "See you guys out there."

"Do you know whose number you have?" Garrett says after we hear the door to the gym slam behind Stef.

I look down at the blue twenty-one on my chest. It has no special meaning to me; it was just the only one in the pile that sort of fit. "I don't know. Kobe Bryant?" I ask because that's the only basketball player I can remember.

"Come on. Like you don't know," she says and goes back to braiding her hair. Garrett's the only person I know who can french braid her own hair.

"What are you talking about?"

"You mean you really don't know?"

I throw my hands up in the air. "I know nothing, G. Isn't that obvious by now?"

She laughs. "Yeah, I guess you don't. Anyway, it's Keeta's. She's had that number all four years she's played. Of course, she has her varsity uniform now, but it has the same number, twenty-one. So, technically, you're wearing the old stinky jersey she wore when she was on JV. Some coincidence, huh?" She winks like she still thinks I did it on purpose.

I look at myself in the full-length mirror again and feel a bit more confident. "That is a cool coincidence." I like that I'm in Keeta's old uniform. It makes me feel closer to her. I try to picture Keeta as an immature freshman who didn't know what she was doing, but that's a joke. She's probably always had it all figured out.

After I pull my hair back in a ponytail that ends up lower on my head than usual, Garrett and I stuff our school clothes into our lockers and head out to the gym. "Yeah, well,"—I look over my shoulder to be sure we're alone—"we may have the same number, but I bet she never shoots at the wrong basket like I'm sure I will tonight."

"You're right, Abbey. Players as good as Keeta never make mistakes." Garrett pushes open the gym doors and a smattering of cheers falls on us. But before we meet up with Stef in the bleachers, she turns and says, "Especially when she thinks she can shoot at any basket she wants."

As soon as the freshman game is over, I congratulate Kate on her good game and then join the JV team as we begin jogging around the gym to get warmed up. While I run, I look up into the stands and easily spot my mom out of the dozen or so fans because she's the only one in overalls and the only one waving a giant foam gila monster above her head trying to get my attention. I don't want to ignore her, but I also really don't want people to know we're related, so I smile and give her a discreet wave. I look for Keeta next. I see her talking with Tai and Jenn by the door. That's right about when Garrett comes up behind me and smacks my butt.

"Keep your head in the game, pervert."

Then, sooner than I would like it to, the buzzer goes off, signaling game time. We run over to Coach Riley and huddle up.

Riley points at me. "Abbey, you know what to do, so do it. No time for nerves, got it?"

I nod and wipe my sweaty hands on my shorts for the tenth time in the past minute.

"Stef, you have to take those threes, and Tori, look weak side. Let's win this, ladies."

"Hands in, you guys," Garrett yells. "Offense on three."

The team yells out the cheer and the four other starters and I take off our warm-up jerseys and head for center court. As my team's center, I have to do the jump ball at the beginning of the game. I wipe my hands again on my tiny shorts and take in a deep breath. It's showtime.

The ref walks over with the game ball. I position myself in front of the Saguaro High School player standing opposite me. She is a supertall black girl with a bright orange mouth guard. She doesn't respond at all when I wish her good luck, but I try not to take it personally.

The ref tosses the ball up and Saguaro's number ten and I leap into the air with our hands reaching toward the ceiling; my body slams into hers like a magnet to metal. I look up and see that my hand towers over hers, so I slap the ball behind me, right into Garrett's hands just like I had done in practice. It's a perfect beginning. In fact, I'm so impressed with my successful jump, I sort of lose track of everything else.

"Brooks! What are you doing?" Coach Riley yells to help me snap out of it.

I look downcourt and see my team setting up our offense without me. I run as fast as I can, but by the time I arrive, a feisty Saguaro High player has stolen the ball from Garrett and is making a fast break to the other end.

"Go, Crutch!" Stef yells.

I obey, quickly change directions, and bolt after the girl with the ball. As she runs downcourt, two more Saguaro players join her, and they start passing the ball quickly back and forth. I reach up as number fourteen lobs it over to number thirty, and as easy as teachers snatch cell phones from students, I intercept the pass. The echoing cheers from the bleachers fill me with energy and I want to do more to please them. I look down at our basket and there's Garrett, and she's very open.

I know it's a little risky, but I seem to like living on the edge these days, so I hurl the ball the full length of the court and pray that Garrett catches it. No one is more surprised than me when it lands perfectly in her beckoning palm. She makes the layup and we're up by two.

"Nice pass, freshie," Garrett says, slapping my butt as she runs by.

"Thanks," I say and run to my place for defense.

After we gain an eight-point lead, Saguaro comes back from a time-out and plays woman-to-woman defense on us. I'm matched up with number thirteen. She's huge, but not chubby in the Miss Piggy sort of way; she is more like scary-strong in the Hulk sort of way. Stef nicknamed her The Fridge last year, and I'm pretty sure she's going to cause bodily injury to me.

But I soon figure out that what I lack in strength, The Fridge lacks in speed. So once I get over my fear, I dribble around her and take a jump shot once and then do it again on our next possession to add four more points to our score. Then, as she attempts a fadeaway shot from the top of the key, I jump up and *bam!* Rejection! And now I've decided that defense is much more fun than offense ever dreamed of being. I want to scream *In your face, Fridge!* but I refrain because that wouldn't be very ladylike of me.

I've played the entire first half, but my body feels no pain. It's like I'm so pumped up on adrenaline I could get shot in the leg and be like, *Hmm, that kind of stings. Oh well. Let's play basketball.* The only thing that's bumming me out is I waited this long to play it. I wonder how much better I'd be if I had just started a couple years earlier.

Unfortunately the halftime break gives The Fridge some time to think about how much she hates me because when the third quarter begins, I quickly find out that The Fridge has a very evil side to her. As soon as I get the ball, she thrusts her bulky torso into me like she's trying to dry hump me on the court. Then, when I defend her, she purposefully crushes my toes with her giant heel and throws a sharp elbow into my chest. After that doesn't shake me off, she jerks her head back, seemingly to try and break my nose. Forget about all that no-pain crap. Now I'm feeling like a featherweight boxer in a heavyweight match.

As we make our way downcourt after a foul is called on one of the Saguaro players during Stef and Eva's fast break, I confide in Garrett about my pain. "G, I think my pinky toe is seriously broken."

Garrett's breathing hard and semi-listening. "I doubt it, Crutch. Suck it up."

"Why aren't they seeing her fouls? She's trying to kill me." I lift my shirt and try to inspect my sweaty back while we line up for Stef to take her shots. "Oh my God, I think there's already a bruise. Look."

"Yeah, she got you pretty good."

"Should I tell the ref?"

We line up for the free throw, and then Garrett leans over and whispers, "Or you could just say, *Oh, baby, you know how I like it,* next time she tries to dry hump you. That always works for me. Gay or straight, it makes them squirm."

"G, I can't do that."

"Well, you asked for my advice. Take it or leave it, but you know I'm always right."

Stef makes both shots and we head back for defense. Then Stef, who's been listening to my complaints, chimes in with what I think might be a voice of reason. "I'll tell you what you're going to do, Abbey. Push her back. Hard."

"Like on purpose?" I pant.

"Yes, like you mean it, *chica.*"

Up to this point in my life, I've never pushed anyone. Growing up as an only child, I haven't even had sibling wrestling matches or slapfests like Kate and Jenn still have. I'm a peaceful kid who once made tiny signs out of toothpicks and address labels alerting sidewalk users that a trail of ants was five feet ahead. And now I'm supposed to push someone? On purpose?

Five minutes into the third quarter, after The Fridge takes another jab at my left boob, I say screw peace and take Stef's advice. Like keeping my kisses with Keeta secret, my next moves seem to be another important lesson in survival. And, like kissing Keeta, I've got to figure out how to get physical with The Fridge without getting caught.

I see my chance when the Saguaro point guard misses a three-pointer and The Fridge pulls down the rebound. I decide to use one of The Fridge's moves against her but add a little Abbey flavor to it. Instead of my elbows, I use my bony butt and shoulders to hopefully leave my mark on her. And instead of stomping on her, I tangle my feet around hers, which causes her to stumble and travel with the ball.

Playing like this is mean, underhanded, and totally unfair. But I'm finding it rather enjoyable.

Now there are four minutes left in the fourth quarter, and I'm at the bottom of the key getting pounded again while trying to fight for position and get open. Finally, Stef bounce-passes the ball to me. I turn to shoot a quick jumpshot, but The Fridge has finally lost patience with our secret battle and blatantly rams me like a bull. I fall to the ground and a whistle blows.

"Red thirteen, pushing! Two shots!"

Garrett and Stef help me to my feet and pat my butt.

"That's what we're talking about," Garrett whispers as she walks me to the free-throw line. "Now you're under her skin. Keep it up, girl."

Even though The Fridge has been pummeling me nonstop, it's my first free throw of the game. As I stand at the top of the key, I feel like I'm at the head of the table at a very important dinner and everyone is expecting me to present a marvelous toast.

The score is 49-46 with one minute left in the game. I know I have to make my shots to put a lid on our win.

"Two shots, ladies. And let's keep it clean out there." The ref points at The Fridge who then scowls at me. Too scared to keep eye contact with her, I look down at the ball in my hands and hope for the best.

My first shot is a total brick.

After I miss it, Garrett comes up behind me and slaps my butt, which has been spanked more in this one basketball game than it has in my previous fifteen years of life. "Come on, Abbey. You make these all the time in practice. You can do this."

"Yeah, I know. Okay," I say and ready myself for my next shot.

This time I *really* concentrate, bend my knees, extend my arm, and release the ball just like I've been taught. It barely touches the rim and easily lands in my enemy's hands. Before any of us can move, the ball is thrown downcourt. Seconds later, Saguaro scores an easy layup while I stand cemented to the floor at the other end.

After that, Coach screams at Garrett to take a time-out.

We run off the court and huddle around Riley. "Abbey, take a seat. Natalie, go check in."

Our team manager, Matti, hands me a towel and a cup of water, and I sit down at the end of the bench. I throw the towel over my head and stare at my shoes, breathing hard to keep myself from crying. Matti tries to console me with a pat on the back, but I shrug her off. I feel so stupid for missing the two easiest shots I had all game. I want to quit and make plans to do so as soon as the game is over. I feel like I let the whole team down. Who do I think I am? I'm a brain, not a jock. I don't belong here.

The teams do their group cheers and run back onto the court.

"Brooks! Get down here," Coach Riley yells.

I prepare myself for the worst and sit in the empty seat next to him.

"Yes, Coach?"

"You better pick up your chin, girl," he yells in a scary whisper voice. "And I better hear you cheering on your teammates. This isn't about you and your missed free throws. This is about working as a team. You hear me?" As he speaks, his neck vein bulges out more than ever. "Do you hear me, Brooks?"

"Yes, sir."

When the buzzer goes off and the clock starts, I stand up with the rest of my team and cheer my heart out.

Neither team scores in the last minute, which means we win our game and no one can blame me for losing it, which also means I can put my plans to quit on hold for now.

After our polite *good job*s to the other team (The Fridge and I slap our hands especially hard), we have thirty seconds to gather our things and meet coach in the locker room for a loud debriefing and lecture. Yes, even though we won, he's sure to remind us of what we did wrong and lay out the punishment we will face tomorrow at practice.

❖

When I come out of the locker room, the varsity team is warming up. Garrett and Stef are taking their time getting cleaned up, so I'm alone as I stand in the doorway in the corner of the gym. I want to send Keeta a good-luck wink before her game, but I don't want to do it in front of my mom or Stef, so I try to will Keeta over with my hypnotic powers. That doesn't ever work, but lucky for me, a loose ball rolls my way. I stop it with my foot and smile as Keeta jogs over to retrieve it. I'm attempting to look casual and calm, but you know how that goes.

"Hey, girl. Good game."

I roll my eyes. "Yeah, right. You must have missed the best part when I totally choked."

"Nah, I saw everything. Nice fall, too." She winks at me and bounces the ball in between her legs. "You okay?"

Her wink sends me spinning, so all I can do is nod.

"Well, see you after the game." She runs off to join her team in a layup drill.

I forget to wish her good luck, but I think she knows I'll be thinking of her. Not that I've ever stopped thinking about her since that day in the Tucson Mall.

As I'm watching Keeta warm up on the court, I get this weird feeling. It's the kind of feeling Garrett described, like my whole world revolves around getting Keeta's attention and being near her. Plus, Keeta looks so sexy in her uniform, which is admittedly easier to do since the varsity uniforms are so much nicer than the JV and freshman hand-me-downs. Theirs shine under the lights and shift smoothly on their bodies as they run. Then I notice it. Keeta's wearing number twenty-one, just like me. I smile bigger and watch Keeta shoot her practice free throws.

Then Garrett comes up behind me and slaps me hard in the back of my head, giving my butt a break. "What the hell, Garrett?"

"Could you be more obvious?" She looks into the stands. "Speaking of being obvious, isn't your mom here?"

"Oh my God. Thanks for reminding me."

I make my way up the bleachers and am greeted with a hug from my mom. "You were so amazing, Abbey," she says and is still flinging around her foam lizard, so I take it from her and sit on it.

She gets this look in her eye like she's trying not to mention what we're both thinking about. That I wish Dad could have seen me play my first game of basketball. But, instead, she clears her throat and says, "I had no idea things would be so rough out there, though. Are you okay?"

"Yeah, I'm fine." I'm actually in a lot of pain but don't feel like crying to my mom about it. Besides, it'll be cool to have some battle wounds to show off at practice tomorrow.

"Well, Abbey Road, I'm not. My butt is totally numb." She stands up and gathers her nacho leftovers and giant purse. "Are you ready to go?"

"Yeah, I guess," I say, glad that no one's around to hear my mom call me Abbey Road. It's still too personal.

But then Garrett makes her way over to us and extends her hand to introduce herself. "Hi, Mrs. Brooks. I'm Garrett. I'm on the team with Abbey, and I'm in her Spanish class."

I can tell my mother appreciates Garrett's politeness since she hasn't been getting much from me. "It's so nice to meet you, Garrett. Call me Susan. You girls were really great tonight."

"I guess you guys aren't staying for the varsity game," Garrett says, pointing to my mom's full arms.

"No, we've got to go," my mom says.

But since my mom's in such a good mood, I decide to take advantage of it like any normal teenager would. "Um, actually Mom, I was kind of wondering if I could stay. It's supposed to be a good game."

"Oh, Abbey, I don't think I can take another hour of these wooden bleachers."

"I can get a ride home from Garrett and her friend Taisha if you don't want to stay. Taisha's a very good driver. Right, Garrett?" If I know Garrett like I think I do, she'll play along.

"Oh, totally," Garrett says, quickly catching on. "It would be no problem. We will have her home right after the game."

"I don't know," Mom says. "Just because it's your birthday tomorrow doesn't mean you can skip out on your homework tonight."

"Please, Mom," I beg. "I'll start my homework right now. We'll work on our Spanish together during the game."

"How can you do homework and watch the game?"

"Believe me, Mom, we can do it."

Garrett confirms that we are supreme multitaskers, which helps persuade my mom. "Well, okay. But don't be late."

"Thanks, Mom." I shove the foam gila monster in her purse. "See you later."

A couple of minutes later, Stef joins me and Garrett on the bleachers.

"You guys are staying?" Stef asks. "God, you're lucky. My stupid mom is picking me up right now."

"Sorry, *chica*," Garrett says, "but it's just as well. I mean, considering your last fight with Keeta."

The words "fight with Keeta" make my ears perk up.

"I know, I know. I should just break up with her already. Whatever, though. I'm moving soon and I'm sure she'll find a replacement, if she hasn't already found one. She never could stand to be alone."

Garrett and I both nod and look out on the court. I wish I knew why Garrett is keeping my secret. It makes me nervous, but I'm not going to argue with her about it. Sure, I'm in love, but I'm not entirely stupid.

As I watch Stef slowly make her way to her disappointed mom standing in the gym entryway, I hope to never have to know what that feels like. In fact, the thought of my mom finding out scares me more than playing against The Fridge again.

"My back is killing me," I say after we stand for the "Star Spangled Banner."

"Yeah, you got worked, Crutch." Garrett digs in her gym bag and pulls out a tube of Ultra Strength Bengay, but her tube has the n scratched off so it says *Be gay* instead. She tosses it over to me. "Here, you'll definitely need this tonight."

"Thanks, G." I apply some to my lower back and slip the tube in my backpack for later.

Then Garrett and I get out our Spanish worksheets and put them next to us on the bleachers. And that's where they stay for about two minutes until Tai makes a three-pointer and Garrett and I jump up from our seats to cheer. My worksheet floats down between the bleacher slots to the gym floor, and Garrett's lands in a puddle of spilled soda. We quickly forget about them and instead watch our girls work up a sweat on the court.

"Hey, Abbey," Garrett says during a time-out, "see number thirty-two?" She motions with her head at Saguaro's varsity center player.

"Yeah, what about her?"

"She was Keeta's first," Garrett says with a laugh. "Weird, huh?"

It feels like Garrett has just punched me in the stomach. I guess I never really thought of anyone except Stef as a girlfriend of Keeta's. I guess I thought I was more special than that.

"And number twenty-four?" Garrett points at another tall blonde sitting on Saguaro's bench.

"Yeah?"

"Keeta's second."

Both the girls Garrett points out are tall and blond like me, but both are much, much prettier. They have boobs, great calves, and their ponytails are high on their heads, dispelling my previous theory that only girls who have low ponytails are lezzies. If only it were that easy to tell them apart from the straight girls.

"So, exactly how many of Keeta exes are out there on the court?" I ask meekly.

But Garrett ignores my question. "See number two?" She points at the girl bringing the ball downcourt.

I sink further in my seat. "Don't tell me. Keeta's third."

"Nope, mine." Garrett giggles into her hands. "Nice, huh? And your good friend, The Fridge, was Tai's third, no first, wait…I dunno, I lost track."

"Seriously? God, does every gay girl in Tucson play high school basketball or something? Is it like a lesbian law?"

She shrugs. "It's not just basketball, Abs. We've always been everywhere. There are a whole lot more of us than you realize. You just never noticed before. You will now, though. Guarantee it." She continues to watch the game like everything is normal, which it's not.

"G?"

"Yeah, Abbey?"

I want to tell her I feel like I'm on the wrong road and everyone around me seems to know exactly what direction to drive, but I'm totally lost. I'm too embarrassed to admit it, though. "Never mind."

"Oh, come on, Abbey, don't get all sad. I'm not telling you about these girls to make you feel bad or inadequate or whatever it is you're sulking about, but you should know something about Keeta."

"Yeah, what's that?" I say, hoping my irritation doesn't show, but at the same time wondering why everyone feels they have the right to get in my business. Maybe I'm lost, but I know exactly where I want to go: Keetaland, USA.

"Look, the only reason I'm keeping your damn secret is because I know what it feels like to have everything in your life turn upside down because some girl makes you feel like you're the queen of the universe. So don't start getting bitchy with me."

"Sorry." I grab the end of my ponytail to twirl. "But what about Stef? You guys are like best friends."

She scrunches up her nose as if what I just said was doubtful. "Yeah, but we have a history." Before I have a chance to ask her more about it, she continues. "It's a long story and I don't want to get into it. Anyway, all I'm saying is have your fun, just make sure you don't get too carried away. Keeta's weird about love. Like, every time she gets close to someone, she screws it up on purpose. It's some sort of abandonment issue she has because of her mom or something like that. I'd avoid asking her about her mom, though. From the little bit I know, it's like Stef and her mom, only a thousand times worse. Anyway, just thought you should know that Keeta isn't exactly a one-chick girl. I mean, I'd hate to see your little freshie heart get blown to pieces."

I hear her but can't quite compute what she's saying because I'm distracted by Keeta's glistening skin and tense muscles as she dribbles in for a layup. She makes her shot and then looks over at us and smiles. I turn to goo like nacho cheese sauce.

"Are you listening to me, Abbey?"

"Yeah, I know, Garrett. Don't worry. I won't get too carried away."

Garrett shakes her head. "Sure, Abbey. Whatever."

Tai fouls for the fourth time and Garrett yells at the ref to get a clue. Meanwhile, back in my twisted head, I'm having a realization. "Wait a minute," I say to Garrett. "I thought Tai was the only girl you've been with."

"Nah. We started dating when I was a freshman, but we broke up for a few months, and during that time she started messing around with some slut from Palo Verde, so I had my own fun."

"Really? God, I'm so far behind everyone else."

"It's not about quantity, Abbey. It's all about quality. And you, my dear, have started with a quality girl."

We both watch Keeta at the free-throw line. She sinks both, of course, and her teammates slap her butt as she runs by to set up for defense. I guess that's about when I finally notice the way Keeta seems to attract everyone's attention; even Garrett's green eyes are tracking Keeta's smooth moves on the court.

"So, why did you guys get back together? I guess you really love each other," I say to help remind Garrett that she's dating Tai, not Keeta.

"Well, that's another long story. The short of it is Tai said she couldn't live without me and I liked how that felt, so we got back together."

"Do you love her as much as she loves you?"

She shrugs her shoulders and opens a bag of Skittles. "Who knows, Abbey? I mean, I'm only sixteen. As far as I'm concerned, high school relationships are just a series of going out, making out, breaking up, and making up. I'm just seeing where it takes me and trying not to get too serious about anything. You should think about doing the same."

She pours a few Skittles in my hand. I munch on them and think about what she said. It seems like a dangerous way to live, but it also seems a lot better than being freaked out by every little thing. Maybe she's right. I mean, except for all the lies I've been telling and the things I've been doing with Keeta behind Stef's back, I'm having fun. Why shouldn't I just enjoy it?

Before I embrace my new rebellious attitude, there's one more question I have to ask Garrett. "But G, how did you know?"

She pops some more Skittles in her mouth. "Know what?"

"About me?"

"You mean that you're family?" My familiar look of confusion must be amusing because she laughs and tosses a green Skittle at me. "You're so cute when you don't know what's going on."

I brush the candy off my lap and put my head in my hands. "Thanks."

"Oh, come on. I'm sorry." She scoots over on the bleacher and puts her arm around me. "Okay, *family* is like, you know, you're my sister because we're similar. We share a big dark secret. We're both into girls."

"Oh," I say. "So, what was it? Is there like a secret sign? Was it the way I wore my ponytail?" I ask, still hoping there may be some validity to my theory.

"Hmm…well, I don't know, you can just tell. It's called gaydar, but just because you're gay doesn't mean you have it. Look at Stef. She never got it. She obviously hasn't picked up on you, but I knew you were one the minute we met in the hall that first day."

"But how?"

"I don't know. I just have really good—"

"Gaydar?" I interject. "Are you making this up, G?"

"Come on, would I lie to you, Abbey?"

I'm pretty sure she isn't lying right now, but I'm not sure she never would. She's lying to Stef, and she's known her a lot longer than me. And, let's face it, I used to be someone I would trust, but now I'm a big liar, too. Yep, Garrett probably would lie to me, but I don't tell her that.

CHAPTER EIGHTEEN

So my dad and I are on a Princess Cruise ship heading toward Canada in search of some rare rock that can only be found in an underground cave on an island off the coast of Vancouver. My mom is at home because she said she had to take care of my twin little brothers, which I don't have, but that's how these dreams always go. After we have dinner on the deck of the ship, my dad says that he's going to go for a swim. Now, I'm thinking he means in the palm-tree-shaped pool, but he's got a different idea. He dives off the boat and disappears into the black water. I freak out and pull an alarm that is conveniently next to our table. The boat stops. I'm screaming, "Help him! He's in the water! Help!" but everyone keeps on saying, "He's gone, Abbey. We need to get going or we'll miss the Northern Lights," which also makes no sense. I see something in the water; I think it's him so I throw a life ring overboard and wait for tension to hit the rope. Nothing. The engines start up and we slowly pick up speed again. I never stop screaming for him. I'm crying and screaming, but no one seems to care.

I finally wake up from this dead-dad nightmare when "Here comes the sun" blares out of my alarm clock. My hand smacks the snooze and I flip over my tear-soaked pillow. That's when I remember it's November 16th. "Happy Birthday to me," I say to myself.

I attempt to make the day extra special by dressing in a new outfit my mom bought for me last week, but so far, fifteen feels like torture. Not old enough to drive, too old to cry from bad dreams, and too tall to fit in most backseats. But before heading out to the kitchen for breakfast, I rub some perfume on my neck from the Victoria's Secret catalog that I got when my mom bought me my first lacy push-up bra, despite her voiced concerns and hesitation.

Since I was five, my big birthday breakfast has always included toast with a heart-shaped blob of raspberry jam in the middle, a book as my first present of the day (the big gift comes at dinnertime), and my choice of sugary cereal. This year I chose Froot Loops because Garrett said since they're rainbow, they're the gay Cheerios.

"Happy Birthday, Abbey Road," my mom sings as I sit down. She places the bowl of Froot Loops in front of me and pours me a glass of orange juice. "How did you sleep?"

"Good. Thanks." I crunch on a big bite of rainbow Os and smile at her so maybe this morning she won't get teared up like she has on every one of my birthdays since Dad's been gone. I pick up the book to try and distract her. "This looks good."

"Well, it's no Dean Koontz, but I think you need to stop with those horror books anyway. Kate Chopin is an amazing writer. It's a love story, which I thought you might like."

I don't get freaked out when she says this because I'm pretty sure she's implying something about my supposed crush on Jake. "Scandalous," I say and laugh. "My mom's buying me smutty novels."

She puts the decorated toast on the table. "Oh stop. It's classic literature, Abbey."

"Something I'll probably have to read in college, huh?" At the mention of college, she starts to tear up. What a stupid thing to say.

"Sorry," she says and goes to the fridge to look for nothing.

"It's okay, Mom," is what I say because it's what I always say when this happens. I munch on another spoonful of Froot Loops and think of a new topic. "So, Golden Buddha tonight? Mmm, I can't wait to devour that garlic chicken. What time are we picking Kate up again?"

Mom recovers, shuts the fridge door, and joins me again at the table. "Seven."

"Okay, I'll tell her during PE." Then Jenn honks outside. "I gotta go, Mom." I grab the toast, kiss her good-bye, and head out to Jenn's car.

As soon as I slam the car door, I receive fifteen quick, but painful, punches to my arm. "Happy birthday, Punkass."

I'd hoped she'd forgotten, but no such luck.

❖

I know from watching other girls on campus walk around with bouquets of flowers, balloons, and giant stuffed animals on their birthdays, that having a boyfriend (or whatever) makes birthdays a bazillion times better. Although, considering we have to act like casual acquaintances in the hall due to the secret nature of our relationship, I wouldn't be able to carry even a single rose around anyway. Still, I'm excited to see if she got me something.

"Keeta?" I call, peeking my head through the music room curtains, but she's not at the chalkboard like usual. She's not in the instrument room either, so I sit on the edge of the stage, look down at the dusty floor, and think the worst: she's rekindled an old flame with one of those ex-girlfriends she saw last night. Or, worse, she and Stef have run away together to get married in California, or wherever gay marriage is legal this month.

"*Dios mío!* That is the saddest birthday face I have ever seen," Keeta says from the hallway. "Who died?"

I hate that expression, but I forgive her immediately. "Hi."

"Sorry, I thought I might be able to get here before you, but Tai picked me up late. *Mensa!* Anyway,"—she unloads her cargo on a desk and walks over to me—"hi, Amara." Then she kisses me, easily making today my best birthday ever. Who needs balloons and flowers? "Okay, close your eyes."

I do as I'm told and stand there smiling foolishly like I'm in line at Ben & Jerry's with a free-scoop certificate because I finally feel like the girl who gets the boy of her dreams in those mushy teen movies, except my boy is a girl.

She's rushing around me, and the breeze from her movements makes goose bumps hit my arms and I shiver. "What are you doing?"

"Just wait. *Sé paciente, Amara.*"

My knees nearly buckle. Everything she says in Spanish sounds romantic. Maybe Garrett's right; I shouldn't get in too deep.

"*Bueno,*" she says, "open your eyes."

On the desk in front of me is a small cake decorated with pink roses and fifteen lit candles. *Feliz cumpleaños, Amara* is written across the top. Next to it is a rectangular jewelry box wrapped in silver paper with a tiny red bow on top.

She puts her arms around me from behind and whispers in my ear. *"Pide un deseo, Amara."*

I lean back into her and close my eyes to think of a good wish. For the first time in a long time, I wish for things to stay just as they are. I take a deep breath and blow out every candle.

"I hope it comes true."

I hug and kiss her. "Me, too."

Next, she puts the small box in my hand. "I hope you like it."

I know some words are supposed to come out of my mouth at this point, but all I can do is stare at the pretty shiny wrapping and smile.

"Come on, you're killing me," Keeta says with an unexpected girly excitement.

Careful not to tear the silver paper, I peel off the tape very slowly. Once the box is free from its wrapping, I open it up. Inside, nestled in red tissue paper, is a dainty silver chain with an A pendant dangling from it.

"It's for Amara, not Abbey. But only we need to know that, huh?" She walks behind me, reaches over my shoulder for the necklace, and moves my hair aside so she can put it on me.

"Thank you, Keeta," I finally say, after it's latched and resting against my chest. I like how it feels against my bare skin. "I totally didn't expect any of this. You really didn't have to."

"Oh, I'm not done with you yet. It's time for the grand finale." She directs me to a chair that's facing the stage. I sit down and tuck my legs underneath to make them seem less obscenely long. "I'm going to play you a little birthday song," she says. "I just wrote it, and it's not perfect, but it's from the heart, okay? So no laughing."

"Okay," I say. "I promise."

She strums a couple of notes and tunes her guitar. Then she clears her throat. "This song's called 'A Girl Named Amara.'"

She starts to sing, and I'm in just as much awe as I was that first night in the guitar store. I can't believe how she makes the music so strong, how she sings each note with such clarity, or how she manages to do it all while staring right at me.

Here comes the chorus again:

And this girl named Amara
She has blue eyes like pools of sky,
And they sparkle and shine
More than any jewel you can buy.

It takes me two times hearing it to realize where I'd heard some of those words before. They were in that letter that Stef wasn't supposed to see, the one Stef shredded in the locker room during one of their fights.

"And what this girl called Amara doesn't know," Keeta continues to sing, "is that I feel the same. Yeah, baby girl, I—"

Ding, ding, ding, goes the bell, and my real-life fantasy comes to an end.

"Pinches campanas," she says, and we hurry to clean up our birthday party.

❖

I manage to make it to my PE locker to hide the little cake before Kate comes over to say hi. Even though she knows about me and Keeta, it's pretty obvious we still feel very uncomfortable talking about it from the way she never asks about Keeta and I never bring her up.

I've already changed into my gym clothes and am putting on my running shoes when Kate sits down on the cold cement bench next to me. "Hey," I say. "What's up?"

She fiddles with the zipper of her Gila High hoodie. "Abbey, I have some bad news about tonight."

I have a sinking feeling that my birthday dinner is about to become a party of two. "What?" I say, shoving my backpack, clothes, and special birthday bra into my locker.

She waits a second and then gives me her lame excuse. "Derrick needs me to go with him to Phoenix tonight. He has to pick up his uncle from the airport."

"And you have to go because…let me see, he doesn't know how to read street signs?" She's not going to get off easy. Not today. "Or is it that he suffers from narcolepsy and he needs you to keep him awake? No, wait—"

"Abbey, don't make this harder than it already is."

"Why shouldn't I, Kate? How long has it been since you came over for a horror movie marathon? Or went out for pizza slices with me?"

"It's not me, it's Derrick," she pleads. "He just doesn't want…"

"Want what?" I yell, just as two Gila cheerleaders walk by. They whisper something to each other and laugh.

Kate turns her back to them and whispers, "Abbey, don't."

But they aren't the first girls to stare at me in a homophobic way. And I know they aren't going to be the last. But, like Garrett did, I'm learning how to care less and less about them.

"Whatever, Kate. Just tell me what you came here to say."

"Well, it's just that..." She pulls at her zipper again. "Derrick, um..."

"Derrick doesn't want you to hang out with me, does he?"

She doesn't even try to make it better. She just keeps saying, "I'm sorry."

"You're sorry, Kate? You're not even going to tell me how stupid that is? It's my freaking birthday."

Then she shuts her mouth, which pretty much says it all.

I slam my locker shut. "I know I lied to you, Kate, but I never turned my back on you like this. And I only lied because I didn't want to lose you as a friend. I don't know what is so special about him, but I hope he's best friend material because you just lost me." I storm off so she won't see me cry, and I leave her sitting there in the dark row of lockers I've become very familiar with.

❖

After PE, I head to my hall locker to find it's decorated with wrapping paper and ribbon just like I've seen on popular girls' lockers, and it's all I need to feel better about what happened with Kate. As I'm spinning in my combo, a confetti egg gets smashed on my head. "Happy birthday, Dear Abbey," Garrett says, as tiny pieces of yellow, blue, and red paper pour down my face.

Before I can recover from the blow to my head, Stef grabs me. "One, two, three, four," Stef counts as she slaps my butt.

"Garrett, help me," I yell and finally get away from Stef around slap number ten.

"So, what do you think?" Stef asks, pointing to the decorations. "We got passes out of first period to do it, thanks to Tai."

"It looks really cool. Thanks, you guys."

"Yeah, well,"—Garrett rubs the confetti into my messed-up hair— "it's not every day our little freshie turns fifteen."

"Hey, this is new." Stef says as she picks the A pendant off my chest and looks closely at it. "Pretty nice. Mom give it to you?"

It's not that I forgot I had on my new necklace, but I did forget I'd have to come up with a good lie about it. Thankfully, Stef did the legwork for me. "Yeah, she gave it to me this morning." Out of the corner of my eye, I think I see Garrett roll her eyes. "So, we're still going to the University Planetarium tomorrow night?" I ask. Although I've been there six or seven times with my dad, I didn't tell them that when they called last night to tell me about our exciting plans.

Stef and Garrett exchange devious looks. "Among other things," Stef says, rubbing her hands together like a mad scientist.

"Don't, you're scaring her," Garrett says and hits Stef in the back of her head.

"I can take it, whatever *it* is," I say, but I am sort of worried that they'll make me get drunk or something, which I am not sure I will ever be ready to do.

"Speaking of parties," Stef says, "did you guys have a party in guitar this morning?"

Oh crap, I think but say, "Sort of. There was a class contest." Apparently, I can now lie without missing a beat.

"Really?" Stef asks. "That's cool."

Garrett looks at me, raises one eyebrow, half smiles, and then adds a slight shake of the head. I recognize this as her *Girl, you are so close to getting caught in your web of lies* look.

But I ignore Garrett and hope Stef will drop the subject when I turn and dig in my locker for my Spanish book.

"Was the prize a cake or something?" Stef asks. No such luck for Abbey.

"Kind of," I say cryptically. "Why?"

"Oh, my mom and I saw Keeta leaving Josephine's Bakery this morning. So I figured it was something like that."

"Yes...exactly. There was a guitar chord quiz contest and the award was some cookies from Josephine's, and"—I'm not sure if the lie can carry me this far, but I say it anyway—"I won."

"So, where's your prize?" Garrett unzips my backpack and starts to dig through it. "Come on, Abs, why you holding out on us? Hey, what's this?" She holds up a card Keeta gave me at the end of class, one I was told to open tonight before bed.

"Nothing!" I grab it from her. "It's just from Kate," I say more calmly. "She told me to open it tonight at dinner. It's probably a gift certificate to some slutty clothing store at the mall. You know how she is."

"That's weird," Stef says. "Why didn't she just bring it with her tonight?"

"I don't know. She's complicated," I practically yell.

"Okay, whatever you say, Abbey," Stef says.

The bell rings, but this time I'm happy to hear it. "Come on guys, we gotta jet," I say and slam my locker shut.

All through Spanish I wonder how much time I have before my snowy mountain of lies melts, revealing the truth underneath. And I wonder if Keeta and Stef started off like me and Keeta. Is this how she seduces all her girlfriends? Am I just another one of Keeta's basketball scores? How can I keep on lying to Stef like this? There are only a few more days to go until Stef leaves, but I'm about to crack. That's when I realize what a hypocrite I am. I mean, I'm a backstabber and a liar. God, I'm worse than Kate.

CHAPTER NINETEEN

"Two for dinner," my mom says to the hostess of the Golden Buddha, our favorite special occasion restaurant.

"Right this way."

My mom links her arm in mine as we walk through the restaurant to a booth in the corner. "I'm sorry Kate had to go to her dad's house tonight, honey. But at least she gave you a really thoughtful gift."

"Yeah, I guess so." I reach up and play with the pendant that my mom thinks is from Kate and that Stef and (maybe) Garrett think my mom gave me. This necklace is feeling more like Pandora's Box than a birthday present.

We get settled at our table and are handed menus and poured tea. My mom looks like she wants to talk about something serious, so I read through the long list of dishes even though I already know I want the spicy garlic chicken and a Coke.

"Abbey Road? You seem so quiet these days. Everything okay?"

I hold the menu up a little higher so she can't see my eyes turn glassy. "Yeah, it's just been a long week. You know, big game last night and all that."

I know she's not quite satisfied with my answer by the way she says, "Hmm," but then she says, "Okay," and looks at her menu even though she knows what she's going to order, too.

Enter uncomfortable silence.

Our waiter arrives and asks if we're ready to order.

My mom and I both say yes a little too enthusiastically.

Once we're alone again, my mom attempts to dissolve the unfamiliar tension between us. "Time for presents," she says and digs in her purse. She unloads its contents on the table and, like Mary Poppins's carpetbag, out comes the oddest collection of items: paintbrushes, a visor, four cabinet-door handles, three tins of mints, and finally my birthday present. She puts a small package in front of me. "I hope it fits."

It's not very big so it's most likely not clothing. I'm sincerely stumped. "You hope it fits?" I ask and inspect the present a little closer.

"Open it!" she says like she knows I'll love it, but I still have my doubts. Not that I'm a brat about presents, but my mom doesn't usually get me anything more expensive or elaborate than school supplies, books, or a Beatles CD.

I pick at the tape and carefully remove the present from its leopard-print paper. I'm blown away. "No freaking way, Mom!"

"I got one, too. I thought it'd be good to have for work." I look at her and she's smiling ear to ear. "Do you like it?" she asks, as if I might not.

I tear open the box and remove the cell phone carefully. I admire it from every angle because it's a work of art. Instead of buying a cheap plastic cover from one of those mall kiosks, she painted my initials on the back in really cool lettering and even added a basketball on the back with my number painted in the middle. No one else in the world will have one like it. "I love it, Mom. Oh my God, thanks!" I climb out of my side of the booth and hug her. "It's perfect."

"Well, it's not that fancy, but it's better than nothing, right?"

I slip it in my back pocket, but then take it out pretending I'm getting a call. "Oh hey, I'm going to have to call you back. I'm having dinner with the best mom ever," I say to no one.

"Now don't go all crazy. You only get two hundred minutes a month, so if you run out, you run out. And, sorry, no web stuff. Okay, kiddo?"

"Got it." Now I'm the one smiling ear to ear because I'm thinking about how I can call Keeta whenever I want. Too bad she doesn't have one, too.

"Who are you going to call first?" Mom asks, like a mind reader.

"Kate, of course," I say, pretending we're still friends. "She'll totally freak out."

❖

It's six on Saturday night and I'm getting ready for my Birthday Extravaganza, which includes going out to dinner, looking at stars at the U of A's planetarium, and something else that they won't tell me about.

My cell phone rings and I jump at the obnoxious ringtone I selected. "Hello, Abbey Brooks's cell phone. Abbey Brooks speaking."

"You're such a nerd," Stef says. "You almost ready?"

I sit on my bed, loving how it feels to be gabbing on my cell like a real teenager. "Almost, punk nugget. When you guys coming over?"

"Like seven. Cool?" Stef asks.

"Yeah. Cool."

"I'm gonna stop by Keeta's before walking over to G's house. I haven't been able to get ahold of her today, so whatever. Wish me luck."

I grab a lock of my hair and start twirling. *Any day now, she'll be gone*, I think to myself like the selfish bitch that I am. "Okay, well, have fun. See you soon."

After we hang up, I stand in front of my mirror and try to braid my hair. It looks pretty bad, so I do it again. But it still looks like I just survived a tornado, so I give up and find my mom.

"Everything all set for tonight, honey?" she asks as she weaves my hair into a perfect french braid.

"Yep. Are you sure you don't mind driving us around?"

"Of course not. Just call me from your cell phone when you're ready to come home." She taps my shoulder for the hair band, wraps it around the end of my braid, and then kisses my head like she always does when she's finished. "There you go."

I look in the mirror and admire her work. It looks perfect, but my mom's niceness makes me feel ugly inside. I fake a smile. "Thanks, Mom."

When I walk back into the living room a few minutes later to wait for Stef and Garrett, my mom's at her easel, working on another large painting. This one's commissioned by the Tucson Public Library. I peek over her shoulder and look for the mini version of me. Once in a while, when she can get away with it, she sneaks in a girl who looks just like me. "There I am," I say and point to a girl sitting on a bench in the front of the library. I'm reading one of my favorite books, *Alice in Wonderland*.

"Yep, there you are." She rinses off her paintbrush and dries it on a cloth diaper that I once wore.

She usually paints me to look like I'm five or six, maybe that's when I looked the cutest, but this time in the painting I'm much taller and I'm wearing checkered Converse. Maybe she's finally accepting that I'm growing up. I sigh because I wish I could be that perfect little girl on her canvas, the one who likes reading and hanging out at the library, not making out with girls in instrument rooms. But maybe I'm making too big a deal out of this whole thing. Maybe she won't even care. Maybe it's time to say something true for once.

I open my mouth and wait for my confession to escape, but the only words that surface are, "Looks cool, Mom."

❖

At around seven fifteen, Garrett calls me. "Dude, is Stef there?"

"She hasn't come by your place yet?" I look out the window of my front door to see if Stef's walking down the street. "That's weird," I say when I see her sitting on the curb in front of my neighbor's house. "She's outside. Call you right back."

Out of sheer insanity or boredom, my mom decided to hang about a thousand bells on the front door to "get in the spirit of the holidays" even though it's only mid-November, so it sounds like Santa Claus's arrival as I open and shut it. Stef looks up at the commotion, but when she sees it's me, she stands up and starts to walk down the street away from my house.

"Stef, wait!" I run after her and grab her arm to keep her from fleeing. "What's wrong? Why didn't you go to G's?"

She turns to face me. The street light illuminates her bloodshot eyes.

I'm very familiar with the look of a recent cry, so I change my tone. "Are you okay?"

Instead of crying on my shoulder like before, she yanks her arm out of my grasp and glares at me. "I should have figured it out. It's always the ones you trust the most that end up stabbing you in the back. You're such a cliché."

"Stef," is all I can say.

"God, Abbey. You know, I actually feel responsible? I should have left you alone about trying out for basketball. Maybe then you wouldn't have become such a two-faced whore."

"Stef, it's not like that. I…"

She backs up and the distance between us forces her to yell even louder. "Let me guess, Abbey. Keeta read you poetry and played her stupid guitar for you. She told you, 'I've never met anyone like you before.'"

I feel an invisible punch hit me hard in my gut.

"Oh my God." She smacks her forehead with her hand. "That present! That was from her, not your mom. And the box from Josephine's…that was for your birthday, too. God, you really had me fooled, Abbey."

"Stef, I'm sorry. I'm really sorry." I really am sorry, but I know *sorry* isn't going to get me out of this one. Mostly, though, I just want her to stop yelling so my mom won't hear us. "Can we talk somewhere else?"

"Why? So you can lie to my face some more?"

"Please?"

She finally lowers her voice. "Abbey, good luck with this messed up life you're stupid enough to take on. I hope your mom is able to accept it. I hope you find a happy ending. But I'll tell you one thing, it's not going to be with Keeta. Everyone tried to warn me about her, but I never listened, and she's going to screw with your head and heart so much you'll wish you were dead just like me. Don't think you're that special, *Amara*."

Stef saying my secret name feels like spit in my face and there's nothing I can say to make it better. But I don't want to make it worse, so I just stand there and take it.

She steps toward me and I brace myself for my first real punch in the face.

"I should totally kick your ass."

At least this is something we both agree on.

"But you know what? Being with Keeta is punishment enough."

With that, it's over. She storms down the street as her words linger and try to penetrate my hard head. Logically, I have no reason to doubt what she said and every reason to believe she probably knows Keeta better than me. But I'm getting used to having what I want, and what I want more than anything is Keeta all to myself. Maybe Keeta treated Stef badly, but that doesn't mean she'll do the same to me.

I head back to my house and try to come up with a way to explain the blowout I just had with Stef in case my mom heard us.

As I walk down the driveway, I see the worst possible scenario: my mom standing at the kitchen sink. Even though a thin pane of glass is all that separates us, she feels a million miles away. It's like the wall I've been working so hard to put up between us has become too large to leap over, too solid to yell through, and too strong to break down.

The jingle bells announce my return as I step into the house and get ready for my next battle.

"Everything okay, Abbey?"

"Um, yeah." I grab my braid and start to paint my cheek with its soft tip. "Well, sort of."

"She seemed pretty upset."

"Yeah, she was," I say, letting out a little sun-ray of truth to counteract the snowstorm of lies.

"Why don't you tell me about it?" She wipes her hands on the dish towel and pulls out a chair for me at the table.

I sit down because I can't think of a reason fast enough for why I shouldn't.

After ten painful seconds of silence, I say, "I didn't mean for it to happen."

"You didn't mean for what to happen, honey? Who's Keeta?"

"Keeta?" I ask, buying time.

"I heard her say something about someone named Keeta."

I look down at the placemat and play with its edges. "Well, see, Stef and Keeta were really good friends. Like, best friends, then Keeta and I started to be friends, and I guess she got sort of jealous. I guess Keeta"—it's beyond weird to say her name in front of my mom—"started hanging out with me more, since we have guitar together and stuff, and Stef started to feel left out, so Keeta and I kept some stuff we did from Stef, but I guess tonight Keeta told Stef about how we lied to her and, so, yeah, Stef was pretty mad at me." I grab my braid again but drop it to avoid looking suspicious.

"Hmm. I guess you know a little about feeling left out," my mom says, picking up her coffee and leaning back in her chair like she's channeling Ms. Morvay.

"What do you mean?"

"It's been pretty obvious, Abbey. I mean Kate hardly ever calls and always cancels her plans with you. That must be really painful for you, too. I bet you can understand what Stef must be going through."

"Yeah," I agree to help speed things along. "I guess I do."

"You know what I think? I think you should cancel your party plans and talk to Keeta about what you guys can do to help Stef feel better. Maybe you can figure out a way to make it up to Stef. That's the kind of good friend I know you are." Then she nods her head and smiles.

But her smile makes paranoia seep into me and I am convinced my mom is messing with my mind.

"Here's an idea," my mom says and then stands to get more coffee. "Since I was planning on having dinner with a friend anyway while you were out, I can drop you off at Keeta's and then pick you back up afterward at around nine o'clock. Unless you and Garrett still want to go out."

If she's messing with me, she's the master. "Uh…" is the only sound I can make.

"Why don't you call Keeta and Garrett and work it out. I'll get ready."

I'm finally able to spit out an okay and run to my room to use my brand-spanking-new cell phone to call my brand-spanking-free girlfriend.

"Hey, gorgeous, I was just thinking about you," Keeta says. For someone who's just broken up with her girlfriend, she's in pretty good spirits.

"Really? Well, I guess my super telepathic powers are improving. Do you know what I'm telling you to do now?" And for someone who has just been given a strong warning about being with Keeta, I sure am being flirty.

"Hey now, don't tease me, Amara. I don't get to see you until tomorrow. Which reminds me, buttermilk or blueberry pancakes?"

I fall back onto my bed and kick my legs in the air before saying, very maturely, like someone who isn't a freshman, "Actually, change of plans. Can I come over tonight?"

"No joke?" She sounds excited, which makes me want to gallop around the house like a pony. "Something go down?"

"Nothing big," I say casually. "It just worked out this way."

"Damn, then get your cutie bootie over here. Not much to do at my house, but I think we'll find something to fill the time."

As Keeta finishes saying this my mom pokes her head in my room. "Abbey, I…"

"Get out, Mom! I'm on the phone!" Lucky for me, my mom doesn't rip the phone out of my hand and toss it in the prickly pear cactus patch outside my window. She does give me a mean mom glare, though, so I say in a much sweeter tone with my hand over my phone, "I'm just getting directions. Be right there." Then back to Keeta, "Anyway, you better give me directions to your apartment or house, or whatever." Of course, I know it's an apartment. Thanks to Mrs. Schwartz and Google Earth, I know exactly where Keeta lives and that there is a brown Buick in the driveway, a tombstone rose bush in front of the window, and a paloverde tree next to the door.

After Keeta and I hang up, I call Garrett.

"No need to explain. Stef already called me," Garrett says, with a tone that tells me she's not mad at me.

"So you don't mind if we postpone?"

"You mean do I mind if you ditch me to slut around with your secret lesbian lover?"

"Right," I say, hoping to wrap up the call so I can get on my way to Keeta's.

"Nah, just have fun. We'll do it some other time."

I hear a click of another call on her line.

"Speaking of whoring around, that's Tai to tell me how sorry she is for flirting with some lame-ass friend of her cousin's. I better go so we can make up already."

"Okay, I'll call you later," I say, looking in the mirror to reassess my outfit.

"You bet your ass you will."

Before going to Keeta's, I reapply some lip gloss, unbutton one more button of my blouse, and undo my hair because I'm pretty sure Kate once told me only little girls wear braids, real women wear their hair down, long, and tousled. I recall her demonstration and flip my head down between my legs, mess it up really good with my fingertips, then come back up to admire it. Kate's right. I do look sexy as hell.

CHAPTER TWENTY

Take a left on Sandalwood," I say to my mom on our way to Keeta's.

She slowly completes the turn. "Then what?"

I look down at the directions I printed out for show. "Uh, it should be coming up, three oh seven Sandalwood, Building A."

We pull up in front of Keeta's apartment, and lo and behold, there's the brown Buick. "Thanks, Mom."

"Her parents are home, right?" Mom says before I shut the car door.

"Uh, she lives with her grandmother, actually. And yeah, she's home." I guess.

"Okay, I'll be back at around nine."

It's a good thing I wait for my mom to drive away before knocking on the door because when Keeta opens it, she holds out a tiny yellow rose. *"Una rosa para ti."*

"Wow, thanks." I put it behind my ear and step inside her home for the first time. It smells like scented candles and looks very tidy. Her grandma isn't visible, which makes me kind of nervous for some reason. But then I get even more nervous when I see how little clothing Keeta has on. She's wearing a tight, racer-back black tank top, boxer shorts, and no shoes. It's the most skin I've seen of Keeta's, and frankly, she might as well be naked.

Keeta closes the door and pulls me to her for a hug. I melt as usual and let my earlier near-death experience with Stef get deleted from my brain.

It isn't until we finally part that I lay eyes on him. "Whoa. That's amazingly…big," I say and point to the giant crucifix occupying the wall opposite the television. Its size and realistic red blood dripping from the feet, hands, and head wounds make me feel very bad for being a backstabbing sinner. "So I take it you go to church."

"If my *nana* asks, then yes I do." She laughs. "I take it you don't."

"Once, when my dad died. It's funny because I hadn't ever given God much thought, but when I sat there in front of my dad's coffin, I decided I hated him for letting my dad die. I guess I never got past that."

"Yeah, I know what you mean." She reaches out and moves the clasp of my necklace to the back of my neck. I smile because I'm glad she notices I'm still wearing it. "But he's not as bad as you might think," she says.

"Oh, I'm sure he's not." I say, but I feel my lies weighing me down again as we walk past him and into the kitchen.

"Water?" Keeta asks.

"Yeah, thanks," I say as I look around. Unlike my house, there are no dirty dishes in the sink, no paintbrushes soaking on the counter, no paint palettes drying in the rack. There's a sense of order I hadn't known I longed for until I saw how possible it was. Every spatula, pot holder, and pan is in its place.

Even the little religious cards are in an exact straight line along the kitchen windowsill. I've never seen anything like them; they're like baseball trading cards of God and his posse. I don't recognize any, but one kind of looks like Santa Claus. One is upside down, but I have a feeling, since everything else is neat and tidy, that it's upside down on purpose.

"Do these all stand for something special?" I ask, pointing to the mini-army of religious folk.

Keeta stops filling my glass with water to look up. "*Claro que sí. Ay*, girl, you really aren't religious, huh?"

I give her a look that says, *Isn't it obvious?* so she puts down the glass and walks over.

"Okay. I'll explain. No need for the dagger eyes, Amara." She comes up behind me and wraps her arms around my stomach, and since she's shorter than me, she rests her chin on my shoulder. She doesn't even seem at all worried that her grandma might find us like this, so I assume there is no one here. "The first one is Saint Sebastian. He's the patron saint of athletes. My *nana* got that one for me when I started to play basketball."

Her face is so close to my neck that when she blinks, her long eyelashes lightly brush my skin like a butterfly's wing. I close my eyes and lose track of my body for a second.

"That's so sweet," I finally say.

Next Keeta picks up the card with a young-looking woman on it. "This is Saint Cecilia. She watches over musicians." She puts Cecilia down and points to the next one. "That's Saint Monica, patron saint of widows."

I take note of that one. Maybe I can get one for my mom. I mean, just because we don't go to church doesn't mean Saint Monica can't protect her.

"The big guy in the middle," Keeta continues, "is…well, I forget his name, but he's supposed to protect us from famine or arthritis or gangrene." She laughs softly in my ear, sending goose bumps down my arms. "Something like that." She holds up another one with a woman who kind of looks like she might have played basketball if she'd had the opportunity. "That's Joan of Arc. She's the patron saint of prisoners, which *Nana* got for my cousin in Texas."

"Cool," I say, but I'm kind of shocked because I've never known anyone who knew anyone in prison.

"This one," she picks up the card of the one who looked like Santa. "This is Saint Nicholas."

"Hey, I knew that."

Keeta laughs on my neck again and I almost fall down. "I should hope so," she says. "He's the patron saint of children."

"Oh, I get it. What about that upside-down one?"

"That's Saint Anthony. You ask him to help you find things that are lost. You say a little prayer and then turn him over. My *nana* has had him turned over since her cat, Mamacita, ran away. It's been three years, but she still thinks Saint Anthony will help Little Mama find her way home."

"Do you believe he will?"

Keeta lets me go, leans against the sink, and nods. "Yeah, I guess I do."

I do, too, but I don't say it because I don't think I have any right to believe in Saint Anthony since I don't pray or go to church.

"Want to see my room?" Keeta asks.

"Sure." I'm trying to act casual, but now my heart is doing double time.

Keeta hands me my glass of water and motions to me to follow her. We have to pass by the giant crucifix again, and I am sure my skin is going to sizzle.

Then we walk down a narrow hallway plastered with school pictures of Keeta. "If you laugh, you'll be sorry," she says.

"Nice ruffles," I say, and chuckle. "Did you pick that dress out yourself?"

"Yes, and now you will pay." She grabs my hand to hurry me along.

I'm still admiring the photos when Keeta suddenly stops in front of a closed door. I walk into her, accidentally spilling half my water down her back. "Oh my God, I'm sorry." I try to wipe it off with my hand.

But she's not mad. She just shakes her head and whispers in my ear, "*Ay,* Amara, there are other ways to get me out of my clothes. Be patient."

Now I'm quietly gasping for air. What am I doing here? I mean, this isn't the instrument closet or the locker room where we sneak kisses between classes. It's her house; it's her private bedroom with a door and a lock and a bed. And now she's talking about taking her clothes off?

"*Nana,*" Keeta says as she pushes the door open, "*estás despierta?*"

Inside the room, a tiny Mexican woman is resting in a giant bed. She's covered with an intricately woven white blanket and is watching an evening soap opera on the Spanish channel, *Los Corazones Perdidos* (The Lost Hearts). I recognize the program because *Señora* Cabrera assigns it for homework, which is pretty much the only assignment I have been keeping up with.

Keeta's grandma has a soft face and her hair is neatly kept together in a bun which looks like a cinnamon roll placed on her head.

Her grandma ignores us, so Keeta yells our arrival again. "*Nana!*"

This time her grandma looks our way and smiles. "*Chiquita,*" her grandma says, and now I halfway know where the nickname Keeta comes from. "*Como estás, mija? Quién es la niña?*"

I see Keeta's eyes in her grandma's, which are just as remarkable. I want to impress Keeta a little, so I introduce myself. *"Soy Abbey Brooks, señora. Mucho gusto. Su casa es muy bonita,"* I say loudly because she's obviously a little hard of hearing.

Her nana does seem impressed. *"Ay, la gringa habla muy bien.* It's very nice to meet you, Abbey." Then she says something to Keeta that I can't translate.

"Mañana, Nana. Está bien?"

"Sí, sí..." her *nana* says.

"Vamos a estudiar en mi cuarto. Do you need anything?" Keeta asks.

"A new hip," Keeta's grandma says and smiles at me. I smile back.

"Ay, Nana," Keeta says, like her *nana* gets on her nerves as much as my mom does to me. "Call me if you need anything," Keeta says to her *nana* then shuts the door. The volume of the television is muffled once more and Keeta takes hold of my hand again to lead me down the hall to her room.

"Make yourself comfortable, Amara."

There's no place to sit except for her neatly made twin bed. I sit on its edge and try not to faint.

"What kind of music do you want to listen to?"

"I'm sure I'll like whatever you like," I say, and while she flips through her CDs, I button up my blouse one button and look around. There's not much to see because Keeta's bedroom is nearly void of all decorations and personal items. Besides her five-drawer dresser, a guitar leans against the wall, and a well-used basketball waits in the corner. Like the rest of her house, everything seems to be exactly where it should be; it seems like if something is moved out of place, an alarm might sound. Then I think that she'd hate my room. It's way too frilly and jam-packed with books, furniture, and stuffed animals.

There is, however, one picture hanging above her bed. It's of two men standing in front of a tree, holding each other in a warm embrace. You can tell they are laughing at the photographer. It's in black and white and the composition is as perfect as the photos I've seen with my mom at the art shows downtown.

The Cranberries begin to play softly in the background, so I turn my attention back to Keeta. She's leaning against her dresser and smiling at me. "Not what you expected, huh?"

I look around again and say, "Well, it's not like I've been constantly thinking about what the lair of Keeta Moreno would be like or anything," hoping she'll pick up on the subtle hint that I have indeed been wondering about the inside of her house. "It's nice in here. I like that picture."

"Those are my uncles, David and Hugo," she says. "*Que descanse en paz, Hugo*. Rest in peace."

"Oh." Now I feel bad for pointing it out. "I'm sorry for your loss."

"Thanks." She walks to her window to lower her blinds. Then she points at the younger one in the photo. "Hugo's kind of why I get what you mean about being pissed off at God."

"What happened to him? I mean, if you don't mind me asking."

"Well, I don't think you'll like the answer." Then she walks over to me, slips off my sandals, and puts them next to her shoes by the door. I like how she takes care of me.

"Well, if you feel like telling me…"

She waits a second and looks again at the two men frozen in time on her wall. "He was killed."

"Really? Was it a car accident?" To me, of course, a car accident is the worst way to lose someone.

"No, my sweet Amara, he was stabbed outside a bar in Hermosillo. See, they were lovers, not brothers."

"That's awful," I whisper.

She shrugs then picks up the basketball and spins it on her finger. "I took that picture."

"It's art-gallery worthy," I say. "And I would know after all the galleries my mom has dragged me to in my lifetime."

"You think?" She drops the ball and kicks it over to the corner again. "I was only five when I took it. The last time I saw them was in Noggie during Christmas break when I was fourteen. Hugo was killed on New Year's Eve that same year."

"Did they find out who did it?"

"All they know is what David remembers—that a couple of asshole guys followed them after they left the bar. They both got beat up, but Hugo didn't make it. They should've known better. They shouldn't have been so open, but that's just how they were. Damn, they were so in love."

"Really?" My eyes feel hot, but I don't let them tear up.

"I used to want to be like them," she says and then looks away. "You know, to be loved and to love someone as much as they loved each other."

I repeat her words in my head—*I used to want to be like them*—and take it personally that she no longer wants to love someone like that anymore. I had planned on ignoring Garrett's advice and asking about Keeta's parents, but maybe I'll have to learn about Keeta in smaller doses.

"Anyway," Keeta says, then shivers and opens her closet, "you got me totally wet, Amara."

"Sorry I got you"—I clear my throat—"wet," and now I'm back to freaking out. Who am I, and what am I doing sitting on Keeta's bed? Then I see her Hot Dog on a Stick uniform hanging on the back of the closet door and remember why I'm here. I want to be.

"Well, I've got to get out of this tank. *Perdón, mi amor.*"

"Go right ahead. I promise I won't watch," I say then cover my eyes but spread my fingers apart.

She likes how I flirt because she's actually doing the blushing for once. "You've been hanging with Garrett too much, naughty girl."

She turns away from me and pulls off her shirt revealing her mocha-brown back and a black lacy bra. I don't know why, but I didn't expect such a girlie bra. As she slips on a gray tank top, her biceps flex. Her arms look so strong, like they could hold me forever. Then she pulls at her hair band and lets her hair down. By the time she turns around to face me again, I'm practically drooling like a Great Dane.

"I guess you liked the free show?" she asks, then closes her bedroom door all the way and locks it.

That doesn't really bother me much because I like the privacy, but when she flips off the lights, I sit upright and lose any ounce of cool I thought I had.

"*Hazte a un lado,*" she says softly, and I move over to give her some room on the small bed.

My heart starts beating fast, like Ringo Starr is playing drums in my chest. I'm positive she can hear my drum solo over her *nana*'s *novela* blaring next door, so I almost apologize but stop myself. Be chill. Be mature.

My eyes adjust to the darkness, and I see Keeta's silhouette. She's leaning back on her elbows and looking at me.

"What?" I ask.

She reaches out to touch my cheek. "You don't have to be afraid, Amara. We can take things slow."

"Slow," I say with a hint of doubt because I'm beginning to think our ideas of slow are slightly different. "I'm not afraid." My biggest lie ever.

"Good." She takes my hand and pulls me over to her, wrapping her arms around me like I have wished for on so many nights. As we lie there, I relax into her, but not too much, so she won't feel how fast my heart is going. "Now," she says, "you wanted to get to know me better…well, ask away. I am an open book." She brushes aside my hair and snuggles so close that when she says, "First question, please," I can feel her lips on my neck.

I caress her back with my hand because it feels right, and then I pull her body closer. Our legs are wrapped around each other like tree roots and I am incredibly glad I shaved this morning. "So, you like to play basketball?" I ask.

"Um," she whispers, kisses each of my cheeks, and then nibbles on my earlobe.

"Yeah, I like to play a lot of basketball. *Y tú?*"

"Yeah, me, too," I think I say, though now I'm feeling too fuzzy to speak coherently. Next, Keeta gently bites me where my neck and shoulder meet. I moan very quietly, even though I don't mean to, and suddenly I am the most religious person ever. I have died and gone to Keeta Heaven.

There's a knock at Keeta's front door, but I don't think anything of it because I'm tangled up in her arms and a million galaxies away from Tucson.

Then my cell phone rings, but I ignore that, too, because the only person I want to talk to is in my arms, kissing me.

The knock at the front door comes again, louder this time, and a voice weasels into my conscience. "Abbey, it's Mom," the voice says.

"Chale," we both say at the same time.

Keeta and I stand up quickly, and I'm temporarily woozy with a major head rush. When my vision clears, I squint at the glowing clock on Keeta's dresser. "Nine fifteen? Where are my shoes?" I feel around the floor for my sandals while Keeta trips over herself with laughter.

"This is so not funny, Keeta."

"Wait, I'll turn on the light," she says between gasps of laughter.

We're blinded once more, but I recover quickly, slip on my shoes, and glance in her mirror to try to fix my tangled hair. It looks like the time I rode in the backseat of a convertible with the top down all the way to Phoenix, only a little worse.

Then my mom knocks again, this time saying, "Abbey? Are you guys in there?" Then my cell phone rings again. I pick it up off the floor. It's my mom.

"You going to answer that or should I?" Keeta jokes.

"Keeta," I whine, silencing my cell phone, which I now regret asking for. "Go tell my mom I'll be right there. Tell her I'm in the bathroom or something. She can't get suspicious."

Keeta frowns. "No way."

"Please. For me?" I bat my eyelashes and stick out my lower lip. "It's the least you can do since I let you kiss me for an hour."

"Okay, I guess you're right," she says and quickly puts her hair back in a ponytail, straightens out her tank top, and leaves. I look in her closet mirror to tidy up and that's when I see it: my first hickey. "Holy, Keeta," I whisper and look at it more closely in the mirror. It's small and low on my neck, and I'm oddly proud of it. But I have to stay focused because my mom is less than twenty feet away, and I have a giant 'fro of blond hair on my head and a hickey on my neck. Not to worry. I'm an honor student. I'll think of something.

I quickly scan Keeta's closet and consider taking her Hot Dog on a Stick hat as a souvenir, but instead grab the U of A hooded sweatshirt (neatly folded on the shelf, of course) to cover my hickey and a Diamondbacks cap to cover my hair.

By the time I walk into the living room, my mom and Keeta are comfortably talking about the weather like they've known each other for more than three minutes.

My mom gets up from the couch when I walk into the room. "All ready, Abbey?"

"Yes. Very ready." I drag my mom to the door. "Thanks for letting me borrow your sweatshirt and hat for Sports Day next week," I say to Keeta with a slight wink, which she hopefully translates as, *You are the most beautiful girl I've ever known, and I wish I could figure out a way to tell you I am madly in love with you,* but I doubt she picks up on it.

"*No hay problema,* Abbey. See you in guitar on Monday."

My mom tries to say something else to Keeta, but I push her out the door before she has a chance.

In the car, I turn my head to the window to try and hide the hickey.

"So, how did it go?" Mom asks as we pull away.

"Well"—I send a smile into the dark desert—"I can honestly say things have never been better."

CHAPTER TWENTY-ONE

Since I had to spend Thanksgiving break in Flagstaff with my mom, aunt, uncle, and my cousins, I didn't get to spend any of my five-day break with Keeta. That's why, when winter break finally arrives, I'm the happiest person on the planet.

Winter break means no homework, no Mrs. Schwartz, no getting up at an unreasonable hour, and no bells to keep me from hanging out/ making out with Keeta. Yep, for the next two weeks, I am going to make sure I get as much Keeta time as I can. I'm either going to be at the mall staring at Keeta in her cute Hot Dog on a Stick uniform or hanging out in the backroom at All Strings Attached. My mom, however, will think I'm at basketball practice or playing hoops with my friends in the park because that's the lie I will tell her.

Everything goes as planned. I use my bus pass like it's the most fashionable card to have this holiday season. But then it's even better than I expected because I forgot there could be postwork kissing at Keeta's house. That's what I like the most. She even gave me my own special knock to use on her door when I come over. With all the time we've been spending together, there's little chance that there's any time for Keeta to spend with any other girl. I guess everyone was wrong about her.

But even though I'm spending more time in her bedroom, and the lacy black bra/panty set Keeta gave me for Christmas has been quickly modeled and admired, my panties have still never left my butt. So, why am I being so prudish? I'm not sure, but I think Keeta wishes I'd figure it out and get over it. I hope she doesn't regret being with someone younger than her, but she assures me my age doesn't matter. I know I love Keeta, like, more than life these days, but going all the way still freaks me out. Despite Garrett's informative geography lesson about girl-on-girl lovemaking, I'm pretty sure I'll do something totally wrong and therefore ruin everything Keeta and I have. Besides, Keeta said she'd wait for me until I was ready. That's how much she must love me, even if she's never actually said the L word to me.

❖

But today is the day I've dreaded; it is our last Saturday before break is over.

At around four this afternoon, I change into sweats and inform my mom of my plans. "I'm heading off to Columbus Park, Mom," I say, leaving out the part that I'm going to be celebrating my one-and-a-half-month anniversary with Keeta.

"Okay, but don't stay in the park after dark, okay?" she nags.

"Yeah, yeah," I say, as I close the front door.

Keeta buys me a mocha shake from the Ugly Mug, and then we walk to the park to play some basketball. We start with a game of one on one, but after she scores her twentieth shot, I get sick of losing, so I shove the basketball up my shirt and run to the playground.

"Come and get it," I yell and scramble up the tunnel slide.

"Like that's hard," Keeta says as she chases after me. "Come on. At least give me a challenge."

I scream like a total girlie-girl and curl up like a pill bug, but she easily plucks the ball out from under my shirt. "It's a girl," she says proudly. "Let's name her Abbey Junior."

I'm too out of breath to protest, so I laugh and lie back on the playground tower platform. As the sun sets, the temperature quickly drops, but I'm hot from playing basketball and running away from Keeta. I strip off Keeta's sweatshirt that I stole from her closet weeks ago and put it under my head.

"The moon looks like your smile," I say and grin up at her.

"You're such a poet." She lies down next to me and tosses the ball into the air like Coach makes us do to practice our shooting form. She's the last person who needs practice at anything having to do with basketball, though. She's Gila's best guard and has had three colleges come by during our winter tournament to watch her play. My stomach sinks every time I count down the months we have left together before she graduates from Gila and leaves Tucson, and possibly me, forever. Tonight this thought makes me angry, so I smack the ball as she's about to catch it. It bounces down the slide and rolls to a stop under the nearby mesquite tree.

She turns her head to look at me. "Yes? Did you need my attention?"

"You're already perfect. You don't need practice."

"Nobody's perfect, Amara." She runs her finger over my lips. "Except maybe you."

"Please. I'm so far from it." I roll to my side and look out as the shadows darken in the park. "Keeta, you're beautiful, talented, smart, and, let's face it, everyone wants to be with you. And I'm just a...totally dumb freshman who...you're probably going to forget all about by the end of June."

"Oh, come on, Amara." She turns me toward her, but I don't look in her eyes.

I don't know why I'm trying to ruin the night.

She lifts my chin and looks into me. "You know I care about you."

Sure she cares about me when we are together and alone. But, when anyone else is around, it's like we're just friends or teammates. I don't know if that's a gay thing or a Keeta thing. I don't know anything about dating a girl and there are zero *Cosmo* articles to help me out. Plus, I can tell Garrett's getting fed up with all my questions, so I have decided to stop bugging her.

I do know, though, that these weeks with Keeta have been the best in my life. I'm completely hooked on Keeta and I'm pretty sure I love her but don't dare tell her that. Not until she tells me first. I don't want to seem like the stupid head-over-heels girl that I am.

"Yeah, I know. I care about you, too," I say and lean in closer to kiss her. The warmth of her mouth makes me shiver (in a good way).

Then Keeta's basketball hits the bars of the platform next to our heads.

I grab her arm. "Oh my God. Who did that?"

"I don't know." She sits up and squints into the dark park. She must see the culprits because then Keeta stands and yells, "Why the hell are you touching my basketball, asshole?"

"Keeta, don't." The story of her uncle pops into my head and I pull at her shirt. "Let's just leave. Come on."

"*Pendejos!*" Keeta shouts, then drops down to cover my body with her own. A second later sharp rocks ping off the playground's metal bars. One hits me in the leg and some hit her in the back of her head.

"Damn queers!" The voice yells back, which feels worse than the handful of rocks; it feels more like a round of bullets.

"Get a room in hell!" a different voice shouts and another shower of rocks and hate falls on us.

"Abbey, stay here."

I try to grab hold of her leg but only end up with her left Nike. She jumps off the platform and runs full speed toward the parking lot. "Keeta, wait!" I yell and climb down to chase after her.

❖

"It's pointless to call the cops," Keeta says after I try again to convince her that we should. "Besides, I couldn't read the license plate before the guys pulled away." Then she explains there's no way of finding out who they are from the description of the car because what jackass homophobe moron in Tucson *doesn't* drive a beat up Chevy truck?

We're walking home, and I'm still recovering from what happened. I've read about things like this online but never thought it could happen to us. Why would anyone even care that we're together? It has nothing to do with them. Then I remember a new law that just passed. "Isn't that anti-hate law supposed to protect us?"

"Yeah, right. Maybe when we're at school," Keeta says and pushes out a laugh. "But have you forgotten that we're both still minors? And according to Tucson, we aren't allowed to be in the park after sundown. If anything, we might get in trouble."

"But you're bleeding, Keeta." I wipe a blob of blood off her arm with the corner of my shirtsleeve. "They can't just get away with this. It's not fair."

"Abbey, stop it. I'm fine." Her raised voice makes my lip quiver, but I don't let myself cry. "Besides, how exactly do you plan on explaining this to your mom? The police will tell her everything. Is that what you want?"

That seals the deal. I do as I'm told and try to forget the whole thing. But I'm still shaking after Keeta walks me to the end of my driveway, after I take a hot bath, and even after my mom kisses me good night. I only let myself cry when I know for sure my mom has taken her sleeping pill and is fast asleep.

As I try to sleep, I finally realize that the lack of public displays of affection from Keeta probably is a gay thing. Even if girls on the team know about us, it doesn't mean they like it, or that they don't tell their boyfriends, or that Coach won't find out and find a way to bench us or make our lives miserable in other ways. And after tonight, I finally realize that some secrets need to be kept. Being out is way too scary and has too many risks. Maybe this was my induction into the Land of Gay. No streamers, no balloons, no songs, just a handful of rocks thrown at me and a damning to hell.

❖

Today is a double-sucky day. It's not only the first day back from winter break, but it's also the day that the second quarter's report cards are sent home. I confess to Jenn on the way to school this morning that this report card is sure to be my worst ever.

As usual, she offers helpful advice on my troubles. "Well, you're screwed."

"Thank you, Captain Obvious," I say and take another bite of my Eggy.

"Well, the only way to keep your mom from finding out is to get the report card from the mailbox first and hope she didn't get the automated call last week that told parents what day to expect it."

For the first time ever, I'm pissed that my mom works at home. There's a slight chance that she won't get the mail, but it's so miniscule that you'd need the Hubble Space Telescope to see it.

But I've been getting away with so much lately that I hold out some hope, as I open the mailbox after getting home from basketball practice. I say a little prayer to the Patron Saint of Students (there has to be one out there), but the mailbox is empty. I'm a goner.

I tiptoe down the front hall to try and sneak past my mom, but just my luck, she's sitting at the kitchen table, waiting for little ol' me, with my report card in her hand.

"Don't even think about going to your room, young lady. Get in here right now and sit."

I silently back up slowly, sit down in the hot seat across from my mom, and twirl a clump of my sweaty ponytail.

She takes in a long breath and then exhales slowly. "Abbey, I don't even know what to say."

"Mom, I promise I'll do better next time."

"Well, that shouldn't be too hard," she says and then reads off my grades. "You got a D in PE? How does one *not* get an A in PE? Really, I'd like to know. And it says here you were tardy ten times last quarter. How big is that school? If you need me to, I can come and personally escort you to class. How would you like that?"

"Not at all," I mutter.

"A pitiful C in Spanish and a D in Social Studies? That's terrible. You've always loved to study history. Oh, but look," she says like she's talking to five-year-old Abbey during an Easter egg hunt, "here's an A. Bravo, Abbey! You got an A in Guitar. Well, I should hope you would."

She has never been this mean to me about anything before, and I think I'd have preferred a slap across the face to her disgusted look of disappointment.

My mom takes another deep breath to recharge her battery—Round Two.

"Abbey, it's one thing to do poorly in classes that I know you can do better in"—she shoves the report card across the table and it stops in front of me like a shuffleboard puck—"but would you care to explain how in the world you failed Biology?"

I look at the report card, and there it is: my first F. I guess doing well on the tests wasn't enough. I guess that 200-point research project really was important. And I guess all those romantic visits to the library had more of an effect on my grade than I thought. I try to swallow the lump in my throat and speak again. "Mom…"

"Abbey, you've always shown respect to me and your father." She pauses because she doesn't want to cry either. "But now I see it's time I lay down some restrictions. I should have done it sooner." She pulls out a list from her pocket and slides it over to me in the same way. "Starting the moment you wake up tomorrow, these are the new house rules. If you fail to follow them, I will not allow you to play basketball anymore and you can kiss your cell phone good-bye."

"Mom, that's totally unfair!"

"This quarter, I will be tracking your grades with a progress report that Ms. Morvay will be sending to me weekly, so don't even think about lying to me about whether or not you have tests or projects due."

I almost scream *I'm not a liar!* but then realize that I am. I keep my mouth shut and read the list:

1. No TV.
2. No Internet.
3. No cell phone use at home—you will turn it in to me every day.
4. You must do your homework at the kitchen table.
5. No incoming house phone calls past nine.
6. No staying after to watch varsity games.
7. You must attend study hall in the Gila library five days a week at lunch.

These I think I can handle, but the final rule sends me over the edge:

8. No friends over and no going to friends' houses.

I pull my sweatshirt away from my neck to try and get some air but quickly let go so as to not reveal my most recent hickey. No Keeta alone-time for nine weeks? I will surely lose my mind, but I don't dare argue with that one rule because my mom might figure us out, and I might not ever see Keeta again. Instead, I take my punishment and sign the bottom. Yes, she makes me sign it like a contract. So clever. She knows I take contracts very seriously.

After I sign it, she posts the new rules on the fridge. They don't really fit in next to our cheery family pictures. Nevertheless, there they are.

I start to get up to mope my way to my room, but then my mom says, "I'm not done with you yet, young lady."

I sigh and sit down. "What now? Do you need to attach my house-arrest anklet?"

She ignores my comment and takes another piece of paper out of her pocket, aka The Pocket of Misery. The paper is a copy of my schedule for third quarter. Next to each class, she's written in the grades she expects me to get: Art/A, Algebra/A, English/A, Social Studies/B, Biology/A+, PE/A.

I think about arguing the A in Art and the five days of lunch study hall, but I don't want to piss her off any further. She makes me sign the schedule, too, and then posts it up on the fridge next to my list of rules.

Finally, after another minute or two of my mom explaining how disappointed she is in me, I'm allowed to take my walk of shame to my bedroom. Where, by the way, I work for a full hour on my English and social studies homework before I start daydreaming about Keeta.

❖

As soon as I see Jenn this morning, I complain about my mom. "I mean, I'm not a baby. I don't need those stupid rules. I can handle it on my own. God, she's being totally unfair. I hate her."

Jenn just laughs.

"It's not funny. I mean, you and Kate don't have any stupid rules."

"Hey, we have plenty of rules—we just choose not to follow them all the time. But I'm laughing at the part where you said, 'I can handle it.' Really? You call a 1.89 GPA 'handling it'?"

"Whatever, Jenn," I say, but she does bring up a good point. Maybe I shouldn't follow my mom's dumb rules. I mean, she can't possibly know my every move. But then, after further deliberation, I finally decide if I'm going to be dishonest to my mom about the whole I-might-be-a-lesbian thing, the least I can do is follow her lame rules.

"Well," I say as we speed toward Gila, "how did Kate do on her report card? How did she handle schoolwork and Douchy Derrick and basketball?"

"How the hell should I know? Ask her yourself."

"Yeah, I'd love to, but I wouldn't want Derrick to worry about me grabbing Kate's butt or anything."

Jenn rolls her eyes. "You guys are going to be so embarrassed when you finally work this out."

"Whatever," I say and pout until we reach Gila.

Jenn's car is barely done pulling into our usual parking spot in the back when I swing open the car door and race toward the performance hall. It's a new semester and I don't have guitar anymore, but Keeta's a TA for Advanced Guitar now.

That means I only have about seven minutes each morning to spend with her before first period. And if I can't be with Keeta during guitar or sneak off to the library with her during fifth period or lunch, I'm going to have to get in as much kissing time as possible before the damn bell rings.

By the time I enter the performance hall, I'm winded and have to rest a second before parting the curtains and kissing Keeta hello. I lean against the wall to catch my breath and that's when I notice a backpack and guitar case sitting on the floor near the stage. I also notice that I don't hear the usual clicking sounds of Keeta writing on the chalkboard. Instead, I hear her tuning a guitar and talking to someone who is behind the curtain with her.

"How long have you had her?" Keeta asks someone.

"Oh, like two years," says a girl, who I hope is butt-ugly. "I've never had a string break like that before. I guess I was whaling on her pretty hard."

"I guess," Keeta says and laughs her flirty-sexy laugh.

On the other side of the curtain, I cross my arms and hug Keeta's U of A sweatshirt close to me. *Keeta's just doing her job*, I tell myself.

"So," the girl says, "How long have you been playing? You really seem to know what you're doing. You're like a professional."

Oh my God. What a kiss ass.

"Anyone can learn to tune a guitar," Keeta says, "but you're right. Not everyone can do this."

Then Keeta plays like Santana for a bit, which I'm still okay with. I mean, she is good and she likes to show off her talent. Then, after stupid better-be-ugly girl applauds, Keeta says, "Yeah, I taught myself how to play when I was ten. It just came to me. You know, like I was meant to do it. Some things just come naturally like that, I guess."

I had no idea she taught herself how to play. I should have known that.

"I totally know what you mean," says Stupid Girl. "The first time I picked up a guitar I was six, and it was like I knew it was for me. I've been at it ever since. It's like, some things are meant to be, and you just have to go for it."

After a few seconds of mysterious silence, Keeta finally speaks, "Yeah, I know what you mean."

I'm getting to know what she means, too, so I clear my throat and make my entrance. "Oh, sorry to interrupt."

"Oh hey, Abbey. I was just fixing Osiris's string."

I bet you were, I think but say, "That's nice of you."

"Hi," Osiris says to me. She's a small, peppy, punk-looking girl wearing lots of eyeliner, with eyebrow piercings, and she has giant boobs stretching out a hipster-band shirt with a studded belt around her waist. Her appearance makes me feel relieved. She's totally not Keeta's type. At least, I hope she isn't.

"So," I say and stare bug-eyed at Keeta. Time is slipping away. We only have three minutes left before the first bell.

"Well, there you go. You're all set," Keeta says and hands the guitar back to the girl. Then Keeta stands up, stretches her arms up, and casually says, "Hey, Abbey, can you help me with something in the instrument room?"

I smile. "Of course."

Once the door is locked, I find my way to Keeta's lips and kiss her desperately. There's no way I can make it through the day without seeing her.

After a minute, she pushes me away to come up for air. "Whoa, Amara. *Qué te pasa?* You're kissing me like you're never going to see me again." Then she traces my lips with her finger. "What's wrong, *chula?*"

I lean back against the door and try not to cry. "My mom got my report card."

"*Chale.*"

"Exactly. Now she has this list of rules, and one of them is no more going to friends' houses for the entire quarter. Can you believe that?"

She brushes my hair away from my face. "Amara, remember when I told you I would wait forever to be with you?"

I nod.

"I mean it, *mi Amara. No te preocupes.*" Then she whispers in my ear, "It will only make me want you more."

I blush and feel stupid for being jealous of that insignificant girl. Even though she's never said it to me directly, it's obvious Keeta loves me. And even though I'm not sure if we are officially girlfriends, I know she'll be loyal to me despite Garrett's and Stef's warnings. They don't know Keeta like I do.

In the remaining minute, I tell Keeta about all my other rules, but she doesn't seem worried. She reminds me of our last two away games, which mean long bus rides home in the dark. The thought of snuggling up with her in the back of the bus makes me smile again.

The faint sound of the bell rings in the other room, and we kiss one more time. Then she presses her lips in my palm and closes my fingers into a fist. "Keep it for later when you miss me."

"Thanks, Keeta," I say and leave feeling more confident than ever.

❖

Since I have Algebra 2 first period and not Guitar/Making Out 101, I get to PE early this morning. And because I'm early to PE, I almost slam right into Kate as she's rushing by on her way to the bathroom stalls. I'm caught off guard and politely apologize before I register that it's her.

She opens her mouth like she wants to say something to me, but I don't give her the chance. I just keep on walking and head out to the field because, now that it's freezing cold outside, Mrs. Schwartz is making us play soccer. Luckily, Kate and I are put on different teams, and we're both made to play goalie because of our long arms and legs. So our chances of having any interaction during PE in the next month are slim to none, and that's fine by me.

After art and English, I run to the cafeteria, scarf down a suspiciously crunchy bean burrito, and report to the library for my first day of study hall.

Mrs. Guzman knows me by name and doesn't look surprised that I'm there for mandatory study hall. "No one spends as much time as you and Miss Moreno in this library. I should have known it could only mean trouble," she says, as she stamps a card, my proof that I showed up and am on time.

I'm embarrassed and surprised that she caught on to our little rendezvous. I guess teachers pay more attention than I gave them credit for. "Well, you won't be seeing me during fifth period ever again," I say and sign my name on the special attendance sheet, meant to collect even more proof that I was there.

"Parents get your grades?"

"Yeah, my mom wasn't too happy. I'm surprised I'm allowed out of the house at all," I joke, but it appears Mrs. Guzman is done with small talk.

"Okay, Abbey, the rules are simple: no talking, no eating, no fun, and—this is a special rule for you—no poetry. Now go sit down and get to work."

The long wooden table she directs me to is placed in the center of the library, next to the floor-to-ceiling windows. When I was a free girl, I used to sit with my friends in the quad and laugh at the losers in the library. Now I'm on the inside, and everyone at lunch has a perfect view of me and the rest of Mrs. Guzman's inmates. How quickly things change.

Since my mom expects an A+ in Biology, I decide to focus my time studying for my chapter test on Friday. It's stuff I pretty much already know, so my studying mostly consists of writing down vocabulary words and definitions. But sooner than I expect, I lose track of my important task and begin to fantasize about my future adventures with Keeta.

"Abbey Brooks!" Mrs. Guzman shouts from her post by the front door. I jump a mile out of my skin. "I can revoke your stamped card and give you a blank one. Is that what you want?"

I flip through my book to look busy. "No, Mrs. Guzman."

"Then I suggest you get back to planet earth and start studying."

A few of my prison mates disguise their laughter with coughs and cover their smirks with the hoods of their sweatshirts. "Yes, Mrs. Guzman," I say, letting out a defeated sigh. And as I sit, writing the definition of homeostasis, my mind is decided: there's no way my life can get any worse.

CHAPTER TWENTY-TWO

My mom asks for my proof of study hall attendance the second I walk into the kitchen, which I guess is going to be her new way of saying hello until the quarter is over.

It's like coming home to the Big House these days, so I say, "Here you go, Warden," and give it to her.

She immediately posts it on the fridge.

"Seriously, you should consider giving up art to become a prison guard."

"Get out your homework," she says, pretending like I'm not hilarious.

"Come on, Mom," I whine, "it's a pain in my butt to work out here, literally. Can't I just sit in my room on my bed? I'll leave the door open."

This is when she leaves the room. Seconds later she comes back with a throw pillow from the couch and puts it on the hard dining-room chair. "There you go. Problem solved. Now get to work."

I try really hard to hate my mom, but of course, I'm a complete failure at that, too. But I have to wonder how someone who claims to love me can torture me so much. I know, she's doing it for my own good, but if she only knew how much it hurts to be away from Keeta, she might be a little less Cruella de Vil about the whole thing.

At least I still get to see Keeta before practice and on our away games, but the season's coming to an end, which means every part of my life is going to officially stink worse than the instant-tan lotion Kate made me try this past summer.

❖

A month of Suckfest-a-palooza finally passes, and I actually have something to look forward to. Valentine's Day is coming up, which is why I've been spending every spare second of my evenings, after my mom is in a deep sleep, working on Keeta's card. It's a masterpiece, thanks to my art teacher, Ms. Chafouleas. Once I finally dismounted my high horse (my mom's a real-life artist, after all) and started to pay attention in class, I noticed Ms. C actually has some mad skills, especially in the art of paper pop-ups.

My card is a large paper heart with the usual doilies and glitter on the outside, but when Keeta opens it, a picture of me will cartwheel across the middle. The caption underneath reads: "I'm head over heels for you!" Finally, I'm going to tell Keeta I love her, sort of.

❖

I get up early on Valentine's Day morning to curl my hair, apply eye makeup, and to dress up in a previously Kate-approved boobage-and-booty-boosting outfit: tight low-rise jeans and a low-cut, light-colored T-shirt with dark push-up bra combo. Then I carefully pack Keeta's card and the cookies I made in my backpack, the cookies I told my mom I was making for my teachers. *Pshyeah.* Whatever.

This morning, I practically skip to the performance hall. This is, by far, going to be the best Valentine's Day ever because, for the first time ever, I actually have a Valentine who isn't related to me.

I'm just about to burst into the room and say Keeta's name when I hear her sexy voice singing "Hey Jude," which is one of my favorite Beatles songs, while being accompanied by mediocre guitar strumming.

Then I hear, "*Así no.* Not like that, like this. *Ay,* let me show you."

My smile deflates like a two-day-old birthday balloon, and flashes of Stef's warning appear in my mind. Keeta said those exact words to me a million times in class. Her showing me how to play a chord or strum the strings gave her the excuse to wrap her arms around me and touch my hands.

Then more horrible strumming starts up again and Keeta says, "That's it. You've got it now. *Muy bien, chula.*"

Cutie? Who the hell is she calling cutie? That's when I storm into the room like I'm the FBI. Keeta and her little *chula* part quickly but remain calm like they aren't doing anything wrong.

"Hey, Abbey. *Qué onda?*" Keeta asks.

"What's going on? I'd like to know the same." I'm sure my face is quickly turning the color of an angry Valentine.

"*Pues aquí trabajando* with Osiris. You know, doing my job," Keeta says and walks toward the stage. "*Nada más*. Help me in the instrument room?"

I should turn around and get out of there, but I worked damn hard on my Valentine and I'm not leaving until I give it to her, so I follow her into the tiny room in the back.

She shuts the door behind us. "Happy Valentine's Day, Amara," she whispers, as her lips near mine.

I turn my head to avoid her poisonous kiss and push her away from me to get a better view of her lying face. "What are you doing with her? And don't tell me you're just helping her because I know that's bull, Keeta."

She takes my hands in hers and laughs. "Amara, are you getting jealous? You're so adorable." Then she leans in to try and kiss me again.

I turn away again so her kiss lands on my cheek. "Just tell me the truth, Keeta." Sure, I ask her for the truth, but in my head I'm praying that the truth is she loves me, and only me.

She steps away from me finally and leans against the metal shelves that hold the violins and clarinets. "The truth about what?"

"You and Osiris."

"Me and Osiris?" It's obvious to me she's stalling. My heart starts to break. Then she almost seems annoyed at my question. "Yeah, we flirt a little. So what?"

"Well, uh," I select my words carefully, "because we're going out and you supposedly *care about me*."

"I do care about you, Amara, but I mean, you and I are not exactly girlfriends."

The truth finally comes out and I can hardly stand how much it hurts. "What…what are we, then?" I ask, my voice shaking from pain and embarrassment while Stef's distant voice mocks me. *Don't think you're that special, Amara.* A tear escapes from my eye.

"Well, it's not like we ever talked about *not* seeing other people." She runs her fingers through her silky black hair. "I mean, I really like you, sweet Amara. You're a beautiful girl."

"That's all I am to you? Pretty?" Another tear rolls down my cheek.

"Come on, Amara, let's not do this. You know what you are to me."

My ears start to ring and I can hardly hear the rest of what she says.

"*Chale*, don't cry." She steps closer and touches my shoulder. "I guess I thought we had an understanding. I mean, I was dating Stef for a long time. I'm not ready to settle down again with one person. Can't we just be...I don't know, special friends?"

I wipe the tears off my face with the sleeve of my special occasion T-shirt, since there's no point in trying to look nice anymore, and my mascara leaves a black smear on the yellow material. "Keeta, I thought you said I was like no other girl and that when you are with me, you lose track of days and months. I don't understand."

"Amara..."

"Don't call me that if it doesn't mean anything."

"This is who I am, Abbey. I thought you understood."

I hear the distant bell and realize I have to hurry to get to algebra. But how can I leave things like they are? I stare at her (with eyes that I am sure are mascara-raccooned) and ask the one thing I have never dared to ask before. "Keeta, do you love me?"

I look at her and wait. I wait for that smile that's only meant for me. I wait for *Yes. I love you, Amara.*

Instead, Keeta puts her hands in her jean pockets and looks sheepishly at the floor. "Abbey, I really love being with you, and I want to keep on seeing you, but..."

As she speaks, I tune her out and finally see how right Garrett and Stef have been all along. "Here," I say and hand her the cookies and the Valentine and then leave the room. She doesn't try to stop me.

Thirty seconds later, I end up collapsing on the front steps of the school, sobbing into my hands. I know...dramatic. But if any other girl were in my Converse, she would have done the same.

The tardy bell rings, but I'm in no condition to go to algebra, and I can't hide in the bathroom because I will surely get caught, get a detention, and get escorted to class anyway, which would make my mom freak out again.

As a last resort, I consider ditching school. I pick my head up to see if there's anyone at the front gate. Dammit. Remembering Jenn's advice, I know there's no way of smooth-talking Mr. Cowen.

All hope is lost, so I start to cry again.

"Abbey, let's go talk in my office." Ms. Morvay's voice is like an angel's. "It's freezing out here," she says, as she lifts me up by my elbow.

I wipe my nose on my sleeve again and try to act like I'm fine, but there's no point in hiding it. I let her help me up and I follow her inside.

In the safety of her warm office, sitting in her comfy chair, I cry and cry until my head feels like it's been pounded with bricks. By the time I can actually talk to her, there are about three dozen soggy tissues in my lap and my eyes are nearly swollen shut.

"It's just, I don't understand what happened," I say between sobbing gasps.

Ms. Morvay gets another box of tissues from her cabinet and puts it in my lap. "Take your time."

I blow my nose and try to breathe like a normal person. "I mean, I don't know why we can't just be together. Why doesn't she love me?" I know I sound pathetic, but I really didn't think anything could hurt as much as when I lost my dad, which is a thought I'm too embarrassed to tell Ms. Morvay.

"I should have listened to my friends. I should've listened to Stef. I'm so stupid."

Ms. Morvay reaches out to touch my hand. "Oh, Abbey, you're not stupid. I can see that you really love her."

I look up stunned. "How did you know?"

"Well, let's just say I put two and two together. Anyway, you can't beat yourself up for falling in love with someone. Falling in love is a natural part of life, and sometimes we get hurt."

Hurt? This is more than that; my heart feels like it's been dragged over a cheese grater. But I don't know how to explain that feeling to her, so I nod.

"Do you want to tell me what happened?" Besides Garrett, Ms. Morvay is the only one I seem to be able to really talk to about this.

I nod again but can't seem to gather any words.

"Just start with the beginning, Abbey."

So that's what I do. I tell her about the deal Kate and I made about basketball. I tell her about making friends with Garrett and Stef. I tell her about how I flirted with Keeta behind Stef's back and about the kissing, the poetry, the necklace, and the special name Keeta has for me. I tell her about Kate and why we stopped talking and how I've been lying to my mom about every little thing. I even tell her about ditching fifth period but leave out the part where Tai abuses her office aide powers.

"It's like, I feel so far away from everything that was once familiar to me. You know, getting good grades, wanting to please my mom, and acting like my best friend's pet. At first, it was really cool, but now I feel like I've lost everything that used to really matter."

After I tell her all that, she furrows her brow a little. "Hmm," she says, in her counselor sort of way, then asks, "Abbey, if you could have one thing back that you think you have lost, what would it be?"

I tear apart a wet Kleenex in my lap and think about it. Maybe Ms. Morvay knows what I'll say, but it comes as a surprise to me that the first person to pop into my head isn't Keeta. I look at her when I finally say the truth. "My mom and Kate."

"It's not too late to get them back. You know that, right?"

"Yeah." And I know exactly what I have to do.

CHAPTER TWENTY-THREE

As I put on my ugly jersey before the game, I tell Garrett the tear-by-tear details of what happened between me and Keeta earlier in the day. She listens like a good friend should but seems pretty unsympathetic to my situation. After all, it isn't the first time a friend of hers has been flattened by the sledgehammer of Keeta's love.

"So, you guys never officially became girlfriends, huh?"

"I guess not. I just sort of went along with falling in love with her. I thought that was what she was doing, too." I put on one sock and then stop to rest my head on my knee. "I miss her so much."

Garrett rubs some of my vanilla-scented lotion on her legs. "Well, at least you know where you stand now. So are you guys still going to see each other?"

I've already spent the whole day in a hazy fog of despair because, in my head, Keeta and I broke up. And now Garrett's asking if Keeta and I are still together? "Did you not just hear what happened to me today?" I ask her like she's crazy.

"Well, you don't have to stop dating her just because she doesn't want to see you exclusively. It's not that unheard of, Abs. Get with the times."

"But I thought Keeta loved me. I thought I was, I don't know, special." I look in the mirror to make sure the word *sucker* isn't written across my forehead. Special? Ha.

"Abbey, Keeta does care about you."

"And how would you know?"

"She told me. We talked at lunch. She feels pretty badly about the way things ended with you guys this morning. Oh, I was waiting for the right time to give this to you. Here." She pulls a folded letter from her gym bag and tosses it on the bench. "She wanted me to give this to you, and you don't have to read it to me. I already read it." She gathers her hair into a ponytail, which is always perfect on the first try because that's how things are for beautiful people like Garrett. "Keeta still wants to see you. That's something, isn't it?"

"Yeah, I guess." I pick up the letter from the graffiti-laden bench and put it in the small pocket of my backpack with my guitar pick and A pendant. I have a game to play, and as much as I want to read Keeta's letter right this second, I know I have to get focused on kicking some butt on the court.

Garrett and I join our teammates on the bleachers to wait for our game, and I silently wonder how it would be to share Keeta with someone else. At least then I wouldn't have to hurt so much. Maybe I could live with the idea of only hurting a little.

As I watch Kate running the court during the freshman game, I'm reminded of my talk with Ms. Morvay. I hadn't noticed before tonight, but Kate is getting pretty darn good at basketball. I imagine how cool it would be if we were on the same team next year. We could dominate the entire city! But mostly I imagine how cool it would be if we could just be friends again. Then the buzzer signals the end of her game and the JV teams start to warm up.

During the first half of our game, I am a total embarrassment to my Nikes because I get three fouls for trying to snag rebounds over the backs of my opponents. Those are cheap fouls, but I can't help it if everyone on Sabino High's team is height challenged. Nevertheless, a foul is a foul and now I only have two left before getting benched for the rest of the game. But, seriously, me trying not to attack the basketball each time it's loose is like telling someone to not close their eyes when they sneeze: it's impossible.

And Coach Riley yelling at me every time I run by isn't helping matters at all. "Brooks, hustle!" "Brooks, screen!" "Brooks, rebound!" God, I swear if he doesn't stop it, I'll have my own commands for him. And they won't be pretty.

I finally get a chance to calm down during halftime because, as if he's sensed my homicidal irritation with him, Riley actually lets me leave the team meeting a couple minutes early to see the trainer about replacing my knee Band-Aid and to shoot around a bit. Then Keeta shows up to ruin my new relaxed mood.

She sits up at the top of the bleachers with Tai and Jenn and just hangs out with them like she isn't a cupid killer. For the first time, I detest the jersey number we share and wish I could trade with someone for the last two games of the season.

So, thanks to Keeta, I get all angry and crazy again and start off the third quarter by "accidentally" tripping one of my opponents, causing the whistles to blow.

"White twenty-one, pushing."

Then Garrett gets all over my case. "Crutch, get it together!"

I try to get it together as I have been instructed, but Sabino's number two is being such a pain in my ass, and part of me wonders if she isn't another one of Keeta's exes, which is why I let myself feel free to push her around and attempt to make her look like she's a sucky b-ball player. When I see my chance, I fake her out, dribble under the basket, and toss the ball over my shoulder showing off my no-look, reverse layup that I have been practicing with Keeta in the park. And I make it! Well, well. Maybe all those afternoons in the park with Keeta weren't a complete waste of time, after all.

Then number two starts to fight back. It begins with a little shoving, but then we both pull out all the sneaky moves when the refs have their backs turned. She's short and thick, so each time she drives to the basket, she lowers a shoulder and ploughs into me like a raging bull, making me hit the floor hard. I look to the ref who surely saw her intentional charge, but the ref claims it was clean. Then, with two minutes left in the game, number two "accidentally" elbows me hard in the face as we struggle for a rebound. A second later, we're both on the ground like dogs fighting for a bone. Finally, the ref whistles and our teammates break us up. I'm pulled up by Garrett and Eva. Along with my reddening eye, I'm bleeding from my knee again and my braid has totally come undone. I'm a mess, literally and figuratively.

"Pushing," the ref says. "White twenty-one."

"What!" I scream and throw the ball I won fair and square against the wood floor. The slam and my *what* echo throughout the gym.

The ref blows her whistle again and throws up her hands to form a T, a player's least favorite letter of the game. And there you have it: my first technical foul.

Coach Riley is too pissed off to even look my way, so I walk to the end of the bench, plop down on the folding chair, and cover my head with the towel Matti hands me. She also hands me an ice pack for my eye, but I tell her to leave me alone because I'm enjoying the intense pain and don't want it to stop. Finally, something else is causing me to hurt besides my broken heart.

Meanwhile, my mom, who came to the game to cheer me on and to prove that she still loves me (even though I'm pretty sure she is just spying on me), is probably confirming her drug addiction suspicions and calling the Solstice House this very second. To make things worse, Kate's actually watching the game, since Derrick got kicked off the team for his bad attitude and she doesn't have to rush off to watch him play. She's probably thinking that I suck at basketball and that it should have been her that got moved up to JV. And, to make things even *more* worse, Keeta is still up in the stands, along with the entire varsity team. She must be so embarrassed to ever have been my non-girlfriend. I hide my face until the game ends. We lose by ten.

On the way home, while we're stopped at a red light, my mom turns off her talk radio program and says, "Abbey Road."

I can't look at her.

"What happened to you out there? It's not just basketball making you so angry, is it?"

But I can't speak either.

By the time I get home, my head is killing me and, instead of heading straight to my room, I walk into the kitchen with my mom to get some water to wash down some ibuprofen. That's when she sees how bad it is.

"Oh my gosh, Abbey. Your eye. That's it, I'm taking you to urgent care." She grabs her purse and her keys.

I take them out of her hands. "Mom, I'm fine. It's just a black eye. Calm down."

"But what if—" she starts, but lets it go. "All right, but let me at least ice it."

I succumb and sit down because I don't have the energy to fight with anyone anymore. She gets a package of peas out of the freezer and wraps them in a soft dish towel, but I still wince when she places them on my face.

"Oh, honey. It looks so bad."

"Thanks, Mom."

"You know, I'm not sure I want you to play next year. It's too rough out there."

I laugh because I already know there's no way I'll let her take basketball from me. Sure, it didn't seem like it was my favorite activity tonight, but I do love the game. I love the feeling of flying downcourt, working up a sweat, sinking bank shots, seeing the faces of my opponents when I reject their shots, singing our songs of victory in the locker room, road trips to every corner of the desert, and even wearing that funky thirty-year-old polyester uniform. After all, it's what says I'm on the team. And, despite everything, I loved tonight's game and making that impossible shot. Then, thanks to my fanatical mind, the thought of loving basketball makes me think of loving Keeta, which makes me think about what Garrett said, which makes me mad all over again. I shouldn't have to share Keeta. If she cares enough about me, she should only want to be with me.

"Abbey Road"—my mom's voice puts the brakes on my manic train of thought—"what made you play like that tonight? Did something happen at school?"

I don't answer until I know where she's going with this.

She adjusts the peas a little and continues. "And what is it that has become more important to you than good grades, or best friends, or me? Is it basketball or something else?"

I shrug. "I don't know."

"That's not good enough."

"It's all I can say, Mom," I tell her, being honest. "I'm sorry."

She puts my hand over the peas to hold them in place so she can stand in front of me. "Okay, but there is one thing I need to know."

I consider fleeing the scene, but I'm also too tired to run from anyone anymore, so I stay. And since my guard is down, I actually consider telling her the truth. I can't believe it, but I'm actually hoping she'll finally ask the big question.

"What, Mom?"

She puts her hands on my shoulders and says, "If you ever feel like hurting yourself, or turning to drugs or anything like that, promise you'll come to me for help?"

All that panic for nothing. I didn't think I'd feel so disappointed, but I guess this stupid secret has worn me out. Why hasn't she seen the signs? Is she totally clueless or just too afraid to say it? I wish I could tell the difference, and I wish I had the guts to tell her myself. "Mom, I'm fine. I just got a little PMS-y tonight. Don't worry. I'm okay."

"Promise me, Abbey."

I take the peas off my stinging eye and look at her. "I promise."

❖

It's two thirty in the morning and I'm no closer to sleeping than I was at eleven or one. I take another dose of ibuprofen because my head is beginning to hurt again. And since there's no sign of sleep in my future, I take out the letter Keeta wrote to me and read it one more time:

Dear Amara,

I just opened the Valentine you made for me. Que bonita está, Amara. *It is by far the sweetest thing I've ever held, besides you, of course. I'm sorry we ran out of time this morning. I really wanted a chance to explain things better. So I guess I'll do it in this letter and hope that I can clear everything up. First, and most importantly, I meant all those things I told you, Amara. You are beautiful. When you're near me, my body melts like ice. I care so much about you and my heart is aching to see you so I can show you how much I care. I want to kiss you* de pies a cabeza; *from your head to your toes.*

Please understand, though, that I just can't commit to you right now. Can't we just keep on going like we were? Nothing's really that different. When I am with you, I am yours. I promise. We have something so cool. Why make it end, Amara? Eres mi amiga y mucho más. *I still want to be with you, but I guess you need to be the one to decide what will happen now.* Asi quedamos. *I mean it, whatever you want. But please remember that I never meant to hurt you.*

I'm thinking about you this very second and I'll be watching you tonight as you run up and down the court (you're so sexy in those little blue-and-white shorts). Don't forget, you're wearing my number. Make me proud.

Besos y abrazos,
Your Keeta

At three forty-five in the morning, I decide it's time to take action or I'll never get any sleep. I choose some plain stationery so I won't look too immature or desperate, and since I don't know what I'm going to write, it's important to stay neutral. I begin her letter very simply:

Dear Keeta,

Then I stare at the paper for about ten minutes.

What exactly am I supposed to say? *It's okay that you're a slut and are using me for cheap thrills.* No, probably not that. Part of me wonders why I'm even wondering. Of course we should go on seeing each other. But there's this nagging part of me that keeps on saying what I already know: I deserve better. I bite on my pen and crumple up my paper. Maybe I should start with something less complicated and work my way up to a decision. I throw the ball of paper across the room into the recycle bin next to my door: two points.

On a fresh piece of paper I draw a handy pro/con chart titled: Dating Keeta.

Cons:
1. She can't commit to me.
2. Why would I want to kiss her if she's maybe kissed someone else that same day? Gross.
3. She'll probably end up breaking my heart even more in the end.
4. I miss spending time with Kate.
5. I have to lie to my mom.
6. Uh, hello? 1.89 GPA?
7. I'm worth more than this.
8. She's never told me she loves me.

The con side ends up being a little longer than I intended. But now it's time for the good things.

Pros:
1. I love her.
2. I need her.
3. I want her.

I don't know what else to write so I add:

4. I love her.
5. I love her.
6. I love her.
7. I love her.
8. I love her.

There. Now at least they're even.

I re-read the con side, and as I get halfway through, it's finally obvious that I need to do something that I've been avoiding for too long, something even more important than Keeta's kisses.

I put my pro/con list aside and ready another piece of paper. This time, I don't chicken out. I know the letter has to be written. So I begin again, simply and honestly:

Dear Kate,

CHAPTER TWENTY-FOUR

Walking past the performance hall this morning feels like that shot I made last night: nearly impossible. After I pass its first set of double doors, I can't help but look back and wonder if Keeta and Osiris are already in the instrument room together. I finally make it up the front steps of Gila, and then to the hallway, and that's when I notice that the rest of Gila hasn't changed at all. In fact, "Oh my God. What happened to your eye?" is all anyone says to me as I walk through the hall. Good thing they can't see how badly my heart has been battered.

Since the second semester began, Kate's taken to using her own hall locker again because it's closer to her new classes, so I look over my shoulder to see if she's coming before I slip the letter in the ventilation slot and head over to algebra. As soon as I let it go, I feel a wave of regret. What if she won't take me back? What if she laughs when she reads it? What if it's too late?

Fifty-five minutes later, I rush over to PE to find Kate. I even take an extra-long time to dress out to make sure that if she does want to talk, she won't have to search all over for me. But then Mrs. Schwartz opens the locker room door and bellows, "Whoever is in here has exactly five seconds to get your butt on your number." Before she turns to leave, she catches a glimpse of my face. "Nice shiner, Brooks, but you're still playing today."

I roll my eyes. After I'm sure the locker room door is shut and she can't hear me, I say, "Whatever." I quickly tie my shoes and run outside, but there's still no sign of Kate, which means she's sick or ditching. Jenn didn't tell me she was sick, but then again, I think Jenn's finally given up on trying to get us back to being BFFs.

While Mrs. Schwartz distributes the softballs and mitts, I sneak a peek at the absence sheet the office sent her and see that Kate missed first period, too. I wonder what's wrong with her. Maybe Kate and Derrick are wandering through the mall, holding hands and wasting the day away at the movies. I find this possibility extremely irritating, but if we're going to be friends, I'm going to have to accept that Derrick's her boyfriend. In the meantime, I'm seriously going to flip out on the next person who asks about my eye.

My classes after PE are sort of a blur because I spend my time daydreaming about the one who shall not be named. After I'm released from English class, I speed-walk to the cafeteria for my five minute lunch. I look at the jock table for Kate in hopes that maybe she was just late to school, but I only see Dumbbell Derrick sitting there with his dumbbell friends. I guess she really is home sick. I'm relieved but disappointed that my apology hasn't reached her yet.

Though no one at the designated Losers R Us table in the library asks, "What the hell happened to your eye?" when I sit down, I do get a lot of raised eyebrows in my direction. But I just shrug, as if to say, "You know how it is," and they seem to understand.

For once, I don't really have any algebra or bio homework to do, so I take out *To Kill a Mockingbird*, which we have to read for English class.

I'm getting kind of into the book when, out of nowhere, someone kicks my shin. "Ouch!" I yelp, and Mrs. Guzman glares at me, so I look down again at my book. I can't take any more trouble or fighting.

Then two minutes later I get kicked again. This time, instead of saying a word, I look coldly up from my book. That's when I lock eyes with the girl sitting across from me, the one I told Garrett about last week when I was trying to figure out if I had been blessed with the gift of gaydar. But when I asked Garrett if she knew about a tank-top wearing girl with a green gem piercing in her nose who might be one of us, she laughed and said, "There isn't a lesbian phonebook that I can cross reference, Abbey. You'll just have to figure it out on your own." Some help she is.

Tank Top Girl grins at me and looks down at the empty table space between us, as if trying to signal something.

I look at the same spot but don't see anything special about it besides the carving of a pot leaf and wonder if she's asking if I want to buy some drugs. Out of the corner of my eye, though, I see Mrs. Guzman look up from her stack of books and glare our way again. I go back to my reading and try to ignore my throbbing shin.

Halfway through chapter two, I feel yet another kick, but at least she's eased up on the strength of it. I'm a little ticked off because I need to read three chapters of the book by tomorrow and my shin is definitely going to bruise. Then I wonder, *Is she flirting with me in some sort of first grade way or something?*

This time she gives up the subtle eye movements and mouths her message instead. "Under the table."

I use my peripheral vision, which has improved exponentially since I started high school, and look at Mrs. Guzman to see if the coast is clear. She's checking out books for a large group of students, so I duck down and pretend to search for something in my backpack.

From everyone else's viewpoint, it looks like Tank Top Girl is hunched over, working on math homework. But from under the table I see a different picture. She's actually slouched in her chair so she can extend her legs as far as possible in my direction. Held between her dusty Doc Martens boots is a note for me to retrieve.

Unfortunately, she's got really short legs, so I have to stretch superfar to get the note from her feet. I nearly fall out of my chair but come up unscathed with a folded piece of binder paper. Before opening it, I look across the table once more.

She smiles, which causes the tiny gem in her nose to catch a beam of fluorescent light and wink at me. Could it be? Could I have developed gaydar? Well, there's only one way to find out. I open the letter in my lap and read it:

Hey. I think you're cute, and I don't just mean that hardcore black eye. You were cute before you had it, too. Do you want to go out sometime? Hit me up if ya do. 345-3247
Signed, your fellow inmate, Mia

Yes! I've got the gift! How cool is that? But then her words hit me. Oh my God! She thinks I'm cute? What's wrong with her? Isn't it obvious I can't handle any more girl drama?

So instead of doing anything normal, like writing Mia back, I fold up the note and try to read the rest of my homework. The whole time, though, all I can think about is how not all the girl-loving girls at Gila play basketball and that I have confirmed, yes indeed, I have gaydar.

When the bell rings, I do all I can, besides hide under the table, to avoid eye contact with Mia. She gets the hint because she doesn't wait around for a response. I don't mean to be rude, but I really have no idea what to say to her. I mean, I still haven't even decided what to do about Keeta, and Mia's note confuses me even more. I do, however, walk with a lighter step to biology.

I'm about to slice open a raunchy-smelling crustacean when Tai comes into my classroom. I start to freak out for three very good reasons:

1. I don't want to go anywhere, especially not to see Keeta.
2. I don't want to see Keeta.
3. I really, really, really don't want to see Keeta.

So, I decide that hell no, I won't go.

I watch as Tai hands Mr. Zamora a note and pray it has nothing to do with me. He opens it, reads it to himself, and calls me up to his desk. Thanks for nothing, Universe.

I quickly look down at the crayfish pinned to my tray and pretend not to hear him. *No, no, no,* I repeat in my head, as if I have the power to change reality. Then he gets kind of annoyed because he practically shouts, "Abbey Brooks, come here now."

The rest of the class stares as I walk over to his desk. I pass Tai on the way, and when she looks me in the eye, she doesn't flash her usual sly smile. Instead, she gives me a sympathetic nod. My stomach instantly tightens and my head starts to spin because this is the same kind of look everyone gave me in the days, weeks, and months after my dad died.

CHAPTER TWENTY-FIVE

Twenty minutes after arriving at the school office and meeting up with my mom there, we arrive at St. Joseph's where Kate is recovering from the appendix surgery she had this morning.

I've twirled my hair into a rat's nest by the time Jenn comes out into the hall to tell me it's my turn to see Kate. Before she lets me pass, she puts her hand on my shoulder. "How important does it all seem now, Abbey?" she says, which is a pretty coldhearted thing to ask me, even for Jenn.

But maybe it's just her way of saying how much she loves her little sister, so I don't give her attitude. "Yeah, I know. You're right, again," I say before entering Kate's room.

I push the curtain aside and find Kate slightly propped up, sucking on small chunks of ice from a pink plastic cup. "Hey, Abbey," she says in a slurred, drugged way.

"Hey, Kate." I check out her room and try to think of something else to say. "Wow, they really knocked their heads against the wall when they decorated this place."

"Yeah. God, your eye looks like crap."

"Thanks."

"You can come closer, Abbey. You can't catch appendicitis, you know."

"I know. I just wasn't sure if you wanted to see me. I mean, after the way I've been acting." I inch a little closer and touch the foot of her bed. I look at Kate with the intent of saying something meaningful, but instead I fiddle with the edge of her blue blanket and concentrate on not crying.

"Sit down," she says, motioning to the chair next to her. "You're making me nervous."

We sit in silence at first, but then I finally say it: "I'm sorry, Kate. Like really, really sorry."

I don't know who starts crying first, but the waterworks are turned on full blast, and we go through the tiny box of Kleenex on her bedside table in a matter of seconds.

"Abbey, I'm the sorry one," Kate says after she blows her nose, which I guess really hurts her stomach because she whines afterward. "Can we have a do-over? But this time be totally honest with each other?"

"Deal," I say. "I'll start."

She adjusts her pillows a little and says, "Okay. I'm ready."

I take in a deep breath and say it for the first time to anyone. "Um, Kate…I like girls and I am pretty sure I'm…gay."

"No way," she says and chuckles a little, but only because it would probably hurt too much to bust out a full-blown laugh.

Not the reaction I was hoping for, but then I start laughing, too.

"I'm sorry," she wipes the laughter tears from her eyes, "you just looked so serious."

"Well, that *was* my first time saying it to anyone, you know." I hope she appreciates the honor, or whatever you would call coming out to someone.

"Sorry I laughed," she says, but giggles again. I figure it's the drugs and let her off the hook. "You did a good job of it."

I roll my eyes. "Thanks, butthead."

"Okay," she tosses the used tissues on the side table. "I guess it's my turn."

"Yep, lay it on me."

"Well, since we're being totally honest, it wasn't Derrick who didn't want me to spend the night anymore. It was me."

I nod but look away from her. I knew it all along, but that doesn't take the sting out of her words.

"Don't be mad, Abbey. I was just freaked out. I'm sorry."

I remind myself of what I wrote in the letter to Kate; we have to forgive and forget. "It's okay. I know it must have been weird. I mean, I was freaking out, too. Speaking of Derrick," *be nice, Abbey*, "where is he?"

She turns her head toward the window, but I can still see her eyes well up with tears. "You won't be seeing him around me anymore."

"Oh?" I try not to sound relieved.

"Don't sound too disappointed, Abbey." I guess I still can't fool her. Then she says, "I know, I know, he was a douche bag."

"Yeah, only slightly."

"If I had the strength, I'd throw this ice in your face."

"Did you guys ever end up, you know?"

"No, thank God. He kept on wanting to and we came pretty close one night, but right when he was, you know…"

"No, I have no idea."

Kate rolls her eyes and whispers, "You know, putting the raincoat on his Jimmy."

My confusion is clear.

"Condom, Abbey. He was putting on a condom. Anyway, Jenn opens the basement door and tells us to knock off all the heavy breathing because we're fogging up the windows, which pretty much ruined the mood."

"Oh my God. She's so crazy."

"I know." Kate fiddles with the empty tissue box. "But I'm glad she did it. He's such a loser. It turns out he was seeing someone from a different school at the same time we were dating. Can you believe that?"

I clear my throat. "Well, yeah. I always knew he was scum."

"I know, but I was too in love to see what he was really like. I guess it felt so good to be loved." Her next words seem to be pulled from my own mouth. "It was like if I wasn't with him, I couldn't breathe."

"Yeah," I agree, thinking that maybe Kate and I aren't that different after all.

"Speaking of being in love with all the wrong people, how is Keeta? Have you guys, you know, done it?"

"Oh my God, Kate," I look over my shoulder. "Shut up."

She taps her fingers on the thin mattress and waits for an answer.

"No, we haven't had sex yet." I'm sure my face turns crimson. "We've come close, too, but…wait, what do you know about Keeta and her being one of the wrong people?"

"Well, all I know is what Jenn tells me, and from what I hear, Keeta's quite the player, and I'm not talking about basketball or guitar.

But I also know, by the way you look right now, you're hopelessly in love with her and you don't really care what everyone else says."

"Did the surgery heighten your mind-reading abilities or something?"

She smiles and says, "When in the world will you get it through your thick skull, girl? A best friend can always tell."

❖

It's after nine when my mom and I get home from the hospital. We're both too tired and hungry to talk, so we eat some leftover casserole and listen to the kitchen clock tick off the seconds. When we hear the knock at the door, we both jump.

"Who in the world?" My mom turns on the porch light, peeks through the small window, then opens the door.

I nearly spit my pasta across the room.

"Hi, Mrs. Brooks," Keeta says. "Uh, I would have called, but I know Abbey is grounded from the phone after nine."

"Oh, that's okay," my mom says. "Come on in."

No, no, no. I look around the kitchen and am so embarrassed at the mess. Breakfast dishes in the sink, my backpack and gym bag on the floor, my lunch study hall cards plastered on our fridge, and a layer of dust on everything. She'll be so grossed out she won't even want to sit down.

As Keeta enters, she continues to explain why she's here. "I heard about what happened to Kate today and was wondering if Abbey wanted me to get her homework tomorrow so she could hang out with Kate at the hospital."

"That's so thoughtful, Keeta," Mom says, and then they both enter the kitchen. "We're just having some dinner. Are you hungry?"

When they come in, I'm at the sink filling it up with hot water and dirty dishes to give Keeta the impression that we aren't slobs. Seeing Keeta in my kitchen is beyond strange, and at first I want to ignore her, but that would be suspicious, so instead I hide my uneasiness with politeness. "Keeta? What a surprise. What are you doing here? Would you like something to drink?" I move robotically through the kitchen while keeping an eye on my mom. Despite my efforts, I'm sure my mom can tell that Keeta and I have been kissing buddies or whatever you would call us.

My mom lets out a loud yawn.

I think Keeta takes this as a hint. "Thanks, Abbey, but I better go. I just wanted to see if you needed anything."

"Gosh, sorry I'm so tired," my mom says as she yawns again. "Long day, I guess. You can stay for a little bit, Keeta. I'm off to bed."

This is the most shocking thing to come out of my mom's mouth since she told me I was grounded, so I stare at her like she's just told me it's okay if I drop out of school and have six babies. "Are you sure?" I finally manage to ask.

"Yep, just don't stay up too late." Then my mom kisses my cheek. "'Night, Abbey Road," she says, before walking down the hallway to her room.

I still have Keeta's glass of water in my hand, but I'm frozen in place by the prospect of spending time with her in my house. And I might have stood there all night staring down the empty hallway if Keeta hadn't walked over, removed the glass from my hands, and placed it down on the table. "So, is Kate all right?"

I step back from Keeta because my brain and heart are still having a bloody cagefight inside me. Plus, I totally expect my mom to run down the hall like the paparazzi and catch me and Keeta in an act of intimacy. Then I wonder what my mom would do if she saw us together. But I'll have to worry about that later. Right now, I have more important matters at hand: Should I kiss Keeta or show her the door?

"Yeah, she's fine now," I say. "They got her appendix out just in time. The best part is we're friends again. I really missed her."

"I bet you did. A best friend is hard to come by." Then that sneaky Keeta takes my hand in hers. "Amara?"

Don't say that unless you mean it. "Yeah?"

"I already miss you so much."

I look at my hand in hers and think about what Kate said—that when she was with Derrick, her whole world disappeared. Like me, she probably couldn't see beyond his face, even though she knew what a jerk he was. And she knew she deserved better, but she also didn't want to lose him, just like I don't want to lose Keeta. But then I think about Keeta's soft kisses and her arms around me and I forget all the lessons I've learned today.

"Abbey," Keeta whispers, "it's your call." Then she gives me that look. The one I can never resist. The one that got me in this mess in the first place.

And I finally come to a decision.

"Come on," I say and pull her down the hall by her T-shirt. "I guess it's only fair if I show you my room, too."

I shut and lock the door behind us, knowing this is probably the wrong thing to do, but I'm a big girl now and am willing to face the consequences.

I watch closely as Keeta glances around my giant spoiled-brat of a room, taking in glimpses of my cheesy life. I look around, too. The Beatles and Marilyn Monroe posters aren't that bad, but the collection of rocks and the giant plant anatomy poster on the wall seem so nerdy. I quickly clean up my bedside table so as not to have her see any really embarrassing items, like pro/con lists about whether or not I should keep dating her.

Then she blows out a long, soft whistle. "You *are* a smarty-pants! Look at these grades," she whispers.

I never took down my report cards from junior high like Kate had instructed, but I'm glad Keeta sees that I'm not some dumb blonde she can push around. "Yeah, that's right. And you don't have to whisper, my mom's out cold thanks to Ambien."

"You'll probably get into any college you want, huh?"

"It's not that big of a deal. It's just middle school and I didn't have a life, that's all." I plop down on my bed but then realize I shouldn't be too presumptuous. Before I can get up, Keeta walks over to me and gently pushes me on my back, which is really what I was secretly hoping she'd do anyway.

She lies down next to me and plays with my hair, then my ear. I prepare for total body meltdown in ten...nine...eight...

"Amara?" she whispers.

Seven...six...five...four..."Yes, Keeta?" It's like that horrible day never happened. It's like we've never been apart.

"I'm sorry I wasn't respectful of your time before. From now on"—she leans in and kisses my cheek—"I promise to let you do your homework without distraction from me." She kisses her way slowly down to my neck. "You just tell me, 'Keeta, I can't see you. I have to study,' and I will totally understand." She reaches over and turns off the light. "Okay, *mi amor*?"

Three...two...one...total body meltdown complete. Zero signs of intelligent life present. So instead of answering her, I pull her body closer to mine.

We kiss and move to a rhythm only we can hear. My shirt is the first to go, and then her shirt gets tossed across the room, too. I love the feeling of our nearly naked bodies pressed together, but I think she knows I'm still not quite ready for the next step. So we enjoy each other like this for a while, and then she gives me one last kiss and holds me in her arms. As we lie there looking up at my glow-in-the-dark stars, I tell myself what I wish I could tell everyone else. Keeta does love me. She's honest, kind, beautiful, and patient. She's perfect.

"Are you insane?" Kate yells from her own canopy bed where she'll have to stay for a few more days to recover. "With your mom in the next room?"

"Kate, it's not like we did it or anything. Stop spazzing out on me."

"What if your mom found you two in bed like that?"

"I locked the door. Besides, she didn't find us, so what's the big deal?" I wish I could take my secret back. I should've paced myself, since Kate and I are barely back on speaking terms. I should have known better than to bring up Keeta.

Kate rolls her eyes and takes another slurp of the soup her mom made for her. "This is so gross, Abbey. I need a fruit slushie. Make your mom stop at Eegee's and get me one the next time you guys come over, okay?"

"Yeah, sure."

"Don't forget—half flavor of the month, half lemon."

She covers the bowl with her napkin and frowns at it, which is my cue to take it away. "You know," she says, "she's going to break your heart. This whole 'I like you, but I can't commit' thing is total bs, and I'm surprised you're putting up with it."

I don't really know what to say to that. I mean, of course Kate is right. Of course, if I can't have Keeta to myself, I'll never be completely happy. But if I can have some of her, I might be sort of happy, and that feels better than utterly miserable.

"You just don't get it," I say, but I don't want to fight, so I start over. "It's just that I like spending time with her, too. So, why not enjoy what I can?"

She shrugs her shoulders. "Well, I guess you know what's best for you. I'll mind my own business then. But promise me one thing."

"What?"

"Don't lose yourself in her because, trust me, it's really freakin' hard to find your way back."

CHAPTER TWENTY-SIX

As Garrett and I warm up at Monday's practice, I tell her about my Friday-night reunion with Keeta, and then how I snuck Keeta in my window Sunday night to hang out some more after my mom fell asleep.

But just like Kate, Garrett quickly questions my sanity. She makes a three-pointer and asks, "So, with one more week before you're off being grounded, you risk it all?"

"Dude, I'm telling you, nothing wakes my mom up. So it's cool. It's like I have the whole place to myself after she pops that magic pill."

She passes me the ball. I shoot a jump shot from the top of the key. I swish it, rebound the ball, and pass it to her.

"So I guess you're over this whole Keeta-seeing-other-girls thing. That was quick." She easily sinks another three-pointer. "Speaking of which, Stef called me yesterday."

"Nice shot," I say avoiding Garrett's last statement. I pass the ball to her again.

"She's fine, in case you were wondering." She dribbles in for a layup and gets her own rebound. "She asked about you, wondered if you were still stupid enough to be with Keeta."

I steal the ball out of her hands and dribble to the three-point line. "And?" I shoot and completely air ball it.

"I told her you were, but I didn't tell her you were a willing participant in Keeta's harem, or whatever it is you guys have arranged."

"Shut up, G. You're the one who told me to go for it. Besides, it's not that big a deal. I mean, when she's with me, it's just the two of us."

Then I almost tell her Keeta's sneaking over again tonight, but Garrett seems annoyed with the topic, so I keep it to myself.

Coach Riley calls us to the baseline, and we line up for our final day of torture. I can't believe it's all coming to an end. Who knew playing this game would mean so much to me? It's like every time I slip on that polyester jersey and walk onto the hardwood court, I feel right at home. Sure, my freshman year isn't over, but I feel like a totally different person already. Suddenly, being tall is a gift, not a curse that makes buying pants impossible. I feel a little more graceful and a little more confident every time I walk onto this court and through the halls of Gila. I guess Kate didn't have to worry after all. I mean, look at me now: push-up bra, lip gloss, sort-of girlfriend, playing basketball, and having fun. I totally own this freshman year.

My mom enters the kitchen with an armload of groceries. "You're starting on your homework already?"

"I know it's hard to believe," I say, but what I don't say is I'm in a hurry so I can entertain my lesbian love muffin tonight while my mom slumbers.

My apparent diligence pays off, too, because for the first time in weeks, part of her after-school greeting doesn't include, "Where's your stamped library card?" Instead, she says, "You want a snack?"

"Mmm, yes please. I'm starving." I'm not sure when the growth spurts will stop, but at this rate I'm going to be the first girl at Gila High to dunk.

She makes me a PB and J sandwich and places it in front of me. Then she asks, "You want to catch a movie tonight? I think there's a new comedy playing at the Rio."

I bite an extra-big piece of my sandwich so I can think up a better response than, "Oh, sorry, Mom. My secret non-girlfriend is sneaking over tonight to make out with me for a while." But the best thing I can come up with is, "Thanks, Mom, but I think I'll go to bed early tonight. You know, since tomorrow's our last game and all."

She smiles and says, "Oh, okay," but I recognize that sad look in her eyes, which means I feel horrible.

"Maybe next week?" I say.

"Sure, honey." She pats my head and leaves me to my mountain of homework and guilt. I'm a bad, bad, bad daughter…again.

I get over the guilt surprisingly fast and, after dinner, I draw myself a bath. I want to smell delicious for Keeta, so I pour in three extra capfuls of cucumber-melon bubble bath, which causes such an overflow of bubbles that I have to spend twenty minutes trying to wash them down the drain when I'm done. Then I brush my teeth and rinse my mouth out two times with extra strength minty mouthwash. The evening is going to be perfect.

But by the time eleven o'clock rolls around, I'm already tired of practicing my surprised happy look that I'm going to have when Keeta taps on my window to be let in. And by the time eleven thirty rolls around, I'm tired of sitting upright in bed so as not to mess up my perfectly brushed hair. And at midnight, I'm just plain tired. Since I've been grounded for so long, I've gotten used to going to bed at ten every night. I think I finally pass out at around one o'clock.

❖

When I wake up at six o'clock this morning, my hair is a mess, my breath is back to normal, and my face has that greasy sheen that I'm unfortunately becoming accustomed to as I progress in my teen years. I roll over, just to make sure, but my bed is empty and the window closed.

I hate myself for falling asleep. What if she came by and I didn't hear her? What if she stood out in the cold, dark night wondering what she did to be treated so badly? Then I wonder if she ever came by at all.

I rush through my usual routine and call Jenn to cancel my morning pickup. I don't want Keeta to get the slightest impression that I've blown her off. So I bundle up in a couple of sweatshirts, jump on my bike, and ride to school to wait for Keeta.

I'm sitting on the curb in front of the performance hall freezing my butt off and rehearsing my apology when I see Keeta get out of a car that isn't Tai's. Then Osiris gets out and takes off for the main hall. I'm suddenly no longer cold.

Keeta sees me and walks over. "Hey, you," she says and then sits down on the steps and puts her arm around me to pull me closer. I let her, too, but I refuse to look at her. She doesn't even say anything like, *I'm sorry I'm such a self-centered hoochie-mama bitch.* She just sits there, like we're waiting for a fireworks show to start. So I finally speak. "Keeta, why didn't you come over?"

She hugs me closer. "I'm sorry. Something came up and I couldn't call your cell since your mom had it."

I only halfway believe her. "Fine, but where were you?" Keeta doesn't get a chance to answer before I ask my next question. "With her, right?" I shrug off her arm and turn my back to her.

Then Keeta says, "Amara, she just gave me a ride to school, I swear. Come on, I'll make last night up to you, okay?"

She could be telling the truth about Osiris, but it seems unlikely. That's when I realize I have two choices: let it go, or let Keeta go. The decision seems too grown up for me, and I miss the days when all I had to think about was what game to bring to Kate's house for our slumber party. I listen to the desert birds wake up and watch the sun illuminate the campus, turning everything pink. I make a decision then, one I know I might regret.

"Well," I say and force a smile on my face, "you owe me big time, you jerk. I even took a bubble bath for you."

"Oh, man, are you serious? I missed that? Okay, I promise I'll make it up to you. What are you doing Saturday night?"

"Going to the movies with Kate." My mention of Kate's name instantly reminds me of her wise words: *Keeta's just going to end up breaking your heart in the end.*

"And after that?" Keeta starts playing with my hair with one hand and slyly slips her other hand up my sweatshirt.

"God, your hand feels like a popsicle," I say, pushing her off me, but in a playful way. "Anyway, after going to the movies with Kate, I think I'll be hitting the clubs. You know, I'm a really big deal around here."

She rests her chin on my shoulder and sighs. "You're not going to make this easy on me, are you?"

Students are starting to take over campus like an army of ants and I don't feel like dealing with their stares, so I get up and stand over Keeta. "I'll check my schedule, Ms. Moreno, and have my people get back to you."

She holds her hand to her heart and falls back onto the gum-splattered entrance of the performance hall. "Oh, you're cruel, but I deserve it." By the time she sits up again, I'm already half way across the courtyard. "I'll wait for your call like a humble servant," she shouts.

I look over my shoulder and flash her a confident, movie-star smile then head to class.

❖

Our last game is against Saguaro again, but this time we're on their court. I've learned there's something wonderful about beating a team on their own turf, so I'm looking forward to pummeling them. This is the team with The Fridge and the team with all of Keeta's ex-flings, so I want to seriously kick their butts. And maybe I'll impress Keeta so much tonight she'll forget about all the other girls and make me her one and only. You never know, it could happen.

In the first quarter, I score five baskets and make The Fridge foul me three times. I only miss one out of six free throws, and Riley actually looks proud. I look up to see if Keeta sees me and smile when she and Tai give two thumbs up for my performance. But Saguaro is scoring big time, too. Without Stef, our best outside shooter, they're able to keep up without any problems.

"Time to run Dust Devil," coach says at the halftime locker-room meeting.

There's a serious hush in the room. Dust Devil is an offensive play that's a thousand times more complicated than conjugating irregular verbs in Spanish. But we've practiced it so much that when I'm not dreaming about my dad or Keeta, I'm dreaming about this play.

"Garrett, you're going to take the three when it's there. I saw you practicing yesterday. I know you can do it." Then Coach points to me. "Abbey, if Garrett misses, I better not see any girl wearing red getting that ball. Got it?"

"Yes, sir."

"Natalie, look inside for Abbey and Tori, and don't forget to look weak side. We can win this, ladies, but only if you want it. Do you want it?"

"Yeah!" we shout in unison.

"I can't hear you," he yells back.

"Yeah!" we scream again.

"Hands in!"

We squish together and put our hands in the middle. One look around the circle and I know we have the game in the bag. My teammates have never looked so determined.

With Dust Devil in full swing, the second half of the game is so much better than the first. Every time Saguaro scores two points, we come back with a quick jump shot or three-pointer from downtown. Seriously, Garrett's threes are sinking like she's just kicking it at home, tossing a pair of socks in the laundry hamper.

And if anyone does miss a shot, I snag every rebound I can. Then, once the ball is in my hands, the only thing I have to decide is if I'm going to turn and shoot, dribble in for a layup, or pump fake and pass to Tori or Eva. Though The Fridge keeps trying to knock me down, not even she can keep me from scoring tonight. And, thanks to the ref's new ability to actually see what's going on, The Fridge fouls out at the end of the third quarter. Maybe it's the reputation I got from the last time we played, or maybe it's my purplish-greenish-yellowish bruised eye, but it feels like everyone is letting me do what I want out here, and I'm loving it. Being in control of the court is almost as good as being in control of my love life.

With three minutes left in the game, Coach calls one last time-out. We're up by seventeen points, so the game is basically over. "Abbey, Garrett, Tori, Nat, Eva, you guys are out," he says, as our subs line up to be let in. "Great job out there."

My big ego nearly causes me to protest, but he's right. We should let the second string in for a while. Besides, I'm drenched in sweat and totally exhausted.

Matti, whom I have decided—with the help of my gaydar—is a total DIT (Dyke in Training), gives us towels and water, and we sit back to enjoy the rest of game.

"Man, you guys kicked serious ass out there," Tai says and rubs Garrett's shoulders like she's a champion fighter, which she kind of is.

"Don't, I'm all sweaty," Garrett says, slapping Tai's hand away, but then she leans back and allows Tai to hug her. "Babe, did you see my three-pointers?"

"*See* them? I think the guy from ESPN is already playing them on tonight's edition of *Slam Dunk*. And Abbey...holy drop shot, girl. Where did you learn that move?"

"Oh, you know, I just picked it up," I say, keeping a serious face for a second, but I can't hold it because I feel like squealing. I've never felt so good about anything I've done.

"Puh-leeze, I taught her everything she knows," Keeta says as she settles on the bleachers behind me and joins the conversation. She sits with her legs spread apart, so I make myself comfortable as I lean back into her and smile up at her. She puts her arms around me and gives me a squeeze. She doesn't even care that I'm all sweaty. "You rocked, Amara," she whispers.

Garrett clears her throat and bumps my leg with her knee, and that's all I need to slap myself back into reality. What the hell am I doing? My mom's probably watching us. I quickly sit up and push Keeta away, pretending I don't want her attention.

Keeta interprets my actions as playing hard to get. So she grabs my wrists and says, "Oh, she's a feisty one tonight, Tai."

I struggle to try and free myself, but when she won't let go, I whisper, "Let go, Keeta. My mom's here."

She looks over her shoulder and sees what I mean. My mom's sitting about seven bleacher steps away, talking to Kate.

"My bad," Keeta says and laughs like it's no big deal. "Well, come on, Tai. We've got to get ready so we can show our girls how the *real* women at Gila High play basketball."

"Whatever, Keeta," Garrett says and shoves them both. "You guys are losers."

As they leave for the locker room, Keeta slips a note onto my lap. But before I can read it, the buzzer goes off announcing the end of our game, so I have to shove it in my sock and save it for later.

My teammates and I all high-five each other, then huddle up together to give a shout-out to the opposing team. We line up, and as I slap each one of the Saguaro girls' hands, I'm already looking forward to next year. I can't wait to stomp them again. Then I'm face to face with The Fridge. I brace myself for a really hard high-five, but instead she moves her hand to the side so I miss her altogether. This only makes me hate her even more.

After Coach's talk, Kate and I get cleaned up because my mom wants to take us out for a celebratory pizza at Magpies. My mom invites Jenn to join us after she plays, but Jenn politely declines and says that after her game, the varsity team has plans to celebrate the end of the season, which really means they're going to go drink Dr Pepper and Bacardi in an undisclosed desert lot near Jenn's house. Keeta's going to be there, so I'm bummed out about not being invited to their party, but it's better this way. I mean, I kind of owe it to both my mom and Kate to spend a little time with them.

But I still need a little Keeta fix before I leave the gym, so I sneak off to the bathroom and read Keeta's letter before we leave:

A,

Cómo estás, preciosa? It's halftime and I have been lucky enough to spend the previous half hour admiring your strength and beauty as you play. You are like a graceful ballerina, a wild stallion, and a ferocious lion all wrapped up in one. It's weird, but out there on the court, I see a side of you that makes me like you even more. But mostly I see how passionate you get about rebounding. Lol. What a turn-on, by the way.

So I know I really screwed up the other night, and I'm sorry I made you wait up for me. I really do want to make it up to you, though, and I will. Actually, I want to make you feel like you do when you're on the court, which I feel very confident I can do, if you'll just give me the chance. (wink, wink)

Well, there you are again in my old twenty-one jersey. Your sexy body is getting it all sweaty, which also kind of turns me on. Hmmm, I am seeing a pattern here. Man, you are in my head, Amara.

Besos all over, lover girl,
(especially on that spot on your neck that makes you moan)
K

I close my eyes and smile. I like being admired. I like being watched. And part of me likes that I somehow manage to turn Keeta on.

"So," Kate says as the two of us wait in line to order the pizza, "does your mom know?"

"About what?"

Kate rolls her eyes. "Come on, Abbey. You know."

I look over my shoulder to make sure my mom's still sitting in the booth across the restaurant. "God, I hope not. Why?"

"I'm just wondering. I mean, you were getting pretty friendly with Keeta at the end of the game. What was that all about?"

"Oh, yeah. I totally don't know why I did that. Did my mom see us?"

"I don't think so, but you have me to thank. I had to distract her with gruesome details of how the staples on my stomach are itching."

I order the pizza and we get our cups for the soda machine. "Thanks, Kate. I owe you one."

"So when *are* you going to tell her, Abbey? I mean, take it from me, it sucks finding out from someone else or, you know, another way. Your mom's so cool. What are you so afraid of?"

"What am I supposed to do, Kate? Just sit down at dinner one night and drop the bomb on her? 'Good evening, Mother, pass the potatoes, and by the way, I like to kiss girls.' You don't get it. It's not that easy."

"Well, you have to do something. Besides, she might already know and she's just waiting for you to say something."

"I know, okay?" *Don't get pissy and defensive*, I tell myself, *she's just trying to help.* "I'll do it when I'm ready. I promise."

We walk back to the table and sit down with my mom, who looks at me, then at Kate, and then back to me. "What's wrong? Are they out of black olives or something? You guys look so serious."

I still feel irritated from Kate's nagging, so I decide to mess with her a little bit. "It's worse than that," I say and then swallow like I'm trying not to cry. "Mom, I have something to tell you. Brace yourself, this may be sort of shocking."

Kate looks over at me with giant Chihuahua-like eyes popping out of her head.

"You're not going to like what I have to tell you," I say. Now Kate's squirming in her chair and gulping down Diet Coke. "But, well, I'm just going to say it…They're out of mushrooms!" I fake sob into my hands.

CHAPTER TWENTY-SEVEN

My mom's sitting at the kitchen table playing Scrabble by herself when I get home from school today. This is a pretty normal scene, but this is no ordinary day; this is my day of reckoning. This is report card day, and my mom actually trusts me enough to let me get it from the mailbox myself.

"Well, let's see it," she says, as soon as I dump my stuff on the couch.

I know what she wants but feel like messing with her, so I say, "I haven't got the faintest idea what you're referring to," in my best Southern belle accent. Of course, I've already hidden the report card in my pocket and I know exactly how I've done, but instead of giving it to her, I open the cupboard and rummage around for a snack, finally finding a forgotten granola bar behind a jar of spaghetti sauce.

She puts out her hand and clears her throat, but at least she's smiling. "Do I have to tickle you for it?"

"Hey, let's not get crazy." I pull it out of its hiding spot and place it in her hand. "You can have it, but I'm sorry to say it isn't exactly what you wanted."

My mom slips on her reading glasses and slowly unfolds my report card. She glances over the class titles and grades, and then puts her hand over her mouth to hide her smile.

I crunch on another bite of bar. "Go ahead and say it because I already know I rock."

She squeezes me so hard that I nearly choke. "I'm so proud of you. Straight As, wow! You even got an A+ in Art and Biology."

"Well, it helps to have an amazing artist as your mom."

"I'm so proud of you."

"Yeah, yeah, I'm incredible, but let's talk about these rules." I tap the fridge of doom. There isn't an inch of the door visible behind all the stamped library cards she insisted on posting. "Am I a free woman again?"

"Abbey Road, it's good to have you back. Yes, you are a free woman. But—"

"I know, I know. Don't let it happen again."

Before she gets all teary-eyed and mushy, I break from her arms, whip out my cell phone, and race to my room, already dialing Keeta's number. "Free at last! Free at last!" I scream before Keeta picks up at her end of the line.

A couple of weeks after being set free from my mom's house rules, Kate and I are lounging in the quad at lunch like lazy lizards in the April spring sun. I'm feeling reflective and satisfied with life. Keeta and I have been spending more time together again, and my mom trusts me. Even better, Kate and I are back to being fulltime BFFs with no chance of ever parting. "Man, we've come a long way this year, Kate."

She laughs but then agrees. "No doubt."

"Don't you feel different? Like, in a good way?" I ask.

"Hmm," she contemplates, "I guess, but mostly I feel stupid. Did you not notice that I wore a pink shirt with blue flip flops today? On a Monday no less? Disappointing."

So, there we are, reclined with our backpacks propping up our heads and our notebooks open on our faces, shading them from the sun's harsh rays. I'm thinking about Keeta (of course) and how there's only one quarter left of the school year, which means Keeta will graduate and leave me behind. I did finally gather up the nerve to ask Keeta about her post-high-school plans, but she said she didn't want to talk about it and that I should stop trying to distract her while she was writing her name on my stomach in permanent marker. I also noticed a pile of unopened envelopes from colleges stacked up by her stereo and wanted to ask why she was avoiding them, but I knew better. Keeta will only talk about stuff on her terms. It took her four months to tell me why she had to work so much; she basically has to pay the rent and the bills for her apartment ever since her *nana* injured her hip.

Back on the quad, a shadow falls over my notebook-covered face. I know it isn't just a random student or Keeta (she's at a senior class meeting in the gym) or a cloud passing by because the person is hovering over me.

When I peek out from under my notebook and see who it is, I feel mega-guilty and a little embarrassed. It's Mia, the girl from study hall who said I was cute. After she wrote me that crazy note, though, I did such a good job avoiding her that I sort of forgot how I blew her off. "Oh hi, Mia."

"Hey," she says and sits down on the grass next to me.

Apparently this isn't going to be a quick visit, so I remove the notebook from my head and sit up. "So, you're out, too?"

She looks at me in a surprised sort of way. "Too? Well, yes, most people know about me."

"I mean, out of study hall. Did your mom let you off the hook?" I clarify.

"Oh, that. Yeah, my mom could give a crap about my grades, or me. Ms. Morvay's the one making me go, but I talked her down to twice a week. I can be very persuasive."

Behind me, Kate clears her throat and elbows me in the back.

"This is my friend, Kate. Kate, this is Mia."

"Mia Thurber." She leans forward and shakes Kate's hand. "You're a junior, right?"

"All right, Mia. There's no need to flatter her. She has a big enough ego as it is." But it's already too late.

"I approve," Kate says to me, then giggles while she packs up her things.

"Where are you going?" I say and telepathically beg her to stay, but she's too busy acting like a junior to notice.

"Gotta find Sarah. See you later, Abbey. Call me!" As she walks off, she tosses aside her long brunette hair and shakes her butt a little more than usual. Oh God, it's going to take a lot of effort to get her back down to earth.

"I didn't mean to interrupt you guys," Mia says looking at me with her intense green eyes. Her short, spiky hair has grown out, and the ends are now dyed black. She seems so comfortable in her skin and it makes me feel nervous for some reason.

Then there's an awkward silence I need to fill, so I blurt out, "I'm sorry I never got back to you that day. Or, like ever. I'm sort of seeing someone. I should've just told you." I try to keep eye contact with her, but she's wigging me out a little, so I bow my head to the lawn and start to hand mow the area I'm sitting in. What a weird habit: making little piles of grass. I'm such a freak.

She stretches her legs out in front of her, and I see she's drawn little red hearts around her ankle, which surprises me. She doesn't seem like the heart-doodling type, but then again, I don't know anything about her except that she thinks I'm cute, so obviously she's mental.

"Sort of seeing someone? Is that like being a little pregnant or kinda dead? I don't mean to be rude, but are you seeing someone or not?" She never seems to take her eyes off me when she speaks, and I feel them piercing the top of my head as I pick at the grass.

What am I supposed to say to that? I mean, who does she think she is, questioning my life? If I need a lecture, I'll call Jenn. "Well, okay. I *am* seeing someone, then. Happy?"

"Oh. Well, that makes it much clearer anyway," she says and smiles confidently. "Well, my offer still stands. I'd like to take you out sometime."

Man, this girl has some major ovaries. I mean, which part of "I'm seeing someone" doesn't she understand?

She looks away from me briefly when a group of girls starts screaming behind her, so I have a chance to sneak a peek at her. She's wearing three tank tops, each one a different color, cargo shorts, and her usual Doc Marten shoes. And even though she's being completely annoying, I can't help but notice her cute crooked smile, which seems innocent and sweet. Then, after reading her tank top, which has a quote from someone named Ani DiFranco, I wonder if she is more trouble than her smile suggests.

Mia is just about to say something, but I interrupt. "Where'd you get that tank?" I point to her tight black top, which actually looks like I'm pointing to her boobs because that's how smooth I am. "I've never seen anything like it around here." In high school, I've learned, originality is pretty hard to find.

"I made it in advanced art."

"Really? It's cool. My mom's an artist."

Mia reclines next to me and puts her arms behind her head. Maybe she's too comfortable in her skin. "Yeah? Well, it wasn't that hard to do. I can make them in my sleep."

"I'm sure you can. You're probably good at a lot of things," I say and am pretty sure I sound a little flirty, which catches me off guard. I look back down at the grass to regroup. Is my life not complicated enough that I have to start flirting with Mia? I need serious psychiatric help.

She's caught off guard, too, I think because then she goes into a long, nervous mini-lesson on the art of screen printing. By the time she's finished, she's back to her old self and is now lying on her stomach.

"Well, I really like that quote." I nod to her shirt again, but since she's on her stomach, mostly what I'm nodding to is her cleavage.

"Yeah. You probably can relate to it. To doing stuff wrong."

"How would you know?" I say, but I have a feeling she knows a lot more about my life than I first thought. I've learned that all the girls on campus, gay or not, make it their business to know everyone else's business. I just wish I knew how much they all knew. Does Keeta kiss and tell more than just Tai? I look down again.

"I can make one for you. I still have the screen somewhere in my room."

I abandon my lawn mowing and give my full attention to Mia again. "Really? That would be cool. But who's Ani DiFranco?"

Mia dramatically drops her head to the ground. "Please tell me you're joking." Then she grabs my leg, which makes me jump a little. "You mean you've never heard her sing?"

True, my music knowledge is lacking, but I've been trying harder. In fact, I just downloaded the new Tegan and Sara album last week, so Mia should give me a break. "You don't have to be such a snob. Just tell me who she is."

She props her head up on her open palm. "No. That would be impossible. I'll just make you a tank top *and* a CD. Geez, this relationship is already costing me more than I'd like."

"Aww, you're already tired of me?"

She smiles. "Never. What color and size top?"

Flirting with Mia is fun, so I continue. "Well, I like the one you're wearing, but I'm not sure if it would look as good on me." That makes her smile even bigger, which feels kind of cool.

Then after we stare at each other for a little too long, she says, "So, let me make sure I've got this. You are, for sure, seeing someone?"

The thought of saying no does cross my mind. I mean, if Keeta's dating half of Tucson's girls' high school basketball players, why can't I go out once with Mia? But it's just not my style. "Yeah, still seeing someone."

"Okay," she says and then starts to dig through my backpack pocket until she finds what she's looking for. "But you should have my number just in case. I'll put it in here for safekeeping." Her fingers move quickly, and within seconds she's entered her phone number into my cell.

"Thanks," I say, "is it under Mia or Thurber?"

"Neither," she says and gets up. After dusting the dead grass off her shorts she stands above me looking like she's trying to decide something. I guess she comes to a conclusion because then she peels off her Ani tank top and tosses it down in my lap. "Here, you can have mine. I have a feeling it'll look even better on you. See you around, Abbey." She starts walking away but then turns around again to give me some last minute advice. "Hey, Abbey."

"What's up?" Yeah, that's right. I'm cool. Inside, though, I'm repeating a Spanish phrase that Garrett taught me today: *Esa mujer es toda una mujersota.* Translation: *She's a totally hot woman.*

"You watch out for those seniors. They're nothing but trouble."

I roll my eyes. "I'll consider myself warned. Thanks for the tank top."

She walks away and I watch her disappear into the hallway. I hold up my gift to admire it and finally come to my own conclusion. Flirting with Mia is fun and I think I might like to try it again. I reach for my cell to find her number. If it's not under Mia or Thurber, then what? Does she have a nickname, too? I click through the contacts and I finally find the number. She added it under Future Girlfriend.

❖

I'm in my room tonight staring at the tank top Mia gave me and thinking about what happened today. As much as I denied it when I talked to Kate tonight, I actually did like talking and flirting with Mia. She's funny, cute, and, as an added bonus, not a senior.

Then Keeta knocks on my window like a nocturnal woodpecker, making me jump out of my skin. Before I open the blinds, I toss Mia's tank top in my closet because I don't feel like explaining it.

"What are you doing here? You gave me a heart attack, Keeta," I whisper out to her. It's almost eleven and I'm just finishing up my biology homework and a long chat session with Garrett.

"*Te extraño, Amara*. Is it such a crime to miss you? *Dame un beso*," she says and leans in to kiss me through the screen.

"No, you can miss me," I say, and then I kiss her.

"Are you alone?"

"Actually, I'm in the middle of a very important strip poker game. Not. Of course I'm alone, baby. Are you?" I look beyond her and into the moonlit night.

"So, can I come in? Or are you going to leave me out here with the crickets and snakes?"

I pretend to ponder for a minute but finally open my window all the way and take off the screen. "I guess you can come in, but I would have worn something without farm animals on it if I had known you were coming. I totally wasn't expecting to see you tonight." I don't mean to sound ungrateful for her visit, but I kind of like to be prepared for these things.

"Amara, you always look good, girl." She hops up on the sill with ease, and I can't help but wonder how many windows she's jumped through in her lifetime, or in the past week.

I walk over to my door and lock it.

Keeta pulls an envelope from her back pocket after she kisses me again. "I got you something."

"What's the occasion?" I ask, as I take the envelope and sit on the edge of my bed. Inside are two concert tickets and a card that reads, *Just because you rock my world.* "Wow, thanks. How cool." The tickets are for an all-ages gig at Hanflings with 36-C headlining the show. I downloaded their album last month and have been playing it every time Keeta's come over. I didn't think she was paying attention, but I guess she was.

"So, there's one ticket for you and one for whoever you want to take. I mean, I know your mom won't let you go with a guy, but you can choose whichever girl you want to take with you."

I put the tickets back in the envelope and then hide them out of habit in my bedside drawer. "Well, I can think of one girl I'd want to take."

"I bet," she says and runs her finger across the spines of my books.

I squint at her. Something's off. Is she drunk or something? "What's wrong with you?" I finally ask. "You're acting weird. *Estás bien?*"

"I'm fine. I was just saying if there's someone else you want to take, it's cool."

"You mean like Kate? Um, I don't think she'd be into seeing an all-girl rock band named after a bra size. Trust me. And I can only imagine what the crowd would be like: way too much girl-on-girl love for my little BFF."

Keeta doesn't laugh even though I think I'm funny. Instead, she kicks off her shoes, crawls past me, and makes herself comfortable under the covers.

"Well, I guess you're planning on staying a while." I smile and lie down next to her. "So what did I do to deserve this surprise?"

"I told you. I missed you." She turns off the light, but I can still see her face from the glow of my computer. "Why does that surprise you?" Then she pulls me close and gives me a long kiss. Her touch sends me spinning like a CD and I soon lose track of up and down and yesterday and today. The only thing on my mind when we're like this is how, with just the soft touch of her hands or lips, she can take me to a place of crazy passion I didn't think was possible.

Then she pulls away and stares down at me with such a serious look that I get a little scared.

"Amara…" she whispers.

"Yes, Keeta?" I say, but in my head I'm thinking, *Don't break my heart yet. Please, just keep me a little longer.*

"Te deseo."

I rack my brain but can't come up with the translation. "What does that mean?"

"Te deseo, Amara. It means I want to spend the night."

That translation clears things up very quickly. Suddenly I'm really thirsty and the words I need have dried up and blown away like dead leaves.

She lowers her head and kisses my neck. "I just want to feel close to you. I want to make you feel good. Will you let me? You know you want me to."

Do I? Maybe I do. I don't know. Besides, what's the big deal? It's not like I'm going to get pregnant.

My lack of response upsets Keeta because she pulls away again. "God, I'm sorry. Look, you're obviously not ready. I shouldn't have asked you. I'll go."

She starts to get up, but I grab hold of her arm and pull her back next to me. "Don't go. I'm the one who should be sorry. I don't know why I'm scared. I want to be close to you, too. I do. Don't go, K."

I reach out and touch her face, but she jumps like my fingertips are the sharp fangs of a rattlesnake.

"Keeta, what's going on?" I sit up and turn on the light. "Come on, just tell me."

She hesitates but then says, "Maybe we should stop seeing each other. I mean, you deserve someone better and I don't want to string you along. You're too good for that."

"Wait. What?" Her kisses always make me feel dizzy, so I don't know if the room is spinning from that or because of what she's just said. "You don't want to be with me anymore because I won't have sex with you?"

"That's not why, Amara. It's just…you should be dating someone your own age."

"It's not like I'm twelve, Keeta. I'm fifteen and you're seventeen. Why is this a big deal now? Is it because you're graduating? We can still see each other, you know? There are phone calls and e-mails and I'll be driving next year."

She covers her face with her hands like she can't stand to look at me. "I just think you should move on."

No, I can't let you go yet. I take her hand in mine. "Keeta, I know you probably don't want to hear this, but…*te amo*," I say in a barely audible voice. After I catch my breath and realize what I've done, I say it again. "I love you, and I know how you feel about me, too, even though you think you're too tough to admit it."

She smiles a little, but it fades quickly. "What about Mia?"

And just like that, she successfully avoids saying that she loves me, too. I guess that's why I quickly get over feeling guilty about the way I flirted with Mia, but I play stupid instead of telling the truth. "What are you talking about? Mia who?"

"Don't lie, Abbey. You're bad at it."

"So I was talking to Mia. She's just a girl I met in study hall. That's all."

"Well, it seems like you two were doing more than talking on the quad today." Keeta's face hardens.

That's when it hits me. "Oh my God, you're jealous."

"Whatever."

"Keeta Moreno, starting varsity guard who averages twenty points a game, the girl who can learn any song on her guitar in less than an hour, the one I dream of kissing every night, is jealous? This is huge. I have to tell Garrett."

I dive across my bed for my laptop, but she quickly wraps her legs around me and pulls me back. We wrestle until she's sitting on top on me, pinning my arms down over my head. I struggle to free myself, but of course I want her to stay right where she is.

"Are you turning into the Hulk, or are you just green with envy?"

"All right, all right. You've made your point."

She releases my arms and I rest them on her legs. "Come on, K. What's the big deal? I mean, you're kinda acting like a jealous *girlfriend*." I tickle her stomach to try and make her laugh, but she just keeps a stoic look on her face.

"How can I not be jealous? She took her shirt off for you."

I try to think of an explanation for that strip scene on the quad and come up with nothing, so I tease her a little more instead. "So were you spying on me? How girlfriendy of you."

"No, I wasn't. Everyone in the library and cafeteria could see you, Abbey. It's not like it took long to hear about it from Tai."

"Foiled again by my nemesis, Tai," I joke, but I can tell Keeta needs some reassuring, which is a nice change. "First of all, Ms. Moreno, I just liked her shirt, not her." It's not a total lie. I mean, she's cute, but I don't know if I *like her*, like her. "And, second of all, you are who I want." I try to pull her down to kiss her, but she resists and leans back. I guess she needs a little more. "Besides, I told her I was seeing someone. She'll probably never talk to me again. And it's not like I wanted to talk to her to begin with. *No te preocupes.*"

"You're welcome to date whoever you want. I mean, it's cool with me."

She's being so stubborn about the whole thing that I put an end to it once and for all. I grab her shirt, pull her down, and give her a long kiss.

When we come up for air, her face has softened. "Man, what am I going to do with you, Amara? You're too much for me."

"This is true, but in the meantime, how about you stay with me for a little bit and hold me close."

"Hmm, I don't know," she says, but one look at me with her beautiful amber eyes, and I know she's mine, at least for a few hours. "Okay, it's the least I can do."

She lies down next to me and covers us up.

❖

"Wake up, Amara." Keeta's voice sounds like it's underneath three thousand gallons of water.

I open my eyes and she's brushing my tear-soaked hair off my face.

"It's just a bad dream, baby girl."

I turn my head away from her and wipe my face with the corner of my pillow. "I'm sorry."

"It's okay. I'm here."

It's four in the morning. The jolt of my body must have woken Keeta up and startled her, but my crying is what seems to be worrying her. I'm so used to waking up this way from my dead-dad dreams that for a second I wonder why she looks so concerned. "God, we totally fell asleep," I whisper.

"Are you okay? Do you want to tell me about it?"

I've never told anyone but Kate about them. I don't even tell my mom because I know it'll just upset her. But if I trust Keeta with my heart, I guess I can trust her with this. "It was about my dad. I've had them before."

"You dream about him a lot?"

"It used to be every night, but now it's like once a month and they're always awful."

"Like what?"

"In this one he was driving our station wagon, and I was with him, but then he dropped me off at a friend's house. Then there was this huge cliff ahead, but he didn't see it because he was waving good-bye to me in the rearview mirror. And, well, you can guess the way it ends."

"Can I do anything for you?" she asks sweetly.

I shake my head. "No. Thanks, though."

"How about I hold you until you fall asleep, then?" She slides her arm under my head and pulls my body into hers.

We fit perfectly together, like LEGO pieces, but I break us apart and turn on my back. "It's late. You should probably go." I want her to stay, but I feel embarrassed. Plus, I don't want to get caught with Keeta in my room. "My mom will be up soon, anyway."

"I'll wait for you to fall asleep, and then I'll leave. Okay?"

I give in quickly. "Okay."

A few minutes go by and I can feel myself about to drift off to sleep again. Then without really meaning to, I whisper, "I love you, Keeta." I don't know if she hears me because she doesn't say anything back, but I feel safe in her arms and fall asleep.

❖

"Abbey? Abbey…"

That's my name, don't wear it out, I think, as I try to open my eyes. Then I wonder, *Who's waking me up and who is this sleeping next to me?*

I turn over and there's Keeta. The same Keeta that was supposed to wait for me to fall asleep and then leave. "Leave" being the most important part of the plan.

"Abbey?" It's my mom at my bedroom door.

I shoot up in bed and look at my clock. It's already seven. Jenn will be here to pick me up any minute. I shake Keeta to wake her up, and the look on her face shows her panic. "Sorry," she mouths as she scrambles out from underneath the covers.

My mom rattles the doorknob. "Why is your door locked? Are you okay? You're going to be late for school. Abbey?" she says, louder.

"Uh," I say, as I gather Keeta's pants and shoes and throw them at her. "Hold on, Mom."

"Why is your door locked? What's going on in there?" she demands.

"Nothing," I say and turn the window handle to let my big lesbian secret out, but the screen is attached and there's no time. I shove Keeta into my closet then run to my bedroom door, unlock it, and swing it open. "Hey, Mom. Sorry, I overslept." I'm totally out of breath and hope she doesn't notice.

"Why was the door locked?" my mom asks with her arms crossed over her chest.

May my lying skills not fail me now. "Well, if you must know, I was reading a really super-duper scary book last night about an ax-murdering psychopath from Maine and got freaked out, so I locked the door. Sorry." Whew, good one.

"Really?" she asks slowly.

"Yeah, why? What do you think I was doing in here? Having an orgy or something? God."

"Okay, you don't have to get all dramatic. I believe you, but I've told you not to read those books. They'll rot your brain."

"I guess you were right," I say, hoping the compliment will help my situation.

"Well, you better hurry if you're going to get to algebra before the late bell. I'll tell Jenn you're riding to school with me."

"Thanks, Mom." I'm about to shut the door on her when she uses her foot to stop it from shutting. "Is that yours?" she asks, pointing to a black bra on the floor.

Keeta's much more developed in the bust area than I could ever dream of being, so there's no way my mom will believe it's mine. "Um, no," I truthfully say.

"Well, whose is it?"

"Keeta's," I say and break out in a sweat. Come on lies. Start snowing down.

"Why is it on the floor?"

I bend down and pick up the sexy bra and resist the urge to smell it. "Well…" I twirl it on my finger and spin it around to make it seem like less of a big deal. "She left it in the locker room and I put it in my gym bag so I could give it to her, and then I forgot it was in there, so when I discovered it in my gym bag last night I put it on the floor so I wouldn't forget to give it to her. And, see? It worked."

My mom looks at my face carefully, and I just smile. I mean, what else can I do?

"I don't think I'll ever understand you, Abbey."

I let out a nervous laugh and fling Keeta's bra over my shoulder. "You're not supposed to, Mom. I'm a teenager. It's my job to confuse you."

She shakes her head and walks down the hall. "Well, you're doing a good job, then," she says over her shoulder. "You might consider giving yourself a raise."

CHAPTER TWENTY-EIGHT

A week later, Kate and I are barely enduring Gila's second day of track tryouts. As we finish our third lap, I'm already regretting my decision to join. How could I have forgotten that I hate running outside?

"Oh my God, how many more?" I pant as we round another corner of the track. "I'm going to die."

"We've only got two more laps to go, Abbey. Suck it up."

"Geez, are you channeling Mrs. Schwartz or something?"

Kate shoves me and I nearly fall onto the grass. "Shut up and run."

"Yes, master."

"So, what did your mom say when you asked her about track tryouts?"

"At first she said no way, of course, but I told her she could put me back on a weekly contract with Ms. Morvay if she wanted. She took that deal but made me promise to go to study hall again."

"That sucks."

"Yeah, but it's my own fault."

We jog in silence for the last lap because neither one of us can spare the air. It's not too hot out, only about eighty-eight degrees or so, but my body isn't used to it yet, which is why I keel onto the grass next to the finish line after our four warm-up laps.

"Am I going to have to give you mouth to mouth?"

I open my eyes and smile because Keeta's standing over me like an Aztec goddess. "You wish. No, I'm fine, but thanks a lot for keeping me up so late last night."

Keeta nods at Kate. "Hey."

Kate nods back. "Hey."

Okay, so they aren't best friends, but I'll take their one syllable exchanges over the way Kate used to totally ignore Keeta.

"Help me up," I whine and extend my arms.

Keeta pulls me to my feet.

"Thanks. So what happens now?" I ask Keeta because she's the experienced one.

"Well, we do a lot of conditioning and drills for the next week until the coaches can determine what strengths we each have. I bet you'll get picked for high jump."

"Hmm, I do like to jump over and into things," I say.

"Yeah? How about you jump in bed with me tonight?" she whispers in my ear. "I'd like to finish off what we started last night."

"Shhhh." I push her away and look over at Kate to make sure she didn't hear.

Keeta's desire to have sex with me hasn't lessened at all, and the more time we spend together, the harder it's getting to stop her before things go too far. She isn't the only one who is wondering why we have to stop, though. The only sense I can make of my half-assed prudish behavior is that the idea of getting even closer to Keeta really scares me. How can I make love with her knowing she's probably sleeping with someone else, too? Plus, I'm just not ready to let anyone see me naked or for her to touch me like that. This all makes perfect sense to me, but when I told Garrett my thoughts on the topic, she said I didn't have to be naked to have sex and if she had the chance, she'd totally sleep with Keeta. I wonder if Tai knows that.

"Well, if you change your mind, you know where to find me," Keeta says and runs off to laugh and flirt with some girls from the varsity basketball team who are also trying out. It makes me wonder how she can turn everything off so easily. Does she just flip a switch in her heart? And what's wrong with me? Why can't I be more like her or Garrett? Why do I think everything is such a big deal?

A whistle blows, and the students on the field all head toward the end line of the football field. "What is it with coaches and lines?"

Kate shrugs. "It can't be too much harder than conditioning for basketball."

She couldn't have been more wrong. For the next hour, we have to do all these crazy exercises up and down the field. First, there's the high skip, then the crab crawl, and finally deep leg lunges that make my butt burn so bad I nearly cry. In fact, I'm in so much pain during our line work I don't even notice Mia is there until after Coach Parker blows his whistle and we are all allowed to collapse again.

Mia uses the opportunity to drink water, and I use it to lie lifeless on my back staring at her. Maybe it's because she always wears her heavy black Doc Martens, but Mia doesn't seem like the kind of girl who would try out for track. Without her boots, baggy shorts, and hand-printed T-shirts, she looks like everyone else. And, for some reason, that disappoints me.

Kate falls down next to me and starts on her own complaints. "What a jerk."

I turn my head to look at Derrick and his friends. They are squeezing their water bottles at some girls who are screaming for the boys to stop, but they obviously like the attention.

"You knew he was going to try out, too, so why are you so upset?"

"I'm not mad. He's a loser, which is obvious, but that doesn't mean I don't want him to see I'm over him. The problem is he hasn't looked at me once so I can show him just how over him I am. It's those skanks. They're ruining everything."

"So, you *are* mad."

"Shut up, Abbey," she says and then sighs loudly.

"Well, if you ask me, I think you just want him to see you in those skimpy spandex shorts they make us wear."

Then, like always, she reminds me that she didn't remember asking me what I thought. She finally closes her eyes to block him out of her sight and her heart. "I hate him."

"He's scum, Kate. Don't waste your time even thinking about him."

"I know." She squirts a gulp of water into her mouth from her water bottle and hands it to me. "I could say the same to you, you know?"

"Ah, here we go." Kate has this annoying pattern: when she finally stops bitching about Derrick, she starts in on Keeta. It makes me miss the days when I was lying to her about it.

"I mean, it doesn't make sense that you're dating a girl who acts like an asshole boy. She's such a player, Abs. Everyone sees it but you. She won't even tell you she loves you. Why don't you date a girl who will treat you right?"

"That is the million dollar question, Kate. But I love her. That's all I can say."

"Are you sure?"

Of all the messed up things that have happened this year, it's the one thing I hold on to as truth. I am sure I love Keeta. But before I get to answer Kate, Coach Parker blows his whistle again and we're back on the end line. As I crab crawl the length of the football field with Mia on my far left and Keeta on my far right, I realize another sure thing: I am seriously into pain.

"You should have seen how scared Mia and I were," I say to Kate as we wobble painfully out of the locker room to the hot track on the fifth day of tryouts. "Mrs. Guzman was so mad she nearly wrote us up, but instead she's going to make us shelve returned books next week. I don't know which punishment is worse. Oh, and guess what Mia's letter said?" I don't wait for a response. "She said she'd be happy to be my stalker any day of the week. She's such a flirt, huh?" I look over at Kate for a reaction, but get zilch.

She's too preoccupied with squinting up at the sky and frowning. "Don't you ever get sick of the blue skies around here? Wouldn't it be nice to have more variety in our lives?"

I look up at the sun and my eyes water. "Um, if you say so."

"And I don't know why you insist on sharing your Mia stories with me. I mean, you know I'd rather you date her than the one who shall not be named."

Instead of having our usual argument about Keeta, I pretend not to hear her.

It's almost three o'clock, and I notice the coaches huddled by the goalpost with their clipboards. I wonder where I'll end up, if anywhere. I had a strong showing the first three days, but yesterday I could hardly walk, let alone run. In fact, I could barely even touch my knees, and my legs were so sore that doing things like putting on socks and stepping into the shower evoked very ungirly, guttural moans.

"He's such a man slut," Kate hisses. "Look at him over there."

Kate's plan is definitely backfiring. Instead of Derrick noticing how over him she is or how bouncy her boobs are when she runs, Kate notices every girl he speaks to or looks at, and it's getting old. At least I'm not *that* crazy about Keeta. In fact, I feel proud of myself for not keeping tabs on Keeta the whole practice. But thinking this makes me look for Keeta. I don't see her and now I'm wondering where she is. I hope she comes soon because, according to Jenn, if you aren't here when they announce the team, you're automatically cut.

"It's one thing to flirt with other girls, but to flirt with Sherice Franks?" Kate continues. "How desperate is he?" Kate spreads her legs and bends forward to stretch. "I mean, she's so stupid, she probably thinks absolute zero is a new vodka drink. And her breasts are so huge they create their own gravitational pull on every guy that tries to pass by. She's like a freaking planet. What a slut."

I nod my head and give my usual, "Yeah. He sucks," but I have my own troubles. Is Keeta coming today? I saw her at my locker after second period, but she didn't tell me she wasn't going to track practice.

Then Mia walks up and distracts me from my worries. "Hey, jerk," I say playfully. "Thanks for getting me in trouble."

"Uh, if I recall correctly, it was you who fell out of your chair. I passed that letter under the table with perfection. You're just a klutz."

"Don't think I didn't see you check out my ass when I was trying to get up."

She smiles. "Yep, you got me. Oh hey, that reminds me. Are you still seeing someone? I'm updating my records."

"Yes!" I throw a handful of grass at her. "And you better get out of here before she kicks your butt."

"Ooh, I'm shaking," she says and pretends to take out a notebook to write down my response. "Still dating loser," she writes in her palm and trots away.

"God," Kate says and rolls her eyes. "You're so freakin' weird, Abbey."

After the coaches call us around, they read off the students who made the cut. Kate and I both make the team and, since she and I are such long-legged mamas, they put us on the high jump and hurdle squads. Running fast and then jumping over scary metal obstacles sounds way too complicated, but I'm willing to give it a shot, I guess.

I'm pretty excited about making the team and get even more excited when the coaches call Keeta's name, too. Because she's a fast runner and strong, she's going to be on the relay and hurdle teams and do shot put. But if she doesn't show up in the next five minutes, she's going to be cut from the team altogether.

I'm determined not to let that happen. I run over to the coaches and tell a whopper of a lie about Keeta feeling really sick and going home early, so the coaches said if she really wanted to be on the team they'd give her until four to get back to campus before they cut her. I'm out of cell minutes, but Keeta doesn't always answer her phone anyway.

I run to Jenn's car after we're all dismissed from practice. "Hey Jenn, can I get a ride to Keeta's?"

"Well, I don't really think I should help you earn your Girl Scout badge of sluttery, but maybe if you give me five dollars."

I look at Kate. "Do you have five bucks I can borrow?"

"God, I'm just kidding," Jenn says and honks her horn. "Get in, dumbass."

"Thanks, Jenn." I climb in the backseat and sit sideways to fit.

CHAPTER TWENTY-NINE

After Jenn and Kate drop me off, I run up to Keeta's door and knock my special knock: three taps, then a pause, then another three.

No one answers.

It's a Friday, which means her grandma is volunteering at church all day, so I don't feel bad about knocking obnoxiously again. Tap, tap, tap. Pause. Tap, tap, tap.

When there's no answer, my imagination gets the best of me. Maybe Keeta is inside and hurt. Maybe she's passed out on the floor bleeding to death. Or maybe she's with that stupid punk girl, Osiris. I knock loudly this time, abandoning the usual taps.

Finally, I hear movement inside, and then the door cracks open a few inches.

"Hey," Keeta says through the small opening. Her braided hair is messed up and frizzy, like she just rolled out of bed. "What's up, Abbey?"

"Didn't you hear me knocking? Are you sick or something?" I ask stupidly.

"No, just, uh, tired. What's up?"

I ignore her unaffectionate greeting and tell her the good news. "You made the track team, but you have to get down there, like, right now or you're going to be cut."

She yawns. "Cool, but I don't think I'm going to join."

"But I talked to the coaches for you. They're waiting," I say and wonder if her behavior has something to do with me and Mia again. Or maybe she's sick of being around me. Maybe I did something wrong.

"Well, I'm sort of"—she looks over her shoulder and closes the door a little more—"busy right now."

Kate's words pop into my head. *She's such a player, Abs. Everyone knows it but you.* "Oh." I don't know what else to say. "Sorry."

"No, it's cool. Maybe I'll go back to school. Thanks for coming by and telling me." She starts to close the door but, borrowing my mom's move, I jam my foot in its path. I don't know what I'm doing or why, but I know I'm over being shocked and sad. Now I'm just plain pissed.

"Can I at least have some water?"

Before she has a chance to react, I push my way in.

"Abbey, wait." Keeta tries to grab my arm, but I dodge her hand.

I look down her hall toward her bedroom, and that's when I see all I need to see.

Just outside Keeta's closed bedroom door is a backpack. But it definitely doesn't belong to Osiris, whose backpack I have recently learned to hate. And it isn't a backpack that I ever expected to see in Keeta's house today. It's a green messenger bag with an upside down rainbow triangle patch and a stupid button that reads *I'm not gay, but my girlfriend is*.

"Garrett?" I say to myself. Then I turn to look at Keeta, but now words have left me.

For the first time ever, I hate being in Keeta's tiny apartment. I feel the stares of the saints on my back, and I know they're laughing at me for being so naïve and for thinking I matter more to Keeta than anyone else.

Keeta reaches for my hand. "Abbey, I..."

"Don't touch me. How could you do this to me?"

"It just happened. I don't know why."

"How does something like this *just happen*?" I shout. "How do you accidentally screw around with Garrett?" My hands start to shake, along with my voice, and I know I have to get out of there before I fall apart. I push past her and head for the door, but she grabs hold of my wrist and yanks me back to her. "Let me go, Keeta." I struggle to free myself, but her grip is like an inescapable handcuff.

"Abbey, listen, we were just hanging out and drinking a little and it happened. It doesn't mean anything to me or to her."

"Then why would you do it?" I don't know when I started crying, but tears are flooding my face. "Why, Keeta? Why?"

"I didn't plan this. I swear. It meant nothing."

"That's your problem. Nothing means *anything* to you. You just use everyone to get what you want. You don't even care who gets hurt." I try to pull away from her again, but she's too strong. "Let me go!"

"Amara…" She looks like she might cry, but my special name now makes me sick to my stomach.

"Go to hell! I mean it!" I yank my arm free.

She looks at me one last time and tries to bring me in with her amber eyes, but my icy glare deflects her attempt.

Finally she steps back and leans against the open door. "You're right, Amara. You're right. *Lo siento, corazón.* I really am sorry."

I steady my hands just enough to unlatch my necklace. "Everyone was right about you, Keeta."

I put the necklace on the windowsill and leave her apartment for what better be the last time.

❖

When I get home, I borrow the side mirror on my neighbor's car to see how bad I look before I step inside my house.

My mom is sitting at the dining-room table playing another quiet game of Scrabble with herself. "Hi, honey," she says as she lays down e-x-c-i-t-e on the board. "How was your day?"

My first obstacle is to speak without sounding congested from crying. "Fine. I've gotta call Kate."

"She just called. Isn't your cell phone on?"

"No." I don't admit I ran out of minutes in the first week of the month.

My mom digs her hand into the letter bag. "And someone else called." She moves her letters around on their wooden tray. "I can't believe I'm forgetting her name."

"Garrett?"

"Yep, that's it," she says and finally looks up.

I've been doing an A+ job of holding back the tears up until that point, but now I'm two seconds away from becoming the blubbering zombie that I was as I walked home from Keeta's.

"Abbey Road, what's wrong?"

"I'm okay," I manage to say and then turn to head toward my room.

My mom and her long legs catch up with me, though. "No, you're not okay. What's wrong? Didn't you make the track team?" She pulls me into her and hugs me tight. "Oh, honey, you can try out again next year."

She holds me until I can catch my breath and stop shaking. Then she walks me to my room and we sit side by side on my bed. She smoothes my hair from my face and kisses my forehead. I didn't know how much I missed my mom until now.

"Okay, what's really wrong with my Abbey Road? Come on, honey, please talk to me."

I can't hold it back anymore. I have to tell her, at least some of it. "It's just...I feel so stupid. I should've listened to everyone." I lean into her again and soak her shoulder with salty tears.

She rubs my back and lets me cry. It's such a relief to not be alone, and I finally realize that I need her. I need her to tell me everything's going to be okay, even if it's not and even if she has no idea what's really wrong.

"I guess I thought I could do it, you know? I thought it wouldn't matter."

I know I'm talking in circles, but my mom just lets me go on without asking questions.

She hands me a tissue and rocks me a little. "I know it hurts, Abbey. I know. It'll get better, though. I promise. It's going to hurt for a while, but it'll get better."

"How do you know it'll get better, Mom?" I ask because right now it feels like my heart is being punctured with knives, and I seriously doubt I'll ever feel okay again.

"Hey, I've been in love before. Even though it's been a while, I haven't forgotten. You never forget your first love."

When she says that my body stiffens and I stop crying. Did she find the letters? Read my journal? Hear Keeta sneaking in at night?

"Besides, whoever this person is that broke your heart is missing out on being with someone pretty special. You just wait and see. Everything's going to work out just fine. I promise."

She says exactly what I need to hear, and I love her more right now than I have in a long time. So, of course, I feel even more horrible. Not just about stupid Keeta, but about how bad I've been treating my mom and all the lies I've told her.

"I promise, Abbey Road. I promise things will get better," my mom says again, which only makes me cry even more.

CHAPTER THIRTY

I don't know why Kate bothers knocking on my bedroom door because she comes in before I even have a chance to ask who it is.

She finds me lying in bed in the tank top and underwear I put on last night after my fiasco at Keeta's because it's way too hot to wear much else. But I doubt Kate wants to hang out with me half-dressed, so I quickly cover myself up with the tangled sheet at the foot of my bed before I turn toward the wall.

"Kate, I'm not in the mood to talk."

"I'm not here to talk." She sits down on my bed. "I'm just here to listen."

I have nothing to say, so I don't know what she's planning on listening to.

"Your mom told me you were pretty upset. What happened yesterday?"

"Nothing. I love my life. See you later."

She pokes me in the back. "Come on. I'm missing a *Project Runway* marathon to sit here, so spill it."

New tears run down my face.

"Okay, I'm going to go out on a limb here and guess your surprise Keeta visit didn't go too well."

I wipe my face with my sheet. "Not exactly. Wait, did you tell my mom where I was?"

Kate gets up and closes the door. "No, but I totally thought you told her about, you know, your big secret. She kept on saying I should talk to you because I knew what it felt like to have a broken heart. And then she used all these generic pronouns when she talked about it. Like, *someone* hurt you and *that person* doesn't know what they're missing. So, anyway, she may be on to you. Wait, do you think she thinks I'm gay, too?"

"No, I don't think she thinks you're gay, Kate. God. Hand me a tissue would you?"

She pulls a fresh tissue out of the box my mom left for me last night and dangles it in front of my hidden face. When I reach up to grab it, she yanks it away so I have to turn to get it.

After she sees my puffed and blotchy face, I figure there's no point in trying to hide anymore, so I turn over and grab the tissue from her hand. Then for some reason when I see her face, I cry even more. "You were right. I should've listened to you. Everyone was right."

"Come on, you can't beat yourself up, Abbey. You fell in love with Keeta. Worse things have happened. Sure, she ended up screwing you over in the end like I said she would, but let's look at the bright side."

I reduce my sobs to a snivel and ask, "What bright side? This sucks." My head's pounding so I rub my temples to relieve the pressure.

"Well, for one thing, now that you're single again, we can spend more time getting caught up on all the horror movies we missed this year."

"Is that all you have?"

She gives me another tissue. "Well, now that you've been with a girl, you don't have to be so freaked out next time it happens. I mean, if it happens again. Or whatever."

I like that she's willing to talk about me liking girls, but I still don't feel better. "Nope, not good enough. If you need me, I'll be here until the end of senior year." I fall back onto my pillows. But being in my bed only makes me think of all those nights Keeta and I spent hanging out in my room, back when I actually believed I was her whole world. And it makes me regret ever saying no to her. Maybe if I had said yes, she wouldn't have wanted Garrett at all. Maybe it's all my fault for being so immature.

Kate squints her eyes and looks strained while she thinks of something else to say. "Okay, I got it. Now you don't have to keep anything from your mom. Since there's no girl, there's no reason to lie and hide who you are. That's cool, right?" She throws up her hands. "See, everything's falling into place."

She's a good friend, but I now realize that there are going to be some things she'll never understand: I'm not done being gay just because Keeta and I are over.

"No. Everything is out of place, Kate." Then I tell her what I walked into at Keeta's house yesterday.

"Damn," she says.

"Yeah."

"Well, I kind of know how you feel."

I doubt it, but say, "Oh yeah? How's that?"

"The same thing happened with me and Derrick."

"Really?" I blow my nose again. "With that one chick?"

"No, it was before that. I caught him kissing some girl behind the gym one day. He tried to deny it even though I saw it with my own eyes. He was all, 'It didn't mean anything. It just happened.' Can you believe that bs?"

"Yeah, I can believe it. Why didn't you tell me before?" I toss my heavy tissues into the wastebasket and she gives me another.

"I was embarrassed."

We don't talk for a while and just listen to the Ani DiFranco CD Mia made for me, which I have been playing all night and morning. Sometimes music makes me feel better, but sometimes I need it to make feeling bad an okay thing, too.

"Abbey, listen," Kate says like she's excited. "Let's just forget everything that happened this year. It doesn't matter anymore. Besides, we have each other. And, you know, you're honestly the only person I can really trust, anyway."

"Really?" I finally smile.

"Really. But you gotta get out of this bed. It's a beautiful day out there and it stinks in here. Plus, you really need to wash your face before you totally break out."

The thought of functioning in the world makes me dizzy, but then my mom comes in to announce that brunch has been prepared. I haven't eaten since lunch yesterday, so my stomach is pretty much digesting itself at this point. "Okay, I'll get up."

After my mom leaves, Kate laughs to herself.

"What's so funny?"

"Well, your hair, for one."

I try to hit her with my pillow, but she dodges the blow.

"No, it's just, I was remembering that promise we made to each other last summer."

I know exactly which one. "Yeah, no basketball and stay away from the lesbians. That didn't go very well, did it?"

She shakes her head and laughs again. "Yeah, you and your cheating lesbian lover and me with my controlling jock boyfriend. It almost makes me not want to play next year."

"Shut up," I say because I'm shocked. I will never give up basketball now that I have a taste for it. It would be like trying to give up mocha shakes or gummy bears. Just plain crazy. "But you can't do that. I was looking forward to playing with you on the same team. We would totally kick ass."

"Hey, I said *almost*. Forget those losers. They may have ruined our freshman year, but they can't ruin basketball. Oh yeah. We're totally going to kick some serious butt."

We high-five like the dorks we know we are.

"But how about we make one more promise," I say.

"I'm still laughing about our last broken promise, but okay."

"How about we stay clear of boys, and girls, for at least the rest of the school year. We're too young for all this drama. It can't be good for our health."

She thinks about it for a second, then sticks out her pinky. "Okay, deal."

We sing our old song and swear in the new promise.

"Now come on. I'm starving."

"I'll be right there," I say.

Kate's right. It smells like misery in my room, so I open the blinds and let some fresh air in. That's when I see the letter taped to my window. I remove the screen and pull the envelope off the glass. My stomach quickly forgets how hungry it is. My heart, on the other hand, easily remembers its pain. The envelope is warm from the intense sun shining on it, and I press it to my cheek and close my eyes, remembering the way Keeta's touch felt on my face.

Inside is the necklace Keeta gave me on my birthday, a poem, and a short note:

There's a word for what I've done to you; the only one that says it all.
This word is as ancient as time, but never loses its sharp edge.
It tells the story of how I lost you in a moment of dread.
It explains why I haven't slept a wink all night.
It describes how one stupid decision has ruined two lives.
Yes, there is a word for what I've done to you; the only one that says it all.
It's what stings and hurts the most, and that word is betrayal.

A, I am so sorry for hurting you. It's the last thing I ever wanted to do. You are still in my heart and on my mind. I hope that we can talk soon. Call me when you're ready.
K

I rest my head against the warm windowpane and wonder when she came by. Did she hear me crying myself to sleep? Why hadn't she been brave enough to knock? But then again, maybe, for once, she was doing the right thing by leaving me alone.

I hold up the necklace and look at the dangling A in the late-morning light. Maybe she does still care. Maybe it doesn't have to be over. Then I hear Kate and my mom laughing in the kitchen. No, I tell myself. A deal is a deal.

CHAPTER THIRTY-ONE

Four weeks have gone by since one of the worst days of my life, and I'm feeling somewhat functional now. It helps that I don't see Keeta around the halls much, or Garrett for that matter. I thought it was all because of my efforts to avoid them, but maybe they're avoiding me, too.

We have a track meet at Tucson High today, so Kate and I are stretching out to get ready for our first race of the day. The sun is shining, birds are chirping, and things seem nearly tolerable. Then Garrett shows up in the stands.

When I see her, I don't want to roll up like a pill bug like I thought I would, and I only have a slight increase in my heart rate and a little bit of the nervous sweats. Maybe time has helped heal whatever happened between us. I have constantly wondered if Garrett and I could be friends again because, technically, she didn't do anything wrong. Keeta and I weren't girlfriends, and even though I wanted to deny it, our relationship was open. Besides, was what Garrett did any worse than what I did to Stef? How could I throw such a huge rock (a boulder, really) in my own glass house? Garrett did call my cell phone a few times, but I ignored the calls. But maybe she wants to apologize as much as I want to apologize to Stef for what I did to her. Could I give her a second chance? Plus, Garrett is my only connection to the big gay world. So even though I have Kate back, I actually miss hanging out with Garrett and being around someone who really does understand and doesn't just pretend. Am I totally insane? Most likely.

Either way, there she is, just as gorgeous as ever, leaning over the bleacher railings and talking to a girl from Tucson High's team. With the way the two of them seem to be carrying on, I think that maybe it's her new girlfriend. Maybe Tai and Garrett broke up after Tai found out about her and Keeta. But then Tai comes up and drapes her arm over Garrett's shoulders, which means either Tai is the most forgiving girlfriend ever, or Garrett hasn't come clean yet.

After Garrett shows up, the day continues to get progressively weirder. First, the sun fades away as the skies become overcast with cumulus clouds. Then, a strong dry wind starts tearing through the valley, blowing dust in our eyes and wreaking havoc on everyone competing.

And that's why in my first race, I nearly biff it on the fourth hurdle as I try to outrun a miniature tornado that seems to be following me. By the time I cross the finish line, I have what feels like sandpaper in my eyes and new bruises on my knees. I end up getting fifth place in my heat, which is especially embarrassing considering that there are only five of us competing.

Then, during the high jump competition, the wind picks up even more.

"Damn it," I yell after landing on the blue mat. A second later the bar falls to the ground. I only have one more try to get over the 4'2" mark. I have been sailing over the 4'3" bar in other meets with room to spare, but today I'm officially sucking and letting down my team.

As the other three girls successfully contort their limber bodies over the bar, I curse the wind, I curse Garrett for showing up, and I curse myself for not being able to get my ass over the damn bar.

Coach Parker gives me some encouraging advice. "Just take your time, Abbey. Watch your steps. You're rushing it."

I nod and set myself up for my last attempt. When I think the wind has taken a brief breather, I propel myself forward, counting out my steps like I've done a hundred times before. But when I push off the ground to jump, something goes terribly wrong. My ankle, the one I wrecked when I fell off my bike, slides oddly in its joint like a doll's plastic limb. The pain jolts up my leg and my body seems to stop in midair. I somehow manage to land on my knee on the asphalt, missing the mat entirely.

I shout an inappropriate expletive and punch the mat.

"Whoa, Abbey. Settle down." Coach kneels besides me. "Let's take a look," he says and squeezes my already swelling ankle. "Does this hurt?"

I shake my head.

"How about this?"

"Not really."

"And this?"

"Ow!" I want to kick him in the groin to show him how much it hurts, but he stands up before I get the chance.

"It's not too bad. Hang on, I'll get some help."

Being carried off the field by a couple of the pole vault guys makes my list of top ten most uncomfortable moments in high school without doubt. At least, so far. And since I'm all sweaty, bleeding from the knee, and haven't shaved for three days, the guys carrying me must be feeling the same way and want the experience to end as quickly as possible, too.

Kate's in the middle of her long jumps, so she can't join the fun, but I give her a reassuring thumbs-up as my entourage and I pass by. She doesn't look too worried. Actually, she laughs at me before giving me a thumbs-up back.

The dudes dump me on a padded table in the trainer's office.

The buff female trainer makes my gaydar go off the charts, but that doesn't help my situation. She gives me a quick look over, gathers some items, and sprays down my knee with antiseptic. "You'll need to ice your ankle for about twenty minutes. Here ya go," she says, putting a bucket filled with ice in front of me.

"Are you kidding me?" I look at her like she's just told me to dip my toes in wet dog food. "I'm not sticking my whole foot in there."

She sighs and crosses her supermuscular arms across her chest. "Look, I can't make you do anything. But if you want to keep the swelling down and heal faster, you'll do it. Don't be such a wimp." Then she walks off to help another injured runner.

I stare at the bucket and paint my face with the tip of my braid for about five minutes. Then I slide my big toe in first but pull it out quickly once it hits the icy slush, which causes my ankle to tense up and throb even more. Another four-letter word slips out of my mouth.

"Do you want me to hold your hand?"

I look up, and there's Mia standing in the doorway watching me act like an enormous baby. She has on her tiny blue silk running shorts and a Gila High tank top. Her hair is haphazardly pulled back in a low ponytail.

"I saw your manly men carry you in here."

"Yeah? Great."

She points to the bucket. "The best way to go in is fast and fearless."

It's not Mia's fault, but her lighthearted attitude that I normally enjoy is only irritating me today. "Don't you have a race to run?"

"Nope, I'm all done." She sits down next to me. "Got second place in the sixteen hundred meter."

She's just trying to help, I tell myself. *Be nice.* "God, how do you run that far? That's impressive."

"Thanks." Her smile is like a muscle relaxant. It's weird, but it seems no matter what my mood, it's always improved when I talk to Mia.

"So, just dunk it in?"

"I'm serious. I'll hold your hand."

"Okay, on three," I say and grab her hand.

She counts with me. "One, two, threeeee…"

As soon as my foot is submerged, the profanities shoot out of my mouth like bullets from an AK-47. I squeeze Mia's hand like I'm giving birth.

"Clean it up, young lady," the trainer shouts.

"Breathe through the pain," Mia coaches.

Thirty seconds go by and I'm ready to give up. "It hurts too much. I can't do this."

"No, no, no. You're almost through the hardest part. Wait. In three minutes, it'll be numb and you'll be like, 'Hey, no sweat.'"

She must be losing blood circulation in her hand, but the stabbing tingles in my foot are getting worse and I need her. I also bounce my other leg to help distract me. "You've done this before?"

"All the time. I've got bad ankles. That's what I get for running so much."

Our conversation is helping me ignore the pain, so I do my best to keep it going. "So you run a lot? For, like, fun?" It's then I realize she probably didn't try out for track just to stalk me. Of course. Who do I think I am?

"Yeah, every morning. I usually run up Sabino Canyon on the weekends."

"My dad and I used to go there a lot. I helped him collect native plant samples for his classes. Did you know the paloverde's leaves are bipinnately compound? They're like that so they won't lose as much water during the summer."

She smiles sweetly at my trivia. "I didn't know that. We should go sometime. You can tell me more about plant survival, and I can show you the best swimming hole in the canyon. Sometimes, after a long run, I just strip off everything and dive in. I haven't been caught bare butt yet."

I look down at my red foot in the icy water so she can't see my blushing face. "You're right. It doesn't hurt anymore." I let go of her hand and she rubs life back into it. "Mia," I start but don't really know where I'm heading.

"Yeah?" She leans forward and rests her elbows on her knees. "What's up?"

"I'm still seeing someone," I say even though it's a total lie and she probably knows it. I don't know why I say it. I guess in my heart I hope it might become true. Because even with Mia sitting next to me, planting naked swimming images in my head, I miss Keeta more than ever. Sometimes, my longing for her is stronger than my longing for my dad. How can that be?

"That's cool," she says without missing a beat. "So am I."

"Oh. Cool," I say, but it's really not. I guess I thought she was going to be my stalker until we both graduated from high school or maybe even college.

She stands and stretches her legs. "Man, I'm stiff. I better go stretch." She points to my icing foot. "Hope it's not too bad."

"Yeah, thanks." She's almost out the door. "Hey, Mia?"

"Yeah?"

"Thanks a lot for holding my hand."

"Anytime, Abbey. I mean it." Then she's gone.

The trainer tosses a towel in my face. "Ten more minutes and you're done. See, that wasn't so bad, was it?"

I wiggle my frozen toes. "No, I guess it wasn't so bad after all."

❖

After my track meet my mom sets me up in my room and makes sure I have everything I need before she goes to the art gallery opening where some of her paintings are being displayed.

"I made some fresh iced tea today. Here you go."

She hands me a glass already sweating with condensation. "Thanks, Mom. Wow, you look really nice." I sound kind of shocked because it's not often that she paints her nails one solid color and puts on makeup and jewelry. She even borrowed my curling iron to add body to her slightly graying blond locks.

"Thanks, honey. I feel nice. It's been too long since I've dressed up," she says and then pats my head. "You be good. I'll be home soon."

Then she's gone and it's completely quiet. I don't know if it's my boredom or the injury or the humiliation of falling on the high jump bar, or even if it's seeing Garrett moving on with her life like nothing ever happened, but as I lie in my bed, I have a sudden epiphany: I can't live without Keeta for one more second.

I grab my cell and speed-dial her number. But then before pushing send, I drop the phone. What am I doing? What do I plan on saying to her? Should I just pretend that day never happened? I wait for some inspiration. I could tell Keeta about the track meet. How I had to put my foot in a bucket of ice. I realize quickly how lame that sounds. But thinking about the ice does get me thinking about more important things. Like how close I am to getting over Keeta. Plus, there's the fun I've been having every weekend with Kate and the love and closeness of my mom. Why would I give all that up for Keeta when I'm almost healed?

Maybe getting over Keeta is like plunging my foot into a bucket of ice. Sure, at first it's painful, but if I just stick it out, I can do it, and sooner than I think, everything will go numb and the pain will leave and my heart will heal. I just need to endure it for a few more days, or maybe a week, and then the stinging will stop. Of course, like the ice bucket, getting over Keeta would be a lot easier if someone was here to hold my hand.

Around eight o'clock my mom returns home and checks in on me. "How are you feeling, Abbey Road?"

"Starving and bored."

"Guess what," she says, smiling bigger than usual. "I sold three pieces tonight." It's been a really long time since I've seen her like this.

Maybe that's because it's been a long time since I've really seen her at all. "And they want to see more of my work."

"Congrats, Mom," I say, and it appears that besides being my mom, she has a life, too. And maybe she might someday need to love someone else again, just like me. Then my stomach reminds me that if she sold three paintings at $750 a pop, that means she just might be willing to splurge. "I know, let's celebrate. Who wants pizza?"

"Mmm. Sounds good," she says. "Call Kate and see if she wants to come. And for God's sake, put on some clothes. You've been running around here half naked since it hit eighty outside."

I find some clean-enough shorts in the laundry hamper and pick out a shirt with sleeves to make my mom happy. Then I call Kate to see if she wants to come, but she's already at Mama's Pizza with her dad and Jenn. I guess everyone is in the mood for carbs.

My mom and I meet up with the Townsends and cram into the booth with them. Jenn's on one side of me and Kate's on the other, so I feel like I'm surrounded by padded walls of comfort, and that's when I get it: I haven't been alone at all this whole time. They've been holding my hand, metaphorically speaking, all year. Then I get a little teary eyed as I look across the table at my mom. She's so strong and wise and knows more about heartbreak than I can ever imagine, and she's made it through this far without anyone holding her hand. Why would I push her away like this? Hasn't she been through enough? Someday soon, I'll tell her the truth. At least, I'll try. In the meantime, I'll admire her for waiting for me to come to her with it.

My mom smiles at me. "You okay, Abbey?"

I nod, but before I get a chance to answer, Jenn butts in with her usual obnoxious sentiments. "Oh, she's just still embarrassed about her back flop on the high bar. That'll teach you to lose track of your steps."

"At least I didn't almost throw my discus into the crowd." My comeback smears the smile off her face rather quickly. "And don't even try to blame it on the wind."

"How did you hear about that?" Jenn leans forward and glares at Kate.

"I have my sources." I give Kate knuckles and we laugh. Nothing brings the two of us closer than making fun of Jenn.

"This sounds like something I should bring up at Jenn's graduation party," their dad says.

"You guys are such punks." Jenn punches me in the side.

When the giant steaming pizza arrives, we all cheer, but before our first bite we pick up our plastic tumblers and toast our successes. We toast my mom's big sales, Jenn's brush with homicide by discus, Kate's third place in the long jump, and finally, we toast my bravery. Yes, I dipped my foot in the Ice Bucket of Doom and lived to tell about it. In my head, I also say a silent toast to myself. For the first time since that horrible day at Keeta's, I really believe I'm going to make it through.

CHAPTER THIRTY-TWO

Tonight is Jenn's graduation party, a night I haven't been looking forward to because I know that Garrett is going to be there, too. I tried to back out last week, but Jenn said, "Do it and die, freshmeat," so here I am.

Before the guests arrive, Kate assures me everything's going to be cool. "You and Garrett are mature enough to give each other a polite nod and then mingle in the other direction, right?"

"Really? You think I'm mature? Have you not been my BFF and seen how wrong this assumption is?" Then the doorbell rings and I don't have a choice other than to suck it up and behave.

So far, the food table and I are getting along just fine, and I'm quietly, yet artfully, piling chips, dip, and brownies on my plate, minding my own business. *See, this isn't so bad*, I think. Then, letting down my guard a little, I look around the decorated basement. Bad move. Garrett's gaze meets mine, and instead of nodding, I freak out and turn around to run but can't get my feet to move.

A few seconds later, I feel her touch my arm which causes me to jump and my tower of Doritos to tumble. My heart begins to race. *Be chill, be chill*, I say in my head like a mantra. I don't want to blow this because maybe it's not too late to make things right. Maybe now's my chance to forgive and forget again.

"Hey," Garrett says.

"Hey," I say to the fruit salad.

"Look, Abbey. About that day."

I grab another handful of chips and add them to my plate. "Yeah?"

"I don't know how to explain it. It just happened. We *were* drinking, but I knew it would hurt you and I didn't stop it."

I nod my head and add another scoop of french onion dip, still waiting for an opportunity to say, *It's okay. I forgive you.*

"I'm sure you're still pretty pissed off at me, but I want you to know I'm sorry."

There it is. The perfect moment. It's time to say it, but instead, I shove a baby carrot in my mouth. Maybe her apology is too late.

"I've really missed being your friend, Abs."

I've missed her, too, but how can I ever trust her again?

Then I guess Garrett gets fed up with my silence because she grabs the overflowing plate from my hands and puts it on the table. "Could you stop communicating with the food and say something to me? Tell me I'm a bitch. Tell me I suck. Just talk to me."

I study the dip on my plate, which is sculpted into the shape of a Hershey's Kiss. I really don't know what to say.

"Say something, Abbey," she pleads again.

"Okay. Okay." I gather my thoughts. "It feels like you did it just to prove how bad she really was for me, which, in a way, was nice of you, but also really, really messed up."

"I swear I didn't think you'd come over. I really thought no one would ever find out, which is stupid because people always find out everything, huh?"

I nod in agreement and notice Kate looking over at us, checking to see if I need her to whisk me away. With a slight shake of my head I let her know I'm fine.

"But I didn't do it to hurt you. I promise. It wasn't even about you."

I look at her finally. "But you knew how much I loved her, G."

"I know. I know. What I did was beyond messed up, but it was about getting even with Tai, not about hurting you."

"Tai? What does she have to do with this?"

"It's complicated," she says, as if that's enough.

My look tells her that she better elaborate.

"Okay," she glances over her shoulder then lowers her voice. "Well, you know that history between me and Stef I didn't feel like telling you about?"

"Yeah."

"Well, it was the same sort of situation, but with Stef and Tai in bed, and me being the one to walk in to be crushed."

"*Chale*."

"Yeah, no kidding," she says and pops a brownie bite in her mouth.

Her Stef/Tai story seems plausible, but things still aren't quite making sense. "But you said you didn't think anyone would find out. If you wanted to get back at Tai, you'd want her to know, right?"

"Yes and no. God, I don't know why I did it. Tai and I got into a fight that day at school about the same stupid friend of hers that we always fight about, and I was so pissed off. I saw Keeta in the hall, and we walked over to her house to talk and, I don't know. We had a few shots and I wanted to feel better and I wanted to hurt Tai."

"I guess you got what you wanted," I say with anger in my voice.

"No I didn't, actually. It was weird. Keeta and I are just friends and we should have stayed that way. But you know what?" She looks over her shoulder again. "You're not going to believe this, but I think I also got jealous of you and Keeta."

"You're right. I don't believe you."

"I know it sounds stupid, but it was like I didn't think it was fair that you got to be with Keeta and I didn't. Plus I was so angry with Tai that day. So it just happened. We didn't plan it."

I take a gulp of Dr Pepper and think about her reasoning, but I still don't buy it. "How does something like that just happen anyway? I mean, you wanted it to happen, that's why it did. It was no accident."

"I know. You're right."

It feels good to be the one who knows what's going on for once. Then I stop congratulating myself and focus back on the matter at hand. "Has it happened again?"

"No, I swear. It was just that one time."

For some reason, I believe Garrett. What else can I do? I miss her and I need a friend who knows how it feels to be afraid of being found out, to be talked about in the halls, and to fall in love with a girl and survive to tell about it.

Then we just stand there munching on carrots like a couple of gay rabbits.

I'm trying to figure out what to say next, but Garrett beats me to it. "You know, she still talks about you all the time."

My stomach does a cartwheel, nearly rejecting all the food I just ate. Then I feel a pull in my heart that I thought was gone for good. "She talks about me?" I grab a lock of my hair and twirl. "What does she say? What a big mistake it was to be with me?"

"No, nothing like that at all."

I can't believe I have to prompt her to tell me more. "So..."

"Well, let's just say I've never seen her so attached to anyone. Whatever it is you guys had was something I don't think she's ever experienced before." Garrett falls silent for a second, eats another carrot, and then says, "If you ask me, she's still totally in love with you."

"In love with me?" I feel myself floating again, but before I can close my eyes to fall into my old Keeta trance, Jenn's mom flicks the lights and calls everyone around.

"Let's all raise our glasses to my beautiful, smart, talented daughter," Jenn's mom says to the partygoers.

"Mom, please," Jenn whines, pretending to be embarrassed.

"May you be successful in everything you do, and may you always remember how much you are loved and adored by everyone in this room. I'm so proud of you, sweetie."

Everyone raises their glasses. "Cheers!"

While Jenn's getting a group hug from her mom, dad, and Kate, I think more about Keeta. I've been so close to getting through the pain, but knowing she might really love me is a different story. Why should we both suffer? But still, things don't quite add up.

"Well, if Keeta's so in love with me, why didn't she try harder to talk to me or apologize after it happened? And why did she mess around with you and Osiris and whoever else if she supposedly loves me so much?"

Garrett shrugs and crunches on one of my chips. "I don't know. I think she's afraid of you."

"Okay, now you're just talking crazy."

"It's not crazy. Not if you're Keeta. Not if you've always lived your life protecting yourself from feeling anything. Especially love."

"Why would she do that?"

Garrett takes my soda and finishes it off before sharing more of her insights. "Maybe because she lost her uncle like that, or maybe because she feels abandoned by her parents. As you know, there are a lot of maybes when it comes to Keeta. She's a complicated girl. Anyway, I think she was afraid you were going to leave her, too."

It almost sounds logical, in a totally screwed up sort of way.

"And I'm kind of embarrassed to admit it," Garrett says, "but I think she was trying to ruin what you guys had by hooking up with me. I think she knew you'd find out and it would break your heart. That way, she wouldn't have to worry about you hurting her. It would be over. Done with. She could wash her heart clean of you. See?"

No I don't see. If Keeta loves me, why would she hurt me on purpose?

Then I'm back to where I didn't want to go, and I'm imagining just one more night in Keeta's arms. Can't I have at least that? It doesn't have to mean we're back together again. But then again, maybe one night could change everything. Maybe we could finally make love, and I could convince her I would never hurt her. Maybe it isn't too late.

The crowd of Jenn fans is mingling again, so I try to look more normal and less utterly confused and love struck. "So, you guys still hang out?" I ask Garrett.

"Yeah, she's freaking out about graduating. She might be playing ball for ASU next year, but who knows. She says she has to stay here and take care of her grandma."

"Yeah, who knows," I say and act cooler than I am feeling inside. We stand there contemplating what to eat next, when I finally get the nerve to ask Garrett one last thing. "Could you do me a favor, G?"

"I think it's the least I can do."

"Could you ask Keeta to come over to my house tonight at midnight?"

Garrett makes a face. "Are you sure that's what you want, Abbey?"

"Just ask her, okay?"

Tai walks over to us and grabs a piece of broccoli off my plate. "Hey, Abbey, where have you been all my life? We've missed your tallness. All my lightbulbs need changing."

I laugh but look at Garrett to make sure I get my confirmation.

Garrett rolls her eyes, which I take as a yes.

"But, seriously," Tai says, "basketball ends and you just drop us like a bad habit. Thanks a lot."

Is that what Garrett told Tai? That it was me? That I was blowing them off? God, she lies as much as I do, or as much as I used to.

"Yeah," Garrett says and laughs nervously. "Well, you know how Abbey is. She's just too cool for us now." With Tai standing behind her, Garrett gives me a pleading look.

Garrett wants me to play along and keep her secret from Tai the same way she played along and kept my secret from Stef. And even though she stabbed me in the back in the end, I still feel like I owe her one. "Yeah, you know how it is, hurdles to jump, ankles to sprain."

"Yeah, I hear ya. Well, will we at least see you at summer league?" Tai asks.

"Summer league?" I ask with my mouth full of brownie because I'm too excited to finish chewing.

"Oh my God, you totally have to sign up. We were undefeated last year," Garrett says while shaking my arm with giddiness.

"I'm so in!" It's just what I need to get through until next fall. I hip-check Garrett with my butt. "But no suicide lines, right?"

"Coach Riley won't even be in a twenty-mile radius. I swear."

Kate carefully walks over to us, balancing a tray of fluted glasses filled with bubbling apple cider. "Ladies?" she asks, keeping her eyes on the drinks.

"Why, thank you, ma'am," Tai says, and we each take one.

I lift my glass. "A toast to basketball."

"To next year's JV team," Kate says.

"And to friends," Garrett adds, looking at me.

"And friends!" we all say together.

Then Jenn barges into our little circle and says, "And to older sisters who are always right about everything."

CHAPTER THIRTY-THREE

My mom and I leave Jenn's party and get home at about ten, but it's still about eighty degrees outside. "I don't think I'll ever get used to these hot nights, Mom."

My mom falls back onto the couch next to me. "How about a strawberry smoothie?"

I consider taking her up on the offer, but after consuming two pieces of cake, a ton of chips, dip, crackers, carrot, cheese, and two servings of lasagna, I have finally reached my max. "No thanks. I think I'm full."

"Wow. I guess there's a first for everything," she says and laughs.

"Ha ha. Very funny. Anyway, I'm kind of tired, Mom. I think I'll just go to bed." I start to get up, but she pulls me down into the cushiony pillows.

"It's your first night of summer vacation and you're going to go to bed early?" She reaches out and tests my forehead for a fever. "Everything all right? You were so quiet on the way home."

I look down at the couch and trace my finger over its pattern. "Yeah, I guess I just need some time to recover from, I don't know, the whole year."

"Yeah, I know what you mean. It's been a long one, huh?"

"Well, it was interesting to say the least."

"Yes, it was," she agrees.

With nothing else to say about it, we sit and listen to the crickets. Even with the screen doors shut, they always find a way into our house during the summer.

Then my mom breaks our silence. "I was afraid, Abbey."

I freak out inside. Does she mean she was afraid she was right about me being gay? And afraid she wouldn't be able to love me?

"I wasn't sure we could do high school without him."

I take a sigh of relief. "Really?"

"You know, he had it all figured out by the time you were five. He knew exactly what classes you should take and which clubs you should join. He even had a curfew figured out. Eleven fifteen. He wanted it to be fair but not too late. Eleven fifteen was the perfect time in his head. Isn't that funny?"

"Yeah," I say and look over at her as she gazes out the window at nothing.

The faint lines around her eyes and mouth seem deeper, and the silver strands sparkling in her blond hair seem to have doubled. I decide I don't like seeing her age. What if I lose her, too? I know now there are things I can make it through, but there's no way I could survive that.

"So, you think this year would have gone better with him here?" I ask.

"Well, this year was going to be what it was no matter what. Don't you think?"

"I guess," I say and don't admit I've been wondering all year about how things might have been different, maybe better, with Dad here. "Yeah, it was what it was."

She looks at me again. "But we didn't do so badly, did we?"

I smile. "No, not too bad."

She reaches over and holds my hand. "He would have been proud of you."

I let out a small laugh because I think it will keep me from feeling sad. "I don't know about that." But my eyes still well up with hot tears.

"And I'm so proud of you, too."

A tear escapes, but I still manage to laugh. "Why? Because I didn't flunk out? That's something, I guess."

"Yes, but it's more than that."

"You shouldn't be proud of me, Mom. I'm not as great as you think I am." It almost feels like the right time. Almost.

"Well..." She hesitates, as if she's trying to find the perfect way to say whatever is coming next. "No matter what you do or who you become, Abbey, I'll always love you, and I'm sure you're always going to make me proud to be your mom."

I can tell she wants to hear it from me, but I can't do it tonight because I'm way too tired. Plus, I have something important to take care of that can't wait.

"Thanks, Mom. I love you, too." I kiss her cheek. "No matter what," I add. "Good night."

I'm light on my feet as I walk back to my room. She loves me. No matter what. When I'm ready, I'll tell her, and I know she'll love me still.

❖

I leave my bedroom window open, but I keep the blinds closed so she won't see me. Then at 12:01, I hear the gravel outside my window crunch under Keeta's shoes.

The footsteps stop and I hear her peel off the letter I taped to my window earlier tonight. I imagine how beautiful she must look holding it up to the moon's light. Then I wait quietly in bed while she reads the note.

You've got your words to describe how I make you feel,
but just so you know, I've got some I also need to reveal.
The first one is lucky, *and* loved *is one more.*
Another is happy *and the next is* adored.
A few aren't as sweet, but they'll dissolve in time
because mostly I'll remember all the nights you were mine.

Dear Keeta,
I just wanted you to know I'm not angry anymore. I guess you could say it's because I think I understand you more than I did before. I hope maybe someday we can be friends again because I do miss you. Plus, I still need to beat you at a game of one on one. So don't leave Tucson without saying good-bye to me, okay? I think that would make me sadder than anything else. But I guess I need a little more time before then. I hope you understand.
You are still, and will always be, deep in my heart.
Love always,
Your Amara

When she whispers my name, I lie perfectly still. So much of me wants to rush to the window to kiss her again, be in her arms again, and be her Amara again. But there's no way I'm pulling my heart out of its ice bucket now. I'm almost healed. My mom's probably right; you never forget your first love, and I can't ever imagine forgetting Keeta. I will probably always love Keeta, but I've learned I deserve more. In fact, I've learned a lot in my freshman year at Gila High, like how to play basketball, how to fall in love, and how to kiss. And (unfortunately) how to lose friendships and trust, but then (fortunately) how to get them both back again. Most importantly, though, I have happily accepted who I am. In fact, maybe next year on the first day of school instead of being freaked out and nervous, I'll sneak into the office (with the help of Tai, of course), grab the PA microphone, and announce to the whole school, "Good morning, Gila High. My name is Abbey 'Chunks' Brooks and I am definitely a you-know-who girl, too!"

About the Author

Annameekee Hesik came out when she was fifteen and has since been obsessed with rainbows. After successfully surviving high school in Tucson, AZ, she went to college for six years and changed her major five times. She earned her BA in English lit from UC Davis and her MA in education from UC Santa Cruz. She is thrilled she finally decided to become a high school English teacher (with a background in anthropology, American Sign Language, world history, and environmental biology). When she isn't helping students learn to enjoy literature or dressing up as the Super Recycler or Grammar Police, she spends her time in Santa Cruz, CA, walking her dogs, napping in her hammock, riding bikes with her wife, slurping down mocha shakes, and writing books that she hopes will help lesbian and questioning teens feel like they're not the only you-know-who girls in the world. To see embarrassing high school photos of Annameekee, read her blog, and to find out what she likes to mix into her macaroni and cheese, visit her website: www.annameekee.com.

Soliloquy Titles From Bold Strokes Books

The You Know Who Girls by Annameekee Hesik. As they begin freshman year, Abbey Brooks and her best friend, Kate, pinky swear they'll keep away from the lesbians in Gila High, but Abbey already suspects she's one of those you-know-who girls herself and slowly learns who her true friends really are. (978-1-60282-754-7)

The Secret of Othello by Sam Cameron. Florida teen detectives Steven and Denny risk their lives to search for a sunken NASA satellite—but under the waves, no one can hear you scream… (978-1-60282-742-4)

Andy Squared by Jennifer Lavoie. Andrew never thought anyone could come between him and his twin sister, Andrea…until Ryder rode into town. (978-1-60282-743-1)

OMGqueer, edited by Radclyffe and Katherine E. Lynch. Through stories imagined and told by youth across America, this anthology provides a snapshot of queerness at the dawn of the new millennium. (978-1-60282-682-3)

Sara by Greg Herren. A mysterious and beautiful new student at Southern Heights High School stirs things up when students start dying. (978-1-60282-674-8)

Boys of Summer, edited by Steve Berman. Stories of young love and adventure, when the sky's ceiling is a bright blue marvel, when another boy's laughter at the beach can distract from dull summer jobs. (978-1-60282-663-2)

Street Dreams by Tama Wise. Tyson Rua has more than his fair share of problems growing up in New Zealand—he's gay, he's falling in love, and he's run afoul of the local hip-hop crew leader just as he's trying to make it as a graffiti artist. (978-1-60282-650-2)

me@you.com by K.E. Payne. Is it possible to fall in love with someone you've never met? Imogen Summers thinks so because it's happened to her. (978-1-60282-592-5)

Swimming to Chicago by David-Matthew Barnes. As the lives of the adults around them unravel, high school students Alex and Robby form an unbreakable bond, vowing to do anything to stay together—even if it means leaving everything behind. (978-1-60282-572-7)

Speaking Out edited by Steve Berman. Inspiring stories written for and about LGBT and Q teens of overcoming adversity (against intolerance and homophobia) and experiencing life after "coming out." (978-1-60282-566-6)

365 Days by K.E. Payne. Life sucks when you're seventeen years old and confused about your sexuality, and the girl of your dreams doesn't even know you exist. Then in walks sexy new emo girl, Hannah Harrison. Clemmie Atkins has exactly 365 days to discover herself, and she's going to have a blast doing it! (978-1-60282-540-6)

Cursebusters! by Julie Smith. Budding psychic Reeno is the most accomplished teenage burglar in California, but one tiny screw-up and poof!—she's sentenced to Bad Girl School. And that isn't even her worst problem. Her sister Haley's dying of an illness no one can diagnose, and now she can't even help. (978-1-60282-559-8)

Who I Am by M.L. Rice. Devin Kelly's senior year is a disaster. She's in a new school in a new town, and the school bully is making her life miserable—but then she meets his sister Melanie and realizes her feelings for her are more than platonic. (978-1-60282-231-3)

Sleeping Angel by Greg Herren. Eric Matthews survives a terrible car accident only to find out everyone in town thinks he's a murderer—and he has to clear his name even though he has no memories of what happened. (978-1-60282-214-6)

Mesmerized by David-Matthew Barnes. Through her close friendship with Brodie and Lance, Serena Albright learns about the many forms of love and finds comfort for the grief and guilt she feels over the brutal death of her older brother, the victim of a hate crime. (978-1-60282-191-0)

The Perfect Family by Kathryn Shay. A mother and her gay son stand hand in hand as the storms of change engulf their perfect family and the life they knew. (978-1-60282-181-1)

Father Knows Best by Lynda Sandoval. High school juniors and best friends Lila Moreno, Meryl Morganstern, and Caressa Thibodoux plan to make the most of the summer before senior year. What they discover that amazing summer about girl power, growing up, and trusting friends and family more than prepares them to tackle that all-important senior year! (978-1-60282-147-7)